QUILLS
WICKED
GENTLEMAN

QUILLS: A REGENCY AFFAIR: WICKED GENTLEMAN © 2025 by Harlequin Books S.A.

Ann Lethbridge is acknowledged as the author of this work
AN INNOCENT MAID FOR THE DUKE
© 2017 by Harlequin Books S.A.
Australian Copyright 2017
New Zealand Copyright 2017

First Published 2017
Second Australian Paperback Edition 2025
ISBN 978 1 038 95577 7

Diane Gaston is acknowledged as the author of this work
A PREGNANT COURTESAN FOR THE RAKE
© 2017 by Harlequin Bokks S.A.
Australian Copyright 2017
New Zealand Copyright 2017

First Published 2017
Second Australian Paperback Edition 2025
ISBN 978 1 038 95577 7

Except for use in any review, the reproduction or utilisation of this work in whole or in part in any form by any electronic, mechanical or other means, now known or hereafter invented, including xerography, photocopying and recording, or in any information storage or retrieval system, is forbidden without the permission of the publisher.

This book is sold subject to the condition that it shall not, by way of trade or otherwise, be lent, resold, hired out or otherwise circulated without the prior consent of the publisher in any form of binding or cover other than that in which it is published and without a similar condition including this condition being imposed on the subsequent purchaser.

All rights reserved including the right of reproduction in whole or in part in any form. This edition is published in arrangement with Harlequin Books S.A. Cover art used by arrangement with Harlequin Books S.A. All rights reserved.

This is a work of fiction. Names, characters, places, and incidents are either the product of the author's imagination or are used fictitiously, and any resemblance to actual persons, living or dead, business establishments, events, or locales is entirely coincidental.

Published by
Quills
An imprint of Harlequin Enterprises (Australia) Pty Limited
(ABN 47 001 180 918), a subsidiary of HarperCollins
Publishers Australia Pty Limited (ABN 36 009 913 517)
Level 19, 201 Elizabeth Street
SYDNEY NSW 2000
AUSTRALIA

® and ™ (apart from those relating to FSC®) are trademarks of Harlequin Enterprises (Australia) Pty Limited or its corporate affiliates. Trademarks indicated with ® are registered in Australia, New Zealand and in other countries.
Contact admin_legal@Harlequin.ca for details.

Printed and bound in Australia by McPherson's Printing Group

QUILLS
WICKED GENTLEMAN

Ann Lethbridge
Diane Gaston

MILLS & BOON

CONTENTS

AN INNOCENT MAID FOR THE DUKE 7
Ann Lethbridge

A PREGNANT COURTESAN FOR THE RAKE 245
Diane Gaston

An Innocent Maid For The Duke
Ann Lethbridge

In her youth, award-winning author **Ann Lethbridge** reimagined the Regency romances she read—and now she loves writing her own. Now living in Canada, Ann visits Britain every year, where family members understand—or so they say—her need to poke around every antiquity within a hundred miles. Learn more about Ann or contact her at annlethbridge.com. She loves hearing from readers.

Books by Ann Lethbridge

Rakes in Disgrace

The Gamekeeper's Lady
More Than a Mistress
Deliciously Debauched by the Rake (Undone!)
More Than a Lover

The Gilvrys of Dunross

Captured for the Captain's Pleasure
The Laird's Forbidden Lady
Her Highland Protector
Falling for the Highland Rogue
Return of the Prodigal Gilvry
One Night with the Highlander (Undone!)

The Society of Wicked Gentlemen

An Innocent Maid for the Duke

Linked by Character

Wicked Rake, Defiant Mistress
One Night as a Courtesan (Undone!)
Secrets of the Marriage Bed

Haunted by the Earl's Touch
Captured Countess
The Duke's Daring Debutante

Visit the Author Profile page at millsandboon.com.au for more titles.

Author Note

In every book, I try to include a little bit of history that might be an insight into a world long gone, but still beloved by so many. The panorama visit by Jake, Rose and Lucy is a description of a real place and event during the time frame of the story. Panoramas were the forerunner of the movies we love to watch today. The size of the building, the care with which the scenes were painted and presented were a testament to human creative ingenuity. Everyone flocked to the Leicester Square rotunda to see the latest panorama offered by the owner, Robert Barker, for nearly seventy years. The painted views provided a window on other parts of the world and were not only painted with painstaking accuracy, but decorated with artifacts to add to the realism. People viewing these vistas often became nauseous because of the realism and unaccustomed scope. Barker's rotunda still exists in London today, tucked in between buildings in Leicester Square, and, fittingly enough, the only way it can be seen is from above.

I do hope you enjoy Rose and Jake's journey to happiness and like reading the series as much as we authors enjoyed writing it for you.

If you wish to know more about me or my books, visit annlethbridge.com. If you would like to dive deeper into the Regency world, visit my blog, regencyrambles.blogspot.com.

Until next we meet, I wish you health, happiness and love.

This novel is dedicated to CanadaLoneWolves, in particular Donmar, Lyon and Katz. Each and every day these awesome people provide me with laughs and smiles. Everyone needs folks like these in their lives and I hope you all have some of those, too.

I also want to dedicate this story to the other three authors in this series. Thank you, ladies, for being such a wonderful group to work with on this project.

Chapter One

Entering the owners' private quarters at the gentleman's club Vitium et Virtus, Jake, Duke of Westmoor, stifled a groan at the sight of the other two founding members lounging in heavy leather armchairs placed around a low table. One of the two empty chairs was his. The fourth supported a small gilded box.

'This was the reason you sent for me?'

Even seated, the brown-haired, brown-eyed Frederick Challenger had a military air. At Jake's words he snapped to attention and glowered. 'It may have escaped your lofty notice, Your Grace, but today is the sixth anniversary of Nicholas's disappearance.'

Jake tensed at the use of his title. The significance of the date had indeed escaped his notice, busy as he was with the affairs of the Duchy, but he wasn't about to admit it. 'I thought we were beyond all this.' He had enough reminders of loss at home without adding to them here. The one place he thought of as a refuge.

'Sit down, Westmoor,' Oliver, the other member of their

group, said, his green eyes snapping sparks in his burnished face.

Jake sighed, but did as requested. Or rather ordered. If Oliver hadn't been such a good friend... No. Not true. He had no wish to alienate these men, his oldest friends. Without them he might not have survived the loss of his father and brother.

He glanced on the gilded box on the other chair. It contained Nicholas's ring, the last reminder of their missing founder of Vitium et Virtus. Could it really be six years since Nicolas's disappearance? It hardly seemed possible. Back then, they'd scarcely achieved their majority. Now look at them. All three of them reaching the grand old age of thirty. The intervening years had passed in a heartbeat.

Yet the shock of finding a pool of blood in the alley outside Vitium et Virtus and Nicholas's signet ring trampled in the dirt beside it wasn't any less raw.

Oliver leaned forward and laid his hand palm up in the centre of the table.

'You seriously intend to do this,' Jake said.

The other two glared at him. Grudgingly, he placed his hand on top of Oliver's, the warmth of another man's skin odd against the palm of his hand. Frederick added his to the pile.

'In vitium et virtus,' they chorused like the bunch of schoolboys they'd been when they started this stupid venture. In vice and virtue. Even after all this time, the words sounded strangely lacking without Nicholas's voice in the mix.

Withdrawing his hand, he picked up his brandy, lifting the glass towards the empty chair in a toast. 'To absent friends.'

The others imitated his action.

'Be he in heaven or hell—' Oliver continued with the words they'd been saying each year for the past six years.

'Or somewhere in between—' Frederick intoned.

'Know that we wish you well,' they finished together. As if anything so nonsensical could bring their friend back.

They threw back their drinks, staring at the empty seat.

'I was so sure he'd turn up like a bad penny before the year was out telling us it was all a jest,' Frederick said.

'If so, it would be in pretty poor taste. Even for Nicholas.' Oliver said, his green eyes dark with the pain of loss they'd all felt since Nicholas's disappearance. A loss Jake didn't want to think about. There had been too many in his life. Each one worse than the last.

'It would have been like him,' Jake said, burying the surge of anger that took him by surprise. 'Nicholas always was one for stupid japes. This club, for example.'

Troubled, he rubbed at his chin and felt a day's growth of stubble. Hadn't he shaved this morning? Surely he had.

'I hear his uncle is petitioning the Lords to have the title declared vacant.' Frederick rolled his empty glass between his palms. 'Bastard can't wait to step into his shoes. I wouldn't be surprised if he didn't do away with him so he could get his hands on the estate.'

Inwardly, Jake flinched, though he kept his face expressionless.

Oliver's eyes sharpened. 'Don't be an idiot, Fred.'

Frederick's ears reddened as his glance fell on Jacob's face.

Apparently, his lack of emotion hadn't fooled his friends.

'Dammit, Your Grace. You know such a thing never crossed my mind.'

He made a dismissive gesture with his hand. 'Naturally not.' But others had whispered words like *murder* behind his back. And it wasn't as if he was entirely innocent.

The night his father and brother died came crashing back with a vengeance. The loss. The horror. The guilt. He leaned back in his chair, needing even that fraction of distance from the sympathetic glances of his friends.

A sympathy he did not deserve.

Oliver frowned at him. 'You look like hell, Jake. When was the last time you had a haircut?'

He couldn't remember. 'None of your business.'

The sound of catcalls and hoots came from behind the thick oak door that separated their private owners' quarters from the public rooms of the club.

Glad of the distraction, Jake raised a brow. 'What is going on out there?'

'It's choose-your-partner night,' Fred said.

Bell, the balding erstwhile butler, now manager of Vitium et Virtus, shot through the door. The noise level went up to deafening.

Bell's face screwed up into an expression of worry. 'Please, sirs. One of you needs to restore order. One of the gentlemen is insisting he wants five of the girls at once and none is interested. I've explained the rules, but he is being most uncooperative. Several other gentlemen have bet on his abilities and are insisting.' He disappeared back through the door. It closed behind him with the faintest click.

'Blast it all,' Jake gritted out. 'It really is time we closed this place once and for all.' It certainly didn't fit with his new position in life. He glanced at the empty place at the table. 'If this wasn't the one place that might draw Nicholas back, I'd be for closing it down.' The club had been Nicholas's idea. He had provided the largest portion of money to get it started.

'I'll go.' Frederick grabbed up his mask and cloak, the required uniform for all entering Vitium et Virtus. While people might guess at their identities, they had never admitted to owning the place.

On his way past, Frederick shot Jake a conciliatory look. 'Water under the bridge, right?'

'Right,' Jake said. He forced a smile. 'It's a good thing Nicholas wasn't here, or he'd be ribbing me about my thin skin for weeks.'

Fred picked up his pace as the door failed to keep out the noise of the rising mayhem beyond.

Oliver pushed to his feet. 'Nicholas would have been ribbing you about your appearance, too. Take a look in the mirror next time you pass one. White's wouldn't let you through the door.'

Jake scraped a nail through his stubble. 'Good thing Vitium et Virtus isn't so fussy. Where are you going? Home?'

Oliver's green eyes sparked mischief. 'At some point. You?'

Jake grimaced, envying his friend his light-hearted grin. The idea of going back to the ducal town house caused his gut to clench. He hated walking through the door, let alone spending time there. He ought to go back, though. Duty called and all that. So much duty. 'Soon.'

He'd have to go soon. His grandmother was expecting him to bid her goodnight. And then she'd look at him with such sorrow in her eyes...

He picked up the decanter and poured himself another glass of brandy. The best money could buy.

'Want to talk about it?' Oliver offered, concern in his gaze.

Sympathy was worse than self-recrimination. 'I'm not in the mood for company,' he said, deliberately avoiding the question, but telling the truth all the same. He rarely was in the mood for company any more. Burying one's family did that to a fellow.

Only when the door clicked, did he realise Oliver had gone.

He swallowed the brandy in one gulp, poured another and headed for the office. These days, work and brandy were the only things that helped him sleep.

Rose stacked the last of the plates in the cupboard, removed her apron and stretched her back. Oh, it felt so good.

'All done, Rose?' Charity Parker, a middle-aged woman and housekeeper at the V&V, as the servants called it, swept a gimlet glance around the kitchen.

'Yes, Mrs Parker.' She hesitated, wondering if there was more to do.

The woman's stern expression softened a little. 'Go on, then, join your friends in the Green Room if you must, but don't be staying up all night sewing their dresses. And be careful, Rose. Things are still in full swing.' She bustled away.

Rose grinned at her back. Mrs Parker's bark was far worse than her bite. But she was right. At this time of the night the gentlemen members were often half-seas-over and could be a little too friendly to anything in skirts. Even someone as drab and plain as her was fair game in their eyes. She certainly didn't want to risk losing her position by breaking any rules. Mrs Parker and Mr Bell were very strict about the servants keeping to their proper places. For their protection as much as anything.

It was just one of the things that made her feel especially lucky to have found this position. The pay at the club was better than anything she'd ever received before and, best of all, she didn't have to live in as she did when working as a housemaid in a gentleman's home. Housemaids risked the advances of any lusty fellow under its roof. Men who couldn't keep their hands to themselves were the reason she'd left her last three positions. She knew the risks of a kiss and a cuddle under the blankets. She was likely the result of one.

No, she was better off going to her own place every night. Her own home, meagre though it was. No matter how kind and respectful the family might be to their servants, she always felt like an intruder. An outsider looking in on a happiness she had never known. Perhaps one day she would have family of her own. She was determined she would. The idea of it sent a chill down her spine.

Enough daydreaming. If she was to do a bit of mending for the girls before she went home, she needed to get going.

She slipped into the Green Room unnoticed. Not green at all, of course. Painted white and blue and lined with mirrors, the large open room was in the basement at the back of the house. It was here the girls who performed at the V&V

changed into their costumes, practiced their acts and rested when not required on stage. Or wherever they performed.

It had none of the lewd pictures and murals covering the walls and ceiling of the rest of the place, or the statues and artefacts, thank goodness. She'd become used to them over time, even got used to dusting them, but at first she hadn't known where to look.

The Green Room was a whole different matter. She loved this room full of chatter and laughter and singing as the girls swirled around in their brightly coloured costumes. It was nothing like the stark cold rooms at the Foundling Hospital where she had grown up. Or the kitchens and servants' halls she'd worked in when she'd gone out into the world. In those places, everyone was afraid of their shadow and talked in whispers.

She sank into the old horsehair sofa in the corner and pulled out the needle case she'd made at the orphanage. A small embroidered book that safely held her few precious needles and pins. She sorted through the mending in the basket beside the sofa and pulled out pair of holey stockings. She loved helping the girls and if they occasionally slipped her a penny or two for her efforts, she was grateful.

From here, she observed the goings-on while she rested her poor aching feet before walking home. With a sigh, she unlaced her half-boots, rubbed at her soles for a blissful moment or two, then tucked her them up under her skirts.

Peace at last.

'I 'oped you'd come by.' Fleurette, whose real name was Flo, plopped herself down beside Rose. Her fair golden locks were arranged in the elaborate hairstyle Rose had helped her with earlier in the day.

It was Flo who had first asked for Rose's help with her hair. When the other girls had seen the result, they had begged for help, too. She did what she could, but Mrs Parker only gave her a few minutes off here and there during the evening. Still, she made a point of helping whenever she had a moment or two, as well as after work. It was these snatched moments that had put the idea into her head that she might one day become a ladies' maid or a dressmaker.

Flo cracked a huge yawn, then exploded in laugher. 'I'm so tired I could fall asleep right here.'

Rose had liked Flo on sight. Apparently the feeling had been mutual. For the first time in her life, Rose felt as if she had a true friend.

Making friends at the orphanage had been frowned upon. They weren't there for enjoyment. They were unwanted children and needed to learn how to make themselves useful as adults.

'Was there something you needed?' she asked after a moment or two of silence.

Her friend winced. 'I wore that new red gown for my first number and caught my heel in the hem. The old besom will fine me when she sees I've damaged it already.'

She looked so downcast Rose wanted to hug her. 'Give it to me. I'll fix it and take it up an inch and then you won't trip.'

'I feel terrible asking. You've been here for hours—'

'And you need it for tomorrow. I'm happy to do it.'

'I'll pay you.'

'No! What are friends for?'

Flo gave her a mock glare. 'You'll take a couple of coppers and like it. I'd have to pay a whole lot more if the old besom had her way.' All the girls called the wardrobe mistress 'the old besom.'

'It is not right that they fine you for rips and such,' Rose said. 'It is not as if the gowns are brand new when you get them. Don't worry, I'll do it before I go home.'

Flo leaned in and kissed her cheek. 'You are a dear. I'll go and fetch it. And don't be offering to sew anyone else's gown for free. Or style their hair, for that matter.'

'I do it because I like doing it,' she said to Flo's departing back. And because it gave her hope that one day she could be more than a scullery maid. A hope that people wouldn't look at her with disdain because she scrubbed floors and washed dishes, and was a bastard to boot.

Within moments, Flo was back with a gown of brilliant scarlet with silk roses adorning neckline and hem.

Rose let the silky fabric slide through her fingers, careful not to let it catch on her work-worn skin and torn nails. 'Leave it with me. I'll have it done in no time.'

'Flo,' one of the other girls called. 'Your gentleman's waiting at the back door.'

A shadow passed across her friend's face, but then she shot Rose a cheeky smile. ''Is lordship's taking me out for dinner.' She glided away.

His lordship, as Flo called him, was Flo's gentleman follower. Rose sometimes wondered if he treated her right. There had been a couple of unexplained bruises that Flo had brushed off as falls.

The girls were allowed to walk out with the club members as long as they were discreet and did not ask for, or mention, any names. Flo lived in hopes her beau would ask her to marry him. Rose had offered dire warnings after seeing those bruises.

In her turn, Flo had instructed Rose on how to avoid unwanted children, just in case.

Rose pulled out the pair of thin cotton gloves she used to keep the silky fabrics the girls wore from getting ruined by her rough skin and set to work.

Slowly the noise around her dwindled to nothing. The wall sconce above her head contained the only candles left alight. A clock struck the hour.

Four in the morning! Already? The repair had taken far longer than she had expected because she'd also found three rips in the gauzy gown's side seams and some of the silk roses bordering the hem had been loose.

She snipped off the thread and held the gown towards the light. So feminine, like something one of the titled ladies who occasionally visited the club would wear, even if it was a little gaudy.

What would it be like to be one of those ladies? Living a life of ease and luxury. She didn't envy them the boredom that Flo said was the reason they came to the V&V, drawn there by the excitement of losing hundreds of pounds at the gambling tables or by the private assignations with one or other of the virile young men who were members.

She pushed to her feet, rubbing at the ever-present ache in the small of her back. Time to go home or she wouldn't get any sleep at all. She carried the gown over her arm to Flo's chest full of clothes. On top was a mask covered in red spangles shaped to cover the top half of the wearer's face. It matched the gown. As Rose moved it aside, she caught a glimpse of herself in the mirror, tired, drab, plain.

Grinning at her image, she held the gown up against her and kicked out a foot, making the red fabric swirl around her ankles. The picture she created was spoiled by the sight of her ugly brown dress as she turned to view herself from the side. She stared at the neckline. Was it too low? Should she have added a bit more fabric? While the V&V was renowned for debauchery and depravity, Flo was a singer not a courtesan.

Perhaps she should try it on before she put it away. For Flo's sake, naturally. She shook her head. Who did she think she was fooling? She wanted to see what she would look like in such a gown.

She whipped off her frock and slid the whisper of a gown over her head. In the mirror, a magical transformation took place. Her eyes seemed to pick up the sparkles at the neckline and her figure seemed more shapely. If it wasn't for the plain Jane face staring back at her, she might have thought herself pretty.

The mobcap had to go. But with the severe bun still in

place, it made little difference. She pulled the pins from her hair and let it fall around her shoulders, then, with a naughty smile, tied on the mask.

She turned this way and that, regarding her reflection. Better. Much better. Why, she might almost pass as one of the girls. And if she really used her imagination, perhaps as a lady. The neckline was not as bad as she had feared. It was a little low, showing the rise of her bosom, but not at all indecent.

Eyes half-closed, she twirled around humming one of the tunes she'd heard the musicians playing in the ballroom earlier that evening, pretending she was waltzing with one particularly handsome gentleman, who had no clue she even existed.

Sore feet and aching back gave her not one twinge.

Returning from seeing his grandmother, Jake passed a carriage standing outside the front door of Vitium et Virtus. Waiting for one of nobility's late-night revellers, no doubt. Usually it was the ladies who kept their carriages at the ready. He went around the side of the club, to the door out of sight of regular members, reserved for the owners.

The porter, Ben Snyder, bowed him in. 'Good evening, Yer Grace.'

Jake froze. The pain of loss held him rigid, followed swiftly by a rage he could scarcely contain.

With a muttered curse Jake slung his coat and hat on one of the four hooks in the shape of aroused male appendages they'd bought as a job lot upon opening Vitium et Virtus.

Snyder handed him a mask and retreated to his chair.

No doubt the man had seen the anger and thought it was directed at him. Jake reined in his emotions. Built the wall of distance that kept him halfway sane. But, God help him, each and every time he heard those two words, his instinct was to glance around for his father. Only to realise it was he who was being addressed. He loathed it.

It was a constant reminder of his father and brother. Of their lives. Of their deaths. Of the reason he was now addressed as *Your Grace*.

It was also why he was here and not tucked up in the ducal bed in the ducal mansion. Here and only here did he seem able to snatch a few minutes' sleep. A slog through the ledgers with a brandy or two in the comfort of the owners' private rooms should send him into the arms of Morpheus. He hoped.

'Any one left above stairs?' he enquired of the porter, trying to sound normal and coming off icily cold.

'A few, Yer Grace,' the man said warily. 'In the gaming room and upstairs in the private bedrooms. Want me to clear them out?'

'No. I am not in. To anyone. I don't care if the place burns down, I do not want to be disturbed, understand?'

'Understood, Your Grace.'

The porter also added a whispered *as usual*, but Jake decided not to hear. The porter would follow orders. He always did and that was all Jake required. He strode along the deserted corridor with its erotic statues and murals seeming to leer at him, the need for brandy an ache in his throat.

He took the servants' staircase down. It would take him to the other side of the house to another set of stairs leading up to where the owners' private quarters were located. Allowing him to avoid any lingering customers.

A sound of soft humming brought him to a halt outside the ladies' dressing room. He frowned. The girls should all be gone by now. They were certainly not supposed to entertain gentlemen here. There were rooms on the top floor set aside for such frolics. Rooms equipped with costumes and toys for every taste.

He donned his mask and opened the door a fraction,

enough to see in but not be seen until he could figure out what was going on.

A petite woman in a glittering red mask was singing to herself, her scarlet gown swirling around her shapely ankles as she twirled in front of the mirrors, each one giving a different reflection of a gown moulded to every curve of a sinuously lush body moving in time to her humming. The smile on her parted lips was not the forced smile of a courtesan, nor that of a jaded widow, or yet the hopeful smile of a debutante anxious to please a duke. This smile was pure delight. Enjoyment.

Her joy at the simple act of dancing spilled over with an infectious feeling of lightness that unaccountably lifted his spirits. He found his own lips curving upwards in response. Even more surprising, he found himself wanting to be the one to waltz her around the room.

A movement in the shadows caught the corner of Rose's eye. She turned and gasped. It was him! The Duke. Though he was wearing his usual mask, she would know him anywhere by his height and breadth and commanding presence. By his dark stubbled jaw and firm chin. By his lovely mouth.

Too many times had she stopped to admire him as he passed her at her work. Of all the owners of the club he was the only one who had caught her attention in that way. He was impossibly handsome, but coldly unapproachable. A proper duke.

Or how one assumed a duke to be.

Not that she would ever mention that she knew who he was. No names were ever spoken. House rules.

Despite his lofty position, something about him had struck her as sad. As if some deep sorrow weighed him down and made her want to offer comfort. A foolish fancy. Someone of her lowly station had nothing to offer a man such as he.

But how often she had dreamed of feeling those strong

arms curl around her while she laid her head on his chest. The very idea of it made her feel strangely weak.

Never before had she felt such a powerful attraction, despite knowing better than to get tangled up with a man. Fortunately, he was nothing more than a fantasy. A man who marched through her dreams like a knight in shining armour. As long as she kept him there, in her dreams, she was safe.

But this was no dream. The crushing realisation pressed down on her shoulders. She should not be here. It was against the rules. She glanced around for an escape route. But he was between her and the door and approaching slowly, his bright blue gaze fixed on her face.

His expression did not reflect anger. Indeed, the warmth of his smile, with a glimpse of white teeth, charmed her into remaining still. She released a breath she had not realised she was holding. A sigh really. Of appreciation.

His smile broadened and he bowed. 'I beg your pardon, my lady. I did not mean to startle you.'

My lady? Her heart fluttered strangely. If only she were his lady. She placed her hand below her throat and shook her head. 'Merely surprised.'

She'd responded with the careful diction she'd taught herself from listening to those of the upper classes as she moved unseen among them, cleaning grates and scrubbing floors.

'I have interrupted you,' he said, cocking his head to the side in question.

'Foolishness,' she said, peeping up at him. Heavens, he was taller than she had thought and broader. And so much more handsome close up. She could scarcely breathe and yet somehow the scent of his cologne filled her lungs and made her feel strangely dizzy. 'I should go.'

'Not before you give me the honour of a dance, surely?' His voice had deepened. His eyes, which had always seemed coldly reserved as he went about the business of the club, were bright, sparkling with mischief.

Dance? With a duke? 'I cannot,' she choked out.

He chuckled, low and deep. 'You certainly can. You waltz as beautifully as you hum.'

Heat rushed up from the neckline of the shocking gown, for now with his gaze upon her, she felt almost naked. Flirting. A duke was flirting with her and every particle in her body wanted to allow it. Nay, wanted to encourage it.

Wanton. Like your mother.

She must say no. But it would never happen again, this chance to dance with the man who haunted her dreams. When she was about her work, he never noticed her underfoot. None of the gentry did. They weren't supposed to. She had long ago realised it saved both the served and the server embarrassment.

What harm would one dance do? This was the first time she had seen the man smile since she started working here. If it would bring him a measure of happiness, and her, too, why not? It would certainly be something for her to dream about for the rest of her life and perhaps tell her grandchildren at some long-distant time in the future.

The night their old granny danced with a duke. The idea of that dream of a family made her smile.

'You know you want to,' he said, holding out a hand.

A moment later, she was in his arms.

The faraway gaze in eyes the loveliest shade of green Jake had ever seen sent blood humming through his veins. Those eyes were limpid and soft as she gazed up at him, as if this was all a dream. To his surprise, not only did their steps meld in perfect unison, it was if they were designed to be partners.

For months he'd been numb to everything around him, going through life by rote, fulfilling required duties and responsibilities hour after brutal hour. Keeping himself busy. But now, here, with this vision of loveliness, he could actually feel the blood coursing through his veins. It was as if he had left a cold dark place to enter a land of light and warmth.

Her light. Her warmth. He basked in it, even though he knew he did not deserve it.

He swept her around a turn at the end of the room, gazing down into her face. What did she look like beneath the mask? Her lips were lush and full, her eyes dreamy, her loose hair a river of thick gilded waves that curled in little tendrils on her faintly flushed cheek.

His body responded to that shadowed glow of pink on her skin. The blood in his veins beat a tattoo of desire.

Her lips parted as if she, too, felt the connection between them. The rise and fall of her generous breasts quickened with each indrawn breath. A pulse beat rapidly at the base of her throat. A place he longed to taste with his tongue.

Awareness sparked in the air. Their steps slowed. Their gazes locked. Hers dropped to his mouth.

With all the old reckless impulsiveness he'd been determined to curb these past many months, he drew her flush against his body. She tensed and, though he wanted to curse, he eased his hold, preparing to let her go. Unbelievably, she smiled up at him and relaxed into his embrace.

A brief kiss was all he intended, a thank you for the respite she'd brought to the darkness of his world, but as the plush full mouth yielded beneath his lips, he lost himself in the pleasure of kissing a willing woman.

Deeper and deeper he delved the soft recess of her mouth, while he felt the warm breath of her sigh against his cheek. A tentative dart of her tongue into his mouth sent a jolt of lust ripping through him.

A groan rumbled up from deep in his throat and he pulled her hard against his body. Feeling pleasure as her belly pressed against his groin.

She gasped and pulled away, staring at him in shock, startled out of her daydream by the evidence of his arousal through the wisp of silk she wore. He cursed his stupidity. Lost in sensation, he'd forgotten the rules of the game. Never rush a woman, especially one he did not know.

He stepped back and bowed. 'I beg your pardon.'

Fingertips went to her lips, covering her mouth, her eyes wide behind her mask, wary, distraught, but also hazy with desire, which gave him a vague sense of satisfaction.

'I mean you no harm,' he hastened to assure her, taking another step back.

'I must go,' she said breathlessly, her glance finding the door. 'I should not be here.'

A married woman then, out for a night of discreet fun. A strange sense of disappointment filled him. Really? This was exactly the sort of entertainment his friends had been recommending would get him out of the doldrums. Before he settled down to find a duchess.

'Allow me to escort you to your carriage.'

She looked startled. 'My carriage?' She swallowed. Smoothed her hands down the front of her gown, caressing the lovely shape that only a moment ago had seared a memory into his skin. 'Oh, yes. My carriage. No need for escort, Your Grace.'

Inwardly he cursed. She knew who he was. Of course she did. There wasn't a person in London who didn't after all that had happened. No wonder she didn't want to be seen with him. To be seen leaving a place like this on his arm would create yet another scandal.

He schooled his expression into cool reserve and looked down the renowned Westmoor nose. 'As you wish.'

She cast him a shy little smile. 'Thank you for waltzing with me.'

That tiny upward curve of her lips, her soft voice with its odd little accent he could not place, caused a pang behind his breastbone. 'You are welcome, my lady. May I see you again?' He froze, startled by the words that had left his lips before his brain caught up to them. Yet he waited for her answer with a sense of hopeful anticipation.

Her jaw dropped a fraction. 'Me?' she squeaked.

He couldn't help but chuckle at her surprise. He took her small hand encased in a silky glove and pressed a kiss to the inside of her wrist. 'Naturally, you.' There was no denying it to himself. He wanted her. And since he hadn't desired a woman since the night of the accident, it came as something of a relief to know he could still feel desire. 'I would like to get to know you better. If it would suit you.'

Heart pounding strangely hard, he waited for her answer. God, he felt like a schoolboy all over again. Shy. Nervous of rejection, yet full of hope.

She looked wildly around as if expecting someone to leap out at her. 'I couldn't.'

She sounded so genuinely regretful, it made him all the more determined. 'You could if you really wished to.'

Her bottom lip drooped. 'It is not possible.'

He'd not flirted and bedded the most beautiful women in London without learning a trick or two. 'It will be our secret. No one will ever know. Not from me. Not if you do not wish. I give you my word.' He ran a fingertip along her jaw and ended up touching her bottom lip still flushed red from his kiss. 'Please.'

'I cannot risk—'

'No risk. I simply want to talk, that is all. There is a garden at the back of the club. Very quiet. The windows on that side are all nailed shut.' He and his fellow owners had decided early on that they would make very sure the club was inviolable to peeping toms and nosy newspapers. Nor did they wish to upset their more respectable neighbours. 'Meet me there tomorrow evening at seven. I will leave the gate beside the mews open for you.'

She looked adorably confused. 'I shouldn't.'

He reached out to touch her mask. 'You came here and you shouldn't.'

Her shoulders sagged and he felt a little spurt of triumph, tinged with a dash of guilt.

'If I can...'

Again the careful diction. Perhaps a foreigner trying to sound English, but not an accent he recognised. 'If you can't come tomorrow, then I will wait for you the next evening and the next until you do.'

'I don't know.' On those words, she turned and fled.

But she would. He was sure of it. He'd seen the longing in those amazing spring-green eyes.

He followed her at a leisurely pace, not wishing to scare her. By the time he reached the front door and looked out, the carriage was gone.

'Anything I can do for you, Yer Grace?' Snyder asked.

Jake smiled at him. 'Nothing.'

The man's eyes widened in shock.

Feeling just a tiny bit smug, Jake walked away, humming.

Chapter Two

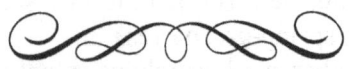

''Ere you are!'

Heart in her throat, Rose swung about, water and suds splashing on the floor. Those were not the deep drugging tones of the man she'd lived in fear would discover her, but Flo's strident angry tones.

She sagged back against rim of the sink. 'Oh, it's you.'

Flo folded her arms across her chest. ''Oo else would it be?' Her expression changed from anger to worry in a heartbeat. 'Wot's wrong?'

'Nothing.' She swallowed the dryness in her throat that had been there since two nights ago. 'I've had extra work,' she mumbled. 'I haven't been able to get away. Perhaps I will see you later.'

Flo narrowed her eyes. 'Oh, no. You'll just go sneaking off again.' She grabbed Rose's wrist and dragged her into the pantry. 'Tell me wot's 'appened. You look like someone died.'

Misery climbed Rose's throat and stuck there in a huge lump at the memory of His Grace the Duke of Westmoor's large hand on the small of her back. The sensation of the tease of his lips danced across her mind and sent chills rushing across her skin. He'd been lovely. So handsome in an unkempt way, his hair a little longer than it should be, his cheeks hazed in stubble, his appearance slightly rumpled. As if he needed someone to care for him.

But, oh, his kisses, they had been truly amazing. Never had she suspected a kiss could be so pleasurable. It was all she'd been able to think about in her bed of a night.

How could she have let him kiss her? Knowing he was one of the owners of the club. Knowing how far above her he was—a duke, no less. How wanton she had been in her enjoyment of his mouth on hers. Worse yet, how she longed to kiss him again.

And she could, if she met him as he'd asked.

She didn't dare, yet the thought of him waiting... She pushed the thought aside. 'Was the dress to your liking?'

'Of course it was. Why do you think I was looking for you?' Flo shoved a handful of coins at her. 'Why haven't you popped in to see us tonight? No one does hair the way you do and the girls have been asking after you.'

She should never have ventured into the Green Room in the first place. If she hadn't, she would never have met His Grace and she wouldn't be walking around with her mind in a whirl and her heart aching.

They'd told her and told her at the orphanage what happened when girls let their emotions and feelings get the better of them. Most of those left there were the product of illicit relationships. As she was. Wanton blood ran through her veins. She'd refused to believe it, until two nights ago. 'I have to go. If Mrs—'

'The sooner you tell me wot's wrong, the sooner you can go back to your dirty dishes.'

She gazed at her friend, at her kind and worried expression. She had to tell someone. Had to. 'You promise you won't tell.'

'Cross my heart and hope to die.'

Rose managed a weak smile at the childish oath. Where to begin? She peeked out of the pantry door. No sign of Cook.

'I met a man.'

Flo squeaked with excitement. 'You are walking out?'

Rose shuddered at the very thought. 'Oh, no.'

Her friend glowered. 'If the bastard took advantage, I'll scratch his eyes out, so I will.'

'Nothing like that,' Rose hissed. 'We danced a bit. He kissed me.' She touched her lips at the recollection. 'He was lovely.'

'So...where's the problem?'

'He's a gentleman. Oh, Flo, I tried on the gown and the mask and he caught me waltzing around in it. I think he thought I was one of the lady guests. He wants to meet me.'

'So meet him. If you like him, that is.'

'How can I?' She gestured to her faded gown. 'He's a gentleman. One of the nobs.' Worse. Far worse. He was a duke, but she did not dare mention that or Flo would guess his identity. 'What would he think if he saw the real me?' The thought of his disgust had her heart sinking to her shoes. All her life she'd been disdained. An unwanted orphan. Child of sin. 'Perhaps he'll think I tricked him on purpose. I can't lose this job.' Or her small room in the boarding house. She was barely able to afford it as it was. She'd have to start all over again and this time with no character. She'd be lucky not to end in the workhouse. Or worse. 'I should never have put on that dress.' She sank on to the hard wooden chair. 'What am I to do? He'd said he'd wait every night until I met him. What if he really is waiting?'

Flo tilted her head, her blue eyes perceptive. 'You like this man.'

She'd be lying to her friend if she said no and that she did not want to do. 'He was nice.' More than nice. He made her heart do somersaults and her body tingle in wicked places.

That last, though, was something she would never admit to anyone.

'Then the real question is...do you want to see him again?'

Dreadfully. The longing in her heart would not be denied. 'I feel horrible every time I think of him waiting.' The back of her throat burned at the idea she would never see him again, except maybe from a distance. 'I should at least let him know meeting him again is impossible. But how could I, dressed like this? I'd be too ashamed. Oh, why, oh, why did I try on the dress?'

Flo ran a glance from her head to her heels. 'You're right. That dress certainly won't do. Leave it to me.' She bustled away.

Rose mopped the water from the floor and she plunged her hands back into the hot soapy water.

Her heart picked up speed at the thought of seeing His Grace again. She took a deep steadying breath. She couldn't. No matter what Flo said. It was an impossible dream. Hadn't she learned long ago dreams were not for the likes of her?

Of course he would not be waiting.

She'd heard all the rumours about him. How he was before he came into the title. He was a man who loved the ladies. All different sorts of ladies. Never faithful to one particular one. Always out for a good time. There were darker rumours, too. Those she'd ignored.

Oh, he might have shown up once, she supposed, shrugged his shoulders at her non-appearance and moved on.

If only her foolish heart didn't keep wanting to know for certain. And hoping.

Only a fool would spend three nights sitting on a cold stone bench waiting for a woman who had made it pretty clear she wouldn't meet him.

A fool indeed.

Not to mention that the last thing he needed was to become

entangled with another man's wife. Dukes didn't do that sort of thing. So what if she'd felt so right in his arms, had eyes the colour of peridots and her kisses tasted of honey and innocence? He had responsibilities now. Duties. The days of dalliance and enjoyment were done.

Besides, he didn't deserve them.

And yet, still he sat here, watching the gate in the wall leading into the garden from the alley. This was the very last time. He'd said it last night, but tonight he meant it.

He got up and paced around the lawn, letting the blood flow back into his backside, rolling his shoulders to ease the tension. Though why he'd be tense he didn't know. All the paperwork he'd ploughed through earlier in the day, no doubt. He needed a drink to relax him, instead of hanging about here like some lovesick swain.

Hell. He didn't even know her name. Had no way of seeking her out. In his mind he called her the lady in red. *His* lady in red, no less, he mocked.

If she didn't come this evening, he'd pin his card to the gate. She could damned well chase after him. He had only come tonight because a gentleman always kept his word. At least, until it was no longer viable. Three nights was more than enough, though he'd likely always regret never seeing her face or getting her name. A feeling he couldn't account for at all. Perhaps it was because of his surprise at seeing her float around in front of the mirror like a goddess come to earth. And the way she'd made him feel something other than numb for those few moments.

Perhaps this was his punishment for all the times he'd missed appointments with his father because he was having such a good time. Just deserts, so to speak. He glanced heavenwards and shook his head. Pure imagination. And wishful thinking.

He returned to the stone bench and eyed it with distaste.

Why not simply give up and return to the comforts of the club and a very fine old brandy?

Better yet, he should go home. The thought of the accusing stares of his household slid a dagger between his ribs and into the hollow cavity of his chest. The same guilty pain he felt every time his grandmother looked at him.

He pulled out his pocket watch and flicked open the case with a thumbnail. Twenty minutes past the hour of seven o'clock. Ten minutes and he was leaving.

Once more he paced the edge of lawn and then shot a glance at the garden gate…again.

His jaw dropped. For a moment he thought he might be experiencing a hallucination. Despite the fact that he'd been waiting, he'd been positive she would not come.

Now she was here, he was slack jawed and speechless. Tonight, she was vision in green wearing a far more modest gown than she'd worn the night they'd met, but it also showed off the sumptuousness of her hour-glass figure, the elegant slope of her shoulders and brought out the unusual green of her eyes. Tonight, instead of a river of hair down her back, her tresses were hidden beneath the crown of a straw bonnet, leaving only one ringlet to fall over her shoulder and draw attention to her magnificent cleavage.

Delicious. He almost licked his lips with the desire to taste every inch of her milky skin.

The hesitance in her expression brought him to his senses.

He bowed. 'Madame.' Dash it, couldn't he sound more friendly and less ducal? What had happened to his famous rakish charm?

'I wasn't sure you would still be here.' She sounded breathless. Shy.

He shrugged. 'I gave my word. Though I must say I was about to leave.'

She winced. 'I apologise. I was unable to…come before.'

Was she toying with him? Hoping that by keeping him

in suspense, she could control him? It wouldn't be the first time a woman had tried such ploys. He was too old a hand at the game of flirtation to be caught in such a way. Then why was he staring at her with a besotted grin on his face? *Idiot.*

He took her hand in his and kissed the back of her glove.

She dipped a curtsy.

Another man of his rank might have deemed her courtesy an insult, for it was neither deep enough or held long enough to be deemed anywhere close to correct. Indeed, it was more of a little bob, as if he held a junior rank or no rank at all.

A deliberate snub? Had she heard the rumours and believed them?

He put his hands behind his back, reverting to the posture his father had so often employed to put him in his place.

She glanced up at him from beneath her lashes. A quick shy little glance before she looked at her feet again. 'I did not intend to come at all,' she said in her soft clear voice, the odd little accent once more teasing at his ear. 'But I did not like to think of you waiting.'

She was pitying him? His spine stiffened. 'I can assure you I have not been waiting long.'

She nodded her acceptance of his words, when he had expected her to flirt and tease. Something he would have been perfectly comfortable with. This honesty left him flat-footed. All at sea. 'Since you are here,' he said, more gruffly than he intended, 'perhaps you would care to take a turn about the garden?'

She glanced around nervously and up at the building. 'If you are sure we will not be seen.'

'I am sure.' He held out his arm.

After a slight hesitation that had him on tenterhooks, she rested her hand on his arm.

A tactical error. By walking side by side, the only way he could see her expressions was to bend forward to peer around the brim of her bonnet. And wouldn't that make him look like some callow eager youth. He led her to an arbour where roses grew over a trellis and some thoughtful gardener had set another infernal stone seat. 'Please, sit for a while. I think you will find the view from here to your taste.' He flicked his handkerchief over the stone surface to ensure she would not ruin her gown.

She smiled up at him. 'Thank you.'

Guileless, that smile, and yet it beguiled him none the less.

She perched on the edge of the seat and he sat beside her, angling his body so he could see her profile while she gazed around.

'I did not expect so large a garden,' she said. 'In London, I mean.'

'When this house was built large gardens were the fashion. This is one of the few streets where they have not been torn down to make way for a square or a terrace. What is left of the garden is only a small part of what was here before.'

'It is quiet enough to be miles from the city.'

'You like the country? What county do you hail from?'

'I have always lived in London, Your Grace.'

'So, you do know who I am. Will you honour me with your name?'

She froze.

Another rushed fence. Curse it, what was wrong with him? He lightened his tone. 'Your first name, if you will.'

'Rose.'

'It suits you.'

'Why? Because my face goes red when I am embarrassed?'

He repressed the desire to chuckle at her defensive tone. It seemed they were both less than at ease. 'No. Because, as you know, a rose is considered the most beautiful of flowers.'

A cheeky grin lit her face. 'Now that's what you call flattery, Your Grace, and I would prefer we was...were honest in our dealings.'

The slight slip in her vocabulary stunned him. It was not

the sort of thing to fall from a gently bred girl's lips. Though a foreigner might make such a mistake, he supposed. 'So exactly where in London do you reside, Rose?'

'I doubt you would know it, even if I told you.'

Or perhaps he was wrong; she certainly sounded haughty enough to be the daughter of a nobleman.

'Are you married?' The question had plagued him from the moment they met.

Surprise filled her expression. 'Mercy, certainly not.'

'So tell me why you were here at the Vitium? Who brought you?'

'I came by myself, on my own two feet.'

He shook his head. She would not win in a war of words. 'Only patrons and their guests are permitted through these hallowed portals.'

She laughed out loud. 'Hallowed. I think not.'

Again, every word was formed with care. Perhaps she was the daughter of some foreign dignitary. Or a very accomplished actress.

He stretched out his legs. 'I am glad you came.'

'Me, too. I wasn't sure you were real. Half the time our dance seemed like a dream.'

He cocked a brow. 'A good dream, I hope?'

Gah, really? He was actually fishing for compliments?

'A lovely dream.'

He found himself tongue-tied by the sweet smile on her pretty lips, the genuine light in her eyes and the blush on her cheek. He wanted to kiss her lips. Badly.

'Shall we walk some more?'

She popped up on her feet. 'I would like that. Do you know the name of all these plants and bushes?'

'Some of them, certainly.'

Rose still could not believe she was doing this. Walking with her hand on the arm of a duke. Conversing as if it was an everyday thing. At any moment he would guess she was an impostor in borrowed clothes and revile her. She'd likely lose her job, too.

What had she done?

She'd let Flo and the other girls talk her into borrowing a gown suitable enough to wear for her gentleman, and helping her with her hair. After all, they had said, twittering in excitement, she had helped them so many times. Gloves had appeared on her hands and parasol on her arm and all topped off by a straw bonnet they all declared was fetching.

Fine feathers did not make a fine bird or a sow's ear a silk purse, but she had desperately wanted to be convinced. Silly goose.

Or she had until she reached the gate.

If Flo hadn't pushed her through, she would have fled.

Now she wished she had run, because she had the sense he was not all that glad to see her. He seemed more reserved than he had the other night, cooler, more distant.

'I really didn't expect you to be here, you know,' she said, lifting her chin.

'You think I would not keep my word?'

Oh, now he sounded insulted. An angry duke was not a good thing. She straightened her shoulders. 'That is not what I meant, Your Grace. It was I who failed to keep our...' What did one call it?

'Our assignation.' He said it casually as if it meant little of import.

Assignation. She savoured the word and stored it away for future consideration.

'So, you see,' she said, 'I assumed you would have far more important things to do beside wait for me.'

A brow quirked as if her words surprised him. 'You are here now.'

Blasted man, could he be any more stiff and starchy? The silence grew heavy. It must be her turn to say something. Oh, dear. What did one discuss with a duke? 'I...um...what sort of tree is this?' She gazed up into the leafy branches that cast a gentle dappled shade over the gravel walk.

'Beech.'

Trees were trees. Though she did know there were different kinds, she had no idea how to tell them apart. She'd seen little enough of them as a child and not much more since starting her employment. 'How do you know?'

While he looked a little taken aback, he stopped to poke at a crack in the paving slabs with the toe of his boot. A strange little shell rolled out, brown and prickly and curling away from the centre. 'For one thing, this is its fruit. A beech nut, if you will.' He pointed at the trunk. 'The bark is distinctive, as are its leaves.' He reached up and pulled down a branch so she could see close up. 'Other trees have serrated leaves, but the combination of all three tells me this is a beech.'

'Did you learn that at school?' The orphanage had taught her to read uplifting sermons and her bible, and how to do sums, but most of her education had been about making herself useful to people with money. Plying a needle, making tallow candles and soap. Sometimes one of the guardians had loaned her other things to read, Gothic tales and such, but the matron had stopped it, said it had given her ideas above her station. Improving texts were best for the likes of her.

But those glimpses into other realms had made her realise that if she wanted to get on in the world she needed to improve herself. She'd emulated the speech of the grand ladies who sometimes came to do charity work among the orphans and read everything she could get her hands on whenever she had a spare moment.

'Actually,' the Duke was saying, 'my family estate has acres of trees of all different sorts. We learned about trees almost the way we learned to walk.'

'We?'

His expression darkened. 'My brother and I.'

'You have a brother.'

'Had. He died.'

While he had done his best to sound nonchalant, she heard pain in his voice and when she risked a glance at his face, saw it in his eyes. 'I am sorry.'

He grimaced. 'I also have a sister.'

'She lives with you?'

'She is a...widow. She and her daughter reside mostly in the country.'

'Your parents?' she said tentatively, then winced. He wouldn't be a duke, would he, if his father was alive? There seemed to be a great deal of death in his family. One always imagined the nobs to be immune from such disasters. 'I'm sorry, I do not mean to pry.'

He stopped and gazed down at her with a question on his face.

Blast. Of course, anyone moving in his circles would know these things. Breath held, throat dry, heart thudding in her chest, she waited for his denunciation.

Instead, he once more held out his arm and they continued walking. 'My mother died when my sister was born. My father, little more than six months ago.'

While he sounded calm enough, tension radiated through him as if the words were hard to say. She had the urge to wrap an arm about his waist and give him a hug. Goodness, he'd probably take a fit if she did any such thing. Still, she patted his arm in silent sympathy and his amazingly blue eyes when he glanced down held a smile. 'My grandmother lives with me. A feisty old lady she is, too. Always trying to boss me about.'

She chuckled, because she sensed that was what he wanted—no, needed—and also because the idea of anyone bossing such a fiercely commanding man about was laughable. 'And what is it that she wants you to do?'

His face became inscrutable. 'Marry. Produce the heir.'

'And you do not want to?'

'I'll do my duty.'

He stopped at a flowering shrub. 'This is gentian.'

A deliberate change of subject. She might not be educated, but she wasn't stupid. 'How pretty.'

'And this is a rose bush.'

'Hah. Very funny.' The blossoms were perfect and a lovely pale yellow.

He dropped her hand and removed his fob from his pocket. He detached a small knife and cut off the stem of a blossom a day or so past the bud stage, but not yet in full bloom. With his little knife he cut off the thorns and handed it to her with a bow. 'While not as fair as you, I hope you will accept it as a token of my esteem.'

She giggled.

He cocked a brow. 'You find me amusing, Madame?'

Oh, dear, had she insulted him again? 'I find such flowery nonsense amusing. It does not sound like you at all.'

Again the strange questioning look. 'So it is honesty your prefer.'

She knew she was plain, but did she want him to say it? Better he said what he thought instead of puffing her up only to let her fall. After all, by the light of the candle, in that gown and the mask, he would not have been able to make out her features. Perhaps that accounted for his reserve. He was disappointed.

'I do prefer it.'

The smile he gave her was so sweet, so endearing, it almost took her breath away.

'Then honesty compels me to say I have never in my life met a woman like you.'

Ouch. Clearly her attempt to be ladylike was failing badly. To hide her embarrassment, she brought the rose to her face and inhaled deeply. The delicate scent brought a smile to her lips. 'And I have never smelled a rose so sweet.'

He opened his mouth to say something, then gave a swift shake of his head as if he thought better of it.

'Tell me about you,' he said, beginning to walk again.

She tucked her hand under his arm. 'There is not much to tell.' Not much of interest to him in any case.

'You have siblings?'

Siblings. Another unfamiliar word. But they had been talking of families. He must be asking about members of hers. She made a stab at the meaning.

'I have no brothers or sisters.' That she knew of. 'My parents are also dead.' Dead to her, for they'd never come to claim their bastard daughter. 'I live with distant relatives.' Liar. But what else could she say? That she lived in London's rookeries? That would certainly spoil his image of her as a lady. Anyway, what difference did another white lie make, when nothing about her was real.

They had come to a wall. The end of the garden, she assumed. She turned back and was surprised to see only the chimneys of the house were visible, through the trees. 'I suppose we must go back.'

'I wanted to show you something.'

The girls had been very free with their advice as they helped her dress. Flo's last warning rang in her ears. 'If he says he wants to show you something, watch out. He might want to show you more than you want to see.'

'Such as what?' she had asked.

The girls had collapsed in laughter. But when they realised she was serious, they had looked worried. 'How did such an innocent come to work in a place like this?' one of them grumbled.

'He might want to show off his manly bits,' one of the others said. She pointed below her waist.

'Not if he's a gentleman,' Flo said severely. 'Not the first time. Still, be careful.'

Rose blushed at the memory.

'I really should go back.'

'Rose,' he said, shaking his head at her. 'It is nothing to fear.'

'The archbishop said to the actress,' Rose mumbled under her breath.

He laughed outright. 'I heard that, you little minx. Where on earth did you hear such a thing? From one of the servants, no doubt. I advise you not to use it in company.' He swept back a tangle of shrub that trailed down to the ground, honeysuckle, she thought, to reveal a swing hanging from the limb of a large tree.

'Oh.' She felt extremely foolish.

'Sit. I will give you a push.' He glanced up at the sky, 'And then you probably should go, before dusk draws in.'

He was right, the sky above was a much deeper blue now and the sky to the west was turning golden and pink.

He held the wooden seat steady by the ropes while she sat. The thing wobbled beneath her bum. She gave a little shriek.

'It is all right. I won't let you fall.' He frowned. 'Hold on to the rope above the knots.'

Right. Of course. She'd seen pictures of this. She could do it.

'Relax.' His grin was infectious and, yes, there was a little dimple in each cheek she hadn't noticed before. Her stomach gave an odd little hop. With a swallow, she eased her death grip on the rope.

He pushed the seat and it swung forward a foot and back a foot. She gasped. He pushed again on the backward swing. This time she went farther and her feet were far off the ground. She felt as if she'd left her stomach somewhere behind her. It caught up to her the moment she started going backwards.

She shut her eyes tight.

He pushed again.

She opened her eyes as the air rushed against her face and

tugged at her hair as the ground fell away. This must be how birds felt when they flew.

'Tell me if it's too high,' he said the next time he caught the wooden seat and pushed off again.

Her body relaxed. It wasn't too high. It was wonderful. She laughed, throwing her head back, gazing up into the tree. The rushing air forced the bonnet from her head, the ribbons caught, then let go and it flew away. A strange sense of joy filled her. She couldn't help it. A feeling of…freedom. She smothered the urge to laugh until she was breathless.

Gently, carefully, as if she was precious, he brought the swing to a stop. He came around to face her a smile on his lips, gazing down at her with such a look in his eyes, she felt seared to her very soul. A feeling something like the one when she had when they danced in the Green Room.

Slowly he dipped his head.

She lifted her face to meet his searching gaze, a sense of wonder filling her heart. A feeling so powerful, it felt as if it would burst out of her chest.

Their lips met.

The magic of his kiss swamped her, so light and tender, a brush of his lips, a touch of his tongue that made her insides tighten and her breath leave her lungs in a rush.

His arm went around her, bringing her to her feet, her body flush with his. She twined her arms around his neck, floating on a cloud of hot sensation, her breasts feeling heavy and full, her heart pounding against her ribs, her whole body melting into his.

One large hand cradled her face, warm, strong. When had he removed his gloves? Why did she care? Feeling his skin warm against hers, his strength held under control yet supporting her with a sureness that made her feel weak, was heavenly.

He nipped at her bottom lip, teased with his tongue until on a sigh she opened her mouth and let him taste.

A Florentine Kiss. She'd always thought it sounded nasty, but this was lovely. It created hot shivers across her skin, wicked pulses low in her abdomen, an expanding sensation of joy that made her heart feel too large for her chest.

A groan rumbled up from his throat and his fingers speared into her hair.

One of her hands had, of its own volition, settled on his chest. It trembled in time to the beat of his heart. The sensation seemed to travel all the way from her fingertips until it took up residence deep inside her stomach.

Her head spun with the onslaught of heat and cold and lightning seemingly happening all at once.

His free hand cupped her hip, pulling her close to his lovely lithe body, so firm against hers. The ridge of his arousal pressed against her belly. Her dazed mind sounded a warning. She pushed at his chest, felt resistance, then, to her relief, he eased away, their lips continuing to cling for a fraction longer. He stepped back.

He was breathing hard.

As was she.

What must he think?

Wanton. Just like your mother.

She covered her mouth with her hand before she said something stupid. Like, thank you. Or, again, please.

With horror she realised her hair had come down and was now a mess of lopsided curls. 'I should go.' She looked around for the bonnet. It wasn't hers to lose.

'Rose.' He held out a hand to her, a careful smile on his lips. 'Sweetheart.'

The sound of the endearment made her want to weep. Couldn't he see, she could never be his sweetheart? She wanted a home. A family. A husband. If she didn't leave now, that dream would be over.

While he had been kind and very sweet, that kiss meant he knew she was no lady. Knew she was not his equal in any respect and he had as good as said he would be marrying soon. A lady. A woman of his own class.

There was no sign of the bonnet. Darnation, she would buy Diana a new one. 'I'm sorry. I cannot do this.' She picked up her skirts and ran.

The crunch of his feet on the gravel followed. Got closer.

She spun around. Backed into the gate. Hands pressed flat against rough wood behind her. 'Don't.'

His expression was puzzled. Perhaps a shade angry. And he had her bonnet dangling from his fingers.

She put up a hand to halt him. 'Please. Let me go. This was a mistake. I'm sorry.'

He froze, his body rigid. 'I beg your pardon, Rose.' He bowed.

The hurt in his eyes stopped her breath. The urge to stay wrenched at her heart, perhaps even her soul, she felt such a pang. Staying would make things worse. If he knew what she was, then it would ruin everything. Spoil the memories.

She whirled around. In seconds she was out of the gate and running. At the end of the alley, she collided full tilt with someone. She let out a shriek.

'Rose!' Flo's voice.

She had waited, despite Rose telling her not to. She almost collapsed with relief.

Flo held her by the upper arms, her eyes blazing as they search her face. 'The bastard. Wot did he do?'

'No, no. He didn't do anything. It was me.'

Flo's gaze went back up the alley. 'Blasted toffs.'

'Please, Flo. I want to go. Now.'

Clearly torn between wanting to seek out the man and needing to help Rose, Flo hesitated.

'Flo, I need to go home.'

With a curse, Flo put an arm around her shoulders and turned down the street heading for Cheapside.

Chapter Three

Heavy-eyed and muzzy-headed, Jake lifted his gaze from the numbers dancing across the page of the ledger and stared at the straw bonnet sitting on the corner of the desk.

What had he been thinking? He was the Duke, not the carefree second son any longer. He had responsibilities and, as his father had reminded him with his dying breath, a duty to the Westmoor name. A duke didn't go about importuning ladies in a hidden garden. Surely even he had too much pride to abase himself before an unwilling woman. His brother would never have considered such a thing.

Besides, even if she was not a member of the *ton*, Rose was innately a lady in every respect. The rake in him had recognised her innocence from the first and he had come so close to scaring her to death, she'd had to run from him. It did not bear thinking about.

After swearing to his father to do his duty by the title, at the first temptation to come his way he'd returned to his old careless impetuous ways. Shame flooded him to the core of his being.

Thank heavens Rose had more sense.

And yet something inside him kept urging him to seek her out.

He could do it. He could find her. A widow or wife living on the edges of society in search of a bit of harmless adventure would be known to someone. As a duke, he had unlimited resources. And he could bend her to his will, make her want him if he put his mind to it, too. He'd charmed enough ladybirds and widows in his salad days to know his appeal to the ladies. A charm he'd never given a second's thought. Until now.

Not that he would. It wouldn't be honourable.

He really ought to apologise, though.

Those last moments with his father floated through his mind.

'You swear you will give up your rakish ways and give the title its due? For my sake.'

'No!' he'd yelled. *'You are not going to die. You must not. I do not want this—'* His voice had broken.

A heavy sigh. *'Do your duty, my son. That is all I ask. Care for Eleanor and my mother.'*

Fingers, clammy and cold, had clenched on his hand.

'Swear it.'

His throat had felt raw. His eyes had burned.

'I swear it, Papa. On my life.'

'I trust you, my son.'

The grey eyes had closed for the last time.

Trust was a heavy burden. Jake squeezed his eyes shut and prayed for respite, for an hour or two of sleep before he returned to the house where his father had placed a life of duty and honour upon shoulders ill-prepared to bear them. Burdens he had never wanted.

How many times during his youth had he rejoiced that the dukedom was his brother's destiny and not his, while he went his merry way.

'You here again, Westmoor?'

He looked up at the impatient tone.

Frederick loomed over him, glaring down. 'Do you not have a home to go to? Oh, wait. You do. A ducal mansion.' He inhaled and curled his lip in distaste. 'God, how much wine have you drunk?' He whisked the decanter off the desk and deposited it back on the tray on the console between the shuttered windows. 'You stink of brandy. Go home. Bathe, for God's sake.'

Frederick's brusque manner hid a caring heart. Jake knew this, but he simply glowered at his friend. 'I have as much right to be here as you do. I am doing something useful.' He glanced down at the ledger. Trying to anyway.

'We employ a bookkeeper for that.'

'Someone has to oversee the bookkeeper.'

What on earth was the matter with him? Fred's advice might not be to his liking, but it wasn't wrong.

Besides, it was a lady's prerogative to choose her protector. A gentleman simply shrugged and moved on if he wasn't picked. He toyed with one of the blue ribbons from the bonnet and twined it around his fingers. Not that he'd suffered such rejections in the past. After all he'd been the second son of a duke, fabulously wealthy in his own right and his reputation for generosity had not gone unnoticed.

Until now. Damn it all, he needed to think about something else. About those in his care. His grandmother, for example.

When had he last seen the old girl? He cast his mind back with effort. Two days ago? Three? She'd be worrying. The thought of her in distress made his stomach roil. Another failure to add to a string of them he dragged behind him like anchors.

Fred peered at the bonnet. 'What is that doing there?'

'Nothing. I found it in the garden. One of the girls must have dropped it. I thought I would ask around.'

'I doubt any of them would want that old thing back.'

'Probably not.' Jake picked it up and dropped it in the rubbish basket.

'Well, I'll leave you to it,' Fred said.

'Not on my account, I hope. I'm leaving.'

'I only came by to check on the state of the cellar, which I have done. See you later, Westmoor.'

Fred left, closing the door behind him.

Jake forced himself to his feet. He was done here. There was no point in pretending to read numbers when he could barely see them. He picked the bonnet out of the bin and hung it on the back of the door. *Just in case.*

He wandered off to the stables. He deliberately did not glance at the garden gate and nor did he utter a word at the reproving glance he received from his coachman for keeping him waiting till some ridiculous hour of the morning. Again. Thank goodness the stables at Vitium et Virtus offered comfort for long-suffering servants.

Once home, he went straight to his room, endured the ministrations of a valet who did nothing but complain about the fit of his coats and the state of his linen, and shut himself in the library, which he now used as his office. Even after all these months, he still couldn't bring himself to use the ducal study.

Instead, he'd had them bring a writing table in here along with the various documents he needed day to day. He'd also had them cover the most recent family portrait. His father, brother, sister and himself. Something about the way his father and brother looked out of that frame made him feel inadequate. And as guilty as hell.

Why had he not done as his father had asked him on that last day?

Such a simple request. For some reason he could no longer fathom, or justify, he had taken umbrage at the implication that he had nothing better to do than dash off to Brighton to curry favour with the Regent.

If only—

He cut the thought off and returned to the pile of correspondence awaiting his attention. Why had he never realised how much work it was, being a duke? Likely because his father and brother had never involved him in the routine running of the Duchy.

Nor had he wanted them to. Had he?

He shut his eyes, briefly. No. He had not. He'd been having too good a time as he'd so often gloated to an older brother weighed down by responsibilities and paperwork.

Too busy enjoying the charms of the fairer sex, his unbelievable luck at the tables and running Vitium et Virtus with his friends. Running it and enjoying its entertainments. Though he had to admit the sameness of it all had begun to pall some time ago.

The library door opened to admit an elderly lady with her hair powdered and her back ramrod straight, despite needing the support of her cane. A pair of piercing grey eyes fixed on his face. Eyes like his father's. And his brother's. His were blue, like his mother's and Eleanor's.

'Grandmama. Good morning.'

A beauty in her youth, she was still a handsome woman in her seventies.

She snorted. 'Don't "Grandmama" me in that cozening tone. It is mid-afternoon. Where have you been? I having been wanting to speak to you for two days now.'

'Out. What can I do for you?'

She pursed her lips, but plucked a letter from her reticule. 'Eleanor asks if she may come to town next week. She wishes to shop.'

Eleanor. Something else his father hadn't seen fit to tell him about. If ever he discovered who the father of his niece was, who the man was who had abandoned his sister to a life of secrets and loneliness, he was going to roast him on a spit.

'She may come whenever she wishes, as I told her.'

'Your father...'

'In this one thing, Grandmama, my father was an ass.'

The starch went out of his grandmother and all of a sudden she looked old and frail and sad. She sank into a chair. 'It was on my advice that we sent her away,' she admitted, sounding miserable. 'I thought it was for the best. You know your father always took my advice when it came to your sister after your mother died.'

Jake bit back a hard retort about his father needing to think for himself and came around to sit beside his grandmama on the sofa.

She reached out and touched his hand. 'You are a good boy, Jake. You have a kind heart.'

Not always. His mind went back to Rose. He'd upset her very handily, when clearly she did not fancy him the way he had fancied her. It was such a spur-of-the-moment thing, he barely understood it himself.

Dash it. He would find her and make sure she had suffered no ill effects as a result of his reckless behaviour. It was the honourable thing to do. But right now his grandmother needed him. 'Shall I ring for tea?'

'No, thank you. I need to get a reply off to Eleanor in the post. I want to assure her right away that she is welcome. Any delay and she will think we don't want her and these days, with my stiff joints, writing is a slow business.'

'Why do you not let me hire a secretary for you or a companion to help with such things?' It was not the first time he'd made the suggestions since her last lady companion had departed.

She shot him a steely-eyed stare his father would have been proud of. 'Your wife would be companion enough, should you deign to obtain one.'

He masked a wince. 'I have to find a willing lady first, Grandmama.'

Her brows lowered. 'Excuses, excuses. Why, I have introduced you to a dozen suitable young women over the past few weeks.'

His hackles rose. He was perfectly capable of finding his own wife. When he was ready. 'It is too soon, Grandmama. We are barely out of mourning.'

'Your father would have wanted you to secure the succession as soon as possible. You danced with Mrs Challenger at the ball you threw for her and Challenger. You could have used the opportunity to meet this Season's crop of debutantes. But, no, not one other lady did you ask to dance.'

His scalp tightened. Every muscle in his body felt tight. He now knew how a fox must feel when chased by the hounds. He forced himself to remain polite. 'The ball was a favour to one of my oldest and dearest friends. Right now, the affairs of the Duchy require my complete attention. Let me get those in hand and then I promise you I will do my duty and attend every ball and assembly from John o' Groats to Land's End. I will leave no stone unturned. No maiden left uninspected for her suitability.'

She laughed and shook her head. 'Ridiculous boy. You always did have a way with words. But...' she wagged a finger gnarled by the ravages of rheumatism '... I will keep you to that promise. Or the spirit of it anyway.'

She limped out of the room.

Eight hours later, Jake found himself entering Vitium et Virtus in search of an hour or two of sleep before the sun rose. Again. He'd forced himself to remain at home, to go to bed like a normal person, under his own roof—and lain awake all through the darkest hours. Now, at almost dawn, he needed sleep to the point of desperation.

Snyder greeted him briefly, took his coat and hat and left him in peace.

If there was peace to be had. The servants would soon be bustling about their chores.

He should have come earlier. He strolled past the Green Room and against his will opened the door and looked in.

Naturally no one was twirling about in front of the mirror. No one was there at all. And in the interim he'd come to the conclusion he should forget about Rose. Seeing her again, he had concluded, would only make his restlessness worse. He had a duty to the Duchy as his grandmother had pointed out. He must make a good marriage if he was to secure the future of his name and the dynasty entrusted to his care. Albeit reluctantly, he'd given in and taken up the mantle and the strawberry-leaved coronet. Blast it.

The weight of that mantle and crown had him dragging his steps towards the owners' private quarters. He passed a maid already at her work in the grand hall, the entrance used by paying members.

On her hands and knees polishing the marble floor, she was scrubbing so hard that her bottom moved in counterpoint to the swish of her cloth.

A very attractive, lushly curved bottom it was too. Drawn by some unnamed instinct, he paused to watch, feeling a strange sense of kinship with that sweetly rounded bum. A palm-tingling urge to stroke and squeeze. And she was humming quietly to herself. A familiar refrain that… No. It could not be.

His gut clenched. He felt ill. She was not… He refused to allow it.

Unable to stop himself, he walked stealthily around her, but she must have seen a movement from the corner of her eye, because she jerked upright, still on her knees, and looked up at him, her face pink with exertion—

'Rose!'

She winced at his shout.

* * *

Staring at the Duke, Rose felt horror roll through her in a sickening tide. Another half-hour and she would have been hidden away in the kitchens for the rest of the day.

He was staring at her as if he expected her to say something. She dropped the rag, wiped her hands on her apron and pushed to her feet.

She bobbed a curtsy, keeping her head respectfully lowered, her gaze on the floor, wishing he'd walk away. Or that the floor would crack open and swallow her up. 'Your Grace.'

All she could see were his feet planted squarely on the patch of marble she'd scrubbed clean. She waited for him to move on. She didn't dare look at his face, at the disgust she'd see in his expression.

Or the anger.

'Well?' he said softly, menacingly. 'Are you going to explain?'

'Explain what?' She winced. She hadn't intended to speak out loud. A glance upwards at his implacable expression sent a shiver down her spine. It was far worse than a show of anger. He looked merely curious. Almost cold.

'Explain why you never told me that you work here.' He looked down his ducal nose. 'You do work here? Have been working here for some time?'

And was unlikely to be working here much longer. She nodded miserably. 'As a scullery maid.'

He folded his arms across his chest. 'So what were you doing in the Green Room the other evening?'

She shrugged. 'I had been mending the gown. I tried it on to see...' Dash it, if she was going to be let go, it might as well be for the true reason. 'I wanted to see what I would look like in such a lovely gown.'

His frown deepened.

She held her breath, waiting for the full force of his wrath.

'You made me think you were gently bred. A lady.' Not angry, disappointed.

What right did he have to be disappointed? 'If you'd thought me a lady, you would not have met me in private or kissed me without permission.' She winced at her scolding tone. What was the point of feeling embarrassed? She was what she was and she cared nothing for his opinion, good or bad.

Only she did. Heat rushed to her face and she let her gaze fall away. 'I apologise, Your Grace. I—I did not set out to trick you. It simply happened. I should never have met you in the garden, however. For that I am sorry.'

His feet did move away then. A few steps and then silence. She looked up, expecting him to be gone, not to find him perched on the second step of the stairs up to the great subscription room.

He gestured for her to come closer and she found it odd when she approached that she was in fact looking down on him by an inch or two.

It made him seem less imposing, less of a threat and more like the man she had met in the garden. As if they were somehow equals. They were not. A fact she would do well to remember.

'This time you will tell me the truth, if you please.'

She clenched her hands at her waist. 'What is it you want to know?'

He narrowed his eyes at her obvious defensiveness.

What did it matter? She was going to lose her job anyway. She shrugged.

'Very well. What is your real name?'

'Rose Nightingale.'

He made a face of disbelief.

'Is too,' she said.

'Very well, Miss Nightingale. How long have you worked at Vitium et Virtus?'

'Four months or so.'

'Do you live in or out?'

She hissed in a breath. Why did he want to know that? Only a few of the employees here lived in. He must know that, being an owner and all.

'Out.'

The answer was received with a heavy silence.

'I will collect my things and leave.' What else could she say? Clearly she had lost any regard he might have held for the woman he thought she was. An ache scoured the inside of her chest. She was wrong to have let herself be swept up in what was really was no more than a foolish dream.

'You want to leave?' he asked.

She frowned at him. A horrid suspicion entered her mind. Did he want to continue where they had left off only…? Now he knew who she was…what she was, would he treat her differently? With less respect?

'I think it is for the best.'

He regarded her for a long moment. 'You are going home?'

'Yes.'

'To your family.'

Truth. She had to tell him the truth. She had said she would. And then he really would despise her utterly. 'I have no family left that I know of.' She lifted her chin.

'Oh, Rose,' he said, shaking his head, sorrowfully.

'I have done nothing to be ashamed of.' Her face flushed again. 'Nothing that has brought harm to anyone else.' Even if she was a bastard. Born on the wrong side of the blanket, the nobs called it. She called it irresponsible.

To her surprise, he looked startled, as if her declaration surprised him. What? Did he think because she had no family, *she* was some sort of undesirable? Or worse yet, a woman of low moral character? She closed her eyes briefly. That was it, most likely. And now, like a lackwit, she had as good as told him there was no one in the world who cared what happened to her. 'Besides, it is none of your business where I go from here.' She turned away.

'Rose, wait.'

She swung back to face him.

He rose to his feet. 'You don't need to go.'

'Are you saying I haven't lost my position?'

He approached her warily, as if she might bite him if he got too close. 'No, I mean. Well, obviously I would find it difficult when…'

She narrowed her eyes at him. 'When?'

He rubbed a palm over his jaw in an odd upward motion. 'I mean, I do not like to think of you…well, scrubbing the floors.' He gestured at the rag and bucket in the middle of the floor.

She frowned. 'There is nothing wrong with scrubbing floors.'

'You could be so much more.'

Anger bubbled up at the disdain in his tone. More? Such as being his mistress, perhaps? What else could he mean? 'I am perfectly content, thank you. I certainly don't need to make my living…' She stopped before she said something really rude.

'I intended no insult, Rose.'

He was the one who sounded insulted. He had gone all ducal, looking down that lordly nose of his.

She was a fool for letting herself be swept up by a dream. Really, she was. 'I wouldn't like Your Grace to feel uncomfortable with my presence. So I will remove it.'

He reached out as if to stop her. She jerked away, and a look of chagrin passed over his face. Followed swiftly by a haughty stare. 'Very well. If you insist. Go.'

She breathed a sigh of relief, tempered by a large dose of despair.

She had liked working here. And the rules had protected her from unwanted attentions, as they had not in the residences where she had worked. Until she'd gone and broken those rules. She was going to miss her friends, too. Especially Flo.

Inwardly she groaned as the full implications of her stupidity landed in the pit of her stomach like a rock. Once her landlord learned she had lost her job, she'd be out on the street, unless she found another one quickly. She would certainly never find another employer as generous as the V&V.

She picked up her bucket and rag. Perhaps if she apologised properly he would let her stay?

When she turned back to ask him, he had gone. For a big man, he moved very quietly. The reason she hadn't heard him when she had been foolishly prancing around in the Green Room and again today when she'd been washing the floor.

Sadly, she shook her head and walked to the lower reaches of the house. If one of the owners of the club wanted her gone, what could be done?

She almost fell over when he stepped in front of her as she was about to enter the kitchen. She backed up hastily. 'I thought you went.'

'I came back.'

She tried not to roll her eyes. 'Was there something else?'

'I—' He huffed out a breath. 'You don't have to go. Keep your job. Just—just keep out of my way. All right?'

It took a moment to process the words. She nodded stiffly. 'Then please be aware, Your Grace, I am required to wash the floor in the front hall every day at five-thirty in the morning and it takes me half an hour.'

'I take note, Miss Nightingale.'

She gritted her teeth. 'It's Rose, Your Grace. Just Rose.' A duke did not offer courtesy to a servant, not if he didn't want to cause talk.

'Rose. Good day.'

Good? What was good about today? This wasn't finished. She could feel it in her bones and down her spine. But the reprieve would give her a chance to find a new position before he changed his mind and she was let go without a character.

As the day progressed she became less worried about him changing his mind. All seemed just as usual. No calls by Mrs Parker to see her in her office. As a precaution, she stayed close to the kitchen, never being tempted into visiting her friends in case she ran into the Duke. When, at the end of the work day there was still no threat of dismissal, she heaved a sigh of relief. It seemed all was well. She scuttled out of the side door as quick as a wink, not wanting to tempt fate by lingering in the Green Room.

'Rose.'

A tall lean shadow detached itself from the darkness in the alley outside the back door.

She swallowed the dryness in her throat. Her heart sank. 'Why are you here, Your Grace?'

'I want to talk to you.'

Here it came then, after all. Her notice.

'Allow me to escort you home. We can talk while we walk.'

'I'm not taking you to where I live. I am a decent girl, I am.' Her landlord would be scandalised. Well, perhaps not. He didn't seem to care about that sort of thing, given what his other tenants were up to. But she didn't want anyone getting the wrong impression about her. It wouldn't take much and coming home on the arm of a toff like him would do it.

The Duke frowned and looked about him. 'You can't surely be intending to walk the streets alone.'

'Today is no different to any other day, Your Grace.'

He looked nonplussed. 'You will, however, permit me to walk you, if not all the way, then at least to the end of your street.'

The firmness in his voice said he was not to be denied.

'As you wish,' she muttered. She'd find a way to be rid of him long before then. She knew the neighbourhood like the back of her hand, whereas he surely did not.

They walked some distance in silence and she kept waiting for him to tell her she was dismissed. Finally she could not stand it any longer. 'What is it you wished to talk about?'

He gave her a look askance. 'I have a request to make of you. Well, more of a proposition, I suppose.'

Her heart stilled. Did she really want this? She gripped her basket tight.

Jake could not figure out what was the matter with him. He was usually so articulate, so charming around women. With Rose, he kept stumbling over his words like an adolescent stumbling over feet too large for a gangly body. And heaven knew, every time he opened his mouth he seemed to put one of those very large feet right in it.

He also noticed that while Rose seemed willing to let him walk beside her, she deliberately kept her small basket over the arm closest to him. Effectively keeping him at a distance.

Well, perhaps that wasn't such a surprise. He'd been so horrified to see her on her hands and knees that morning he'd been unable to think straight. A nap had sorted him out, somewhat. After all, finding her, knowing where she was, had enabled him to relax enough to actually close his eyes without being haunted by images— He cut the thought off. Nonsense.

He had been able to relax merely because loose ends drove him to distraction. Rose was no longer a loose end. That was all.

'What is this…proposition?' she asked, clearly irritated by his continuing silence.

'It is a matter of some delicacy,' he said, trying to frame what he wanted to say in a way she would not take amiss. He'd rehearsed it a couple of different ways in his mind, but as her responses to him in the past were always such a surprise they threw him off stride, he wasn't quite sure how to put it.

'Are you asking me to keep your confidence in this matter, Your Grace?'

There, that was what had intrigued him about her. Her quick understanding. Her sharpness of mind.

'I am. More than one matter, actually, but we will take them one at a time.'

She nodded firmly. 'I am no gossipmonger.'

He tried to squash his scepticism, given his intimate knowledge of the female gender, and was conscious of squaring his shoulders. 'It is with regard to my current living arrangements.'

She looked at him sharply. 'Go on.'

They turned on to Cheapside. He gritted his teeth. The idea that Rose walked these streets alone had his anger building again, as it had when he'd learned of her address from the housekeeper. The woman had frowned at him mightily when he'd asked for it. Worse yet, she'd more or less told him to leave the girl alone, as if he had the reputation for being some sort of lecherous beast who preyed on servant girls.

A look of the sort his father used to give *him* when he was a lad had put her in her place. An incivility for which no doubt an apology would be required at some time in the future. The woman had told him all he needed to know without further demure.

'To be honest the house has seemed empty since my—' he forced the words past his lips '—since my father and brother died. It needs a feminine touch. My grandmother is rather elderly and cannot cope.' He grimaced. 'With anything really. She keeps mostly to her rooms.' Only emerging to nag him about getting married. About the need for a legal grandchild to inherit. But that was not Rose's business. That was his problem to solve in the future when he had mastered his ducal duties.

He plunged on, surprisingly anxious to have her answer. 'I wanted to offer you the position.'

A small silence ensued. His throat tightened. He risked a

peek at her face. Her lovely mouth was set in a thin straight line. 'You want me to live in your house.'

'It wouldn't work any other way. You will be well paid, of course. Far more than your wage as a scullery maid.'

For a moment she looked torn, then her chin firmed. 'I cannot.'

Cannot? He didn't understand. 'I will, of course, provide you with a suitable wardrobe. You do not have to worry about—'

'This is my street. I bid you good day, Your Grace.'

And before he could say another word she took her heels and ran into the nearest alley.

Not her street.

A long way from her street.

In one of the worst neighbourhoods in London.

Damn it all. Why had she run, when he'd likely made the best offer of a job she had ever received in her life or was ever likely to receive?

I cannot.

A strange feeling entered his chest, sharp, ugly. Did she have a husband? A child? Such impediments would account for her reaction.

Face it, man. She didn't want the job. There were lots of women who would be thrilled to get such an offer. Find someone else and leave Rose to it.

Yet what had he said to make her upset enough to dash off down a street nowhere near where she lived? At the very least he ought to ensure she had arrived home safely and that she understood her current position at Vitium et Virtus was secure.

Did he really want to know what was stopping her from taking what had been an outstandingly generous offer?

He sighed. He really had no choice if he wanted to sleep tonight, though why that was the case when he barely knew the girl, he could not fathom.

Chapter Four

Rose perched on the edge of the small truckle bed tucked beneath the eaves in her rented chamber.

Pressure built behind her cheekbones. A lump formed in her throat while the backs of her eyes scalded. She clenched her hands together trying to breathe. She would not cry.

A sob escaped.

She swallowed it down and glanced around the shabby room. At the brave flutter of floral fabric covering the window. At the scrap of carpet beside the bed she'd bargained for at the market. At the worn-out broom she'd salvaged from the rubbish bin at the V&V. She could not help comparing what she had to what the Duke of Westmoor had offered.

She didn't know if she was upset because he had made such a dreadful offer, or because she had turned him down.

A bitter smile pulled at her lips. Likely a bit of both.

He was such a handsome, charming man. Sometimes. When he wasn't making tempting offers that undermined her efforts to maintain the standards she'd set for herself so many years ago.

She dashed a tear from her cheek that seemed to have escaped without her knowledge.

What was she to do? Her stomach pitched. This time he would see her dismissed. She was sure of it. She shouldn't have run. She should have thanked him before refusing.

The thought hit her like a blow.

She should have explained why she did not want to be his mistress. He wasn't a bad man. He was simply man who expected to get his way in all things. She had met enough of those in her time and he was, after all, a duke. But she did not think him deliberately cruel. If she had explained, he might have understood.

Or not. But at least she would have had her say instead of running away like a coward.

Truth be told, if she had stayed, she might well have said yes. The thought of his kisses and the tender way he'd held her in his arms when they danced had tempted her sorely.

That same temptation had led her into the mistake of meeting him in the garden, of seeing him one last time to tell him they should not meet again. Clearly he now thought her a low sort of creature, given the way she earned a living.

The rosy dreams she'd been clutching to her heart since the hours spent in the garden turned to ashes before her closed eyes.

Not that she'd expected to see him again. She really hadn't. She'd simply enjoyed the dream. It made the day pass faster and the drudgery of her life seem less hard.

This offer made a mockery of those innocent imaginings. Didn't she know better than to have dreams? Had she not learned to live day to day? To survive by hard work and keeping herself to herself? She'd let herself be lured into the pitfall of wanting more and look what he'd offered. Hope. It was such a stupid thing.

A cacophony, louder than usual, drifted up from the street

below. An argument. Someone run afoul of her landlord, no doubt. Someone unable to pay their rent.

She shivered. She'd seen more than one family evicted from this house for that crime.

Heavy footsteps thumped their way up the stairs. She expected them to stop on the floor below. More than one set, she thought. No one ever came all the way up to her little garret. And yet something about the determination in those steps brought her to her feet.

They did not stop until they arrived at her landing. A fist thumped on her door.

'Who is it?' Her voice was not as firm as she would have liked.

'It is I, Miss Nightingale.'

The cultured accents were unmistakable. Westmoor. How on earth had he found her?

''E says 'e's a friends of yourn,' the belligerent tones of her landlord added. 'Shall I throw 'im down the stairs?'

'I'd like to see you try, my good man.'

'Would yer? Put 'em up, I says.'

Goodness, they were going to come to fisticuffs on her landing.

She rushed to slide the bolt and open the door.

The Duke, with nary a hair out of place, was grinning conspiratorially at her landlord. Money went from a ducal fist to a grimy grasping hand. Blast the man.

'Miss Nightingale.' The Duke removed his hat and bowed.

'You tricked me.'

'As you tricked me. May I come in?'

'I did not trick you.'

A movement on the staircase caught her eye. Old Mrs Carter was at the forefront of a growing group of spectators. Oh, this really was too much. Her reputation was going to be ruined.

She opened the door wider. 'Please come in.' She certainly

did not want her neighbours listening to the conversation that was about to ensue.

The Duke ducked his head beneath the lintel and entered. The ceiling was too low for him to stand fully upright. Wincing, she gestured to the only chair in the room. 'Please, be seated.'

He eased his large frame on to the rickety chair as if fearing it would splinter beneath him and looked around.

Shame filled her.

Followed by anger.

She'd been proud of her little room. Her own place, rented with the money she'd earned. 'What are you doing here?'

He started to rise. 'A gentleman may not sit in the presence of a standing lady.'

They couldn't? There was nowhere for her to sit but on the edge of the bed. She perched there and clasped her hands in her lap to stop herself from throwing something at him. Or perhaps to hold herself together from flying into a thousand miserable pieces now he knew the full extent of her poverty.

'I came to make sure you arrived home safely.'

She stared at him. 'I manage to arrive home safely every day without any help. What you have done is made every occupant of this house wonder about my respectability.'

He gave an impatient sigh. 'This is not where you should be living, Rose. You deserve better.'

'What would be better about being your mistress?' The words were out before she thought about them. Heat scalded her cheeks. Her stomach twisted in a knot. She fixed her gaze on the patch in her carpet. 'Please. Go. You can let Mrs Parker know I won't be working at the V&V any longer. I have found another job.'

She clenched her hands harder and prayed she would be able to do so.

'Rose.' His voice sounded grim.

What now? Would he strike out? Like the first gentleman

whose advances she'd refused. She'd left that position. And several more after it.

She risked a glance at his face, ready to run or to defend her honour. Not easy when one was already sitting on the bed.

The stern, aloof Duke stared back at her. 'I beg your pardon,' he said stiffly. 'My behaviour led you to misconstrue my intentions.'

Misconstrue? She frowned. Not a familiar word.

'Misunderstand,' he said as if realising the source of her puzzlement, 'from the Latin *construere*.'

'What is to misunderstand?' she asked, quelling her interest in his explanation.

He tugged at his neckcloth. 'The position I was offering in my house was not as my...' He pursed his lips as if he had a bad taste in his mouth. 'It was as something else.'

An odd feeling pierced her chest. A feeling of hurt. Because she wasn't good enough or pretty enough or something to be his mistress?

'You want to hire me as a servant in your house?' She felt queasy at the thought of making up the fire in his room as he slept, possibly not alone. Of cleaning and polishing his floors as he walked passed her, unseeing with his friends. Of said friends pinching her bottom. They were the sorts of things that had kept her moving from one job to another. It was also the reason why the V&V with its rules and regulations for servants and customers alike had been so perfect.

She shook her head. 'I—'

'I want to offer you the position of companion to my grandmother.'

As the words began to make sense, she couldn't help a bitter laugh. 'A companion to your grandmother? Is this some sort of jest?'

Even she knew such a position was well above her station. She wasn't even good enough to be his mistress, for heaven's sake.

'She's lonely. She doesn't go out much. Normally such a position would fall to an indigent relative.' He shuddered. 'The only such females available are not those I would wish under my roof. You won't find it onerous. Grandmama rarely leaves the house, but she needs someone to help write her letters, fetch and carry and make sure she eats. That sort of thing. My duties mean she is frequently without any company at all. Or any…supervision. My sister is busy with her young daughter, or I would ask her. I honestly think Grandmama would take to you. You are honest, kind and, Mrs Parker informs me, one of the few under her supervision who can read and write well.'

Mrs Parker. Of course, that was how he had discovered her whereabouts. Why hadn't she thought of that? Still, she couldn't help but approve of a man who so obviously cared about his grandmother. Cared about his family. How could she not? It was all she had ever longed for in the deepest regions of her heart. A home. A family who loved her.

For one blissful moment acceptance hovered on her tongue, then the enormity of what he was asking struck her. Yes, she could read and write, but she was nowhere near well enough educated to mix with her betters. 'I'm sorry, it wouldn't work. I wouldn't know how.'

He gazed at her from beneath lowered brows, his jaw a determined jut.

This was a man to whom people did not usually say no. She steeled herself for an argument. 'Truly, I cannot. Your grandmother needs a proper lady. I couldn't possibly—'

'Rose,' he said, his voice deep and dark and delicious as he interrupted her speech. 'You are every bit as much a lady as one who bears the title. You speak as well as any lady I know, act like a lady and no one would think otherwise unless they knew. I certainly didn't.'

'I don't always speak like a lady. I don't understand all

those long words you use. And what if your grandmother learns I am one big fat lie. Wouldn't she be angry?'

He shook his head. 'Who will tell her? We shall say you were previously employed by a distant relative on my mother's side.'

'And what of your friends? Will you tell them that, too?'

'What I do, who I employ, is no one's business but mine.'

'How arrogant,' she muttered. Inwardly, she smiled at finding a use for the word she'd read in the newspaper that morning. When he pressed his lips together, she thought she might finally have annoyed him enough to make him leave her in peace.

But, no, he continued to view her with that intense gaze of his, as if he saw right through her. A look seemed to melt her from the inside out.

'At least speak with my grandmama before turning it down. Who knows, she may not offer you the position. She can certainly be a bit difficult at times.'

The poor man looked…worried. She almost felt sorry for him. Fortunately, his grandmother would have more sense than he had and she would not look at Rose with such hopefulness, either. 'And when she turns me away, you'll leave me in peace? Never speak to me again?'

He inhaled a quick breath. 'I will never speak to you first. However, should you speak to me, I will respond.'

Like that would ever happen. 'And I will keep my position at the V&V if she does not decide in my favour?'

'Naturally.'

Strangely, she had every faith he would keep his word. Which was odd, because she rarely trusted anyone. 'Very well, then. Let us go and meet your grandmother.'

He gave her a startled glance. Clearly he had not expected her to give in so quickly. She smiled sweetly. 'Is something wrong?' Like the drab gown she was wearing? Or her rough work-reddened hands?

'Not a thing,' he said more cheerfully than she expected. 'While we walk, I will explain a few of the niceties of meeting a duchess, if I may.' He gave her a piercing blue stare. 'You do plan to give this a good shot, I hope.'

Fair was fair. 'I will do my best.'

'That is all I ask.'

As he escorted her down the stairs and out into the street, she had the feeling he was smirking as if he thought he had won, though his face showed nothing. Hah. One look at her servant's garb and his grandmother would show her the door. And that would be that. Life would go back to the way it was before.

The thought gave her a queer little pang in the centre of her chest.

At the sight of his own front door, Jake breathed a sigh of relief. All during their long walk, he'd half-expected Rose to bolt again. If she had, he had no doubt she'd do everything in her power to make sure he didn't find her a second time. And then how would he ever be free of his irrational worry for her safety.

He still couldn't stop thinking about what might have happened to her if some other man had caught her waltzing around in that particular dress with that particular look on her face.

It was a sight no red-blooded male could have resisted. He certainly hadn't had the strength of will. He couldn't help thinking about what had almost happened to her at *his* hands because he had completely misread who and what she was. He'd not had a clue she was an employee.

It had been pounded into his head by his father from an early age that a gentleman never exploited a servant beneath his roof. It wasn't done. Yet he'd come far closer to breaking that rule than he liked to think.

Of course, he could have ignored her once he did know and

simply thanked his stars for a lucky escape. He would have, too, if she hadn't seemed so damnably vulnerable.

Simply watching the sensual movement of her body while she was washing the floor had heated his blood to boiling. Sooner or later one of the coxcombs who haunted Vitium et Virtus would have spotted her and, rules or no rules, taken advantage.

Jake could not abide the thought. The tightness the idea caused in his gut was not jealousy, could not possibly be jealousy. It was merely the need to protect a good but naive young woman from harm.

When he'd gone to her lodging, he hadn't quite known what he intended, but the moment he'd seen the bright scrap of fabric fluttering at the window of her shabby room, along with the worn bit of rug so neatly patched on the floor, every instinct within him rebelled at leaving her there.

He'd felt so strongly he'd ridden roughshod over her objections. Was still riding roughshod, truth to tell.

When a footman opened the door at the ducal mansion, Jake stifled a grin at the way the man hid his surprise at the sight of Rose who was also in for a surprise.

While his grandmother could be starchy, she had never considered herself above her fellow man—or woman. She was the direct descendent of a yeoman long-bowman who fought at Crécy, as she would tell anyone who cared to listen.

He waved the butler away when he stepped forward to take his hat and gloves and instead deposited them on the hall table. The less intimidating things seemed, the more likely he was to win this round.

Rose, who had no outer raiment to remove, kept her gaze fixed straight ahead, her chin up in brave defiance.

Yet tension stiffened her shoulders and a twinge of guilt at her discomfort assaulted Jake's conscience. He pushed the notion aside. After all, she was the one who had issued the final challenge.

'Her Grace?' Jake enquired of the butler.

'In her withdrawing room, Your Grace,' the butler said.

Jake winged an elbow at Rose. 'Shall we, Miss Nightingale?'

'We shall,' she said, her voice little more than a whisper and tinged with dread.

Damn it all. She was far more nervous than she appeared on the outside. 'She doesn't bite, you know.'

She didn't relax.

They climbed the stairs up to the first floor and into the east wing. His rooms were in the west wing. Or rather that was where he still kept his things. The ducal chambers were also located here in the east wing. He never used them.

The first time he had entered his father's bedroom he had felt like an intruder. Or an impostor. Or perhaps a very bad actor. The underserving villain in a play.

He opened the door to his grandmother's suite and ushered Rose in with a light touch to the small of her back.

'Grandmama, I would like you to meet a young lady introduced to me by a distant relative of my mother's. Your Grace, Miss Rose Nightingale. Miss Nightingale, Her Grace, the Dowager Duchess of Westmoor.'

Rose sank into a curtsy fit for royalty, but since his grandmother was related to some of those, it was not completely out of place.

Startlement appeared in those ancient grey eyes for the merest moment, then Grandmother smiled. 'Miss Nightingale. What a pleasure. How delightful. Are you visiting in town?'

'Miss Nightingale is seeking employment,' Jacob said, as he informed Rose he would during their walk to his house. 'Her present position is unsuitable.' It was the truth. He ignored Rose's gasp of shock.

Rose blushed, but her gaze held anger when she shot him a glance.

'My dear Miss Nightingale,' Grandmama said, 'anyone

instrumental in bringing my grandson to see me is welcome in this house.' She frowned at Jake. 'I so rarely see him these days.'

'Grandmama,' Jake scolded, with an apologetic smile. 'Miss Nightingale will think I neglect my duty.'

'You neglect your pleasures, my boy, you are so busy fulfilling your duties. Ring the bell for tea, do. Miss Nightingale, please, be seated.' She patted the sofa cushion on her right.

A good sign. If she had been dismayed or displeased she would have pointed to the chair at the end of the tea table. A chair known for its discomfort. No visitor stayed long seated upon that chair.

As long as Rose didn't decide to reveal exactly where she had been employed all should be well.

He tugged at the bell pull and reclined in his usual armchair.

'Grandmama, I believe Miss Nightingale would make you an excellent companion. I am sorry we did not give you any advance notice, but it did not occur to me until this very morning.'

His grandmother looked intrigued. 'What sort of employment have you undertaken in the past, Miss Nightingale?'

Rose lifted that stubborn little chin and Jake had the urge to nip at it. And then to kiss her luscious lips even though he knew by the martial look in her eye she planned to foil his plan.

'I have been working as a scullery maid.' She sounded as if she expected to be thrown out on her ear. Extraordinary bravery.

His grandmother stiffened. His stomach dipped. It seemed he did not know her as well as he thought.

The elderly lady narrowed her gaze on Rose, but there was a gleam of amusement in those faded eyes Jake hadn't seen for many months. 'A scullery maid.'

Rose nodded firmly.

'Good honest labour, Miss Nightingale, but beneath you, I think. My grandson was right to bring you to me.'

Rose's jaw dropped. 'But—'

The butler entered with his usual troop of footmen who glided about until the tea tray was properly presented before departing on silent feet.

'Please, Miss Nightingale,' Grandmama said, 'do pour. My hands are a little shaky at times and it makes it all such a chore.'

With a startled glance directed at Jake, Rose did as directed, making an exceedingly creditable job of it, too.

'Where did you learn such skills, Miss Nightingale?' Grandmama asked gently.

'I trained as a housekeeper,' Rose said. Her expression held surprise as she set the teapot back in its place. 'My age has precluded my obtaining such a position as yet.'

'Trained where?'

'The Foundling Hospital.'

'I see.'

It was his grandmother's turn to shoot him a look that spoke volumes, or it would have were he able to translate its meaning.

'Do you know anything about your parents, Miss Nightingale?' Grandmama asked.

Rose stiffened. Looked uncomfortable.

Jake had the urge to stand between her and his grandmother's probing questions, but it would not do. If she could not stand up for herself, then her grandmother would dismiss her as missish.

Grandmama's eyes narrowed. 'I beg your pardon, my dear. I do not wish to pry. I was merely curious.'

Rose drew in a breath. 'I know nothing at all.' From her pocket she drew out a little pouch. A needle case that looked as if it had been stitched by a child. She unfolded it and brought forth a broken mother-of-pearl button.

'I have this half-token. But no one returned to claim me.'

Grandmama's eyes swam with tears for a brief instant. So brief, Jake thought he might have been mistaken and Rose did not see it at all, since she was busy tucking away her treasures. At the thought of her always being alone in the world his throat felt deucedly tight.

Grandmama sipped at her tea, her expression thoughtful.

Rose handed him his cup. Nothing ventured, nothing gained. He took a mouthful. Perfect. He glanced at his grandmother over the rim. 'Well, Your Grace. What do you think? Will you accept Miss Nightingale as a companion? Knowing someone is keeping an eye on you will relieve my mind of a worry while I toil away at the mountain of paperwork on my desk.'

Rose kept her gaze firmly fixed on her hands in her lap. She had not touched her tea. Clearly she expected rejection.

Grandmama shot him a glance. 'Highly recommended I think you said, Jacob.'

'Very highly recommended.'

'By a relative of your mother's? One you have confidence in?'

'Indeed.'

Grandmama smiled. 'Miss Nightingale, do you think you can bear the company of a crotchety old lady day after day?'

Jakes shoulders felt suddenly a great deal lighter.

Rose's jaw dropped. 'You actually want me to be your companion? Surely some lady of rank would be better suited—'

'A lady of rank would likely drive me to distraction within a week,' Grandmother said. 'Sniffing about each request. Complaining about lost advantages. Tippling at the brandy when she thinks I am not looking.'

Jaw dropping, Rose looked at him for confirmation.

'Her Grace is right,' he said lazily, casually. 'Cousin Susan, before she went home to her mother, was always half-seas over. It was why Grandmama sent her packing.'

'That wasn't the half of it,' Grandmama said. 'I caught her snooping about in my correspondence. Not something Miss Nightingale would be about, I am sure.'

Rose shook her head.

'And you won't be stealing the silverware either, I'll be bound.'

'Grandmama!'

'Well, that nurse you hired certainly did.' She adjusted the shawl over her shoulders with a little twitch at the fabric. 'I'm missing one of your grandfather's snuffboxes. His favourite, to boot.'

'Perhaps it is simply misplaced,' Rose said with a placating smile.

'Perhaps,' Grandmama admitted. 'And perhaps you will help me find it. That is, if you will accept the position?'

Rose's eyes widened.

Jake watched with bated breath as she considered the offer. Finally she nodded slowly. 'Yes. I will, Thank you. Thank you both. I will do my very best to please.' Rose smiled. It was bright and happy and hopeful. It came from within and seemed to shove warmth at the cold empty feeling in Jake's chest.

'Excellent,' Grandmama said, beaming. 'Jake, you will inform the staff and have Miss Nightingale taken up to her room. The same one Cousin Susan used. Once she is settled, she and I will go through Eleanor's wardrobe and see what clothes are suitable for making over.'

It seemed Grandmama had found a project. She already looked brighter than she had for weeks.

Rose glanced self-consciously at her drab skirts. 'Really, I couldn't impose on your generosity.'

'Nonsense. You must and you will, for I cannot have my companion looking as if she is underpaid. People will think me a nip-farthing and that I cannot allow.'

'People?'

'Well, there are bound to be callers now we have put off black gloves. And morning calls when you are up to snuff.'

The look on Rose's face said she thought that would never happen. He wanted to grin at her, or chuck her under the chin; instead he simply nodded his agreement.

Grandmama turned on him with a sly smile and a gleam in her eye. 'It is certainly time the new Duke took up that side of his duties. He needs to find a bride.'

Jacob's stomach sank to his shoes. Blast the woman. He'd been hoist by his own petard. But he could see from his grandmother's determined expression that if he wanted to haul Rose out of that dreadful slum, he was going to have to bow to his grandmother's wishes in this matter. He should have guessed she'd turn matters to her own advantage.

He became aware of Rose watching him with an air of hope. Hope he would turn his grandmother down, no doubt.

'I shall look forward to it.'

Warily Rose edged into the stables at the back of the house and passed the first stall. The beast with its head hanging over the halfdoor was enormous. Terrifying. It rolled its brown eyes and blew a hay-scented breath in her direction. Where was the blasted man?

These past few days had moved far too fast for Rose's comprehension. Her Grace had swept her along on a tide of dressmakers, milliners and hairdressers, not to mention shoemakers and assorted other tradesmen indispensable to the companion of a duchess. The worst part of it all was not understanding why Westmoor, as she was now to call him, really wanted her to take this position. Nor why a footman followed her all the while like a lost puppy, making privacy impossible.

When she had tried to send the young man about his business, he had looked anxious. Her Grace's orders, he had said. In case she became lost.

Only until she knew her way about, Her Grace had informed her, when she had asked. For example, did she know she was not to visit a gentleman alone? Should a lady ever, even by chance, you understand, be alone with a gentleman, then the door was to remain open at all times with a footman hovering a few feet away.

As if *she* was some sort of lady.

Finally, she had tracked the Duke down. After seeing him from her chamber window return from his morning ride, she had slipped out of the house by the side door and made her way to the stables.

She inched past the hind end of another large animal, this one nosing around in its manger. To her relief, the next stall contained the man she sought. She blinked. Busy grooming a horse, he had not noticed her presence and she paused, not sure if she dared interrupt. She'd heard much about the eccentricities of the nobility, but this menial work seemed a little odd, even for a duke who owned the most disreputable gentleman's club in London.

Coatless, with his shirtsleeves rolled up to the elbows displaying strong forearms dusted with dark hair, she had an excellent perspective of a pair of broad shoulders displayed to advantage. And a delicious view of a muscular rear end as he brushed the horse's glossy brown coat with long sweeping motions. Her insides clenched. Warmth suffused her skin.

She ought to close her eyes or turn away, she really ought, but she stood silently burning up inside, watching the elegant strength of him. Longing crept through her, as it did every time she encountered this man, despite the way he kept his distance.

The way she felt around him did not seem to lessen with familiarity, either. The more she saw of him, the more attractive she found him. Never before had she been so tempted by a man. It was the reason for her need to speak with him.

To hand in her notice. She had to leave before she was overcome by desire.

Thank heavens he was not the least affected by her presence. When he noticed her at all, he seemed coolly amused.

The thought gave her courage.

'Your Grace?' It came out more of a whisper than actual words. She swallowed the dryness and tried again. Louder. 'Your Grace.'

He swung around, his eyebrows climbing to hide beneath the lock of dark hair that had fallen forward over his forehead. Something flashed in his eyes, gone too fast for her to be sure what it meant. The sweat trickling from his temple and trailing down his cheek riveted her attention. A sudden urge to taste that trail with her tongue stole her breath and left her speechless.

'Miss Nightingale.' His dark brows crashed down. 'What are you doing out here?' He seemed to be looking around for someone else. 'You should not be out here alone.'

The horse stamped an enormous hoof and she leapt backwards.

He patted the animal. 'Steady, boy,' he said gently, soothingly. 'You'll get your turn. Right now we have a guest.'

He gave her an encouraging smile, causing dimples to appear each side of his mouth, and her stomach to flutter. 'Old Sev, here, thinks I should be paying attention to him, instead of talking to you.'

She steeled herself against his charm. 'If you hide from him, the way you hide from me, it is no wonder.'

The frown returned. 'I do not hide from you, Miss Nightingale. I see you at dinner when I am home. And in the drawing room afterwards. I very much enjoyed your reading from Gray's "Elegy" the other evening.'

Right. He'd enjoyed it so much he'd bid them goodnight after half an hour. 'I mean, we have not had an opportunity to speak privately.'

His lips thinned. 'Nor should we. As my grandmother's companion—'

'That is precisely what I wanted to talk to you about.'

He looked puzzled and perhaps even a little angry, or was it something else she saw reflected in his gaze? 'Is there a problem? The servants lacking in respect? If so—'

'No, no. Everyone has been most kind.' Extraordinarily respectful, in fact. As if she was some sort of duchess. Honestly? The only thing making her uncomfortable was him. Knowing he was there in the house, sensing his presence and feeling the disturbing need to seek him out as if there was more between them than employee and employer.

There wasn't. There could not be. Yet no matter how often she told herself not to think about him, her mind kept going back to his kiss until she could barely sleep of a night. Taking this position had been a very bad idea indeed. The last thing she needed was to be led astray by a nobleman. She knew where that would lead.

He grimaced, put the brush down on the top of the rail and wiped off his hands on a rag. 'Something is troubling you, Miss Nightingale, for you to seek me out here.'

He left the stall to loom over her. A half-step back and she was up against the central pillar. A snuffling from behind her made her jump and look around at yet another great beast observing her over the top of a half-door.

Westmoor put out steadying hand. A brief warm clasp on her elbow that sent hot shivers racing over her skin. She tried to ignore the reaction.

'Steady on.' He spoke in much the same tones as he had used on his horse. 'They wouldn't hurt you even if they weren't all safely gated and barred.'

She inhaled a deep breath. Tried for calm. All she succeeded in doing was breathing in the scent of horses and him. The spicy scent of his cologne overlaid with the clean sweat scent of a male engaged in hard physical labour. A man who bathed regularly, ran a dukedom, yet took pleasure in grooming his own horse.

She gripped her hands together. 'I want my old job back.' *Please let me go back.*

Normally, Jake would have been far from pleased at being interrupted. The stable was one of the few places people left him alone. Gave him space to himself and his thoughts. His initial delight at seeing Rose in what he considered his domain had taken him aback. He'd been certain the distance he had created between them had solved the problem of his fascination. After all, a gentleman did not importune the females living under his roof.

He stared at her face, at the determination reflected in her eyes and her hands clasped tightly at her waist. He had no wish to keep her here against her will, but nor could he abide the thought of her returning to Vitium et Virtus or her old lodgings. 'You would really prefer to go back to scrubbing floors and living in that dreadful building rife with rats and dirt and surrounded by thieves and vagabonds than work for my grandmother?'

She stiffened as if insulted. 'There were no rats in my room.'

She had avoided his question. He moved a step closer. She had nowhere to go given the horse behind her. A suspicion arose in his breast. 'Is it my grandmother? Has she been too outspoken? Too testy? She's not the most patient person. Too used to getting her own way. Shall I speak to her for you?'

'Your grandmother is the soul of patience.' She gazed at him with pain in her eyes. 'But I feel like such a fraud. She has to explain the simplest things. A real lady would know these things.'

This was reason for her anxiety? 'I am sure she is only trying to be helpful.' He saw from the way she recoiled this had not helped. He shrugged. 'You catch on very quickly.' That did not seem to help, either.

He reined in his anger at the idea she wanted to leave and called upon reason. 'My dear girl, your fears are unfounded. A woman does not need a title to be considered a lady. I promise you no one would mistake you for anything else.'

She did not look in the slightest convinced.

'And besides, you can't leave, not when, for the first time in months, Grandmother is acting more like her old self. It is you who has wrought this change. It is not only your help she needs, I realise now, it is your company. She was lonely.'

Her eyes widened a fraction and for a second he saw a crack in her determination. She shook her head. 'Surely when your sister arrives—'

If only it were so. 'Eleanor will stay for a short time only and then Grandmama will be alone again.'

Rose gave him a look filled with suspicion. 'Could you not prevail upon her—?'

'No.' He stiffened, realising he was about to be rude when he wanted to be conciliatory. He knew he was overly defensive where his sister was concerned, but he feared he had said more than he should. 'I beg your pardon. Eleanor would not brook my interference in her life. Nor could I lay my duty on her shoulders. She has enough—' He shook his head at the urge to unburden himself about his sister. These were his concerns and not to be shared. 'My sister's business is—' Damn it all, now he was being rude.

'None of mine,' she finished. 'You don't have to mince words with me, Your Grace. But what will she think about the likes of me currying favour with your grandma when she arrives?'

'I can assure you Eleanor will be as glad to see Grandmama come out of the doldrums as I am.'

She shook her head. 'It isn't right. Just look at this gown.'

'You look...' He stumbled over his choice of words. She

looked divine in primrose yellow. The gown skimmed her lovely figure, emphasising her curves, without being immodest, and brought out the amazing light green of her eyes. They had a gold sunburst in the centre, he realised. Her blonde hair, professionally cut and coiffed, framed her face, enhancing her beauty. 'You look perfectly acceptable to me,' he temporised, not wishing her to take umbrage. He might as well have not bothered judging by her glower.

'Fine feathers do not fine birds make and it will take every bit of my wages to pay for it.' Her eyes glistened with moisture. She blinked it away.

His heart sank at the sight of her misery. 'Rose.' He wanted to hit something. 'The gown is a gift from my grandmama. Would you hurt her feelings and throw it back in her face?'

She shook her head. 'No,' she whispered. 'I just want to go back to the life I know.'

He leaned his forearm on the pillar, gazing into those worried green eyes, certain she was keeping something back. 'Tell me what is really troubling you.'

She swallowed the lump in her throat. 'Your grandma is talking about taking me with her to call on proper ladies. I am sure to put her to shame and then what?'

'Nonsense. You are making a mountain of a molehill. Nothing could be simpler.'

'To you, maybe. You were born into it.' Panic threaded through her voice.

A feeling of triumph went through him. Finally he had discovered the source of her worry. For this he had the perfect answer. 'Then I will go with you and make sure you do not make any fatal mistakes.' Though it would be a risky business spending too much time in Rose's company, for she offered far too much temptation. Hopefully his presence nearby would be enough to steady her, for it would not do to pay her too much attention with the old biddies looking on.

'She accepted an invitation to a Venetian Breakfast at Greenwich.'

He flinched.

Her expression turned to one of satisfaction. As if she knew she'd played a trump and won the trick. Well, he would not allow it. 'All the more reason for you to accompany her. If Eleanor were here, she would not go. It will be the first gathering Grandmama has attended since—' He took a deep breath. 'Since I came into the title. I must certainly go along and both she and I would be most grateful if you would agree to bear her company.'

She stared at him as if nonplussed. 'Grateful?'

'It will be hard on Grandmama, Rose. There will be condolences and sympathy. She will need your support as well as mine, for I cannot be at her side at all times.'

Her shoulders slumped. The urge to kiss away her fears was overwhelming. Especially since there was no one about to see.

'It is nothing to worry about, I assure you,' he said instead. 'A few old dowds and their menfolk having a picnic beside the river. I'll see you through it.'

'You promise?' she said grudgingly. She grimaced. 'It would please your grandma to have your escort, for sure. She worries that you are becoming reclusive.'

He felt distinctly disappointed that she had not said it would please *her* to have him along. 'It is my duty to escort you both.'

Her gaze slid away. 'Very well, I will stay, but only until she finds someone better. More suitable.' She narrowed her eyes. 'And you must promise me you will look for such a person.'

She really didn't trust him. Or was it men in general she didn't trust? Trust was something a man had to earn. He certainly hadn't earned his father's. Yet he was not prepared to give in on this. Not yet. 'Let me offer you a compromise. If you are still of the same mind in four weeks, I shall not put forth another objection to your departure. I will guarantee you your old job back and will pay you everything I promised. But please, for my grandmother's sake, give this opportunity a fair chance.'

She swallowed.

The salary he had offered her as a companion was more than she could earn in five years at the V&V and had been out-and-out bribery, but he didn't care. One of the few privileges of being a duke was getting what you wanted.

'Well?' he said.

Slowly she nodded. 'Three weeks more then, since I have already almost completed the first week.'

He stopped himself from laughing at her audacity. Damn, but he liked her spirit. 'It is not exactly a prison sentence, you know.' He put up a hand to prevent her from saying another word. 'All right. Three more weeks.'

He stuck out a hand. She clasped it, as if intending to shake on their agreement. Instead, he brought it to his lips and pressed a fleeting kiss to her knuckles. Her little shiver heated his blood. She was not as indifferent to him as she pretended. A heady blood-stirring thought he did not need.

Yet, unable to resist, he flashed her a charming grin. 'I will see you at dinner, Miss Nightingale, where we shall discuss which invitations we shall answer in the affirmative.'

'Affirmative?'

'Those to which we shall say yes.'

Her eyes widened for a second, but nodded. 'At dinner.' With wary glances at the horses, and a less-than-happy expression, she left as quietly as she had arrived.

He frowned. Was he being purely selfish in encouraging her to stay? Hardly. Being constantly in Rose's company and unable to do more than be polite would be hellish.

This was for his grandmother's sake. Nothing more.
So why was he now looking forward to the dinner hour more than he had in weeks?

Chapter Five

Chin pointed ceilingwards to permit the placing of an emerald in his cravat, an emerald much darker than the colour of Rose's light green eyes, Jake became aware of a strange sound issuing from his valet.

'Are you humming, Clacket?'

The sound stopped. 'I believe I am, Your Grace. I beg your pardon.' Clacket stepped back to admire his handiwork, his brown eyes bright in his round baby face.

'And what has you lifting your voice in joy, may I ask?'

Jake felt a bit like humming himself, which was odd. It was only dinner, but the prospect of sharing a meal with Rose always lifted his spirits and without the aid of brandy.

'Joy, Your Grace?' Creases formed between sandy brows. 'I supposed I am somewhat pleased. After all, it is the very heart and soul of a gentleman's gentleman to see his gentleman departing from his care well turned out. It has been a while since Your Grace has taken much of an interest in his appearance.'

And tonight he had permitted the man to trim his hair

and shave him clean before dinner. 'So you deem me well turned out?'

Clacket pursed his lips and brushed a hand across Jacob's shoulder as if to smooth the material. 'Reasonably, Your Grace. Perhaps we might ask for a slightly better fit of the coat, but it would be nothing to take a seam in here or there, the coat being a little less snug than was your wont in the past, but otherwise...'

The coat was a little loose. Before the accident, Clacket would have struggled to get the coat on him. It had fitted like a second skin, as fashion demanded. Now, he slipped it on with ease. He must have lost weight. He frowned at himself in the pier glass. He'd dropped a stone at least. And he looked paler than normal. When and how had that occurred?

He was also hungry. It seemed his appetite had returned with a vengeance. Or was it simply that he was looking forward to crossing verbal swords with Rose? He had no doubt she would fight him every step of the way, when she realised just how many invitations he planned his grandmother would accept.

Invitations that six months ago he would have scorned as being a bore, given as how they tended to be small family affairs for those left in town over the summer. Card parties, the odd musical evening, or picnic, as well as the obligatory morning visits his grandmother deemed essential to a man seeking a wife.

Not that he was. Not yet. He wasn't ready to tread the path to the altar. But he was ready to get back on the social horse. To show his face in polite society on a regular basis. He'd not been to a single event since he'd thrown the ball for Fred and Georgiana. And curse any of them who muttered behind his back about his culpability. Or about Rose.

Indeed, the best part of it all would be escorting Rose to those events. He could not help but wonder what she would make of it all and was secretly looking forward to hearing her candid opinions.

Perhaps all the gadding about would also help him sleep. Clacket finished inserting his diamond shirt buttons and began the task of tidying up.

Humming under his breath, Jake went down to the drawing room to await the ladies of the house.

Oliver joined him a few minutes later. His friend eyed him up and down. 'You are looking better than the last time I saw you.'

'You are not.' His friend looked rather harried.

'Why the urgent note to come to dinner?'

'I need your help.'

Oliver eyed him askance. 'Spit it out, man.'

'I have a young cousin up from the country. She's agreed to act as companion to my grandmother, but she needs a bit of town bronze. A formal dinner will bolster her confidence before we set out into the shark-infested waters of the *ton*.'

'Trying to pass a country bumpkin off on to the *ton*? Can't be done, old fellow. Sorry. They will spot her a mile off.'

He hadn't. 'I'll trust your judgement on that after you have met her, but I am sure Grandmama or I can help her over any rough spots.'

'Like a horse? Of all the queer starts you've ever had, Westmoor, this takes the cake, I must say, but I'm happy to spend an hour or so with Her Grace. She's a good old stick and has always been cordial.' His eyes gleamed. 'Besides, if you are going to poke a stick in the *ton's* eye, I don't mind being part of the action.'

Not everyone was forgiving of Oliver's background. As a boy he had taken great pains to never give them an opportunity to criticise him by maintaining the highest standards of good breeding. He would know if Rose was ready to face the *ton* and would not hesitate to say if she was not. 'I will abide by your opinion.' He poured them each a glass of sherry.

Oliver sipped his and nodded his approval. 'Nice vintage.' He turned as the door opened to admit the ladies and bowed. 'Your Grace.'

'Oliver. How lovely of you to join us,' Grandmama said. 'Miss Nightingale, let me make Mr Oliver Gregory known to you. He is a good friend of my grandson's.'

Rose curtsied the perfect depth for a non-titled gentleman. Grandmama had obviously started the task of moulding Rose into shape. She didn't want Rose to suffer embarrassment any more than he did.

'Can I pour you a sherry, Grandmama? Rose?' Jake asked.

'Miss Nightingale does not imbibe, Jake. But I will take a glass.'

'Perhaps some ratafia, or orgeat, Miss Nightingale,' Oliver said. While his expression was bland, Jake had no doubt he was inspecting her from her head to her heels and his tone indicated he was not displeased with what he saw.

'Thank you,' Rose said. Her smile was a little too warm for Jacob's taste. He forbore from saying so, but once she had her drink in hand he drew her towards the window and left Oliver catching up on gossip with his grandmother.

'When you reply yes to a gentleman you can be a little more haughty,' he said. 'No need to look as if he has offered you a special gift when he is simply doing his gentlemanly duty.'

'Sorry.'

'And no need to apologise for anything. A lady is always right. About most things anyway. Under the right circumstances.'

She frowned. 'I have no idea what you mean.'

And no wonder. He scarcely understood himself. Blast it. He had to stop thinking of her as his lady in red. She was now a female under his protection. Out of bounds. Was that not half the reason he had offered her the position in the first place? The other half, the need to protect her, was an aberration he must ignore. 'Never mind. You'll get the hang of it.'

The butler announced dinner and Oliver went ahead with his grandmother, while Jake brought Rose in on his arm.

Arm in arm they watched while Oliver demonstrated how to seat a lady and Grandmother demonstrated how a lady took her seat. Standing there with her on his arm, a strange sense of comfort filled him. Mentally he shook his head and held out Rose's chair. She accomplished the whole sitting down in skirts to the manner born. He felt an odd sense of pride at her elegance and style. As if he'd had something to do with it. It was all Rose herself. He had been foolish to worry about such a simple thing.

The rest of the meal was taken up with polite conversation and Jake desperately trying not to bash Oliver on the nose when he flirted with Rose—all in the cause of helping her get some polish, damn him.

By the time they partook of dessert, Rose was flagging. Her eyes were shadowed by effort and her smile strained.

'And now we ladies will retire for tea,' Grandmother said with a kind smile for her charge. 'We will leave these gentleman to their port. Will you be joining us in the drawing room later, Oliver?'

'I greatly beg your indulgence, Your Grace, but I have a previous engagement elsewhere for the rest of the evening.' He rose and came around to help Grandmama rise. Jake did the same for Rose.

Oliver bowed over Rose's hand. 'A pleasure to meet you, Miss Nightingale. I hope I have the felicitation of meeting you again.'

Rose frowned for a second as if puzzling out his meaning, then smiled her sweet lovely smile that had Jake once more wanting to shove the far-too-handsome Oliver out of the room.

Rose dipped a little curtsy. 'If you are going to Lady Dearbourne's Venetian Breakfast you will indeed be felicitated.'

Oliver's eyes danced. 'I would not miss it for the world.'

Rose followed his grandmother out of the room.

When the door closed behind them, Jake turned to Oliver. 'Well, what do you think?'

Oliver gave him a hard look. 'I think she is a delightful young woman. I have only one doubt.'

Jake tensed, concerned she had not passed muster in his friend's eyes. 'And that is?'

'Your intentions. Are you toying with that sweet *innocent* female?'

He bridled. 'Certainly not.'

'Good,' Oliver grunted. 'I saw the way she looked at you. Don't break her heart.'

Jake bristled.

Oliver cut him off. 'I really must go, old chap. By the way, my visit to the Club Plaisirs Nocturnes in Paris provided some novel ideas.'

'Thinking of bringing them to Vitium et Virtus?'

'I am. We are losing custom.'

'Boredom setting in. I'm bored with it myself. Not to mention up to my ears in work for the Duchy. Perhaps we should divest ourselves of it.

Oliver grimaced. 'I'd hate for Nicholas to come back expecting it to be here and...'

It always came back to the same thing. Their hope, forlorn though it was, that Nicholas would return. 'You are right. We should probably wait.'

A bit of a pall descended on them as Nicholas's ghost intruded. They'd kept it going in his memory after all.

Jake saw Oliver out and climbed the stairs to the drawing room. Only when he reached the top step did he realise he had left his port untouched in his eagerness to join the ladies. Or one particularly lady.

Damn it.

* * *

Rose lay in bed, looking up at the canopy. Blue silk, no less. How on earth had this happened? When would she wake up and discover it was all a dream?

Nightmare more like. Women like her did not end up under the roof of a gentleman for no good reason. Though his stated reason was for the sake of his grandmother, how could she believe him?

A strange uncomfortable feeling in the pit of her stomach made her roll over on to her side.

Moonlight poked fingers of light through the gaps in the curtain, casting strange shadows in unexpected places and forming bars of brightness across the counterpane.

Sleep seemed further away than ever. She should have brought the book of sermons she'd been reading to Her Grace. She'd been desperately trying not to yawn then, and Her Grace had actually dropped off for a minute or two. Bless the poor old dear, she'd had a very busy day.

Perhaps she should go and fetch the book from the drawing room. Another dose of that would surely have her eyes closing in no time.

Better yet would be a book she would actually enjoy reading. The house boasted a library. Her Grace had pointed it out, but they had never gone in there. Since Her Grace had a store of books in her chambers, there was no need to seek out more. Yet all of them were exceedingly dull.

Feeling too warm for comfort, Rose clambered out of bed and poured a glass of water from the jug on the nightstand. As she sipped she walked to the window and looked out.

The last time she had looked out she had seen the Duke heading out, probably to the V&V in pursuit of more manly entertainments than listening to her read to a sleepy grandmother.

She hated the idea of him going to the club.

There were girls there who would—she pushed the thought aside as an image of Flo came into her mind. She had sent Flo a note saying she'd found employment elsewhere, but little more by way of an explanation, which made her feel guilty and sad. Flo would miss her, she was sure, when no one else gave a fig for what became of her.

Somehow she would find a way to meet her friend and tell her the full story. One day.

She headed back for the bed, then changed her mind. There was no point in tossing and turning for hours. She'd get a book or two from the library and read until she fell asleep.

Another wonderful indulgence of this new life of hers. Books. Hundreds of them.

She pulled on her dressing gown, lit her bedside candle from the one in the sconces outside her door and headed downstairs.

The library was in the other wing. Passing through the dimly lit grand entrance hall, she was surprised at the lack of a footman on duty at the front door since His Grace had gone out.

Perhaps he had his own key.

The corridor to the rooms on the west wing's ground floor ended at the library, if she recalled correctly. She pushed open one of the great double doors and was delighted to see shelf upon shelf of books lining the walls in highly polished glass-fronted shelves. She lifted her candle to better see the titles.

At a sound her heart gave a hard thump. Her breath caught in her throat. She whirled around.

'Your Grace,' she gasped.

Chin resting on his palm, he stared at her from behind a table piled high with ledgers. His shirtsleeves glowed a startling white in the light of the moon coming through the window as he rose to his feet. 'Rose.'

So intent on her task, she hadn't seen him on the other side of the room. 'Why are you sitting in the dark?'

He made a soft sound and arched his back in a stretch. 'The candle must have gone out.' He sounded surprised. 'I must have nodded off.'

She drew closer. 'You were working? I thought you left the house after dinner.'

'Keeping track of my movements, Miss Nightingale?' Now his voice sounded frosty.

'Not especially. You do pass right beneath my window on your way to the stables. I happened to be looking out when you headed that way.'

'I beg your pardon. You did indeed see me. I had intended to go…to go…well, out, but I changed my mind.'

She couldn't stop the glad little feeling that lifted her heart a fraction. 'What are you working on?'

He dragged his gaze from her face to the papers and account books. 'This month's reports from various properties and tenancies the Duchy owns.'

'Do you not have employees to do that sort of thing?'

He nodded and a small smile curved his lips. 'I do, but they are employees. It is important to check their work from time to time.'

As the housekeeper always checked the maid's work once a day to make sure no one was shirking their duties.

'And what brings you to my office in the middle of the night?'

His office? 'I was told this was the library.'

He shrugged and glanced around. 'It is more comfortable than the estate office where my man of business and my secretary are in and out all the time. Here, I can work without interruption.'

Unless someone like her started prowling around at night. He didn't say it, but she could imagine the words coming from his mouth without any difficulty.

'I should go.'

'Please don't. You came for a book. Perhaps I can help you find one.'

She gazed longingly at the lovely full shelves. 'I didn't expect quite so many to choose from. I am not even sure where to start. I'll come back another time.'

'I insist you take something with you.' He came around to her side of the desk. He lit his candle from hers. 'What did you have in mind?'

He was so tall.

And his shadow danced across the books, stretching up to the ceiling the closer he came. The scent of his cologne filled her nostrils. The warmth of his body penetrated her flimsy robe.

A small shiver passed down her spine. Not fear, but something altogether different. Pleasurable. She forced her mind to focus on their conversation. 'Something other than the books of sermons your grandmother enjoys.'

He smiled slightly. 'We have all kinds of books. Travelogues. Atlases. Flora and fauna. *The Farmer's Almanac. La Belle Assemblée.* Or if you would like something a little more entertaining, there are novels by Walter Scott or Fielding.'

She forced herself to listen to his words, rather than the dark and delicious cadence of his voice that seemed to beckon her closer. With some effort she kept her distance as he wandered the shelves naming the various works. So many books. She had no idea where to start.

'Of course there is always dear old Hannah More, if you feel in need of a bit of moral uplifting.'

'"*Forgiveness is the economy of the heart...forgiveness saves the expense of anger, the cost of hatred, the waste of spirits,*"' she quoted and chuckled ruefully. 'I have read lots of her work,' she said. 'They provided them at the—' She cut herself off. Her Grace had told her never again to mention the Foundling Hospital.

'It's all right, Rose. You don't have to pretend with me.'
'I shouldn't have to pretend at all.'

Jake did his absolute best not to look at Rose's sumptuous figure wrapped about in a lace so sheer he was sure as she entered the room he had seen... No, he was not going to think about it. He was a gentleman. She'd given him her trust.

Even as he quelled the urge to stroke a finger down the rope of plaited hair lying over her left shoulder and breast, he could not prevent himself from inhaling the scent of lavender from her evening ablutions rising from the warmth of her body,

That was too much to ask of any man. Especially with a woman as attractive as Rose. In the light of their candles, her skin had a translucent quality. Like very fine china with a light behind it, yet the glow was all her own.

He would not give in to his urges.

He hoped.

For that would be a betrayal.

'Are you in the mood for entertainment or sleep?' he asked, forcing himself to focus.

'Oh, something of each, I think.' She smiled. The pretty curve of her lips took her face from merely lovely to beautiful, the gold in her eyes seeming to reflect candlelight. 'I am not being very helpful. And I certainly do not wish to disturb you at your work. I really did think you were out.'

'No matter.' He had gone to the stables, found all there asleep including his horse and come back again. Restless, he had decided to work on some of the paperwork he had not got to during the day.

For a moment he thought he was dreaming when Rose floated in, for he had dreamed of her more than once. Dreamed of kissing her.

But a gentleman did not kiss a lady companion.

'I decided my time would be better employed going through one more ledger before I retired.'

She glanced at the desk. At the brandy decanter and the empty glass. Her gaze skittered away. 'Your grandmother worries about the hours you spend working.'

He grimaced, putting distance between them, as much for his own sake as hers. 'I have a great deal to learn and not much time to do it.' If the Duchy wasn't to end up in a great deal of debt. His father had worked equally hard, but Jake was fast coming to realise that his father did not have much of a head for business. He had simply followed the methods his own father had employed.

Methods that were no longer working as well as they had once done.

Each year the income had declined and each year it had declined more than the year before. There were improvements that needed making, in farming, in buildings, in husbandry. All of which took money. And the coffers, while not empty, were not up to the task, either.

Rose wandered the shelves, cocking her head from time to time to read a spine that caught her eye. The wall opposite the windows did not contain any cabinets, because of the fireplace. As she walked past it, she glanced up at the portrait covered in black crepe above the mantel and then over at him with sympathy in her gaze.

'Another picture of your family?'

Grandmother must have told her about the one in the drawing room. 'My mother. My father couldn't bear to look at it.'

Understanding filled her face. 'Your father and brother were killed in an accident, your grandmother said.'

He stiffened. So Grandmother had gone into detail. He wondered what more she had said. Whether she had spoken of who should really have been in the carriage with Father that night.

The coldness he'd felt when he learned of the accident rose

up like a fog. Surrounding him. Chilling him to the bone. Guilt pressed down on his shoulders. He turned away, headed for his desk. Pushed papers around. Aware of her watching him. Aware of her sympathy.

'You miss them,' she said. Not a question.

Yet for some reason he could not quite fathom, he answered, 'Like the very devil.' He closed his eyes. 'I beg your pardon.'

'It is all right, Your Grace,' she said, her voice soft but clear in the silence. 'You don't have to pretend around me, either.'

He shouldn't have to pretend at all.

A moment later she was by his side, slipping her arm around his waist, leaning a cheek against his shoulder and giving him a squeeze. Never in his life had he felt such comfort. He brushed his lips against her temple, felt the beat of her heart against his ribs and knew without a doubt this was a supremely bad idea.

As they turned towards each other she tipped up her face. She was a petite woman, barely coming up to his shoulder, and while robust, there was a fragility about her. Perhaps that was the reason he felt such a need to protect her from her world.

A heartbeat later, their lips met and he wasn't thinking at all.

He was feeling. Relishing the soft curves pressed against his chest. Enjoying the way her waist dipped beneath her ribs as his hand roamed her back. Tasting the honeyed sweetness of her mouth as their tongues tangled and danced.

A sweet sigh brushed against his cheek and she moved closer into his embrace until they melded into one.

He'd missed her kisses like the very devil, too. He just hadn't let himself realise it. 'Rose,' he said, drawing back to look down into her face. 'This is a bad idea.'

'Yes,' she agreed softly, moving not one inch and gazing at his mouth with a hunger that drove claws into his own need.

And when she lifted up on her toes to press her lips to his, he took what she offered.

To Rose, the sensation of being held remained a novel experience. Few people in her life had put their arms around her as far as she recalled. And only this man had ever embraced her with such gentle care. His touch seemed to reach into her very soul. And the way his kisses made her feel was heaven on earth.

A heaven she hadn't known existed, or that it could be shared with another. Her body trembled and yearned and her heart seemed to want to pound itself free of her chest. She twined her arms around his neck, for support and because she wanted to touch him, too. The feel of his silky hair against her fingers was enchanting and wicked.

Pressed against his chest, her breasts felt full, heavy, sensitive, and the only thing between them was her night attire and his shirt. The heat of him through the fabric was lovely. His hands on her buttocks as he drew her close were firm yet gentle. No rough pawing and scrabbling, simply a closing of the distance between them in a way that made her melt helplessly against him, submitting to his strength.

The way he nibbled at her bottom lip sent a piercing sensation arrowing deep into her body. And when his tongue swept her mouth, hot shivers raced across her skin and between her thighs flutters and tiny pulses made her moan.

This was the delight between a man and a woman that the wardens at the Foundling Hospital had warned against. And that the girls at the V&V had whispered and giggled about. Why had she never understood?

Could anything so heart-stoppingly beautiful be evil? But this was only the beginning. The start. Against her belly, she felt the hard ridge of his arousal. The male flesh that, when joined with the female, made babies.

Something that ought only to happen between wife and

husband, if those babies were not to be cast out unwanted and alone.

Before, when she'd thought he was going to ask her to be his mistress, she'd fled. Now held in his embrace, his kisses made her weak, needy and full of a longing she was not sure she had the strength to resist after all.

For long moments she let herself whirl in the maelstrom of sensations, heat, jolts of tension and tingles in nameless places. But this man was a duke who needed to marry and get himself sons. Over and over his grandmother had talked of his wedding with such wistfulness it pained Rose to hear it.

While he might enjoy dallying with her—indeed, it was clear the enjoyment was mutual—he could never marry a foundling. A bastard without a name. He would marry someone of his own class. A noble girl with noble connections.

And if she let this thing happen now, between them, he would eventually cast her off, as he had cast off many before her according to her friends at the V&V. She'd paid close attention to the gossip after their dance. She'd learned about his mistresses and what he gave them when he bid them farewell.

None of his women had ever complained about his generosity, according to the girls, and none had ever lasted more than a year. She might not be worldly, but she knew what happened to those women. Ultimately they ended up in places like the V&V, plying their *trade*.

She'd sworn she would never tread that particular road even if she was starving. Yet here she was very close to...

She broke their kiss. 'Your Grace,' she pleaded.

The haziness in his gaze dissipated in a flash of understanding. He straightened, his lovely blue eyes full of regret. Gently, reluctantly, he held her arms firmly in his hands, as if he sensed her weakness, and stepped back with a grave smile. 'Choose as many books as you like. I will see you in the morning.' He left without a backward glance.

Rose watched him leave with a heavy heart. Knowing he

had more sense than she did, more control, did not help settle the unsteady beating of her heart, or the sense of loss as he left. Not in the least.

Nor the embarrassment curdling in her stomach.

By her boldness, her wantonness, she had ruined what should have been the simple offer of sympathy for a man who felt the loss of his family keenly.

Women in his class of society did not do things like comfort a man with a kiss. Nor did they wander the halls in the middle of the night dressed in their nightclothes. She had taken pride in having standards and yet she had succumbed to the first handsome man who had shown interest. She had let herself down. Flooded by the heat of mortification, she picked a book at random and returned to her room. She didn't bother to open it, but simply blew out her candle and huddled beneath the covers.

Why, oh, why had she kissed him? Had what she had seen in his expression been regret or disgust? A painful certainty curled up in a tight hard ball in her chest. Whatever it was, an impetuous kiss had likely ruined her one chance to make more of her life.

Chapter Six

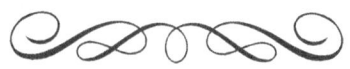

The next morning there was no sign of the Duke at breakfast or when they entered the carriage to leave for Lady Spear's At Home, despite his promise to go with them. Clearly he had been disgusted by her wanton behaviour. Misery rested heavily in her chest. She hadn't realised how important she found his good opinion. And now she had lost it.

They were admitted to Lady Spear's house by a very lordly-looking butler, who announced them to the company assembled in the drawing room in sonorous tones.

'Lend me your arm, dear Miss Nightingale,' Her Grace murmured as they lingered on the threshold. 'I am feeling less than steady on my feet.'

Thus she and Rose swept into Lady Spear's drawing room together instead of Rose following at a discreet distance and remaining unnoticed. She'd been outmanoeuvred by a frail old lady with a will of iron. As she looked about her, she realised there were far more people in attendance than she had been given to expect.

A large-bosomed woman in deep purple hurried forward to greet them. 'Your Grace.' The woman curtsied. 'You honour us.'

The Dowager Duchess accepted the homage without blinking an eye. 'Dear Lady Spear, I would like to introduce my companion, Miss Nightingale. Rose, this is Lady Spear, our hostess. Miss Nightingale has kindly consented to join my household.' She smiled fondly at Rose. 'She is most helpful.'

In other words, she was held in esteem by Her Grace, so don't be treating her badly.

Rose stilled. Apparently she was becoming adept at deciphering the politics of society manners, after all. But then she had good teachers in the Dowager Duchess and the Duke. If only she hadn't messed it all up. She pushed off the feeling of impending doom. There was no sense in worrying about what could not be changed, she'd decided in the wakeful early hours of the morning. Practical advice she was having trouble following.

'And how is His Grace?' Lady Spear asked.

While her voice held sympathy there was a gleam of something less kind in her hazel eyes as she peered at the Dowager Duchess, who released Rose's arm to make a careless gesture with her hand. 'He'll be along shortly, so you may ask him for yourself. He would have come with us, but urgent business delayed him.'

Rose swallowed her surprise. It was the first she'd heard of urgent business. Or was the old lady telling a fib?

Lady Spear's eyes widened. 'Oh, I—' She visibly pulled herself together and beamed. 'That is wonderful news. I will be honoured.' Her tone turned a little sly. 'It has been such an age since anyone has seen him.'

Rose found herself clenching her fist at the woman's insincerity. Forcibly, she relaxed her fingers and once more took Her Grace's arm. It trembled a little beneath her hand.

Worry replaced irritation. 'Perhaps you could find Her Grace a chair, Lady Spear,' she said quietly but firmly.

'Yes, Eloisa, do find me a chair,' the old lady added imperiously and gave Rose a conspiratorial smile.

'Oh, pardon me, Your Grace. Please, come this way.' She led them to a group of other elderly ladies seated around a low table.

Having seen Her Grace settled, Rose took the wooden chair placed by a footman off to the side and a little behind Her Grace. She breathed a sigh of relief. Here in the corner, she could observe without being noticed, just as Her Grace had promised.

A dark-haired gentleman approached Her Grace and bowed. With a start, Rose recognised him. Mr Oliver Gregory.

Such a handsome man with his dark skin and startling green eyes. But nowhere near as handsome as Westmoor. Not in her eyes. Her heart gave a funny little skip.

Mr Gregory bowed with elegance when he reached their group, his brief smile encompassing all the ladies in the circle and somehow included Rose, too. How did he do that? 'Ladies. I bid you all a pleasant day.'

The ladies murmured their greetings with much fluttering of fans and adjusting shawls. There was something odd about their reaction. As if they would prefer he had stayed away. All except Her Grace, who greeted him with a warm smile and an outstretched hand. He bowed over it. 'Your Grace. How delightful to meet you here and with Miss Nightingale, too. A great pleasure.'

The other ladies turned to look at her. Exactly what she had hoped to avoid. Heat flashed to Rose's cheeks. She stammered something in reply.

He bowed as befitting her station. 'Are you quite well, Miss Nightingale?' His eyes held concern.

Dash it all, her sleepless night must be showing. 'Perfectly, I thank you, sir.' She spoke a little more stiffly than she had intended, but once more he had drawn other gazes to her little corner.

He gazed down at her, with a slight frown. He leaned a little closer. 'You know, it is the strangest thing. I keep thinking I have met you somewhere before our dinner the other evening, but it isn't possible.'

Of course he'd seen her before. He'd often been in the room when she'd cleaned out the fireplace in the owners' private parlour. All the owners had. Once, this man had kindly opened the door for her when she was struggling with her buckets and brushes. Guilt swept through her. How would he react if he knew who she really was? She clenched her hands in her lap. 'The first time we were introduced was at dinner with Her Grace.'

His lips tightened as if he had noticed the subtle change in her answer, but to her relief he turned back to Her Grace. 'It really is good to see you out and about again, Your Grace, isn't it, ladies?'

The other ladies nodded and twittered their agreement. 'I thought Westmoor was to accompany you? It was part of my reason for being here. I needed a word.'

'He will be along shortly, I am sure,' Her Grace said, sounding more haughty than was her usual wont with this gentleman.

Mr Oliver's eyes narrowed a fraction, hinting at displeasure. 'Unfortunately, I am unable to await his arrival. I have another appointment.'

'It seems that you are fortunate, young man,' Her Grace said, nodding at the door. 'Here he is now.'

A gasp rippled around the room as the butler announced the Duke of Westmoor. Rose's heart lifted and, as his gaze caught hers, she couldn't help but smile.

'Careful, Miss Nightingale,' Mr Gregory said in a low

voice right by her ear. 'Smiles like that will start the gossips wondering.'

She blushed and looked up at him. His green eyes were dancing with amusement, but there was also a question there and that shadow of puzzlement.

Her heart sank. He was a clever man. He was going to remember. And then what?

The Duke's arrival triggered a great deal more rushing forward and curtsying by Lady Spear and various other women, while the men bowed their greetings. Outwardly, the Duke seemed to take it all in his stride, but Rose saw the shadows in his eyes and the faint lines of strain around his mouth.

She wanted to go to him to offer her support, but how could she? She was merely his grandmother's companion. Which reminded her, she was neglecting her duty. Rose tucked the shawl she was holding around the Dowager Duchess's shoulders. 'In case you feel a draught,' she murmured.

'Such a kind, thoughtful girl you are,' Her Grace said with a smile. 'I am very fortunate to have found you.' She turned to the woman at her side. 'Finally, I have found a companion worthy of her hire.'

The other lady's glance skimmed over Rose. 'Who is her family?'

Rose held her breath.

'Distant relatives of my son's wife,' the old lady said.

A gasp almost escaped Rose's lips. That was an out-and-out bouncer. She opened her mouth to deny it, then closed it again. What would it serve? She would only embarrass the old lady by revealing the lie.

She inched her chair back a little farther into the shadows of the corner.

While Her Grace exchanged gossip with her companions, Rose sat as still as possible, her hands folded neatly in her lap, and tried to disappear into the background. Yet over and over her gaze was drawn to the Duke holding court with a group of young ladies. Her heart squeezed painfully. She forced herself to look away, yet somehow she could not stop herself from being aware of his every movement, every expression on his face, no matter how brief.

He wasn't happy.

Also, though his gaze never strayed her way once, she had the oddest feeling she had his undivided attention. But it wasn't possible. Not for a moment.

A footman arrived with a dish of bohea for Her Grace, added cream and sugar, according to the old lady's likes, and placed it in front of her. By the time he had served Her Grace, the footman, clearly aware of her lowly status, had moved off, though no doubt he would come back around when everyone else was served.

Indeed. His next stop was the Duke, whose expression was now a picture of grim dissatisfaction. Another footman arrived with fancy little cakes and Rose filled a plate for her employer who was deep in conversation. She placed the plate at Her Grace's elbow and retired to her seat.

A moment later, the footman returned with a cup of tea for her. Surprised, she stared at him. His face was bland, as was the face of the footman behind him waiting to offer her a plate of cakes.

Something made her glance in the direction of the Duke and for a moment their gazes met. With a slight nod of satisfaction, he turned to speak to the lady at his side and Rose wondered if she had imagined their exchange of glances, so attentive did he seem to be to the lovely young lady.

She glanced at the clock. A mere twenty minutes had passed. Her Grace had promised they would not stay long and wondered how she could possibly manage with a plate of cakes in one hand and a cup of tea in the other. Fortunately, a fair-haired gentleman standing nearby seemed to realise her dilemma. He came over with a smile and bowed. 'I fear we have not been introduced. I'm Faxford—Spear's eldest. Perhaps I may be of assistance.' He signalled to a footman. 'Fetch a table, would you, John?'

The footman scurried off, returning a few moments later with a piecrust table, which he set within arm's reach of her chair.

'Sorry about that. Stupid fellow should have seen you needed somewhere to set your cup down,' the young man said, taking her plate and setting it down.

She smiled her gratitude.

Her Grace turned around. 'Faxford, Miss Nightingale is my companion and you will cease your flirting immediately.'

'Miss Nightingale,' Faxford said with a cheeky grin and a bow. 'A pleasure to meet you. I knew I'd winkle an introduction eventually.'

Heat flooded Rose's face.

Jake cursed under his breath at the sight of Faxford hovering over an embarrassed Rose. He hadn't asked the footman to provide her with a cup of tea in order to give the blasted fellow an opportunity to show off his gentlemanly manners.

He shouldn't have done it at all. Servants gossiped.

He resisted the urge to join his grandmother and give Faxford a set down. A kindly employer ensuring his mother's companion got a cup of tea was understandable, just. The same employer acting like a jealous fool would be quite another.

And now she was smiling at the fellow, albeit shyly. He clenched his jaw so hard, his back teeth ached. He turned away, only to see a matron with her marriageable daughter in tow striding in his direction.

Avoiding catching the woman's eye, he sauntered to his grandmother's side and bowed to the ladies. 'You will let me know when you are ready to leave, Your Grace?'

His grandmother hid her surprise. 'I will, dear boy. Thank you.' She turned back to the lady with whom she was conversing.

Faxford, blast him, grinned cheerfully. 'The ladies love their gossip.'

'Indeed,' he said repressively.

The young man shifted from foot to foot. 'What do you think about this business in the north?' he blurted out, clearly trying for another topic of conversation. 'This riot.'

'I read about that,' Rose said. 'Some are calling it a massacre. It warrants some sort of official investigation, I should think.'

Faxford blinked his surprise. 'By Gad, Miss Nightingale, are you a bluestocking?'

Jake raised a haughty brow. 'You raised the topic, Faxford. Hardly fitting in mixed company.'

The young man visibly wilted. 'Oh, right. I beg pardon. My mistake. If you will excuse me, my mother is trying to catch my attention.' He bowed and to Jake's satisfaction scurried off.

Rose frowned at him. 'Surely such an important event is everyone's concern?'

Jake's jaw dropped at her challenging tone. He gave her the same haughty look he had given Faxford. 'I have no intention of engaging in rumour-mongering, Miss Nightingale and that is what it would be since I do not as yet have all the facts.'

She frowned, clearly undeterred. 'Hardly a rumour. Troops called out to quell a riot, if you believe the government. A massacre of citizens, if you believe those present. The real question is how is the truth to be discovered, Your Grace?'

Rose was right of course. Her argument was the same as that he had presented to Prinny that very morning. Not something he could bruit abroad, however. Discussions with the Prince Regent were confidential. 'You suggest some sort of impartial enquiry, I assume?'

She wrinkled her brow thoughtfully. 'Is it even possible?'

'It certainly ought to be.'

She glanced up at him. 'What did he mean by calling me a...a stocking, was it?'

Jake lowered his voice. 'We can discuss it later.'

Anger rose in Jakes's throat at the worry on her face. He wanted to march over to Faxford and make him apologise. Yet with the old biddies looking on, they would find themselves the subject of gossip in a heartbeat should he do so. He set his jaw and said nothing.

'Why, we have been here half an hour already,' Grandmama said, smiling up at him and filling the awkward pause in their conversation. 'Jacob, would you have the carriage brought around?'

Jake bowed. 'It will be my pleasure.' He tried not to notice Rose's anxious expression. He would explain it later.

Westmoor joined his grandmother and Rose in the drawing room after dinner, though he had not joined them for the meal itself.

'Will you explain what is meant by bluestocking, Your Grace?' Rose asked once the servants had withdrawn. She hadn't found the word in the dictionary she had borrowed.

Her Grace looked up, her mouth wrinkling as if she'd tasted a quince. 'Did someone call you that, Rose?'

'Faxford,' Jake answered. 'The idiot.'

'I gather, then, being a bluestocking is not a good thing,' Rose said, her stomach falling away. Oh, why, oh, why had she said anything at all? And just when she'd begun to feel more comfortable in her new position.

'It means a young woman who is more interested in politics and education than she is in gowns and dancing,' the Dowager said.

'A lady is not supposed to be interested in the events of the day?' It hardly seemed right. 'Shouldn't soldiers attacking women and children concern everyone? Not to mention the unrest it has caused. There is talk of revolution.'

The old lady's chin trembled. She looked at her grandson. 'Jake, is this true? Are the peasants rising against us?' She shuddered. 'One cannot but help think of France.'

Rose's stomach pitched. 'I am sorry, Your Grace. I did not mean to scare you.'

The Duke's lips thinned. 'We do not have peasants in England, Grandmama. And let us not jump to conclusions. That was your advice, was it not, Rose?'

Rose wished she'd never opened her mouth. Anyone of nobility would be scared witless after what had happened in France.

The old lady fixed her grandson with an intense stare. 'Cooler heads must prevail, Jacob. I am relying on you to speak to the Prince. To make him see reason. This is England. Our soldiers do not run roughshod over the populace. Now, if we have quite exhausted this topic, I find I am tired. Ring the bell, Jake. I wish to retire.'

Her heart sank. How could she have been so thoughtless as to upset the old lady? 'I am sure it will all be resolved satisfactorily in the end. I am sorry if my careless words caused you worry.'

'Nonsense, child. My weariness has nothing to do with politics. I need my sleep after all our gadding about today.'

Jake rang the bell, then went to help his grandmother to rise. 'I will escort you up, Grandmama.'

'No need. Previs is here now. Finish your tea, Jake. Entertain Miss Nightingale. Perhaps you would read to her for a change.'

The elderly butler had indeed arrived and was handing the old lady her cane and offering an arm. They staggered out, closing the door behind them. An unusual mistake. Should she get up and open it? Would it not seem distrustful? She glanced at Westmoor for his reaction and was surprised at his strained expression.

'I am so sorry, Your Grace. I would not upset your grandmother for the world. She has been so very kind.'

When he said nothing, she felt compelled to continue. 'I told you I'd muck things up. Me pretending to be a lady is such a...' she waved a hand to encompass everything around her '...farce.'

She had never seen a farce at the theatre, but she'd read them. Shakespeare's *A Midsummer Night's Dream* and *As You Like It*. People dressing up as what they were not. While as funny as all get out, things often ended badly.

'Rose,' Jake said.

There was something in his voice that made her look at him more closely. He was laughing? She bridled. 'What? Do you find me amusing?'

'Not at all,' he said, laughter dancing in the depths of his eyes. 'Poor young Faxford. The brainless idiot didn't have a clue what you were talking about. That is why he called you a bluestocking.'

'How mean. I promise to be more careful.' Something inside her shrivelled a little.

'You certainly don't want people to think you have any sort of brain,' His Grace said, agreeably.

She glared at him. 'Why must women act like foolish creatures without a sensible thought in their heads?'

He must have realised her distress, for he reached over and patted her hand. The touch of his bare skin on hers sent tingles rushing across her skin.

'I'm teasing, Rose. I like you just as you are. Unfortunately, one derogatory remark can be picked up and passed from person to person until one's reputation is in tatters. Men love to deride intelligent women. It makes them feel superior.'

'Derog...' She frowned as she tried to get her tongue

around the unfamiliar word. 'Derogatory. I assume it was something intended to hurt.'

'From the Latin, *derogatorius*, meaning impairing in force or effect, criticising.'

Her head whirled. 'You speak Latin?'

'I learned Latin. No one speaks it any more. But that is beside the point. Faxford is a twit, whereas you are eminently sensible.'

A feeling of pride at his praise swelled her heart. 'Which account do you believe?'

'The prognosis is not good.' He winced. 'I apologise, I forget you have not had the same opportunity to—'

'Oh, I know what that means. It is a medical term for the course of a disease.' She had heard the doctors at the orphanage use it. 'You think there is cause for concern?'

'I do. I ran into Tonbridge, a military man with friends in the army. He believes the press has the right of it, for a change. Resentment among the people is building.'

She gasped. 'Revolution?'

'No need to look so hopeful, my dear.'

They both burst out laughing.

When their laughter died away, once more Rose looked so adorably serious, Jake wanted to kiss her.

'You really think it will come to that?' she asked.

'Let us hope not, though there is talk of Acts which will not be popular with the people.'

'You will speak against them in the Lords?'

He ignored the pang of guilt. 'I have no seat.'

She frowned at him. 'You are a duke, are you not? A peer?'

'I am. But there are customs and processes to be observed. I haven't bothered.' He hadn't felt he had the right or the need. Against his will his gaze flicked to the swath of black crepe covering the picture over mantel. 'I have been otherwise occupied since gaining the title.' If one could call it a gain. He frequently felt he had been much better off as plain Lord Jake.

'Did your father take an active role in politics?' she asked casually.

'He did.' A memory made him want to smile. 'He and I were not always in accord with how the country should be run, but he was...assiduous in voting his seat.'

She glanced down at her hands. 'Assiduous.' She rolled the word around her mouth. 'I see.'

What did she see? Guilt pricked his conscience. A feeling he resented. 'What are you thinking, Miss Nightingale? That I should take up the cause of our northern citizens, perhaps? Insist that any soldier who used his sword on a member of the public be tried for murder?'

'Not the soldiers,' she said quickly, softly. 'Those who gave the orders.'

'Men like me.'

She stiffened. 'You are offended. I do not agree with those who call for an uprising, you know. Too many people will be hurt, most of them women and children. I do, however, believe the way the country is run must change. Ordinary people must have more say.'

'By Jove, you really are a bluestocking, Miss Nightingale.' At the sight of her hurt, he touched a finger to her nose. 'I mean that as a compliment.'

'And you will...vote your seat, is it called? On this matter?'

'I do not know.' A very shameful truth. 'I really do need more information.' But he would speak to Tonbridge again. The man seemed to have more knowledge and intellect than most and he was also a ducal heir. 'I will think about it, certainly.' But to sit in his father's place in the Lords, the very idea made him nauseous.

'You still grieve for them,' she said softly. 'Your father and your brother.'

Shock rippled through him. At the words. At the look of

understanding rather than sympathy that somehow made their deaths all the more real, when most days he still did not fully believe it. He forced his gaze away from the black crepe that hid nothing of their faces from his mind's eye. 'Shall we read that poetry as Grandmama suggested?' He reached for the book.

'No, thank you, Your Grace.' She was already rising to her feet with a small smile. 'It has been a very long day, with more than its share of excitement. I think I, too, will retire.'

Frowning, he shot to his feet. Had he said something wrong? Now he looked at her, he realised she was a little pale and drawn. Naturally she would have found her first foray into society daunting. Yet she'd still had the wit and the energy to debate politics with him. 'Very well, I shall escort you up.'

'No need.'

'It will be my pleasure.'

Without further demur she placed her hand on his arm. He walked her sedately up the stairs to the door of her chamber.

She stopped and he opened it. About to step inside, she hesitated, looking up at him. 'You do not think my error today is irredeemable, then? I would hate to give Her Grace cause for embarrassment. I—I have come to like my position here.'

Wonder of wonders. 'I think your little *faux pas* will scarce make a ripple.'

'Foh-pah?'

'It is French for error. A minor mistake.' He spelled it out.

She shook her head. 'How will I ever learn all of this?'

'You have made great strides, Miss Nightingale, do not doubt your ability.'

She swung around to face him, a smile on her face. 'You know I don't think I ever thanked you properly for this opportunity. Indeed, I came most unwillingly, I believe.'

'You did. Believe me, no thanks are required. Your presence is a boon of the highest magnitude. I haven't see Grandmama in such good spirits for a long while.'

'You are good man, Jacob Huntingdon, despite your attempts to hide it.'

Surprised, he stared at her. 'Why would you think I—?'

She touched a fingertip to his lips. 'You hated that event today, yet you came to please your grandmother.'

Not only his grandmother, but he wasn't about to admit that to Rose. 'It was my duty.' He sounded stilted. Uncomfortable. But what was new about that? Nothing in his life was comfortable. Except perhaps his private moments with Rose, when he could be himself.

She shook her head at him. 'You really deserve more than duty, Your Grace.'

His breathing quickened at her teasing tone. The urge to smile back pulled at his lips. He closed the distance between them. 'What would you suggest?'

The delicious scent of her body filled his nostrils, her warm smile was an unexpected welcome. He wanted to bask in that warmth. To drink his fill of her sweetness. He should not. Must not.

As she placed her hand flat on his chest, he found himself wanting to hold it. He clenched his fists behind his back instead. He would not treat her as if she was anything less than a lady, even if she could never be his lady, in red or any other colour. He steeled himself to step back. 'I beg your pardon. A gentleman should not importune a lady under his roof. I—'

'If I was truly a lady,' she interrupted softly, 'you would not have kissed me last night.'

Regret speared him. An apology leapt to his tongue. But that little hand gripped his lapel tight enough for her knuckles to show white through her skin. 'And if I was any sort of real lady I would not have kissed you back. I don't want you to go.'

She rose up on her toes and pressed her mouth to his.

Unable to stop himself, he swept her into the circle of one arm, deepening the kiss, while opening her door with the other. He edged her inside and closed it behind them. A long moment later, he lifted his head, breathing hard.

'Rose. That is what I call an ambush. And it is not the first time I have been ambushed by a lady. So don't think it.'

She was panting and staring at his mouth with the kind of raw hunger that called to him on a very basic level. 'You really do kiss beautifully, Your Grace. I have missed those kisses.'

'Call me, Jake, sweetheart, please.'

'Jake, right now, I would love it if you would kiss me again.'

He had never been propositioned so sweetly or so devastatingly. He fought to find some rational thought, some reason why he should walk away and...found nothing but the desire to kiss her again.

A groan rumbled up from his chest. Where Rose was concerned when it came to kissing, he had almost no willpower. A kiss, that was all it would be, and then he would leave.

He touched his lips to hers.

Chapter Seven

Rose wasn't quite sure when she had decided she could give up her long-held principles and take this daring step with a man who could never really be hers.

Perhaps the sight of him in such delicious and tempting undress as he groomed his horse, or the way he treated her like part of his family, or patiently explained the meaning of a word she had never heard before, had made her feel this overwhelming fondness.

Or perhaps it was the terrible loneliness she had sensed in him in that drawing room this afternoon when, despite the crowds around him, he had seemed to stand alone. Surely the man deserved someone to care about him, the way he cared for his family. While she could not stand at his side, in private she could offer him affection.

And, yes, gain something for herself. A feeling of being needed.

Truth to tell, she really had missed his kisses.

Clearly, he was far too much a gentleman to press for what she had indicated was unwelcome so it was up to her to take the first step. Another thing to be grateful for in a life where so few decisions had been her own.

And Jake's kisses were blissful. Intoxicating. A word she now understood, though she had never imbibed strong drink.

She opened her lips to his tongue's gentle request along the seam of her lips, sighed as their mouths melded. Aching deep in her heart, she let her fingers wander through the silk of his hair, absorbing every whisper of sensation against her skin. The hard bulk of his broad chest pressing against her breasts. The hand caressing her back as he drew her close, the feel of his arousal against her belly.

Each breath she took was not enough. Dizziness made her head swim and her knees feel weak, yet she had no fear of him letting her fall. His heat and his strength surrounded her like a barrier against the world. Nothing and no one would harm her when she was in his arms. Safe as she had never been safe before.

What wonderful memories they would make and for a while, he could forget his duty and be himself. A good kind man. She cupped his face in her hands and he broke the kiss, looking down at her, breathing almost as hard as she was. That he wanted her, she had no doubt.

His hazy gaze sharpened. His expression became enquiring. 'Rose?'

'Jake,' she whispered.

He shut his eyes for a moment. When he opened them, they were clear, his emotions bare. He looked tortured. 'Do you know how rarely anyone calls me by my own name?'

She brushed back the lock of dark hair that liked to fall on to his forehead. 'Jake, I…' How to say this without sounding forward?

He stepped back. 'I should go.'

She caught at his hand. He glanced down at where their fingers intertwined, then lifted his gaze to her face. The muscles in his jaw flickered. 'I am not made of stone, Rose.'

'Nor am I.' The thunder of her heart made it impossible to speak, so she smiled at him. Swallowed. 'Stay. Please?'

His eyes widened.

She'd been too forward. Or had she? The heat flaring in his gaze said otherwise.

He put his hands on her waist. 'Do not say it, if you do not mean it.'

Relief flooded through her. She could not stop the chuckle of delight that bubbled up in her throat. 'I never say things I do not mean.'

A small smile curved his lips. 'Never pretend, was what you said.'

She nodded slowly. 'Never.'

He shook his head slightly, but his smile broadened. 'You are lovely. Delicious. Gorgeous. Delightful.'

All words she recognised. Words that made her heart swell with an odd kind of pride that he would use them to describe her. She felt almost…precious. As if this moment was as important to him as it was to her. She twined her arms around his neck, gazing at his lovely mouth that formed such lovely words and her body tightened in anticipation of his kiss. 'Jake, I…'

'Mmm?' he murmured, nuzzling against her neck, tasting a spot beneath her ear that sent strange surges of that same tight feeling rushing between her thighs. She rolled her hips against him, pressed closer.

'I forget everything when you kiss me.'

'Me, too.' He drew in a breath. 'You are sure you want this?'

She chuckled. 'I have never been more certain of anything in my life.'

A shudder rippled through him. 'A gentleman really does not take advantage of the women in his household. I do rather pride myself on being a gentleman, you know.'

Only too well. It was one of the things about him she found

so endearing. Irresistible. But not when it held him back. 'Can't we just be Jake and Rose tonight? No titles. Not employer and employee. No rules. Merely two ordinary people enjoying each other's company.'

He stilled as if considering the idea. So cautious, her Jake. So very thoughtful. 'I would like that, Rose. Very much. You have no idea how much.' He chuckled. 'Jake the footman. I think it sounds well, don't you? A devil of a fellow I am below stairs, too. But you...' he rubbed his nose against hers in a gesture of affection '...are the only one I want.'

Want in the carnal sense. She understood his meaning and could not help but smile at his rascally grin. He could not know how her heart ached to hear that she was the only one he wanted. She'd had so few friends in her life, she would treasure his declaration even knowing he was being his usual flirtatious self. He had a family who loved him and could not possibly understand how lonely her life had been until now.

She was starting to feel as if she belonged somewhere.

She instilled laughter into her voice. 'Lawks, now. Wouldn't that be something? You a footman and me the upstairs maid.'

'Who have ducked into the upstairs linen closet while everyone is at breakfast.' Now he sounded mischievous.

'We must be very quiet,' she murmured, stroking her fingers through his hair. 'We wouldn't want the housekeeper catching us. We'd cuddle in the dark and you would whisper about your dream of becoming a butler, while I talked grandly of being the housekeeper.'

'And in between, I would steal a quick kiss.' He pecked at her cheek and she turned her face to catch it on her lips. The kiss was not in the least quick.

She melted against him, wanting to burrow into his skin, to feel him close.

He groaned, lifting his lips from hers and letting his mouth cruise her cheeks, her nose, her forehead, their bodies limpet tight.

'You will have to kick me out, Rose,' he muttered. 'I swear I do not have the will to leave of my own volition.'

Volition. He did say such funny things. But she knew what he meant. 'Then stay, Jake. I am not one of your noble misses with a reputation to guard.' Though she had guarded herself for years. But then no man had offered her the least temptation.

She could see from the expression on his face that he was torn between doing the honourable thing and fulfilling her request. And while this was not what she had ever intended—indeed, was against the rules she had set for herself—it would hurt if he turned her down. She would not give him the chance. Not now that she had made the decision.

This might well be her only chance to be with him. His sister could arrive at any moment and likely her presence in the house would preclude her and Jake from finding time to be alone.

She worked down the buttons of his coat and then his shirt, longing to reveal that wonderful expanse of chest. It did not take long for her to lay his torso bare, for he helped her pull the shirt over his head between plundering kisses that never seemed to end.

He was a beautifully constructed man. All lean muscle and lithe sinew. His arms were as defined as any sculpture she'd seen in a book. From grooming horses, no doubt. And his chest and stomach above his waistband made her mouth water with the desire to run her tongue along each ridge and shadowed dip. To see if he tasted as good as he smelled.

She eyed the buttons holding his falls at his waistband, but he spun her around, holding one arm about her waist while plying her nape with whisper-soft kisses.

'Let me take your hair down.' He barely waited for her nod before pins went flying about her feet and the curls she had spent an hour or more to fix in place were spilling around her shoulders in mere seconds.

Fair was fair.

God, Jake couldn't believe how much he desired Rose, when he hadn't wanted a woman for weeks or maybe months. Unable to resist, he bent and buried his nose in her golden tresses, breathing in the scent of lily of the valley. Sweet and innocent like her, but also incredibly alluring.

He swept her hair aside and gently sank his teeth into the tender skin where her shoulder joined her neck, loving the taste of her on his tongue and caught up by a primal urge to leave his mark. Though he would never do it in truth, the idea sent what little blood remained in his brain rushing south.

'Have you known many saucy footmen, Rose?'

She gave a low sensual chuckle 'Enough, Jakey-boy.' Her low husky voice sent tingles down his spine.

Relief. He'd had the suspicion—but ordinary people did not need to worry about such things as lineage and family blood. Saints preserve him, what he wouldn't give for just a few hours to be Rose's ordinary footman, without responsibility or duty to anyone but himself. Free to choose.

Not six months ago he'd been ordinary as far as the *ton* were concerned. The second son of a duke who led an idle life mostly unnoticed on the marriage mart. Safely hidden in his brother's shadow, he'd even kept the wealth derived from Vitium et Virtus and other investments a carefully guarded secret. Neither his father nor his brother had known how large he'd grown his personal fortune.

He would have been able to make Rose an honourable offer, had he been so disposed. Would he have been disposed? Unlikely. He'd never been one with marriage on his mind. He liked his independence too much. A pang twisted in his chest. He'd gone through life pleasing himself. Utterly selfish and thoughtless. Ultimately others had paid the price for his rottenness and would continue to do so.

He pitied any woman who became his wife. He simply wasn't cut out for marriage and yet he'd do as required by duty. He'd promised.

He didn't deserve Rose, but nor could he refuse her what she wanted. He wouldn't refuse her anything if it would make her smile, for if he was good for anything, it was bringing a woman pleasure. More pleasure than any footman ever had or ever would, of that he was certain.

She sighed at the touch of his lips and bent her head forward in a submissive posture that had nothing meek about it. This was a demand.

He could not help the smile the small gesture brought to his lips, any more than he could help kissing the lovely tender flesh at her nape one more time.

Slowly, he undid the buttons of her gown and the tapes of her stays, exposing the filmy fabric of her chemise, through which he could see the delicate nobs of her spine and the sharp-angled shoulder blades. Rose had not always eaten well.

The thought caused a stir of anger in his gut.

Gently he turned her to face him. She tipped her face up, a teasing smile on her lips and a softness in her expression that made him ache with need.

But this was not about him and his desires, it was about Rose. He took her lush lips, carefully, tenderly, as he pushed the gown and stays down over her arms and the lovely swell of her bottom, to slide to the floor with a little sigh. Echoed by Rose against his cheek.

Her arms went about his neck and he plundered the dark heat of her mouth, tasting her, feeling her melt against him, moving her hips against his erection in an erotic dance that practically had him coming apart. He broke the kiss on a groan. 'Let us at least make use of the bed.' He kept his voice light, but it was a heartfelt plea none the less.

She patted a cheek. A gesture of affection he couldn't recall anyone ever doing before. It was comforting. Familiar. Kind. Friendly. When were his lovers ever friendly or kind? Or anyone else for that matter.

'I'll be back in a moment,' she said and whisked herself behind the screen. 'You can finish undressing if you like.'

He did like, very much, and he guessed much of the reason for her disappearance was modesty. The thought of Rose being shy was almost too erotic for his sanity.

It didn't take him long to strip down and hop into bed, discarding all the covers but the sheet. Several moments passed. 'Rose, what—?'

'Precautions,' she said from behind the screen. 'No unwanted mistakes—' A small sound of triumph. 'Sponges and what not.'

Heaven have mercy on him, she was taking charge of the whole business. And what a relief it was to know she thought as he did and her preparedness eased some of his doubts about taking advantage. 'What a competent woman you are, Rose.' But responsibility was not hers alone. 'You know there is no guarantee.' He almost kicked himself for his honesty. His lust almost kicked him, too. He ignored those selfish male urges. 'I, too, will take precautions.'

She appeared from behind the screen looking adorably flushed with embarrassment. 'Then we should be doubly sure.'

He lifted the sheet with a welcoming grin and she skipped up the steps and on to the bed and into his arms.

'Now,' she said, sounding very pleased with herself, 'where were we?'

He gazed up into her sparkling eyes, so full of mischief, the glossy strands of her hair falling around them trailing across his chest like tormenting fairy fingers. 'You were kissing me.'

She ran a fingertip along his eyebrow and then patted the end of his nose, the admonishment startlingly novel. 'Was I, now?'

He couldn't resist, he flipped her on her back and leaned over her, grinning like a fool. 'Or perhaps I was kissing you.' He nipped at her earlobe. 'What do you think?'

She shivered. 'I think,' she said solemnly, 'we were kissing each other.'

She wrapped her arms around his neck and pulled his head down, even as she rose up to meet him.

Such sweetness. He gave himself over to the pleasure of her lips and her tongue and the feel of her tiny fingers wandering his back, tracing his spine, exploring the shape of his buttocks beneath the sheet wrapped around his hips. He wanted those fingers on another part of him, but this wasn't one of the many bold lovers he'd had over the years. Ladies knowledgeable in the art of *amour*.

Her modest blushes were a testimony to hurried couplings in the dark of an evening off. The housekeeper at the ducal estate where he had lived as a boy had explained this to him and his brother when they reached thirteen. She had warned them off all the maids in the house with threats of dire consequences. Something he'd taken to heart, until his brother had introduced him to a local widow who knew all the tricks required to keep a lusty boy happy.

He'd never bothered the maids in the house. But here he was bothering his grandmother's lovely, adorable and terribly sweet companion.

Which was worse. She was under his protection.

He broke the kiss. 'Rose, are you really sure you want this?'

The dreamy smile on her lips as she gazed up at him was enough to drive a man mad. 'I am really, really sure.'

The words drove his conscience into a deep dark corner

even as it noticed there was a touch of sadness in her voice his desire refused to examine in detail.

Learning how to please Rose, when likely she did not yet know the answers, was going to be a pleasure and a delight.

He pressed a swift kiss to her lips, her chin, her jaw, then swirled his tongue around the rim of her ear.

She squirmed, her hip nudging against his painfully hard erection, making his head swim. He sucked in a breath and she stilled.

'You liked that,' he managed to ask.

'It tickled.' She sounded bemused. 'Everywhere.'

'Including here?' He laid his palm over her breast, slowly letting her take the weight of his hand, feeling the tightly furled nub against his palm with a smile.

'There, too,' she said, arching up into his hand, encouraging him to stroke. He paid careful attention to that breast, teasing the nipple lightly through the sheer fabric of her shift, while watching the reactions flutter over her face. Surprise, pleasure, desire. Never had he seen anything quite so erotic as a woman learning her pleasures.

Having patience was going to kill him before he was through.

He moved to her other breast, performing the same gentle motions with hand and fingers while he lowered his mouth to taste the tightly furled nub of the first.

Then he suckled. Her thighs parted, her hips rolled into him and he pushed one knee between her legs, giving her the pressure she sought at the apex to her thighs. She moaned her pleasure.

He came up on his knees and gradually eased her shift upward until he could get his lips and tongue on her naked breasts. Beneath him, her hips arched towards what instinctively she knew she wanted, but he refused to be rushed, no matter how much delayed gratification pained him. He gritted his teeth and with his hands still playing with her breasts, he kissed his way down her ribs to lay his cheek upon her flat stomach.

She flattened her hands over his still cupping her breasts, as if she feared they would wander off elsewhere. They wanted to. He eased one out from beneath her clutching fingers and showed her how to stroke her own breast, while he continued to tease the other. He combed his fingers through the golden little triangle of curls and her hips came up in response.

The sensuality in that simple little twitch had him wanting to drive deep within her heat. Soon. He promised it would be soon as he gently parted her folds and felt her heat and the damp on his fingers.

She froze for a second, then lifted her head to see what he was about. He pressed a kiss to her stomach, swirled his tongue in her navel and she sank back against the pillows, parting her thighs wider in an invitation he had no hope of refusing.

Not if he wasn't to disgrace himself entirely this first time.

And there would be many other times when he could take it more slowly, no matter what she thought.

He rose up on one hand, took her hand and guided it to his shaft. 'Tell me where you want me, sweetheart.' Let there be no mistake about who was in charge. He had been robbed of what he had thought were his choices; he would take none from anyone else.

Her small hand closed around him.

He watched the delight in her face with puzzlement, for not only was she delighted, she was also surprised. And curious. She rose up on one elbow to look at him, rapping him on his nose in the process. He ignored his pain and watering eyes, because he was entranced by her look of wonder.

'I'm supposed to do that, too?' she asked, letting go of his shaft and cupping him, exploring the texture. Hadn't she ever been given the chance to feel her partners?

He swallowed at the pleasurable sensations rippling up through his body as she caressed him, her gaze focused on what her hand was doing.

'Only if you wish,' he said, hoping she did with a longing that caught him off guard. As if the memory would be something to treasure for years to come.

Grasping him again, she frowned in concentration and guided him in the right direction. He nudged forward into her folds and, as he slid forward another fraction, she made a small sound, a cross between a sigh and a squeak of fear.

He froze.

She reclined back on to the pillow. 'More,' she demanded.

He gritted his teeth against the urge to drive into her and eased forward another fraction, into the heat and the wet. It snugged around him, so hot, so tight, it was so unbearably delicious his head spun with pleasure. His hips jerked a little more than he'd intended and she gasped.

Pain?

He lifted his gaze. She was biting her bottom lip. Her eyes were squeezed tight shut.

'Did I hurt you?'

He wasn't a small man, but he had never encountered a woman so small and tight and— 'Rose!' He wanted to curse.

She flexed her hips experimentally. 'My. That is nice. I think I am getting the hang of it.'

Well, damn it all, not for one moment had he expected this. To be her first. 'Rose, we shouldn't—'

She wrapped her legs around his thighs, effectively holding him in place. He shouldn't. He really should not.

'You cannot stop now,' she said, flexing again.

Even if he wanted to, with her holding him fast, he could not. And he really did not want to.

Slowly, gently, he eased deeper into her body, too slowly for her it seemed at times, but he refused to let her hurry him, he was not going to cause her pain. To distract her, he kissed the lovely mouth that would urge him to go faster. He teased her breasts to keep her focused elsewhere. Finally he was seated fully. Only then did he rise up to look into her face.

What he saw in her expression almost undid him. The haze of desire, the pleasure, the sensuality of her smile—all were so much more than he could ever deserve.

He started rocking against her and she quickly picked up the rhythm, lifting her legs up around his waist to bring him closer and harder against her, and there was no longer any hope of doing anything but taking her into bliss. To do anything else would be a crime.

He suckled at her breast while she met him stroke for stroke and he heard by her cries and soft moans that she was so close, yet she did not know what her body sought.

He reached between them, sought out the place he'd found on his earlier exploration and circled it with his thumb. She writhed against his hand with a sound a protest.

'Let it go, my sweet,' he crooned. 'Let it happen.'

A second later she fell apart.

He held off long enough for her to spasm tightly around him, to draw on him and then somehow his brain managed to wrest back a measure of control. He withdrew and spilled on her belly.

He collapsed. Wrecked. Overcome. And feeling for the first time in a long time that he wasn't completely alone.

Whatever that meant.

Languid in a haze of warmth, her body lax, Rose became aware of a heavy weight pushing her into the mattress. Jake. Lovely Jake. Who had just—

Heaven help her, she'd gone and done it. Something she had always said she would not. And she'd enjoyed it, too.

Without a smidgeon of regret. Indeed, there was a whole lot of joy bubbling strangely inside her, trying to escape. Not that she'd ever dare express how she felt in such terms. He'd likely think her foolish or some such, mock her for being silly, and then she'd be mortified.

Mortified. Such an interesting word. She'd read it in a book and looked it up in *Johnson's Volume II*, an enormous set of tomes Jake had placed on tables in the library for her use. She stretched, luxuriating in the strange new feelings coursing through her veins.

Jake threw the sheet back and went to wash himself off. He shot a considering glance from across the room, rinsed out the cloth and came stalking back. 'Your turn.'

Tenderly he washed her belly and her thighs with his mouth set in a thin grim line. He had more smiles while brushing his horse. 'What is wrong?'

'If I had known, I would have been more careful.'

More careful? Everything had been too lovely for any sort of words she could think of.

'You will likely be sore come the morning.' He tossed the washcloth across the room and it landed with a *thunk* in the basin. 'Why did you leave me to believe this was not your first time?'

She must have looked as blank as her mind felt, because he tapped her nose with a finger, much as she had done to him earlier. It was as if they had their own private language. The thought pleased her.

'Rose, this is no smiling matter,' he said sternly. 'You have never been intimate with a man before.'

'Not like that I haven't. Had the odd kiss and a cuddle, but that was all. Never met anyone I liked well enough. Besides, live-in servants can't marry and...' She bit her lip.

His expression became thoughtful. 'Is that what you want?'

'I haven't given it much thought.' Not quite the truth, but really a husband and family had been little more than a dream.

'You deliberately misrepresented matters.' He sounded bemused.

'Mispre— What?'

'Misrepresented. Made me think you were something you weren't.'

She pulled the sheets up to her chin. 'Are you accusing me of lying?'

He pulled her close and kissed her forehead. 'Misleading me. You said you'd known a great many footmen.'

'I was a housemaid. Houses are full of footmen.'

'Then it is my mistake.' He petted her hair where it lay across her shoulder. 'I should have been more direct. When I asked you if you knew them, I meant in the biblical sense.'

'The biblical...' She shot upright. 'You meant had I swived them?'

'Yes. I'm afraid I did.'

'Then you should have said so.'

'Indeed.'

She frowned at him and realised he was smiling, but not in a mean way. He looked pleased.

'Come here, sweetling. Cuddle up. I find I am too tired to think, right at this moment. I want to hold you.'

She snuggled into his embrace. 'I didn't mean to misrepresent,' she whispered against his chest.

He stroked her back. 'I know. Are you comfortable?' He shifted his arm.

She moved so that one leg draped across his thigh. 'I am now. Are you?'

'Very.' His head moved as if he was trying to see her face. 'Rose, you would tell me if you weren't happy here, wouldn't you?'

Would she? They had promised to be truthful. 'I will.'

'I worry that I might have been a little high-handed.' He gave her a little squeeze. 'I would not like to think of you feeling trapped.'

'I like it here. I just fear making a terrible mistake and putting you all to shame.'

'You couldn't.'

If only she could be as confident.

'Rose?'

'Yes.'

'Was it your dream to become a housekeeper?'

She recalled her playful words of earlier. Clearly he had been listening. 'Once it was. More recently I have been thinking of becoming a dressmaker.'

'A seamstress,' he said with a yawn he tried to disguise.

'No. A proper dressmaker. To the fashionables. Like Mrs Gill of Cork Street. The girls at the V&V said I do wonders with their gowns.'

'Would you rather—?'

'I am fine where I am at the moment. What about you? Did you dream of becoming a duke?'

He stiffened. 'It was the very last thing I dreamed of, I can assure you.' He sounded offended. Cold.

'But—' She bit the words off as she recalled it was his older brother who should have inherited. 'I am sorry, Jake. I did not mean—'

'Forget it. I had better leave now. We don't want anyone finding me here.' He threw the sheet back and pulled on his breeches and shirt.

She winced. Somehow she had ruined the moment. Gone was the easy camaraderie of moments before. The autocratic Duke was back—cold, efficient and displeased.

'I did not mean—'

'I don't wish to discuss it further.'

In moments, he was dressed and walking out of the door. 'Goodnight, Rose.'

He didn't even kiss her.

'Goodnight,' she whispered, but he was already out of the door and would not have heard.

It seemed it was all right for him to ask her questions, but not all right for her to do the same.

Well, they had promised to be honest with each other, and

if she had trespassed somewhere he did not want her to go, then it was right he should let her know.

Still, his refusal to talk about himself hurt. A great deal.

Jake slowly came to his senses, taking more than a moment to recognise the unfamiliar feeling of well-being spreading throughout his body. And then he did.

The sense of loss at the realisation that he wasn't still with Rose was surprising and none too welcome. He'd always been a rolling-stone sort of chap when it came to women, making good his escape at the earliest opportunity, and had been true to form last night. He could still recall the hurt in her eyes when he'd left.

Her question had touched him on the raw. Now he wished he'd stayed. Not that he could or would explain. Thinking about it made him feel ill. He certainly wasn't going to tell anyone else.

He stared at the light coming through the window. By Jove. It was morning. He'd slept all night, once he'd crawled into his own bed. He couldn't remember the last time he had awoken in his own bed, let alone slept there for several hours on the trot.

Or when he'd last awoken feeling remarkably at peace rather than desolate. It would have been even better if Rose had been here to share his good mood. He stilled. Not something he should want. Not now. Not ever. Good lord, he'd been wrong to let lust carry him away in the first place. It would never happen again.

He wished he believed that, truly he did, but he knew beyond a doubt that things had not yet come to their natural conclusion. Unless after his rudeness, Rose decided to turn him away.

He shrugged. She wouldn't be the first one and likely not the last. It meant nothing. But he couldn't help hoping that she would forgive his lapse in manners.

His valet entered and started. 'Your Grace!'

Jake sat up. 'That is me.'

And for the first time the very idea of it didn't make him want to hit something.

'Shall I fetch a tray, Your Grace?'

'No. I'll go down for breakfast. Fetch some hot water. would you? There's a good fellow.'

It didn't take him long to shave and dress, though he was held up by his valet, who insisted on trimming his nails. When he entered the dining room he was surprised to discover his grandmother and Rose already eating.

'You are rather early this morning, are you not, Grandmama?' He leaned forward to kiss the papery wrinkled cheek she presented.

'Have you forgotten the Dearbournes' Venetian Breakfast is today? You were to escort us.' She swivelled in her chair and looked up at him. 'You look different. What have you done?'

'Nothing.'

'Rose, does he look different to you?'

Rose cast him a swift glance, then looked down at her plate, a rush of colour across her cheekbones. 'He looks the same as always, Your Grace.'

'Hmmph.' His grandmother went back to her eggs. 'You hadn't forgotten you promised to escort us, have you, Westmoor?'

'I had not.' He just hadn't recalled it was today. He'd been too busy feeling good about beginning the day feeling so cheerful and well rested. 'We leave at eleven, do we not?'

'We do. Which is why Rose and I are eating now. It might be three in the afternoon before Lady Dearbourne puts out a morsel of food.'

He groaned. 'Truly?' He'd gone last year with a couple of friends while his grandmother had gone with his father and brother. Jake had only stayed an hour or so before heading off for more enjoyable pursuits. This year there would be no departing early.

He filled his plate and sat down at the head of the table. Something that usually made him feel like a usurper. This morning it gave him the chance to sit between his grandmother and Rose and charm himself back into both ladies' good graces. 'Are you well, Grandmama?'

'As well as can be expected at my age, my boy,' she said, narrowing her eyes at him.

'Glad to hear it.'

'And how are you this fine morning, Miss Nightingale?'

Again he received only the briefest glance. 'Very well, thank you, Your Grace.'

'I do wish you would call me Jake, or at least Westmoor, or people will think it strange.'

The pink in her cheeks turned a darker shade. She pushed her eggs around on her plate. 'I prefer to maintain the proprieties, Your Grace. May I pour you some tea?'

Grandmama looked from Rose to him. Her gaze sharpened. She raised a brow. 'You seem very cheerful this morning, Jacob.'

'I am.' He glanced at Rose, couldn't stop himself, but she kept her gaze fixed on her plate.

'I'm glad to see it,' Grandmama said, looking pleased. 'Very glad. Aren't you pleased, Rose?'

Rose jumped. Her gaze flew to his and back to his grandmother. 'I am sure it is not my place to offer an opinion, Your Grace.'

Jake felt nervousness like a kick to the gut. Clearly she was not feeling the same *joie de vivre* he was this morning. At least, not with him. Women were such sensitive creatures.

She continued to poke at the food, barely eating a mouthful.

'Hmmph,' Her Grace said. 'And here I was thinking you and my grandson were getting on so well.'

Rose looked ready to hide under the table. 'His Grace is very kind, Your Grace.'

Kind. Was that what she was calling it? He realised his grandmother was watching him and forced his frown away.

'Young people,' Grandmama said with a snort.

'What about young people, Grandmama?' he asked.

'They cannot see what is beneath their noses, that is what. Jacob, you will have the carriage brought around at eleven, if you please. Are you finished, Miss Nightingale?'

'Quite finished, Your Grace,' Rose replied, putting down her knife and fork.

She'd barely eaten a thing. Blast it. But what could he say? He got up and held his grandmother's chair. Rose did not wait for his assistance, but came around the table to take his grandmother's arm and support her progress out of the room.

Devil take it. So much for feeling better than he had in days. Now he had a sense of impending doom.

And then there was Eleanor and Lucy's arrival to be considered. He wasn't sure if having them here would make things better or worse for Rose. But he did know one thing—last night must not happen again if it was going to make Rose unhappy.

Suddenly the day did not seem quite so bright.

Chapter Eight

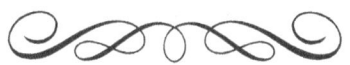

To Rose's relief, Jake had seen her and his grandmother into the town coach and had ridden on ahead. She wasn't quite sure how she would have managed if he had travelled with them in the carriage. Awkward did not begin to describe the way she felt. It wasn't that she regretted their lovemaking, exactly. It had been something beyond her girlish imaginations. Quite wonderful, in truth. But she did feel as if she had let herself down. She had always assumed she was far too smart to let her attraction for a man overcome her good sense. That she was no better than the mother she had blamed for her situation came as a disappointment.

In addition, she did not like the feeling of keeping secrets from his grandmother, who was regarding her intently. Not in an unfriendly way, more a sort of knowing glance, as if at any moment she might wink. Imagination, surely? Or a guilty conscience. Her Grace would probably toss her out on her ear if she so much as guessed what Rose and Jake had been up to.

Not Jake. His Grace. Using his name would be a terrible

slip in public. Besides, it had all ended rather badly, so it wasn't as if it would continue. If only she hadn't made such a stupid comment. Of course he hadn't dreamed of being a duke. Still, there was no reason for him to get so stuffy about it. She hadn't meant anything by it. She could only hope he wasn't regretting offering her this position.

A feeling of excitement took up residence in her stomach as the carriage turned into the drive. Her Grace had tried to explain what a Venetian Breakfast entailed and it sounded like it might be fun. She would just have to be careful what she said and did and not make any more silly mistakes where Jake was concerned.

He was waiting to greet them when the carriage set them down at the front door and escorted them around the side of the house. The Marquis and Marchioness of Dearbourne met them on the terrace and directed them to lawns that sloped down to the River Thames at the back of the house where the guests were assembling.

The scent of late-summer roses swirled around them. Bunting fluttered from bushes and poles in the light breeze on what had turned out to be a day of blue skies and a few puffy clouds.

The drive had been a scant five miles from the ducal town house to Dearbourne Villa, but Rose, despite her misgivings, had enjoyed every moment. It was the first time in her life she had been what she thought of as *out in the country*, though Her Grace had assured her this was, by most, considered as an extension of London. Why, the old lady had exclaimed, they were going nowhere near as far as Windsor.

The villa was not as grand as the Duke's mansion, but it was no paltry affair, either. It had the look of a fairy castle, in fact. Pennants flew at the top of turrets and one could almost imagine armed knights standing on the tops of walls decorated with crenulations.

Since Jake had very properly taken his grandmother's arm, Rose was free to wander along behind them taking in the sights. There were tables set out in the shade of trees that clustered at the edge of a field that the Marchioness had called the lawn. There were also open-sided tents in bright colours, providing shade and seats as well as blankets for those who liked to sit on the ground.

Some of the tents shaded tables full of bottles and glasses, while footmen and maids strolled among the guests, looking dreadfully hot, offering trays of full glasses or carting away the empty ones.

Rose could not help feeling sorry for those servants and their heavy clothing in the summer heat, while the ladies were in the lightest of muslins. Some of the gentlemen lounging on the blankets had stripped down to their shirts and waistcoats.

Al fresco. Rose savoured the exotic Italian words.

Jake organised a chair for his grandmother beneath one of the canopies and offered Rose the one beside her. Instead, she took one to the rear and shook her head when he looked as if he might argue with her choice. She leaned forward to murmur in the Dowager Duchess's ear, 'Is there anything you need, Your Grace?'

'A glass of champagne wouldn't go amiss.'

Jake grinned. 'Leave that to me.'

He strode off, looking every inch the nobleman. Utterly gorgeous. Rose hoped her face didn't betray her thoughts. She fixed her gaze on her hands. The last thing she wanted to do was draw attention to her feelings about him. 'Do you need your shawl, Your Grace? Out of the sun, you might find the breeze a little cool.'

'Not at the moment, my dear, but thank you for your kind thought.' She gestured with her cane at some ladies and gentlemen wandering around with what looked like mallets. 'Have you ever played pall mall?'

'I have not, Your Grace.'

'You should try it. It is all kinds of fun.'

Rose frowned as one of the gentlemen put his hands around a lady to help guide her mallet as she swiped at the ball. Games. When did a maid have time for such games? Or an orphan for that matter?

The Duke returned with a waiter bearing several glasses. He handed one to Her Grace, then attempted to offer one to her. 'No, thank you.'

'Try it,' Her Grace said with an encouraging smile. 'You will find it refreshing.'

'I prefer not,' she said, surprised at the old lady's warmth of tone.

'Persuade her, Jacob,' the old lady said.

Jake frowned. 'Miss Nightingale must decide for herself.' He sounded so aloof the chill of his voice sent a shiver down Rose's back.

His grandmother frowned. 'Jacob, really—'

He waved the waiter off as if he hadn't heard. Of course he wouldn't encourage his grandmother's companion to indulge in strong spirits. It had been something they had complained about with regard to her predecessor. And as for his coldness in front of his grandmother, she was glad of it. The old lady saw too much. More than once she had asked Rose if she didn't think her grandson a most handsome fellow.

He sipped at his drink, arranging himself beside his grandmother's chair. Rose could not see his expression, but she could well imagine the aloof look on his face.

A few minutes later, the Marchioness bore down on them. With her was a young lady in a white sprig muslin. Glossy chestnut locks framed the girl's oval-shaped face shaded by a wide-brimmed straw hat decorated with flowers. She looked lovely and fashionable. The trim on the hem of her gown, a festoon of lace held in scallops by pink silk roses, was gorgeous. The gown must have cost a fortune.

'Your Grace, allow me to present my niece, Lady Alicia Pettigrew.'

The young lady curtsied deeply and batted her eyelashes at the Duke as she rose.

'My lady,' Jake said coolly.

Her lips curved in a friendly smile. 'How lovely to meet you, again, Your Grace.'

She had a slight lisp and spoke in little more than a whisper.

He blinked as if trying to recall her. 'Indeed. Delightful.'

'This is my companion, Miss Rose Nightingale,' Her Grace said into the uncomfortable pause.

The young lady nodded and Rose inclined her head in acknowledgement of the other's superior status.

'Lady Alicia is seeking a partner for a game of pall mall, Your Grace,' the Marchioness said pointedly.

'It would be my pleasure,' the Duke said, looking anything but pleased. He hesitated, glancing briefly at her, then set down his glass and held out his arm to Lady Alicia. 'Shall we?'

It took great effort not to show any emotion. Indeed, she was not sure what emotion it was that made it hard to breathe and had her stomach twisting. Gladness that he had not asked her to join them?

'Don't they make a lovely couple?' the Marchioness cooed.

Her Grace pursed her lips. 'You might say that.'

The Marchioness looked affronted. 'I do indeed. And she is very well connected, you know. I hope you will excuse me, Your Grace, more guests are arriving.' She bustled off.

'Do you think they make a lovely couple?' Her Grace asked, watching her grandson with narrowed eyes. 'I suppose he could do worse. The Pettigrews are a family almost as old as ours. Not to mention the gal has a considerable dowry.'

Was that hope in her voice? Rose gritted her teeth and ignored the clench of pain around her heart. Was Her Grace making a point? 'She is lovely.'

'Lovely.' The old lady turned slightly in her seat with a strange smile on her face. 'They do say beauty is in the eye of the beholder. There's no accounting for people's tastes.'

Did she like the match or did she not? Rose couldn't make up her mind. Not that it was any of her concern. Except it was, because if Jake did decide on a lady to marry, Rose would not be remaining under his roof. She clenched her hands in her lap. She just couldn't.

An elderly lady of enormous proportions wearing a turquoise dress and a wide-brimmed hat tottered over, waving her fan. 'My word, Your Grace, it is warm today. How are you? I heard you were out in company again. About time, too.'

'Sit, Elizabeth, and tell me your news,' the Dowager Duchess said.

The woman collapsed on to the empty chair and dived into a discussion of people Rose had never heard of. Her gaze drifted off to the game of pall mall.

They did make a lovely couple. Rose wanted to take the mallet and bash Lady Alicia over the head with it.

The girl stumbled over what could not have been more than a pebble, or perhaps a worm cast. Rose glowered as Jake caught her before she fell to her knees and set her back on her feet. A trill of laughter wafted across the lawn to grate against Rose's ear.

She could not bear to watch them, yet try as she might her gaze still wandered in that direction. He was her lover and while she accepted the fact that they could never be more... she certainly did not want to watch him flirt with another. It hurt.

She stared at her gloved hands gripped in her lap until there was a lull in the ladies' conversation. 'Is there anything I can get for you, Your Grace?'

'Nothing at all, thank you, Miss Nightingale.'

'Would you mind if I went for a short walk? I feel the need of some exercise.' She needed to be as far from Jake and Lady Alicia as possible. At least until she got her emotions under control.

'I do not see why not.' The expression on the Duchess's face held concern. Rose had the feeling the old lady knew why she needed to get away. Surely not? 'Young people, always so restless,' Her Grace said to her friend. 'Stay within sight of the house, Rose,' she added in a low voice. 'And do not be gone too long. They are sure to serve food at any moment.' Her Grace spoke louder. 'Take your parasol. The sun is very bright today.'

Parasols and gloves and delicate little slippers not at all suited to walking conspired against anything but the daintiest steps, when she wanted to march off at great speed. As far away as possible if the truth were told. But she did not want to cause Her Grace any embarrassment, so she strolled towards the river. Fortunately the grass was dry and would not mire the hem of this very expensive gown. She shuddered every time she thought about the cost.

She wandered towards the bank. The Thames here was very different to the busy river running through the city. Here, there were boats, but none of the tall ships that docked south of London Bridge and none of the ferrymen shouting for custom. It smelled a great deal better, too. It was quiet and it was peaceful.

Slowly she began to calm. Seeing Jake with that other woman had been a painful tug on her heart, even though she had known it would happen. Perhaps she simply needed time to get used to the idea. After all, she was merely an employee. They could certainly never be more than lovers.

It wasn't as if he'd made any promises. As someone abandoned as a baby, she knew better than to expect loyalty from anyone in her life, least of all a man. After all, only a woman lacking the support of a man would give up her child as her own mother had done. And while she might not be all that different to her mother when it came to Jake, she certainly was going to do her very best to ensure no unwanted children would result.

The day was too lovely for such dark thoughts. She took a deep breath. Tried to focus on her surroundings. The air here in the country smelled fresh, like a bouquet of flowers, and if this was not exactly the countryside, it was as close to it as she was ever likely to get.

And yet she couldn't quite shake off her unhappiness or the need to avoid the company of those clearly enjoying the day.

When Jacob returned to his grandmother, after a very tedious forty-seven minutes with the vapid Lady Alicia, he was pleased to find her surrounded by a group of her cronies and having a grand conversation. Of Rose, however, there was no sign.

When his grandmother caught sight of him she waved him over. 'Are you looking for Miss Nightingale?'

He smiled at the assembled grande dames and bowed. 'Good afternoon, ladies. I see you are looking in fine fettle. Our debutantes should beware.'

They smiled with girlish pleasure and there were even a couple of giggles. 'You always were a charmer, Lord Jake,' one of them said, flailing her fan.

Her grandmother gasped. The lady who had spoken flushed. 'I beg your pardon, Westmoor. I haven't seen you since…the accident. My condolences.'

She lowered her voice on her last words. Was she another who doubted his honour? 'Where is our dear Miss Nightingale?' he asked cheerfully, as if he had not noticed the inflection in her voice.

'She went for a walk.' His grandmother frowned, looking

around. 'Quite some time ago, now. Not long after you left. I asked her not to wander too far, but I no longer see her.'

Jake's heart gave an uncomfortable thump. She should not have wandered off alone. Nor should Grandmother have allowed it. 'I'll find her and bring her back to you safe and sound.'

Grandmother's face paled. 'She walked towards the river. I did not think to warn her about the current.'

'Please, Grandmama, do not concern yourself. I am sure Miss Nightingale simply went a little farther afield than she intended.' He bowed and strode down the sloping green sward towards the jetty where several young men lounged about, no doubt hoping to encourage some unwary female to board one of the punts.

Was that where Rose had gone? This urgent need to find her surprised him. In all his relationships with women, he had always been the one in control. With Rose he felt like a ship lost at sea.

How easily she'd abandoned him to Lady Alicia, while she went off having fun. Disgruntlement stirred in his chest. And worry.

Rose was too much the innocent to be safe around these young rakes. Rakes not unlike himself only a few months ago. He had no trouble imagining the sort of things they might get up to.

'Westmoor. How fortunate to meet you here.'

Inwardly, Jake groaned as he realised the source of the hail-fellow-well-met voice with its distinctive lisp. This was a man he'd prefer not to meet anywhere, though he wouldn't give the fellow the cut direct since he was also one of the Marquis's guests. Nor did he wish to appear overly anxious about Rose. Damn the gossipmongers.

He tamped down his impatience and gave a sharp nod to the thickset fellow. 'Bowles.' He'd known Nash Bowles since university. The man lived on the fringes of society. His reputation was, if not tarnished, then not highly polished. He was rumoured not to have paid his debts. Worse yet, he had attempted to entrap Fred's wife into marriage and Nicholas had held him in low esteem. All of which put him beyond the pale as far as Jake was concerned.

Now the blasted man was eyeing him with a narrowed gaze. Like a predator spotting prey? Damn his impudence.

'I have a business proposition for you,' Bowles said sotto voce, glancing around as if he was imparting some great secret.

'Really, Bowles? At a party?' The man was an idiot. He moved them a couple of steps away from anyone who might be within earshot. 'Send a note to my man of business, why don't you?'

Bowles smiled with the great bonhomie that some ladies found charming. It set Jacob's teeth on edge. 'I want to talk to you about Vitium et Virtus.'

Here? The man wanted to discuss the club in a public place, with ladies present. He glared. 'I have no idea what you are talking about.'

The man bridled a little, then caught himself and flashed another of his oily insincere smiles. 'With Bartlett gone, you have need of another partner, I should think. What if I told you I learned things in Europe that would bring in fabulous wealth? Special offerings for those with unusual tastes.'

Jake kept his hands loose at his sides. He would not let this jackanapes make him lose his temper. He curled his lip in a perfect imitation of his father when disgusted. 'Not interested.'

Bowles shifted from foot to foot, glancing about him. 'Think about it. That is all I ask.' He bowed. 'Good talking to you, Your Grace.' He sauntered away, with a strangely graceful gait for so thickset a man. He flourished his cane as if he wasn't the most irritating man in London.

Jaw clenched, Jake watched him make his way across the

lawns, bowing here, and pausing to exchange a word there. Gall. The man certainly had gall. Jake shook his head. He wasn't going to let an idiot like that ruin his day. What was ruining his day was not finding any sign of Rose.

She was nowhere near the jetty. Nor was she one of the ladies lounging beneath parasols in the little flat-bottomed boats being wooed by eager young gentlemen in straw hats.

Rose would not have got into a boat with a stranger.

His stomach settled at that certainty. He looked along the bank. Upstream the edge of the river became reedy and the path petered out. Downstream the path meandered into a small stand of trees intended to look natural, but carefully planted to provide dappled shade. He chose that direction and set off with a lengthened stride.

Around a bend in the path he found her seated on a wooden bench looking out over the river to the fields on the other side. Though she sat with shoulders straight with her hands in her lap, she looked so forlorn his heart wrenched.

And the relief he felt was out of all proportion to discovering her whereabouts.

She did not turn her head when he sat down beside her, but he had no doubt she knew that it was he.

'Rose,' he said softly.

'Your Grace,' she replied, her voice calm.

'Jake when we are alone, remember?' he said in teasing tones, unsure of her mood.

'Are we alone?'

'It would appear so, unless you are hiding some other fellow in the bushes hereabouts.' He gave her a gentle shove with his shoulder.

She cast him a glance of disdain. '*I'm* not hiding anyone.'

'Nor am I.'

'You and Lady Alicia make a very striking couple.'

He winced. 'I would much rather have played pall mall

with you, you know, but—' Curse it, how did he put this without making things worse?

She lifted her little chin and looked him in the eye. 'But we both know she is the sort of girl you are expected to marry.'

Thank God she understood. Even so, her understanding didn't provide any sort of relief. It made him sad. 'At the moment I have far too much to do learning how to manage the Duchy without adding a wife to my list of duties.' At least that was what he kept telling himself, despite his grandmother's urgings.

She stared down at the white linen. 'Your grandmother wouldn't agree.' She took a deep breath. 'I suppose her anxiety is natural after what happened.'

He froze as guilt rose in his gullet, making it hard to breathe. 'Are you saying you agree with her?' Damn it, did he have to sound quite so defensive?

'I beg your pardon. I should not have said anything. I know you do not like to speak of it. I understand how dreadful you must feel.'

'I doubt that you do, actually.' And now he sounded harsh. How the devil had they ever got on to this topic?

She stiffened. 'I, too, lost my family.'

He gazed at her, shocked for the moment. It simply hadn't occurred to him she would see her orphaned state as that sort of loss. Not when she'd never known her parents. 'Rose. I am sorry.'

She gave a brave little smile. 'Of course, they may still be living. I sometimes wonder.'

He had the urge to find out for her. 'Do you know their names? Does the Foundling Hospital have records?'

She shook her head. 'Only my last name. There is no other information. It must have been a difficult thing to do, give up a child.' She glanced up at him, doubt in her eyes.

'Of course it must have been difficult.' He honestly couldn't imagine it. 'There has to be some way to find them.'

She shook her head sadly. 'It is not the way it works. If the mother wants you, she comes back. Otherwise...'

Surely not? Perhaps a man in his position could do what another could not. But he certainly didn't want to make a promise he could not keep.

She gave him a smile. 'So you see, I do understand a little of what you feel.'

He winced. They were back to him. And it wasn't the same at all. Unlike him, she had no reason to blame herself for their loss. They had abandoned her. 'I really prefer not to discuss my family, Rose. It is not the same case at all.'

Her wide eyes and startled gasp said he had hurt her.

'I beg your pardon. I did not mean to pry.' The coolness in her voice made him want to curse, as did the little sniff that made him think she might be trying to hold back her tears. The last thing he wanted was to hurt her.

What he wanted was to hold her, pull her into his arms and kiss her silly. Yet while there was nothing risqué about sitting side by side on a bench in so public a place, anything more would land them both in trouble. And there was nothing he could do about the future.

The most comfort he could offer was a promise. 'I swear I will not make an offer of marriage without letting you know first. Not that I intend marriage in the near future. I scarcely have time for the work of the Duchy as it is.' He handed her his handkerchief. When she did not refuse it, or throw it back at him, he could only assume she was satisfied.

He breathed a sigh of relief. 'I am glad that is settled.' He risked a brief kiss to her temple.

She shivered and leaned into his shoulder. The slightest movement unlikely anyone else would notice. 'Lady Alicia is pretty.'

He hated hearing the sadness in her voice. 'Rose, at this sort of event, a gentleman must do his duty unless he wishes to be thought the worst sort of cur. Her aunt made it impossible for me to refuse. Honestly? I was bored nigh unto tears.' A thought occurred to him. 'How old are you?'

'Twenty.'

Barely a couple of years older than Lady Alicia. 'You have more sense in your little finger than she has in the whole of her body.'

'She's never had to do for herself.' For all that she defended the other girl, she sounded pleased.

Rose would never have to do for herself ever again. When it was time to let her go, he'd make sure she would want for nothing. Not that he would say anything of the sort. Instinct told him that Rose would see such an offer as a bribe. He would have to find a way to accomplish it without hurting her pride.

Since he wasn't marrying any time soon, there would be lots of time to figure it out. 'Shall we go back? We don't want to start tongues wagging.'

She blew her nose and offered him his handkerchief.

'Keep it,' he said, smiling down into her face, seeing her courage in the lift of her chin.

She tucked it into her reticule, picked up her parasol and put her hand on his arm, the way any perfect young lady would, and while he desperately wanted to kiss her, Jake knew that any sign of disarray would be noted and commented upon and he would not have Rose embarrassed for any number of kisses, though the temptation be nigh irresistible.

They strolled back along the path and out into the open.

Rose nodded at the house where flags and turrets and crenulations abounded. 'It is almost as grand as the Tower of London, isn't it? It must be very old.'

Bless the girl for not making a scene and for trying to make the best of it.

Now he had to decide if he should destroy her image or... Rose was always honest with him. It was one of the many things he adored about her. 'The Marquis had it built scant five years ago.'

Her jaw dropped. 'Really?'

'A sort of Gothic-revival design.'

She frowned. 'He wanted to live in a castle?'

'Like a knight of old. Luckily we weren't asked to dress up in medieval costume and masks.'

She frowned. 'Why would they do that?'

'Why do the very rich do anything? For amusement.'

They were approaching the riverbank where punts and rowboats hung with bunting bobbed merrily against the jetty. Several gentlemen and ladies milled about, waiting their turn to board. One of them waved. 'Your Grace. We are having a race—will you join us?'

Curiosity was rampant on Rose's face. For one wild moment he thought about asking her to take part with him. He grinned at the young man and shook his head. 'Sorry, lads. My grandmother requires Miss Nightingale's services.'

She glanced up at him with regret in her eyes. 'Thank you for your discretion,' she said softly. A bell rang off in the distance. She smiled. 'It seems food is about to be served.'

Damn. He would make up for it later. When they were alone.

Exhausted by her day by the river, Her Grace had retired the moment she arrived home, taking her dinner on a tray. So Rose and Jake had dined alone in ducal splendour. Or as alone as anyone could be attended by several footmen and the butler. The servants had hovered around them like the flies that had hovered over their picnic, darting in every now and then to remove a dish or add a new one. She and Jake had spoken very little.

With the prospect of the night before her, Rose had barely been able to eat a mouthful. Jake hadn't fared much better.

Then, when he'd bid her goodnight, he'd leaned forward and whispered in her ear. 'Leave your hair down for me.'

Now Rose sat on the edge of her bed in her dressing gown, transfixed by indecision. Did she go to him? Or would he come here? Her heart pounded in her chest. Her mouth was so dry she might have swallowed coal dust. Questions buzzed around and around in her brain. Had her fit of the megrims beside the river made him regret taking up with her? How could she have as good as admitted to jealousy when she knew very well they would never be more than lovers? Why did he never want to talk about his family?

Should she apologise for bringing it up? Or should she try harder to get him to speak of what troubled him?

Her door creaked open.

Jake sauntered in, a bottle of wine and two glasses dangling from one hand. He wore only his shirt tucked into his pantaloons, but his hair was damp, as if he'd come from his bath.

She had also bathed, but had not washed her hair, since it had been washed first thing this morning.

He lifted the bottle. 'Care for some champagne?' He set the bottle and the two glasses on the table by window, where two armchairs made a cosy little nook. When she was not waiting on his grandmother, she liked to sit there and read, since Jake had commandeered the library for his office.

She perched on the edge of one of the chairs.

He gave her a charmingly boyish grin. 'Don't worry, my sweet, I am not going to descend upon you like a ravening wolf.'

'That's a relief, I must say.'

He laughed. 'Did I hear a note of regret, my dear? It really isn't my style, I'm afraid, but I can always give it a go.'

She grinned and eased back into the chair, relaxed by his teasing. Now she knew the answer to one question. He would come to her. Obviously. Of course, no one would take notice of the Duke wandering around his own house. Or if they did, they would say nothing if they valued their positions. And since, as his grandmother had complained from time to time, they ran on a skeleton staff with many of the rooms shut up and the furniture under holland covers, he was unlikely to run into anyone at all.

He popped the cork and poured them each a glass and raised his in a toast. 'To us.'

'To us.' She sipped. Tart and a tickle on her tongue. 'So that is what champagne tastes like.' She made a face.

'The more you drink, the better it gets.'

She wrinkled her nose. 'Are you trying to get me tipsy?'

'Not at all.' He pulled her to her feet and sat down in her chair, lifting her on to his lap. 'Well, perhaps a little. You looked nervous when I came in.' His fingers cradled her jaw and he gazed down into her eyes. 'You aren't afraid of me, are you, Rose? I would not hurt you for the world.'

Not physically, at least. Though she had no doubt she'd be devastated when he married. But if this was all she would ever have of him, shouldn't she take it? 'Not in the least bit afraid.' She inhaled a shaky breath and wondered if that was what her mother had thought, too? Well, at least she wasn't leaving the issue of conception to chance. Or to him.

Then there was no more room for doubts, for he was kissing her, tenderly at first, gently, but when she parted her lips his tongue went questing and tasting and the sensations inside her were almost more than she could bear.

She twined her arms around his neck and went questing on her own account, inhaling the clean scent of him, soap and something earthy. His cologne. Stroking the inside of his mouth with her tongue, she was entranced by the slide of their mutual tasting.

Sensations rippled through her body, heat, tingles, shivers. Her skin felt alive and aching for his touch. Her palms wandered the breadth of his shoulders, her fingers slid through the tendrils of his hair at his nape. His heart slammed a beat against her breasts and made them feel full. She pressed hard against him.

Breathing heavily, he eased away from her, brushing her hair back from her face, gazing into her eyes with a slumberous heat that she felt all the way to the place deep between her thighs.

Even if she had wanted to resist him, she couldn't. And not because of the attraction, the primal desire she felt for him, but because she sensed he needed her help to forget his duty and responsibilities for a short time.

It made her feel important. To him.

Something she had never felt before. She'd been useful, yes, but never had she felt as if it was *she* who was needed, not just because of what she could do with her two hands, but because of who she was as a person.

This was how it must feel to be part of a family. To mean something to another person. And she was going to make the most of it while it lasted. She would not think about the future.

She brushed the errant lock of hair back from his forehead and kissed the tip of his nose.

He grinned and gave her an affectionate squeeze. 'That's more like my Rose.'

His Rose. It sounded wonderful. Heart-wrenchingly so.

She pushed the thought aside. She would enjoy the moment. And if that was what her mother had done, then so be it. For if she had not, Rose would not exist at all, now would she?

He reached around her, picked up her glass and handed it to her. She took another sip. Fewer bubbles, less tart on her tongue. 'You are right, it is quite pleasant when you get used to it.'

'Like many things.' He nuzzled into her neck, kissing and nibbling until shivers raced this way and that all over her skin. 'I want to lick you all over, you smell so good,' he said against her skin.

The idea sounded intriguing. Her insides fluttered alarmingly. 'You wouldn't!'

He groaned. 'I would. In a heartbeat, were you ready for such games. The very idea of it makes me—' He choked off what he had been going to say.

She pushed away from him. 'Makes you?'

'It arouses me to the point where I can no longer think.'

There was no mistaking the bulge of his erection beneath her. She burrowed a hand between them and shaped his length with her fingers. He arched into her hand, eyes closing, his expression intense as if he would savour every touch.

Recalling some of the talk she'd heard among the girls at the V&V, she set her glass down and slid one knee between the outside of his thigh and the chair and then twisted to straddle him, holding his face between her hands and kissing his lips. She shifted forward to seat herself on his lap.

His hips lifted and the contact of his hardness against that particular spot was startling, and so delicious, she wiggled herself more firmly against him.

He groaned and cupped her nape and deepened the kiss, while rocking his hips in a rhythm that had her moaning into his mouth and trying to get closer. In a surge of movement that took her by surprise and made her squeak, he rose from the chair. She clung on for dear life.

He took the two steps between the chair and the bed and, leaning forward, lowered her on to the counterpane. Reluctantly, she released him and lay back. With a smouldering glance at the way she lay sprawled before him, he toed off his shoes, and stripped out of his clothes.

She let her gaze wander over his magnificent body. A virile healthy male who was rampantly aroused. 'I want to lick you all over, too,' she whispered.

His member jerked.

Her gaze whipped up to his face.

He nodded. 'Your words caused that.'

And if she suited the deed to the words? She reached out to trace a fingertip down the hard length until she encountered the soft springy hair at the base. Then she cupped him beneath, wondering at the softness and vulnerability. He must trust her to let her handle him in this way.

He put his hand over hers and showed her how to caress him firmly, curling her fingers around his shaft and sliding them up and down. He released her hand and she tried it for herself, keeping her grip firm, revelling in the hard shape of him beneath the surprisingly silky skin.

He grabbed her hand and raised it to his lips. 'Enough or this will be over too soon.' He climbed up beside her and pressed one thigh between hers while his hands buried themselves in her hair.

Her eyes reminded him of the soft green that heralded spring. Alive and lively, but mysteriously opaque. He'd done his best to stay away from her, to be honourable, but one crook of her finger and here he was. No other woman had ever had him dancing on a string the way this one did. Though there was no triumph in her expression. Or greed. Only affection.

She asked for nothing, when others would have bargained for the moon. Had she done so, he might have tried to get it for her, too.

He shook his head at the astonishing thought. If he ran true to past form, now that she wanted him the way he had wanted her, he would grow bored very quickly and be ready to move on.

Not that he'd ever really encountered another woman like Rose. She was innocent, but wise beyond her years, intelligent, but ill schooled, lovely but without artifice. And she was his.

For now.

Most humbling of all was that she had chosen him to be her first lover.

Guilt racked him. He'd been selfish the last time. Presuming and unthinking when he should have known better. This time he would make it perfect.

She reached up and stroked her small hands over his shoulders. Down his back. His skin shivered at her touch.

He bent his head and took her lips, kissing her until neither of them had breath. His heart pounded against his ribs. His body fought for control, but this time it was all about her. About Rose. He shifted his attention from her lips to her ear, his tongue tracing the delving deep. On a soft cry, she arched up, pressing her lovely soft breasts with their hardened peaks against his chest.

He cruised down her throat, tasting her collarbone, licking at the pulse points on his way, until he nuzzled into her lovely cleavage, intent on gifting her with every bit of his skill. She deserved that and more after he'd been so careless the first time, thinking her experienced.

It still made his stomach knot when he recalled how thoughtless he'd been. And how awed at her gift.

She shuddered and moaned, her fingers digging into his back. Encouraging him to greater efforts.

He smiled.

'Why are you laughing?' she asked, her voice husky with passion.

'I'm *smiling* because I am happy.' He licked first one nipple, pausing to watch it bead into a tight little nub, then the other. He cupped her breast in his hand and swirled his tongue around that hard little peak, flicking at it until she squirmed beneath him, then taking it into his mouth, letting her feel his teeth in a gentle graze before suckling.

Her hips rolled against his groin, so sweet an appeal it almost undid his good intentions. He shifted away and let his hand drift down her flat belly to the sweet little triangle of blonde curls, stroking and petting while she moaned and tried to increase the pressure of his hand on her mons.

He pressed down with the heel of his hand and when she sighed her approval he gently parted her folds, one fingertip slipping inside her warm damp heat. Hot silky smooth softness. Still so damned tight. He caressed and stroked until she opened her thighs wider, giving him deeper access.

A quick learner his Rose. He licked and teased the other nipple. She pressed down on his nape, telling him silently what she wanted. He suckled. Drew hard. She cried out and her body tightened, before climaxing in a rush of heat and dampness and tight muscles around his finger.

Breathing hard, she lay lax, looking up at him from beneath lowered lids, her lips parted in a smile of surprise and pleasure. Something in his chest tugged. As if a part of him had attached itself to her.

Not possible. He had no wish for deep attachments. Never had. People he cared for always abandoned him when he needed them most. His mother, Ralph, even his father. All right, so it wasn't their fault, but the pain of it had been intolerable. He refused to go through that again.

When he married, it would be to a woman to whom he would not be emotionally attached. As long as he liked her, that would be all that mattered.

He didn't like Lady Alicia and her ilk. A woman like her would drive him mad in half a day, but there were other women he'd met who were not so silly. Sensible women. He was sure of it.

But he really liked Rose.

He froze as he realised the depth of that liking. At how deep she had got under his skin in such a short time. The way Georgiana had with Fred. Their happiness was almost painful to watch when one stood on the sidelines.

His father and Ralph would turn in their graves if they

knew he was wishing for such a thing. Typical irresponsible Jake, they'd be saying. He could hear their voices in his head.

He could no longer be that man. He had a duty to the title. He'd sworn to do his best. Rose as anything more than a mistress was out of the question.

But he would do his best for Rose, too. Here in this bed and hopefully outside of it where he'd find out what had happened to her family. She'd like that, he was sure. It was something he could give her that no one else could.

Right now, though, he needed to be inside her, buried in her warmth and surrounded by her loving self. Tenderly, he eased his knee between her parted thighs and nudged them farther apart. She welcomed him into the cradle of her hips. Deep satisfaction filled him, a sense of belonging as he entered her body.

'That's better.' She sighed, lifting her legs around his waist, opening to him, arching up to kiss him deeply.

He slid home to the hilt and gave himself up to the pleasure and the bliss and the peace of mind that he only found with Rose.

Later, when they lay in each other's arms, his mind once more turned to the future. Her future. It seemed he could not prevent himself from being concerned. He spooned around her and knew she was smiling, and she snuggled back against him.

'Have you thought about where you would like to open up your dressmaking shop?' he asked.

'Near Bond Street.' She yawned. 'Somewhere ladies will feel comfortable. Cork Street, perhaps. Nothing too large to start.'

He tucked the information away. 'You will need to advertise.'

She glanced over his shoulder. 'You are very interested in this enterprise that may never come to pass.'

'I have every faith in you, Rose.'

She sighed. 'I will try to get *La Belle Assemblée* to use one of my gowns in their articles on fashion. One can advertise, but their recommendation would be the best.'

'Grandmama would be able to assist you there.'

'Do you think she would?'

'I know so. She is very fond of you.'

'She might not want me to leave.' A little pause. A little hitch in her breathing. 'But I expect she would see it as for the best, once you marry.'

He wasn't going to touch that with a barge pole. He didn't even want to think about it. 'She will want what is best for you.' Even if he did have to explain.

She sighed. Not unhappily. A sound of contentment. 'Go to sleep, Jake.'

He close his eyes and drifted off.

Chapter Nine

Three days after becoming Jake's mistress, Rose sat with Her Grace in the drawing room. It was the only public room in the house not closed up. And as usual, because the old lady's eyes were failing, Rose read and Her Grace pretended to embroider. A little snore indicated that also, as usual, the old lady had dropped off. Rose stopped reading and let her mind wander.

Her days seemed to so idle now. Writing a few letters to Her Grace's dictation in the mornings. A bit of fetching and carrying during the day. Not to mention the wonderful food she ate at every meal. It was all so very easy. But it was her nights that she lived for. More and more. And each time Jake came to her chamber, he seemed more attentive, more loving.

Yet she always felt a sense of distance, too. He never shared any other part of his life. A brief mention of the V&V from time to time. An odd reference to other estates in other places as they undressed each other, or lay sated and touching and stroking.

While he listened endlessly to her plans for a dressmaker's shop, he never spoke of his hopes or dreams. And each time they made love, he seemed a little more desperate and each time he left her before the sun rose, he seemed a little more reserved.

Only once, when he'd come to her, had she asked him what troubled his mind. He'd closed up tighter than an oyster tapped with a knife. Clearly, whatever was on his mind, he had decided it was not the business of his mistress to enquire. With a heavy heart, she had passed it off with a smile and a kiss.

He'd relaxed then and been his usual wonderfully attentive lover. What more could she ask? Why should she hurt that he did not want to share? That was not their arrangement.

Yet she was not sure how much longer she could bear their growing distance. Perhaps it was his way of showing he was ready to be done with her.

A commotion at the front door brought the old lady awake with a start. She patted at her hair to see if her cap was straight. Rose put the book aside and went to assist, replacing a couple of pins that had come adrift.

'Great-Grandmama!' A dark-haired little girl lunged across the room and buried her face in the old lady's lap. 'I thought we would never get here, Mama made so many stops along the way.'

Rose retreated behind the Dowager Duchess's chair at the same moment an elegantly tall woman swept into the room. An eyebrow lifted at the sight of Rose, but a sweet smile curved her lips, and her eyes lit up when they fell on Her Grace. 'Grandmother. Here we are at last.'

Rose sidled out of the room. This was a moment for the family, not for her to intrude. Head down, hurrying towards the stairs, she would have collided with Jake had he not caught her by the shoulders.

'Rose? What is it?'

She gazed up into his face, unable to explain why she hurt

so bad inside and forced a cheerful smile. 'Good news. Lady Eleanor has arrived.'

He glanced eagerly towards the drawing room from where a high-pitched voice was to be heard, though the words were indistinct.

'And Lucy, too. I'm glad. I thought she might not bring her, after all.' He frowned. 'But where are you going?'

'On an errand,' she said vaguely, not wanting to admit she was running away from her own feelings. 'I will see you at dinner.' She slipped out of his grasp and headed up the stairs.

He followed after her, then stopped, one foot on the bottom step. 'Rose. Is something wrong?'

'Nothing is wrong, Your Grace,' she said, hoping she sounded calm and sensible instead of full of inexplicable tears. 'Go and greet your sister.' She turned and carried on.

He did not follow. He couldn't. Not with half the household standing in the hall looking on. But she did think she heard him curse softly.

She kept going. She needed a bit of time alone. Time to remember who and what she was.

By the time she needed to help Her Grace down to dinner, she was perfectly composed. As they had when Mr Gregory had joined them, they gathered in the drawing room. Jake was already there with Lady Eleanor. Rose curtsied deeply when he introduced her to his sister. Inside, she winced as the young woman took her hand. What on earth would she think if she knew the truth about her and Jake?

'Rose has been such a help to me these past few weeks,' the Dowager Duchess pronounced. 'I do not know how I managed before she came.' To Rose's ears she sounded a little defensive. Did she know? Cold fingers walked down Rose's spine.

Heat travelled up to her cheeks. 'Thank you, Your Grace.'

She risked a glance at the statuesque Lady Eleanor, who seemed to notice nothing amiss.

Strangely, Jake looked rather stiff and starchy. Tense.

If the circumstances had been different, she might have given him a poke in the ribs and told him to relax. But it wasn't her place.

She helped the Dowager to sit and stood behind her with the old lady's shawl over her arm, ready to place it around her shoulders if she showed the least sign of feeling a draught.

Eleanor smiled at her. 'I am so glad to meet you, Miss Nightingale. Someone needs to care for Grandmama. Jake has a great deal to keep him busy, these days.'

'Are you hinting that I am neglecting Her Grace?' Jake asked. There was a twinkle in his eye. Clearly, despite his unbending posture, he was fond of his sister. Rose couldn't help feel a pang of sadness. The man had a family, yet could not seem to fully enjoy it.

A footman walked around with a tray of drinks. Sherry. Rose shook her head when offered a glass, but the others partook and Jake raised his glass. 'Welcome to London, Eleanor.'

'Where is Lady Lucy?' Rose blurted out, realising they were one person short.

Jake frowned.

Eleanor looked down her nose very much in the way Jake did when he was displeased. 'Miss Lucy,' she said, her voice calm. 'No title, Miss Nightingale.'

An awkward silence descended, finally broken by Lady Eleanor. 'My daughter is in the nursery. She was tired after the journey and I gave her an early dinner and put her to bed.' She straightened her shoulders. 'I hope you don't mind, Your Grace, but she does usually eat dinner with me.'

Jake stiffened. 'Do we have to stand on ceremony, Eleanor?'

Rose flinched at his stern tone.

Eleanor seemed to take it in stride, though her expression held sadness. 'The sooner you get used to who you are, Jake, the easier it will be for you and the rest of us, but, no, we do not need to observe the formalities at home if you do not wish it.'

Jake put his drink down with a snap that spoke of irritation. 'Then, since Rose is as good as family, we can all be comfortable without titles and such.'

Rose's heart gave an odd little thump. *As good as family.* How delightful that sounded, yet how foreign. What wouldn't she give for it to be true. She swallowed. She could not imagine calling the Dowager Duchess by her Christian name. Not for a second. She risked a quick glance at Jacob's sister and saw that her smile was encouraging.

'Dinner is served,' the butler announced.

Jake took his grandmother's arm and Rose followed Lady Eleanor into the dining room. No, she *would* think of her as Eleanor, or Jake would be displeased.

Once they were seated, the Dowager at one end, Jake at the other and Rose and Eleanor on each side, the footmen served them their dinner.

'How was your journey?' Jake asked. 'Not too arduous, I hope?'

'Not at all. Lucy was a treasure. Hardly any complaining at all, but I took Grandmama's advice and took it in small stages with lots of walks in between. We even visited a couple of castles along the way. The child is fascinated with the idea of knights and maidens in distress. I fear I have read her too many stories.'

They discussed the proper reading for Miss Lucy, speaking of books Rose could only have dreamed of as a child. Some of them sounded wonderful. She wondered if there were any of them in the library. Not that she'd ever dare venture there again. Jake had made it clear it was out of bounds for everyone.

* * *

Towards the end of the meal, Eleanor put down her dessertspoon. 'Why on earth are we eating in here?'

Jacob's eyebrows shot up. 'It may have escaped your notice, sister mine, but this is the dining room.'

'Don't be ridiculous, Jake. This room holds forty people. It is like eating in a mausoleum. We should be using the breakfast room, where we always dined *en famille* when Papa was alive.'

In response Jacob's gaze became frosty, his shoulders stiff.

Her Grace made a face of distaste. 'Most the rooms in this wing, apart from this one and the drawing room, are under holland covers. It *is* like living in a mausoleum. Don't you agree, Rose?'

'Many of the rooms are indeed closed up, Your Grace.' She had asked Jake why it was so and he had shrugged her question off. She certainly wasn't going to offer her unwanted opinion on it. The Quality did what they did and people like her simply accepted it.

'What is the point of opening up a lot of rooms when they are never used?' Jake said.

'This room won't do for Lucy, if she is ever to join us for a meal,' Eleanor said. 'The poor child will be overwhelmed.'

'Jake has taken to using the library for his office,' Her Grace grumbled. She waved off a footman's offer of dessert, though Jake and Eleanor accepted several of the dishes.

Rose also accepted a small portion on her plate. A lovely fruit pudding and custard. She loved the sweets they served after dinner, but tried not to appear too greedy.

Eleanor took a small bite. 'The library, Jake? Is there something wrong with the estate office?' Eleanor sounded scandalised. 'Is it also true you do not yet sleep in the ducal apartments?'

What would his sister think if she knew he slept either at the V&V or in the bed of his grandmother's companion?

She'd likely be horrified. Rose wanted the floor to open up and swallow her.

Suddenly the dessert tasted like cardboard.

Jacob's eyes turned bleak. 'Gossiping with the servants, Eleanor? Isn't that beneath you?'

Eleanor flushed.

Jake stiffened even more. 'I beg your pardon, but surely where I sleep is my business.'

'Never fear, he will take over the ducal suite when he marries,' Her Grace said with the certainty of old age. Her gaze flickered to Rose and away. 'His wife will see to it, of that you can be sure.'

For a long moment, Jake stared at his grandmother, his face an expressionless mask. He glanced around the table. 'If everyone is finished, shall you withdraw, Grandmama?'

Her Grace blinked and smiled vaguely. 'Tea in the drawing room, ladies?'

Jake helped his grandmother to her feet. The attending footmen assisted Eleanor and Rose with their chairs. Eleanor took her grandmother's arm.

Jake bowed them out.

When they reached the drawing room, Eleanor took Rose's accustomed placed behind the teapot. She poured with the graceful elegance of one who did not need to give a second's thought to what she was doing or how she did it. Unlike herself, who agonised over each part of the ritual, each movement, fearing she'd display clumsiness or ignorance.

She seated herself a little distant from the other two ladies, not wishing to appear intrusive or above her station.

Jake did not join them and while the two ladies chatted, she heartily wished she had pleaded tiredness and gone to her chamber to await him there.

Jake strode along the deserted corridors. One of the first things he had done when becoming Duke had been to do away with the night-duty footmen. Not because he envisaged needing to sneak about under his own roof in order to visit a lady, but because it made no sense in this day and age.

It was a medieval practice, requiring men to sit on hard chairs at the corner of every corridor in case the sleeping occupants might be in need of some service.

The remaining two took turns below stairs watching for a bell to ring. The rest, he'd either pensioned off or found other positions.

He halted on the landing between the two wings. He had told himself he would not go to her tonight. Not with his sister under his roof. Seeing Eleanor and his niece had reminded him of his own obligations to the dukedom.

It was not fitting for a duke to keep his lover under the same roof as his family. His father would never have done such a thing. Nor would Ralph. He would have set her up in her own little house at the edge of town. In New Town or across the river. Ralph had never put a foot wrong when it came to doing his duty.

Jake gritted his teeth. How could he send Rose away when his grandmother had come to rely on her?

He stopped outside her door, a wry smile twisting his lips. His reluctance was nothing to do with his grandmother. It was his own selfishness. Something his father had accused him of that last day when he had convinced Ralph to go in his place. Selfish and feckless was what his father had called him. It seemed he hadn't changed.

He turned the handle and walked in.

Seated by the fireplace in her nightgown, Rose looked up from her book and smiled. The gladness in her eyes warmed his heart, making the cares of the day disappear. The cold lump in his chest shrank and became less weighty.

She put her book aside. 'I wasn't sure you would come tonight.'

Guilt intensified. 'Would you like me to go?' The hurt in

her eyes made him want to kick himself. 'I'm sorry. I'm a little out of sorts.'

She rose and opened her arms to him. 'It is all right. I am a little out of sorts, too.'

'Because of Eleanor's arrival?'

'Your sister is lovely. And her daughter is quite delightful.'

Ignoring her avoidance of his question, he sat in the chair, as he did most nights when he first arrived, and pulled her on to his lap for a lovely satisfying and arousing kiss.

He was relieved to discover not a scrap of hesitation in the way she melded her lips to his. He ran his hand over her back and down over the lovely swell of her hip, feeling the change in her breathing against every inch of his body, sensing her relax into him, bringing her breasts flush with his chest. Her fingers combed through the hair at his nape and his mind seemed to settle, even as his body came awake in a surge of hot blood.

Finally, breathlessly, they broke apart. She rested her head upon his shoulder as she always did. A gesture of trust, but the hand clutching at the lapel of his dressing gown spoke of possession. Of need.

He needed her, too.

The only time he slept well was in her arms. As often as he had tried to tell himself it was ridiculous, it was the truth.

He didn't deserve it. He didn't deserve her. But he could not bring himself to give her up. Not yet.

So often in the past he had found himself bored to tears by a woman within a very short space of time, a week or two, sometimes even within days. With Rose he never had the slightest urge to be anywhere else. Not even when they sat silently as they did now.

Rose released her grip on his dressing gown and patted his chest. 'How was your day?'

Such a small thing to ask, but it always soothed him, let

him talk of things he never discussed with anyone else. 'I heard from the steward at Maston. The sheep have foot rot.'

She shuddered. 'That sounds horrible.'

'It is. We are likely to lose the whole flock.'

'Lambs, too?'

He had told her about lambs. The way they pranced around each other and the way their little tails wagged when they nursed. 'All of them.'

'That is…so sad.'

'It is. It is also a financial disaster.'

He hadn't realised until he came into the title how close to the edge of bankruptcy the Duchy operated with its heavy reliance on the land for income.

She frowned. 'One flock can make that much of a difference?'

'It is the same for everyone. Since the war ended, more and more men are leaving the land to work in factories. I have fewer tenants and therefore less income from rents. Not to mention the price of wool has plummeted. A loss like this will make things even worse.'

It was why his father had asked him to go with him to Brighton to charm the Regent into selling them an attaindered estate. It would have added to their financial security for years to come, not because it would allow them to expand their farming, but because of what they suspected lay beneath the soil. Coal.

Perhaps if Father had couched his demand in those terms, Jake might have acquiesced. Instead, Father had simply ordered Jake to accompany him instead of wasting his time on what he called frivolous nonsense. Never mind that his investment in Vitium et Virtus as well as other businesses had resulted in Jake's considerable wealth. Enough for a gentleman to live very well indeed, but a drop in the bucket compared to what the Duchy needed.

It wasn't until he took over that he realised how difficult

things had become. His father had done a fine job according to his lights. And Ralph no doubt would have known how to turn things around. While, despite his man of business's assurances to the contrary, Jake felt as if he was floundering on the brink of ruin.

By the time he'd had the reins of the Duchy in hand, the opportunity for that other estate had been snatched up by another. Today his man of business had suggested he sell himself to the highest bidder on the marriage mart as the quickest and easiest financial solution. He'd actually suggested an American heiress.

Was it his just deserts?

'Is there no way of saving them?' Rose asked.

Sheep. She meant the sheep. 'The steward and the shepherd are doing everything they can. I have every faith in them.'

'But you are worried.'

'We need the income. Plus we have a contract. Defaulting is not an option. I will have to buy the wool elsewhere in order to keep our side of the bargain. If word of our loss gets out to the marketplace, we will end up paying a premium on the price of those sheep and lose even more.'

'You will lose money in order to keep your word?'

He nodded. 'A man's word is his bond. And besides, break faith once and no one will ever trust me again.'

She patted his shoulder. 'I read today that the price of wool is depressed.' She wrinkled her nose. 'Is that the right word?'

'It is. But if word of my need gets out, and it will, prices will rise immediately.'

'What if you bought it now, before word gets out.'

'Then I'm left with a load of wool no one may want.'

'Someone must want it, if they contracted for yours.'

He frowned. Kissed the tip of that wrinkled nose. 'You are right. First thing in the morning...' His brain raced ahead. 'You know, I have been thinking of buying a factory to make our own cloth. It is risky. If we lose all our sheep, we will have no wool to weave.' He closed his eyes. 'We won't lose them. I read something somewhere. A way of cutting the losses. An article. Where the devil did I put it...?'

She captured his face in his hands. 'Jake. It will still be there in the morning. There is nothing you can do tonight.'

'I can send a message.'

'To a man who is likely in his bed. It will get there faster if your messenger sets out in daylight.' She kissed his lips. 'You are exhausted, my dear sweet Jake. Tomorrow is quite soon enough.'

He was exhausted. Had been for weeks. The only time he slept was in here in her arms. He gazed at the expression of concern on her face, the sweetness, and relaxed. Let go with a sigh. 'You are right.'

'Make love to me, Jake. Please.'

What man, least of all him, could refuse such an enticing request? Even if he did not deserve such bounty.

He rose to his feet and carried her to the bed.

Held in Jake's arms, Rose felt treasured. Being held had been a rare enough event in her life. Most of the people at the orphanage had been kind enough. They had done their best for unwanted children, but they'd had families of their own on whom to lavish affection.

This sense of being wanted, of belonging, was completely new. Even though she knew it wouldn't last, she wanted to wallow in it. Pretend that she was the princess in a fairy tale, instead of the example held out to orphans of what would happen to them unless they were good.

While Jake pulled back the sheet, she clung on to his shoulders. When he set her gently on the bed, she opened her arms to him, welcoming him to lay beside her.

And when he untied his robe's belt, she gazed in awe at his beautiful masculine body. Aroused for her. His lips smiling for her. Him needing her. At this moment she could pretend it was only her he wanted.

She welcomed him into the cradle of her hips, drawing him to her with her legs high about his waist.

He dipped a finger into her feminine folds and groaned. 'So wet and hot. So ready.'

'For you, Jake,' she whispered in his ear. Only ever for you, her mind echoed back. She stilled. Was it true? Was he the only one for her? And what did that mean for her future? She pushed the unwanted doubts aside. All would be well, as long as she didn't visit her own needs and desires on an innocent child.

His lips roamed her breasts, his tongue teasing and tormenting, his hands glided over her body in a trail of heat and sensual tingles.

The desire in her built until she could not bear it any longer.

'I need you,' she groaned. 'Inside me.'

'You are impatient tonight.'

Impatient. Yes. He had read her correctly. Meeting his sister, the Lady Eleanor, so beautiful, so cool and reserved, had given her an odd premonition that time was running out for her and Jake and she didn't want to waste a moment.

Likely because his sister had agreed with his grandmother. Jake needed to wed. He seemed to take more notice of his sister's words.

'I want you.' And no matter what happened in the future, one thing she knew for certain, if a child did result, despite all their precautions, she would never ever leave it to grow up alone.

He took her mouth in a searing kiss and she gave herself up to the pleasure she planned to hoard as if it was miser's gold.

He broke the kiss, gazing down into her face. She sensed the deep weariness of soul he tried to hide from the world.

Perhaps he, too, was feeling the future closing in. 'Jake, is something wrong?'

He smiled and kissed her forehead. 'What on earth could be wrong when I have you in my arms?'

What indeed. Whatever it was he did not intend for her to know and for some reason that made her feel sad. And distanced.

She wished there was something she could do to share his burdens. There was always this, of course. Whenever they made love he seemed to forget the outside world for a time. But she wanted to do so much more. To lessen the shadows she saw in his eyes.

She recalled the discussions of the girls at the V&V. Some of the naughty things they'd talked about doing with the men at the club.

Perhaps all men liked such things? Would he think her terrible if she offered?

She flattened her hands on his chest and pushed.

A look of disappointment crossed his face, but he obligingly broke the kiss and raised up on his hands. 'Not in the mood tonight, sweet?'

The girls had been right. A real gentleman never forced himself on an unwilling woman, lady or not.

A wicked smile pulled at her mouth. 'It isn't that.'

He frowned and if anything looked more disappointed. 'Indisposed?'

She tilted her head in question.

'It is your time of the month?'

Oh, that. 'Not until next week.' She gave his shoulder a hard push and he rolled on his back, his erection arrowing up against his belly.

'Tired, then,' he said, throwing an arm over his eyes. 'You should have said when I first arrived. I promise, you are entitled to your peace if that is what you want.'

She leaned over him, her hair falling forward to brush over

his chest. He moved his arming, frowning up at her. 'Don't tease. It doesn't become you.'

She threw one leg over him and came up on her knees so she straddled his thighs, but not sitting down.

His whole expression changed. No longer disgruntled, but intrigued and hopeful. 'Rose?'

He sounded hopeful, too.

She glanced down to see him beautifully aroused. When they joined she knew it would feel wonderful. But first she wanted to do a little exploring.

Heat rushed to her cheeks at her wanton thoughts.

But when she looked up to see his face, to read his expression, his gaze was fixed on her breasts.

A hand reached out to cup her and it felt wonderful and gentle, tender.

She grazed a thumb over his flat nipple, ran her fingers through the rough smatter of hair in the centre of his chest. His breathing hitched at her touch.

He grinned. 'I see what you are about. Trying to seduce an innocent young man.'

She circled his nipple with a fingertip and watched in fascination at the way the nipple furled up tight the same way hers did when he touched them. She leaned forward and licked. The little bud felt like a bead against her tongue. He moaned softly.

'It is hard to imagine you as innocent,' she said, sitting up to regard the result of her efforts.

He tried to look insulted, but his pout was adorable. 'I was until my brother Ralph introduced me to a local widow looking for a young man to make her happy. She taught me all I needed to know.'

'She pleased you?' She bent forward to lick the other nipple as if she could swipe away memories of that other woman.

He groaned. 'What were you saying?'

The girls had been right. A man with lust on his mind lost the ability to think. 'About the widow.'

He gasped as she grazed the hard nub with her teeth. 'Rose!' He stroked her hair back from her face. 'How sensual you are,' he said. 'She was a kind lovely woman. I was very fond of her. Also very disappointed to come home from university and learn she had married again. But then I hadn't met you.'

Her heart gave an odd little squeeze. 'Don't try your charming ways with me, your Dukeship.'

He laughed and that sound, that rascally look on his face, was what she had been looking for. As a reward, she bent, intending to give his lips a brief kiss before setting about completing her plan, but he caught her around the nape and held her while he deepened the kiss and they both became breathless.

But she wasn't about to be deterred. Once more she rose up on her knees, working her way backwards.

His eyes widened. He reached out as if to stop her, then let his hands fall away. 'Leaving already, Miss Nightingale?'

'I can't leave, this is my bed.' She swooped down to swirl her tongue in his navel.

He gasped. 'Oh, you really don't want to—'

The gravel in his voice made her insides clench. The girls were right about this also. She slid back another few inches, until her prize was right where she needed it. She grasped it firmly, pausing to admire the pulsing life of it, the darkness of the skin, the rigid length, and dipped down to swirl her tongue around the blunt head that gave her so much pleasure.

The taste was remarkable. Salty, male, hot against her tongue. His hips came up in silent plea. She glanced up to see the agony of extreme pleasure etched on his handsome features as he watched her with hot eyes.

She took him into her mouth and he cried out, a rough feral sound from deep in his throat. As she swirled and licked this most pleasurable part of him, she learned what made him gasp and what made his hips buck out of control, and in the end, that when she drew hard on that part of him, learned what drove him to a pitch where he could hold out no longer.

In a flash of movement, he lifted her up and had her beneath him, driving home to the hilt. She gave herself up to his pleasure with an indescribably joy.

Sometime later, as she lay scarcely able to breathe, their hearts pounding in tandem, he cuddled her in his arms and stroked her hair. She felt...blissfully happy. Safe.

A dream, of course, but lovely none the less.

'Rose,' he whispered against her ear.

She smiled. 'Jake.'

'Do you ever think about your parents? Wonder what became of them?'

She tensed. 'I used to wonder about them all the time as a child.'

'And now?'

'Who wouldn't be curious?'

'That is what I thought.'

He sounded oddly pleased. 'Why do you ask?'

'I wondered, that was all.' He rose up on one elbow and kissed the tip of her nose. 'It is time I left.' He slid out of the bed and slipped on his robe.

The chill left by his departure stayed with her for some considerable time. It was the way it had to be, without question, but that didn't mean she liked it. Still, she had him for small snatches of time and those times were all that mattered.

Chapter Ten

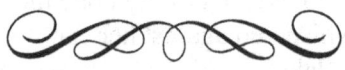

Jake entered the bright breakfast room at the back of the house for the first time in six months. As had been the case under his father's rule, chafing dishes were laid out on the sideboard. The occupants, his sister and his grandmother, had already helped themselves.

Where was Rose? He kept the question behind his teeth, discretion being the watchword.

'I'm sorry, Grandmama,' Eleanor was saying as he browsed the offerings on the sideboard, 'but there is nothing I can do. I have no power to cure the ague.'

Jacob's heart clenched. 'Is Lucy ill?' He turned from the scrambled eggs to eye his sister.

'No it is Nanny who is ill. Grandmama and I planned to go shopping, but I refuse to leave Lucy in the care of the upstairs maid as Grandmama suggests. Lucy doesn't know her and, besides, the girl is much too young.'

He spooned scrambled egg on to his plate and added another dollop for good measure. Clearly his appetite had returned. He moved on to the bacon, then frowned. 'We were left with the maids often enough after Mother died.'

'Do not tell me you don't recall the mischief we got up to,' Eleanor said, 'because I won't believe you. If it hadn't been for Ralph that one time, we would have set the house afire.'

His heart clenched painfully at the sound of his brother's name. 'You lit the blasted thing.' He hoped she didn't notice the rough edge to his voice.

'I understand your fears, dearest,' Grandmama said. 'But we won't be gone above a couple of hours, surely?'

'Two hours will run into three.'

'And three to four,' Jake finished. 'Why don't I take care of Lucy?'

Eleanor's doubtful expression cut at him. He'd seen how little trust she placed in men these days. Did she put him in the same category as the man who had abandoned her and her child? Instinctively his fists clenched, not for himself, but in his need to protect his sister.

'It is not that I don't trust you, Jake,' she said quietly, obviously understanding his reaction. 'There are some things a young lady requires where an uncle cannot be of assistance.'

Of course there were. *Idiot.* 'I will enlist the help of Miss Nightingale, then.'

'A lady's companion, Jake?' Eleanor scoffed. 'I doubt she'd consent to play nursemaid.'

He took his plate to his seat, only to stand up again as Rose entered. She handed his grandmother an amethyst ring.

'You found it.' His grandmother beamed. 'Clever girl.'

'It was under the dressing table caught in the rug's fringe.'

'Oh, thank you so much, I had Parrot on her knees for half an hour with no success.'

'Poor Parrot,' Eleanor said.

His grandmother's dresser was older than his grandmother.

'Not at my request,' his grandmama said. 'She was upset about dropping it.'

'I told her all is well before I came down,' Rose said, going to the sideboard and filling her plate before taking her seat.

Eleanor poured tea for her. It pleased Jake no end to see Rose being treated more like family than employee. More than it should.

'Rose, my dear,' Grandmama said. 'Jake has offered to look after Lucy while Eleanor and I go shopping, since Nanny is ill. May we impose on you to help him for a few hours?'

As predicted by Eleanor, Rose looked doubtful.

Jake frowned. He hadn't expected that from his Rose. His Rose. He liked the sound of it in his head. If only.... He shook the thought off.

'It is not that I mind, your ladyship... I mean, Eleanor,' Rose said with a regretful smile. 'But I have very little experience with the needs of young children.'

'No need to worry about that,' Jake said, smiling at her. 'I practically raised Eleanor single-handedly after Mother died.'

With Father and Ralph busy with the dukedom, the two younger siblings had been left to manage for themselves.

'You were a wonderful big brother, Jake.'

Jake felt stunned at his sister's compliment. He felt heat sting his cheeks. 'Well, I helped Nanny a bit, anyway.'

'You help me.' She turned to Rose. 'It is all right if you don't wish it, Miss Nightingale. Indeed, it was wrong of us to ask. You have your own duties.'

'It is only for a couple of hours, Rose,' Jake said quickly, then winced. 'Unless you would prefer to accompany Grandmama and Eleanor to the shops?'

Rose shook her head. 'I thought to catch up with my mending.'

'You prefer mending to time spent with Lucy and me?'

'Enough, Jake,' Eleanor said. 'If Rose—'

Rose put up a hand with a smile. 'His Grace is right. Mending pales in comparison to spending the morning with Lucy in the schoolroom. Truly.'

Jake raised his brows at her. 'The schoolroom? Really? What sort of uncle would that make me? We are going out.'

'It needs to be something educational,' Eleanor said sternly, 'If you intend her to forgo her lessons.'

Jake made a face.

'What about the Elgin Marbles?' Grandmama suggested.

Jake winced. 'Some of those might be a little too risqué for an uncle to be explaining.'

'I know the very place!' Eleanor said, her eyes alight. 'Lucy has been learning about famous explorers. The Panorama in Leicester Square is exhibiting the North Coast of Spitzbergen. We talked about it just the other day. Would it interest you, Miss Nightingale?'

Rose looked fascinated, the way she looked fascinated when she discovered a new word.

Mentally he grinned. There was no way her natural curiosity would let her allow such an offer pass her by.

She glanced his way, but he kept his gaze fixed on Eleanor. 'Educational, Eleanor?'

'I would like to see it,' Rose said.

'Everyone should visit Barker's Panorama,' Grandmama pronounced with a stern look at Rose. Dear old stick. If he hadn't known better he might have thought she was championing his cause with Rose. Really? He narrowed his gaze on her, but her expression was completely innocent. Suspiciously so.

'In the upper chamber they have a view of St Petersburg,' Eleanor said, drawing his attention to her. She looked more animated that she had for a while. His offer had pleased her and he could not help but feel glad. Mostly these days she simply looked sad. 'I read in the paper that it is even better than going to visit the actual city,' she continued. 'Apparently one can see the whole thing, though it is quite a climb to the top.'

'You had better eat a hearty breakfast, Rose,' Grandmama said, with a chuckle. 'You are going to have your hands full with those two.'

'Two?' Rose asked.

'Lucy and Jake,' the old lady said, her eyes twinkling with mischief.

Rose smiled such a sweet smile his heart gave a strangely painful little thump. It meant nothing. He was glad for her, that was all. He simply wanted to give her an opportunity that might never present itself again.

What was he letting himself in for? An expedition alone with Lucy and Rose, that was what. Something he was looking forward to far more than he should.

The morning was warm, the sky blue with only a few puffy clouds sailing along on a light breeze when Jake helped Rose into his town carriage. A grand black affair with its wheels picked out in yellow and the ducal crest emblazoned on the door. Once she was settled, he handed Lucy in as if she was a grown-up young lady.

The child spoiled the impression with a giggle. Once inside she hopped up on the forward-facing seat beside Rose, wiggling around until she was comfortable.

After giving instructions to the coachman, Jake climbed aboard and took the seat facing them.

'How long will it take to get there?' Lucy asked.

'Half an hour,' Jake said. 'Depending on the traffic.'

The coach pulled off.

'Exactly what should we expect to see when we visit this Panorama?' Rose asked. 'Perhaps you should explain it to Lucy.' She'd looked up the word, but it hadn't been listed. His grandmother had waved a vague hand and called it a vista, which Rose had learned came from the Italian word for *view*.

Jake gave her a rather mischievous look. 'It's a surprise.'

He looked younger with that expression on his face. More handsome than ever. Somehow more dear.

The nervous flutter in her stomach increased. She had hoped he would give her some guidance as to what to expect.

There were so many traps to avoid when moving among the members of the *ton*. But clearly he wanted to surprise his little niece. Who was she to want to spoil the occasion? And, truth to admit, she was really looking forward to accompanying Jake on this adventure. For that is what it would be.

'Oooh!' Lucy exclaimed, bouncing off the seat and lurching towards the window. 'Birdies.' She grabbed the ledge and pulled herself up to lean out, pointing.

In a flash, Jake leaned forward and pulled her back to sit on his knee.

'Uncle, you made me miss the birdies,' Lucy grumbled.

A second later a horse and carriage going in the other direction passed so close Rose recoiled from the noise and the swirl of air that swept into the carriage, raising a cloud of dust in its wake. Her breath caught in her throat as she realised it could easily have hit the little girl's head.

'What did I tell you about leaping about inside a moving vehicle?' Jake growled. He sounded so severe the little girl visibly shrivelled. Poor little thing.

Rose recalled one of the maids telling her that his father and brother had died in a carriage accident. No wonder he looked so fierce.

He cared for this child. Deeply. Rose couldn't help admiring his protective streak even if he had spoken too harshly.

Then she saw that he had softened the effect of his admonition with a gentle touch, one hand holding the little girl gently but safely on his knee while the other rubbed comforting circles on her narrow little shoulders. He shifted so she could once again see out of the window, but this time in safety.

'You know if you stick your head out like that you will frighten the horses coming the other way,' he said.

Lucy gave a nervous little giggle. 'They would be scared of my head?'

'Certainly,' he said. 'Horses are stupid creatures. They are terrified of rabbits and can shy at the mere sight of a ribbon fluttering on a hat.'

'Did Grandpapa's horses see a hat?'

Rose's heart stopped. Jake never talked about his father. He became positively remote if the subject came up.

His hand on the child's back stilled. His shoulders tensed. A little muscle in his lean jaw flickered.

For a long moment, Rose feared he might stop the carriage and walk away.

He inhaled a slow breath and blew it out. 'I don't know. Perhaps they did,' he finally said.

'I miss Grandpapa,' Lucy said quietly, sadly. 'And Uncle Ralph.'

'Me, too, poppet,' he said in a low voice.

The pain in Jacob's eyes was hard for Rose to see. She wanted to offer comfort, but all she could do was look down at her hands so he would not see her sympathy. She did not want to intrude on his grief. She did not have the right.

Oh, but she did understand their sense of loss.

There was an empty space in her heart where a mother and father should have been and perhaps one or two siblings.

She blinked the mist from her eyes. Perhaps she was the lucky one after all. Seeing the depth of Jacob's sorrow made her think it was better to have never known her family, than to have had them wrenched out of her life in such a cruel way.

'How much farther is it?' Lucy asked, returning to her bright eager self in the wink of an eye.

Jake smiled at her fondly. 'Not far now.'

What a wonderful father he would make. Wealthy. Protective. And best of all, loving. The woman he married would be fortunate indeed.

She on the other hand would likely never have children. For that she would need a proper home and husband, but women in service rarely married, because if they did, they lost their positions and income.

No, what she had with Jake was the best she could ever expect. Sadly, it would not last for ever, but when it was over she would have the most wonderful memories, including those of today.

'Time to go back to your seat, young lady,' Jake said, lifting Lucy as if she was lighter than air and setting her beside Rose as the horses slowed, turned the corner on to Cranbourn Street and halted.

Jake climbed down and helped them to alight to the pavement. He crouched on his haunches so he was eye to eye with Lucy. 'You will hold my hand at all times,' he said, once more his tone stern. 'Your mama will spank my backside so hard I won't be able to sit for a week if I lose you.'

Lucy roared with laughter at the thought. Rose couldn't help smiling at the image her mind conjured up, though she had the feeling Jake meant every word.

The entrance to the rotunda was rather small, though it proudly proclaimed its exhibition and promised delight and amazement. The porter at the door tipped his hat.

'Westmoor,' Jake said. 'I am expected.'

'Indeed, Your Grace.' The man bent almost in half, his bow was so low. 'This way if you please. All is ready for your party.'

Rose frowned at him.

Jake raised a brow. 'I sent word ahead. The place is reserved for us.'

'Reserved for...' She gasped. 'You mean no one else can come in while we are here?'

'One of the benefits of being a duke. Privacy.'

She eyed him with suspicion. There was a little too much smugness in his voice. But with Lucy able to hear every word there was little she could say.

Jake held out his arm, she hooked hers through his and, with Lucy holding his other hand, they followed the porter through a door.

The narrow passage in which they found themselves was dimly lit. There was absolutely nothing at all to see in the chilly gloom of the corridor that twisted and turned like a labyrinth.

'Not much of a vista,' Rose, said savouring the unfamiliar word.

Jake patted her hand. 'Wait. You'll see.'

The shadowy passage arrived at a set of equally badly lit stairs winding upwards. Finally, at the top, they stepped through a black curtain and on to a platform. Rose blinked at the sudden brightness.

Her jaw dropped as her eyes finally focused. Speechless, she stared at the…the view. She was standing in a blazing white wilderness of ice that was not just in front of them but all around, no matter which way she turned. She shivered, despite that she was not cold. Chills ran down her spine.

'Oh, look,' Lucy cried. 'Mermaids.'

Fearful for the child's safety, Rose made a grab for her, only to realise there was a railing between the edge of the gallery where they stood and what seemed like a gaping black hole beneath them.

She stood behind the child, gazing at the scene spread out before her. 'Oh, my.' There were icy mountains and a ship heeled over, held fast between two blocks of ice, and men in small boats or standing around conversing on the snow. The whole thing made her feel slightly dizzy.

She swayed and Jake put an arm around her waist, steadying her. 'Give it a moment,' he murmured. 'You'll get used to it. They say Princess Charlotte was seasick for a week after viewing a sea panorama.'

The feel of that strong arm supporting her was blissful. She took a deep breath and looked up to find Jake grinning at her, though much of his face was in shadow. 'Now you know what panorama means.'

She took in the scene before her in wonder. 'Yes. Yes, I do.'

'And how would *you* explain it?'

She shook her head. 'I couldn't. Not in a hundred years, if I was to try ever so hard.'

He leaned forward and brushed his lips along her jaw, a fleeting warm touch over almost before it began and shivers broke out all over her body. Pleasure and desire.

Naughty man. She glanced down at Lucy, who for once was silent and clearly transfixed, unaware of the adults behind her. She was terribly tempted to kiss him back. Out of gratitude. Out of deep affection. Out of love.

It could not be. She forced herself to remain still.

Lucy turned and tugged at her skirts. 'What are those things there?' She pointed through the railing.

Jake pulled a sheet of paper from his pocket. 'I have a guide.' He angled the paper towards the light that somehow seemed to emanate from the scene itself. 'The ship you see is the *Dorothea*, caught in the ice.'

'But the creatures, Uncle Jake.'

'Give me a moment, child.' He scanned the paper. 'Those are walruses. See their curving tusks.'

'Where are their legs?'

'No legs, pet. They don't need them for swimming.'

Lucy ran a little farther along to take in another part of the scene. Jake tucked Rose's hand beneath his arm and they strolled after her, he reading from the guide and pointing out the items of interest.

'They have dogs,' Lucy announced.

'Not dogs,' Jake said. 'Polar bears.'

'Bears aren't white.'

'These are.' He went on to describe the explorers and their ships as they promenaded around the railing, until they had gone full circle.

To Rose, it felt as if they were a real family. A man and his wife and their child. A lump forced its way into her throat.

Longing. She wanted to weep for longing. She turned her face to the panorama, hoping Jake would not see.

She took a deep breath. Swallowed past the lump and pinned a smile on her lips. 'Why is some of the ice blue?' Her voice sounded brittle.

Luckily in the dim light, Jake seemed to notice nothing amiss.

'Honestly, I don't know. I would have to read more about it. It is hard to believe this happened last August. The middle of summer, no less. They were lucky to survive a huge storm, I understand.'

'They are very brave men.'

'I'm going to be an explorer when I grow up,' Lucy said. 'And go on a ship. And get stuck in the ice.'

Jake glanced down at her.

Rose expected him to tell her that women did not undertake such daring adventures. Instead he merely smiled. 'I expect you will, pet.'

And then they were back where they came in. 'Shall we go down?' Jake asked. 'There is another staircase leading up to the other view, but it is a very long climb to get a view of St. Petersburg. Not nearly as exciting as this.'

In other words, not something that would interest a child. 'No, I think it might be best saved it for another day.'

'I want to go,' Lucy said, pouting.

Jake crouched down. 'Very well, I will give you a choice. A long hot climb for a view of an old city with streets and buildings or ices at Gunter's.'

'Ices. I want raspberry.'

Jake chuckled and came to his feet.

Rose breathed a sigh of relief, having expected floods of tears or a tantrum. The man was so lovely with the little girl. He would indeed make a wonderful father.

Again her heart squeezed.

'Shall I carry you down the stairs, Lucy?' he asked.

'I can do it myself,' the little girl said. She bustled ahead.

'Hold on to the banister,' Rose reminded just before Jake spun her around and kissed her on the lips.

She melted against him and kissed him back. When they finally broke apart, she smiled up at him. 'Thank you.'

His eyes sparkled. 'Thank you. Now, *you* will allow me to help you down the stairs, will you not?'

Chapter Eleven

To Jacob's disgruntlement, the heat of the day had brought every member of the *ton* left in London to Gunter's Tea Shop. Didn't they know they were supposed to be residing in the country at this time of year?

Glancing around him as he stepped out of the carriage, he realised he had made a fatal error. The place was riddled with biddies who would have a field day when they saw him escorting Rose without the company of his grandmother.

He could bring the ices into the coach, but it was far too hot to be sitting inside a stuffy carriage. And besides, he didn't want the seat cushions ruined just because of a lot of gossipy old besoms.

To hell with them. He had promised Lucy an ice and he wasn't going back on his word.

With the skill born of long practice, along with the newly acquired ducal stare, he contrived a seat in a corner beside an open window where what breeze there was would help keep them cool until their ices arrived.

He made his ladies comfortable, seating himself between

them and relaxed. Sitting here beside Rose seemed right somehow. With her at his side, he felt more settled inside himself than he had for months.

He smiled down at his niece, who was sitting with her hands folded in her lap as if ice cream would never melt in her mouth, let alone on her frock. 'I know Lucy wants a raspberry ice, but what about you, Rose?'

Rose looked thoroughly uncomfortable. He turned in his seat. Blast it.

Everyone present was looking at them, some covertly, others openly interested. 'Don't worry about them,' he said with an encouraging smile. 'I can assure you, they are ogling me.' Probably regurgitating the stories around the accident, if he knew them. He handed her the menu.

She gazed at it with what he could only describe as awe. 'I have no idea what to choose.'

'Have raspberry. It is the best,' Lucy pronounced.

Rose lifted her gaze to meet his. 'Is that your opinion also?'

'I like them all.' A wicked idea formed in his head. 'Trust me?'

She nodded.

He hailed a passing waiter and turned aside so Rose could not hear while he placed his order.

Lucy frowned. 'Raspberry, Uncle Jake.'

He grinned. 'I didn't forget.'

'What a lovely place this is,' Rose said. 'They are even taking ices out to that carriage.'

'An open carriage is the only place a gentleman can be alone with a single lady of marriageable age,' Jake said, 'and not cause talk. On a hot day like today an ice will make a gentleman very popular with his lady.'

A moment later, the waiter returned with a tray full of small glass dishes, each containing a different flavour, and one large one with red ice cream. He arranged them on the table, making sure Lucy had her favourite, the smart observant chap.

Rose gasped and looked at Jake in dismay. 'They must have made a mistake. These can't all be for us?'

'They are. There is one of every flavour for you to try. You like tasting things.'

Her face went fiery red and her expression became mortified.

He cursed. He'd meant to tease, not embarrass. What was the matter with him? He seemed to be behaving like an awkward schoolboy. 'Rose, I mean it as a treat. These are samples. Look, over there, they are doing the same at that table.'

Her eyes widened. 'Oh.'

The other table did not have quite as many dishes, but they had several. Her feathers settled. She picked up her spoon and he breathed a sigh of relief.

Lucy was already tucking in to her ice. He grabbed her napkin and tied it beneath her chin. 'Your mama won't be pleased if you ruin your dress.'

Lucy nodded. 'Which one will you try first, Miss Nightingale?' she asked.

'This one.' Rose drew the white one closer and inhaled. 'Vanilla?'

'Indeed,' Jake said and the next moment, watching her scoop a small amount into her mouth and seeing her eyes go particularly dreamy, he was as hard as a rock.

'Oh, my word,' she breathed, staring at him. She gave a little shiver. 'It is cold, but it simply melts on my tongue.

He wanted to melt on her tongue. He couldn't stop recalling how she had licked…

He looked down at the dishes, trying not to shift on his seat. 'Try that one. It is strawberry.'

And so it continued, the sensual torture of Rose's first experience of ice cream.

Her surprise at the taste of lemon made him laugh.

One or two people sent startled glances their way and Rose's face mirrored worry.

'I told you,' he said. 'Pay them no mind.'

'It is not that,' she whispered. 'Mr Challenger just walked in, with a lady.' She swallowed. 'What if he...?' She glanced at Lucy and winced.

'People only see what they expect to see.' He shifted so he could see the door. 'Mr Challenger is my friend. He won't say a thing. The lady with him is his wife.'

They made a lovely couple, too. Imagine, Frederick married. The first of the founders of Vitium et Virtus leg-shackled. And happily so. Times were changing. He, too, would have to marry. But not for a long while yet.

'What flavour will you choose next, Rose?'

'Have the raspberry,' Lucy said with the wisdom of the very young. 'You will like it the best of all, I promise. It tastes just like raspberries and it is pink. The first time I came here, Uncle Jake said raspberry was the best.'

He gave Rose's hand a squeeze where it rested on her lap out of sight of any of the watching crows. 'Why not let Miss Nightingale choose for herself.'

'It is all so extravagant,' Rose said.

He loved the way she rolled the word of her tongue as if tasting its meaning.

'But I hate to think of it going to waste, when it must have cost a fortune.' Her spoon hovered over the raspberry ice.

He also loved it that she was considerate about spending his money. So different from any other lady of his acquaintance, he realised with a sense of deep admiration.

'Do not worry. I'll eat anything you don't want, so nothing will go to waste.' He wanted to kiss her again. Taste all those flavours on her tongue. And not a sneaking kiss in the dark as he had at the rotunda, but a possessive this-lady-is-mine sort of kiss for all the world to see. Wouldn't that be scandalous? He grinned inwardly at the thought, even knowing he would never embarrass her that way.

'Westmoor.' Fred stood looking down at him. Jake rose to his feet.

'Challenger.'

'Well met, old chap. Can we impose ourselves on you? There's not a table to be had and we walked over, so I cannot even offer my lady a carriage in which to partake of her ice.'

'Please, do join us.'

While Fred went for a couple of chairs, Jake bowed over Georgiana's hand. 'It is good to see you again, Georgiana. Please, allow me to introduce my grandmother's companion, Miss Rose Nightingale, and my sister's daughter, Miss Lucinda Robertson. Ladies, this is Mrs Challenger.'

Georgiana smiled warmly at both of his ladies. 'How lovely to meet you. And please, call me George. Everyone does. What luck for us, meeting you here, Jacob. I feared we would have to leave without our ices and I would have been most disappointed.'

Rose visibly swallowed and took Georgiana's outstretched hand. 'I am pleased to meet you, Mrs um… George.'

A flush stained her cheeks and she looked nervous, her gaze flitting to his face and back to Georgiana as if the sky was about to fall. A feeling of impatience took Jake by surprise. He didn't want her feeling embarrassed when meeting his friends. He wanted her to feel…comfortable. At ease.

'I am pleased to meet you, too,' Lucy added. 'Can I have another ice, Uncle Jake, if the waiter ever comes back? I am still hot.'

Jake gave her a mock-stern look. She had been such a good girl today and he didn't want to crush her high spirits as long as they stayed within bounds.

Georgiana, bless her, looked indulgent. 'It is hot,' she said.

He became aware of Fred giving Rose a narrow-eyed stare and his stomach knotted. Not much slipped by Fred.

'Why don't I go and order at the counter?' Fred said. 'It might be faster.' He gave Jake a pointed stare.

'I'll come with you,' Jake said. Might as well hear what he had to say.

He followed in Fred's wake, the man's shoulders militarily straight and an aura of disapproval distinctly visible. When they reached the counter, Fred gave him a chilly stare. 'Nightingale? I recognise her name. She's employed at Vitium et Virtus. Damn it all, I'm sure I have seen her there. You certainly have a nerve to introduce her to my wife?'

'To the devil with you, Fred,' he said in a low voice. 'You joined us. Don't you think that if she's good enough for my niece, she's good enough for your wife? And besides, she worked there as a maid, nothing else.'

His friend looked mollified. Slightly. 'What on earth is she doing as the Dowager's companion?'

'My grandmother likes her and she is doing a very good job. First one the old lady has agreed to tolerate, in fact.'

'If that's the case, where is your grandmother?'

'I don't see that it is any of your business.'

'I saw the way you were looking at her when we came in.'

'The way... Blast your eyes, man. You are as bad as all the other gossips in this place.'

'So you don't have seduction on your mind? Or do you plan to make an honest woman of her?'

That was the question, wasn't it? He'd promised his father he would be the Duke his brother would have been. Sworn it. His brother, Ralph, would have done his duty. Married for political or financial advantage, for the sake of the title. He would not have married a scullery maid, even if he had fallen in— He froze. Cut off his thought before it could fully form. Love was not an option for him.

He'd keep his promise.

Fred thrust out his chin, wanting an answer.

Jake glared at his friend. 'Miss Nightingale is a perfectly respectable young woman, Fred, and if you say one more word suggesting otherwise, I swear I will draw your cork.'

Fred stared at him for a long moment. He let out a long sigh. 'Have it your way, Jake. But I advise you to be very careful. She seems like a nice girl.'

Rose was a nice girl. Very nice. The nicest girl he had ever met. Fred was right. Much too nice for him. He ground his back teeth.

Across the room, the ladies were engaged in a lively conversation.

Rose really was amazing. It didn't matter where he took her, she could hold her own.

He had never felt prouder.

Or, given Fred's admonition, more miserable as reality struck home.

Rose had spoken of children and family and he had heard the longing in her voice. Under the circumstances in which he found himself, he could never give her that. And children out of wedlock were out of the question. No child of his would suffer the way Oliver had.

He ought to stop what he should never have started. Send her on her way with a generous gift and wish her happy when she found a good and decent man who could make her an honest woman.

The thought of Rose in the arms of another did not sit well in his gut as he maintained his outward calm beneath Fred's stare.

Fred waved at one of the servers behind the counter who was looking around for his next customer. 'Over here, man.'

They placed their order and returned to the table, but all through the chatter and pleasantries, Jake could only worry about Rose and what he should do.

* * *

On the way home in the carriage, Lucy leaned against Rose's arm and closed her eyes. Rose pulled her close and made her comfortable. 'Dear little soul. She's fast asleep.'

'It has been an exciting day for her.'

Rose raised a worried glance to his face. 'I met Mrs Challenger once before, you know. At the club. I don't think she remembered me.'

'You did what?' He realised he had raised his voice when her eyes widened.

'I helped her dress. Mr Challenger was most annoyed with her at the time.'

Jake could only imagine. Good for George. Perhaps she'd shake Fred up a bit. He'd become far too stuffy since coming back from the war. 'You must never mention the club again and especially in relation to Mrs Challenger.'

She paled. 'Oh, I would never...' She turned her face away. 'I would not want to put you to shame.'

Dash it, now he'd upset her. Fred was right, he was bad for Rose. He could never offer her what she truly deserved. Things could not continue as they were. The resolution came to him in a flash. 'I have to go to Hertfordshire. To my estate. Something has come up there that requires my attention.'

Surprise filled Rose's expression. 'Has something gone wrong there? I thought you seemed distracted.'

He might have known she would sense his mood, though he'd been careful to keep his thoughts hidden. But her concern was misplaced. She should be worrying about herself. Guilt twisted in his gut. He really did have to make this right. 'My steward has written concerning problems with the harvest. I need to see for myself.'

Her brow cleared. An understanding smile curved her pretty lips. Her gaze softened. 'Will you be gone long?'

The longing not to go at all shook him to his core. Never before had he had any trouble parting from a woman. He took a deep breath, kept his expression cool. 'I am not sure how long I will be away, actually. A week or two. Maybe longer.'

'Oh.' She looked nonplussed. 'I see.'

'I am relying on you to care for Grandmama in my absence. She depends on you.'

She gave a nod. 'Anything I can do to help, I will.'

'I am most grateful.' The words sounded stilted and formal and he saw the hurt in her eyes, but he could not let that sway him. The risks were too great no matter what precautions they took. He needed to make a clean break of it. To set her free of any obligation she might feel to him so she could get on with the life she had planned for herself. 'I will leave the moment we arrive at the house.'

Rose's little gasp of shock, quickly hidden, cut his heart to ribbons. He ignored the pain. 'If I leave right away, I can make it there before it is dark.'

The evenings were already drawing in, but he could do it, if he rode hard. The staff would be surprised to see him, but it was a ducal household and they were always prepared.

The days after Jake left were the longest of Rose's life. There had been one letter from him, a single line to his grandmother announcing his safe arrival in Hertfordshire and no mention of when he might return.

The household had continued in its usual routine, despite the strange emptiness the house evoked without him. She missed him terribly.

On the third afternoon, Rose sat with Eleanor and her grandmother in the drawing room, the other two ladies sewing and chatting as if nothing had changed, while an uncomfortable thought kept going around and around in Rose's mind.

Did Jake's departure mean something more than a need to visit one of his estates? He'd decided so suddenly. And had been so distracted in the carriage ride home from Gunter's. Had he intended that she should hand in her notice in his absence?

Every time that thought crossed her mind, as it had several times since he'd bid her farewell, her heart squeezed with a pang so painful she couldn't breathe. Over the past few weeks, she had grown to love his grandmother as if she was her own. She adored Lucy. And wondrously, Eleanor treated her as an equal. She had the feeling they might have become friends if things had been different.

But she could not allow it. Not when she was living a lie.

Eleanor would be disgusted if she knew the truth of her history, what she was. Not to mention her horror if she learned of Rose's relationship with Jake. What decent mother would want someone like her near their child?

Shame rose up in a horrid wave. She ought to leave before Jake returned. A voice inside her, a niggling discomfort, kept reminding her that as sure as eggs were eggs, the truth would come out. A servant would see him entering her room. Or Mr Challenger would say something. Or...

'Your Grace,' the butler said, walking in with a silver salver. 'A note came for you. Hand delivered. The messenger said it was urgent.'

The Dowager Duchess took the paper with a smile of thanks and spread the paper open. 'Well, fancy that.'

'What is it, Grandmama?' Eleanor asked.

'We are all invited to a musicale evening at Lady Buckhurst's.'

Rose rested her embroidery frame in her lap, intending to refuse any attempt to take her along.

Eleanor frowned. 'Why would that be considered urgent? When is it?'

'Tonight. A last-minute affair. Lady Buckhurst discovered that Signora Calvetti, a brilliant soprano fêted in Paris and Rome, is visiting London. She is due to depart on the morrow. Lady Buckhurst has managed to get her to agree to one performance only. Quite the coup, from her note. Shall we go and add to the consequence of the evening?'

'You may go if you wish, Grandmama,' Eleanor said softly. 'I prefer not.'

'You need to go about more, my dear, now that we have put off black gloves. It is not right for someone so young to be cloistered away.'

Eleanor sighed. 'I am perfectly happy as I am, Grandmama. You will not flex your matchmaking muscles on my behalf. You have enough to do with Jake.'

Her Grace frowned mightily. 'Rose, you *will* add your pleas to mine.' The old lady turned to Rose. Her hopeful expression pulled at Rose's heartstrings more than it should. The old lady was right, though. Eleanor was too young to remain a widow. She ought to be out among society, seeking enjoyment.

'You told me you like music, Eleanor,' Rose said, a little weakly even to her own ears. She forced confidence into her voice, along with a dab of persuasion. 'You might regret not hearing this singer if she is as good as your grandmother says.'

Eleanor grimaced. 'I don't know.' Her face brightened. 'I will go, if you will. You have been moping about, since my brother left.'

Jake. She meant Jake. Shock hit her hard. She couldn't believe Eleanor would have noticed. And now her cheeks were hot and she couldn't meet the other woman's gaze for fear she would give herself away. More than she already had.

'It is true, Rose,' the Dowager Duchess said. 'You have not been your usual cheerful self. An outing will do you good.'

Oh, no. She had noticed, too. Why was she not demanding she leave? Instead she looked…sympathetic?

'I know nothing about opera, my lady,' she managed to mumble. 'It would be better if I stayed here with Lucy.'

Eleanor looked startled. Perhaps even shocked.

Oh, dear. Was opera a part of every young lady's curriculum? The only thing close to what she thought might be opera were the bawdy ditties at the V&V.

Her Grace wagged a gnarled finger in her direction. 'A lack of education in a young lady such as you will not do, Rose. The sooner you add music to your repertoire the better, my gel.'

Her repa— *What?* A young lady such as her would likely be on the next ship to Botany Bay if Her Grace ever guessed the lies she'd been told.

She opened her mouth to refuse again.

'Please, Rose,' the Dowager said and the hope in her old wise eyes made Rose feel as if she'd stepped into a bog and was floundering around for an excuse when Her Grace knew Rose would never refuse her anything she wanted. As an employee, she didn't have the right.

Still she tried. 'I don't think—'

'Oh, please don't say no,' Eleanor said. 'Grandmama is going to insist I go, I can see she is. Having you with me will make it bearable. It doesn't matter in the least that you don't speak Italian. It is the music that counts.'

Italian? Heaven help her.

How could she refuse? These people had been good to her. So good that sometimes she forgot herself and thought of them as family. And to have the chance to hear such music... What a treat it would be. She raised a hand. 'I give in. I will go.'

Hopefully they would not run into Mr Challenger. As kindly as his smile seemed, that man unnerved her.

Seated between Her Grace and Lady Eleanor in Lady Buckhurst's opulent music room, Rose had never heard anything quite so beautiful as Signora Calvetti's singing. True, she did not understand the words—but, oh, the feelings her voice evoked. They tore at her heartstrings in nameless ways.

Sorrow. Loss. Joy. It was all there in the music. Rose sat entranced. Thrilled they had persuaded her to accept the invitation.

Nothing in her life had prepared her for the sounds issuing from the woman who stood at the front of the room with diamonds glittering in her hair, at her throat and on her eloquent hands.

The music came to a close and the audience clapped heartily.

The dark-haired voluptuous flashing-eyed singer, curtseyed and blew kisses to her audience.

'Encore!' someone shouted.

The cry was picked up around the room.

The singer smiled but shook her head.

Lady Buckhurst hustled up to stand beside the woman, signalling for silence. 'Thank you everyone. I promised the *signora* we would understand that she has a long journey tomorrow and must guard her voice for a performance in Paris booked many months ago. If you would like to follow my major-domo, refreshments are served in the conservatory.'

The crowd, good-natured if disappointed, began to shuffle their way out. Someone tapped Rose on the shoulder with a fan.

Wondering who it could be, she turned around. It was the girl who had played croquet with Jake. 'Oh,' she said surprised. 'Lady Alicia.'

The girl's smile was less than friendly. 'He won't marry you, you know.'

Rose blinked. 'I beg your pardon?'

'The Duke.' She nodded to the back of the room. Jake was standing there, talking to another gentleman.

Rose's heart soared.

He was looking a little haggard. Something like the way he had looked when they first met. What could have happened during the past few days to make him appear so? Or was it merely weariness from his journey?

'He won't marry a nobody from the country,' the girl hissed in her ear as people shuffled around them as if they were an island in the middle of a fast-flowing river. 'A libertine and a rake he may have been, but he will do his duty by the title. You'll see.'

Rose glared at her, her hackles rising at the scornful tone. 'You don't think he will marry you, do you?'

The girl primped the cluster of curls resting on her cheek. 'If my father has anything to say to it he will. After all, it is his fault I didn't get to marry his brother.'

'His fault.' Rose's jaw dropped. 'What on earth do you mean?'

'He wanted the title and he arranged to get it. Everyone says so.'

Rose's fists clenched. Was one allowed to strike a horrid girl in the face at a musicale evening? Likely not. But, oh, how she was tempted.

'How could you believe such horrid gossip?'

The girl sniffed. 'There's no smoke without a fire. He owes my family a marriage. And my papa isn't one to leave a debt unpaid.'

She flounced away to join an older lady who was looking daggers at Rose. The girl's mother.

Instead of shrinking beneath that stare as she might have a few weeks ago, Rose straightened her shoulders. Poor Jake, if that young woman was his ultimate fate.

A horrid suspicion crossed her mind. Was he aware of this family's expectations? Was that why he had played croquet with the girl?

Rose sat in the chair beside the window, looking over the gardens. Night had fallen a good two hours before and still Jake had not come to her.

Not only that, while he'd been his usually gentlemanly self in the carriage on the way home from the musicale, he'd returned to his former coolness. He'd barely spoken to her and only answered his grandmother's enquiries as to the affairs at his estate with brusque brevity. In the end, Eleanor had taken him to task for his rudeness and he'd made more of an effort.

Had he finally realised how unsuitable she was as a companion for his grandmother and was trying to pluck up the courage to let her go? Mr Challenger had recognised her. She was sure of it. And if he had not, she had certainly seen the reservation in his gaze, despite that he'd been the soul of politeness and his wife had been lovely.

And noble.

Her hands clenched in her lap. That was the sort of woman Jake would marry. A girl of good family. One who would not cause him to be ashamed. She just hoped he didn't choose Lady Alicia for a bride. That girl would not make him happy. And no matter what happened, she did want him to be happy.

A knock at the door startled her. She shot to her feet.

Jake strode in. Fully clothed.

He usually came in a dressing gown of green silk covered in golden dragons.

Her stomach fell away at the grim look on his face, the intensity in his eyes as he took in her *dishabille*.

'Rose.' His voice had a rough edge to it.

'Jake?'

'I came to tell you...'

She held her breath, her heart balanced on a knife-edge of expectation, ready, but in no way prepared for the pain of his words of parting.

He closed his eyes briefly, stepped into the room and closed the door behind him.

'You came to tell me?' she prompted in a whisper, tipping

her face to meet his gaze, seeing heat there, desire flaring between them as it always did.

He kissed her, hard and deep, a low growl rising up from his throat. Feral. Not tender, not sweet, but wild and hungry. Full of dark passion.

A rush of desire ran hot through her blood, her heart picked up speed, her body trembled. She twined her arms around his neck and kissed him back hard. How could she have thought she had lost him?

Their tongues tangled, her heart pounded against her breastbone making it hard to breath and she sank into the fire of a blazing kiss. Moments seemed like for ever until they fell apart, breathless.

He attacked the ties of her robe, she tore at the buttons of his coat. He shrugged out of his jacket, then his waistcoat; she let the dressing robe slide to the floor. He tore off his neckcloth. Ripped his shirt off over his head.

She jerked at the ribbon holding her bodice closed.

He groaned as the gown dipped down one shoulder, pulled her close and kissed her again. In a movement so swift and effortless she felt weightless, he picked her up and carried her to the bed, depositing her carefully on the mattress. It took him mere seconds to strip out of his nether garments and, gloriously naked, he joined her on the bed, giving her no time to admire his rampant erection and manly physique.

Never had she seen him so demanding, so urgent, so fierce.

It called to something inside her she had not known existed. The need to be overpowered, to feel vulnerable, yet powerful in a different way. As if in breaking through his control, he had given her something strange and wonderfully exhilarating.

Without thought, without modesty, she drew her nightdress off over her head and brought his mouth to her aching breast.

He drew deeply on the aching nub. A pain of such piercing sweetness arrowed deep to the heart of her femininity.

She cried out. Her hips arched, pressing into him, feeling his hardness against her mons. Seeking him inside her.

A knee pressed between her thighs and the pleasure of opening herself to him made her heart lift and soar.

He settled himself between her legs and drove into her body with a groan that welled from deep in his chest.

She shattered, melting around him, surrendering beneath him.

He stilled. A shudder ran through him, so strong it resonated in her bones.

Him, too? Never had he shown such urgency.

But, no. She could feel him inside her, still hard.

He slowly rocked his hips. Tension inside her began to build. A ripple of pleasure spread outward from her core, intense, soul stirring. Again?

And still he had not—

He moved again, slow easy thrusts of his hips, gradually increasing the tempo. The restlessness started up again, tightening every nerve in her body. He drove deeper and again she reached the pinnacle and let go.

Overwhelmed by the beauty of the sensations he instilled, a joy so vast filled her and tears leaked from the corner of her eyes. Supported on his hands, looming over her, the rigid tension of his body, the ripple of hard muscle and the straining of tendons in his neck left her in awe.

Balancing on one hand, he lifted her buttocks, opening her more to his penetration, filling her completely.

Somehow she managed to lift her head to nibble at his earlobe, to trace the outer ear with delicate strokes of her tongue, then plunged into the depths of it, tasting salt and inhaling the scent of his soap.

His hiss of indrawn breath sent shivers across her skin.

He raised his head, gazing down at her, his eyes dark with passion, his expression strained by longing and need. The same longing and need echoing in her heart.

As if their souls had merged into one.

'You undo me,' he rasped, driving into her harder.

I love you, she whispered in her mind, finally recognising the truth of the depths of her feelings and revelling in them even as she grieved that he would never be fully hers.

She closed her lips on the words, held them tight to her heart, for she had a shred of wit left to know that to admit them out loud and see rejection in his eyes would tear her apart.

Instead, she showed him all she could never say with her hands and her body and her lips.

Feeling him unravelling inside her body was the greatest joy of all. And the saddest moment of her life. Because in a moment of clarity at the moment before she followed him into bliss, she sensed he was saying goodbye. '*I will always love you.*'

They lay tangled together, damp with sweat, hearts beating a wild rhythm, breathing harsh in the quiet room.

After several moments he shifted. Moving away. She reached to hold him, but he slipped from her grasp, leaving the bed in a surge of movement. She rose up on her elbows and was startled to see him hastily dressing. He glanced over his shoulder.

'I am so damned sorry, Rose. I did not intend this.'

Her heart stopped beating. Her breath caught in her throat. 'What is it? What did I do?'

He straightened, now fully clothed, his expression stern, closed off. 'You did nothing wrong, Rose. You are everything that is—' He choked the words off, made a slicing gesture with his hand. 'I actually came to tell you I have business at Vitium et Virtus this evening and cannot stay.' He closed his eyes against her surprised gaze. 'I am sorry.'

He bowed and, with his shoulders straight and his steps determined, he left.

While he had said nothing of any import, Rose had a strange feeling that everything between had changed.

He'd donned the reserve he'd worn when they first met like a coat, or some sort of suit of armour, as if he sought protection.

Protection from her?

Chapter Twelve

Jake could not stop thinking about the expression of Rose's face when he had left her last evening.

Flushed, sated, seductive. Words of love barely discernible above their pounding heartbeats and ragged breathing. He wasn't sure she'd realised what she'd said. But the words had carved a path through his heart to his very soul.

He had tried to convince himself that the words meant nothing, that she had spoken them in the heat of passion. After all, other women had said similar things in the same circumstances, but he knew deep within him that Rose wasn't like other women. She did not say things that were not true.

She'd given him everything and he had been so stunned, he'd been unable to think, let alone speak what was in his own heart.

Thank God he had not.

In bringing her into his home, he'd made a grave mistake. The sort of mistake he might have made as a green boy new upon the town. Feeling more than he should for a lover. Wanting to keep her, when all he could do was keep her safe. Not only that, he'd stolen her innocence. Stolen her lack of worldliness which had made her so attractive to him in the first place.

His heart twisted. He did not deserve a woman like Rose. He could not allow his own feeling to colour his decisions. His life was not his own.

If things had been different— He squashed a thought that kept intruding where Rose was concerned.

Things, he thought bitterly, would have been different had he been a little less selfish. A little less headstrong. A little more willing to do his father's bidding instead of leaving it to Ralph to fill the breach. As he always had.

On the other hand, had he done as he'd been asked that day six months ago, he might never have met Rose. Anger balled in his chest. A hot, hard lump. At himself. At whatever fate had decided his world should be turned on its head.

The stupidest part of all of it? He'd never been happier than he had been these past few weeks. A happiness he did not deserve.

Last night, seeing her waiting for him in her nightgown, her skin golden in the glow of the candles, he'd been unable to resist her allure.

She loved him. The wonder of it had shaken him to his core. Left him speechless and wanting what he could not have.

Today, in the cold light of day, he would lay out the future. The best he could offer, given his circumstances. A carte blanche.

A house of her own across the river, where they could be together whenever they wished. A house where he could entertain his friends and they could be themselves, instead of sneaking around late at night. She'd have a carriage and clothes as befitted her beauty. He'd settle her financial affairs so when it was over, perhaps when he married, she would be comfortable for the rest of her life. Able to do just as she pleased. Perhaps find herself a husband.

Icy fingers clutched at his heart.

He fought off their chill. It was only fair. Because the one thing she wanted, the one thing he could not give her, were children. No child of his would suffer the taint of bastardy, though as a duke he could likely get away with it more easily than Oliver's father had.

He steeled himself for the coming interview. Fortunately, his grandmother and sister had taken Lucy shopping for clothes. It was the perfect opportunity for him to talk to Rose without the fear of interruption.

He entered the drawing room with a smile and a yawning pit of dread in his gut.

Rose had her back to him, concentrating on—

'What are you doing?' His voice was loud, harsh, in the silence. He kept his gaze fixed on her, not on the portrait above the mantel.

She spun around. Put a hand to her heart. 'Jake. You startled me.' She turned back to the painting, denuded of crepe, which she must have pulled down and now held in her hand.

'In this painting, you look more like your sister than your father or your brother,' she mused with a smile in her voice. 'They seem quite stern, the way you do most of the time, whereas here you look ready for any kind of adventure. A right proper rascal. You can't hide it, though. Sometimes that rascal peeks out and you seem more like this boy.' She turned back to face him, her face alight with interest in the truth she'd instantly seen.

Her words struck a blow at his heart. At the essence of everything he'd tried to be these past few months. A flash of unreasoning rage raced along his veins. 'How dare you remove that without permission.'

Her face blanched. She glanced guiltily over her shoulder

and winced. 'I wanted to see the other members of your family. This is the only likeness of them in the house.'

Unable to stop himself, he glanced up. The faces of his brother and father gazed down on him with their usual self-assured gravity.

The Duke in his regalia and his heir, squaring his shoulders beneath the weight of the father's hand and the responsibilities he would bear with dignity when his turn came around. And Eleanor, little more than a baby, holding her father's hand. A hand that had been ripped from her grasp.

And then there was himself. Looking out with the expression of devil-may-care that had always been an irritant to his brother. After all, he was the younger son with all the privilege and none of the duty. A careless attitude that had destroyed everything he and Eleanor had held dear. A stark reminder of his failings.

He snatched the crepe from her hand, intending to replace it, but could not reach the top of the frame. Cursing under his breath, he went for a chair.

'Why do you hide it?' Rose asked from behind him, her voice full of puzzlement. 'It is a beautiful portrait. Your father's obvious pride in his children is heart-warming. Surely—?'

His hands gripped the chair arms, his knuckles white, his heart beating an unsteady rhythm. He didn't need the portrait in order to recall his father's face, it was there in his mind's eye every time he took a decision on behalf of the Duchy, every time he drew a breath he had denied his brother.

Along with the shame he felt every time he thought about his father's request and the way he had sloughed it off on to good old dutiful Ralph so he could go to a masked ball at Vitium et Virtus. It made him feel ill. How could he tell her what he had done? How could he ever explain what the look on his father's face did to him when he couldn't explain it to himself?

He chilled the heat of his emotions. Slowed the beat of his heart. Turned to face her. 'You don't understand.'

She stood her ground, eyeing him with concern and confusion. 'How can I understand? You always keep me and everyone else at a distance. I do understand one thing. I would give anything to have a likeness of my family even though they didn't care enough about me to keep me.' Her voice filled with tears. She swallowed them down, fumbling with the hem of her sleeve to produce a dingy bit of linen tied in a knot, which she undid. The little half of mother-of-pearl button dropped into her palm. She held it up between forefinger and thumb, her hand shaking. 'This is all *I* have of *my* family. No memories, only this. And I had to beg for it to get it. I keep it to remind me that I did once belong to someone.'

She turned to look up at the picture. 'I thought that if you saw them it might help you feel better about—'

'This really is not your concern.' The words were hard and cruel and intended to stop her questions. Intended to maintain his appearance of strength in the face of the guilt eating away at his insides.

Her eyes filled with hurt. The same hurt he'd seen the previous evening when he'd left her so abruptly.

Her shoulders straightened. Her chin came up. Amazed, nonplussed, by her dignity, he could only stare in silence. This woman was no longer the little maid who had polished the floors at Vitium et Virtus or the giddy girl who had laughed on the swing, she was a woman with a sense of herself.

Such strength. She put him to shame.

'I apologise. I should not have put myself forward,' she said coolly. She glanced up at the picture and back at him. 'You are right. It really is none of my business, but if I had had a family like yours, I would want the world to see them. To celebrate their lives, not hide them like some shameful secret. You don't deserve a family at all, if you cannot see that. I am done with you.'

He froze, waiting for the next words out of her mouth. The words that would part them for ever. But he could not allow it. 'You are not leaving. We have a bargain.'

Anger sparked amid the sadness in her eyes. 'I know my responsibility as well as my position.' She took a deep breath. 'I am your grandmother's paid companion. Nothing more. Henceforth, my chamber door will be locked.'

It was as if an arrow had struck his heart. She'd seen him for what he was and she no longer wanted him.

'I apologise if my words were overly harsh, Miss Nightingale.' His gaze slid up to the portrait. 'I—' The gesture of his hand expressed the impossibility of trying to explain. 'It is complicated.'

She nodded. 'Too complicated for someone like me. I understand perfectly. Please excuse my transgression, it will not happen again.'

She bobbed a curtsy much like the first one she had given him. This time, she knew it was an insult and he could only admire her nerve. 'I bid you good afternoon, Your Grace.' She swept out of the room.

He closed his eyes at the odd painful pang in his chest and the sense of emptiness left by her departure. When he opened them again his gaze fell upon the portrait everyone had said was a perfect likeness. Everyone had agreed that the artist had perfectly captured the character of his subjects.

Rose had seen it, too. What he lacked. It didn't matter that he'd done everything in his power to emulate his father and his brother, his relationship with Rose was proof he could never live up to their example. He didn't have it in him.

No wonder disappointment had lurked in the grey depths of his father's pain-filled eyes that last night. 'You really didn't expect me to make a go of this, did you, Pater?' he said to those eyes looking down on him now. 'You must have known I'd muck it up.'

He was a terrible substitute for his brother. He glanced down at the fabric in his hand. He balled up the scrap of cloth and threw it into the empty coal scuttle. 'To hell with it.' It wasn't like he could hide the truth from himself. 'I'm for the club.' And a nice bottle of Nicholas's best brandy.

Thank God he had work to do. There were always mountains of paperwork, both here and at Vitium et Virtus.

Again his unwilling gaze was drawn back to the portrait. He remembered the endless sittings, the admonishments from his father to stand his ground like a man, and Eleanor's chatter. He frowned at it.

He would leave the picture undraped as a reminder of his shortcomings and the promise to his father.

More to the point, what was he to do about Rose?

Seated at the escritoire in Her Grace's private sitting room, Rose waited, pen poised, while Her Grace reread the letter in her hand. This was their usual after-breakfast ritual. Replying to Her Grace's correspondents. For an elderly lady Her Grace certainly had plenty of letters in want of reply.

'My dearest Wellington...' the old lady said.

Rose's eyes widened. She was writing to the Duke of Wellington? The most famous man in England, after the King and the Prince of Wales? She carefully formed the salutation below the date.

After a long pause, she looked up to find her employer regarding her somewhat sadly.

'Is something wrong, Your Grace?'

The old lady's lower lip trembled. 'It is Jacob. For three days now he has been shut up in the library with his papers and his man of affairs. He doesn't even come to dinner any more and I thought things were improving.' Her brow furrowed. 'Did something happen, Rose? You seemed to be getting along so well and now you rarely look at each other, let alone speak? I had hoped...'

Rose's fingers clenched on the pen. A large drop of ink dribbled off the nib on to the paper. 'Bother.' She snatched up the sheet of blotting paper. Too late. The blot had already spread across the words she had written. 'I am sorry, Your Grace. I am afraid I shall have to start again.' She set the sheet aside to be cut smaller and used for notes and lists and drew another sheet from the pigeonhole in front of her. She readied her pen.

'You did not answer my question,' Her Grace said gently. While her eyes might be old and short-sighted, they were not in the least bit vague. She wanted a reply.

What could she say? That she had tossed him out of her bed? Hardly. Indeed, she had missed him so badly she was scarcely able to force food past her lips. Had Her Grace noticed that too?

'We had an argument.' It was the truth.

Her Grace tipped her head on one side. 'Put him in his place, did you? Hmm. Well, it might serve, I suppose.'

'I do not understand.'

The old lady's lips pursed, the wrinkles around her mouth deepening. 'I have my hopes pinned on you, Rose. Now, where were we? Ah yes. My Dearest Wellington—have you got that?'

Her hopes? What did she mean? 'Yes, Your Grace.'

'Very well, then. Let us continue.'

And continue she did for another hour. Rose's hand was cramped by the time she had returned the writing implements to their proper places and closed up the writing table. 'Will there be anything else, Your Grace?'

'Yes, Rose. I have come to a decision.' Her voice was strangely tight as if she was holding back some sort of emotion. 'I am going with Eleanor to Hertfordshire. I wish to spend more time with Lucy.' She picked up her fan and waved it briskly. 'Not to mention, it is far too hot at this time of year to remain in town.'

'We are going to Hertfordshire?'

The old lady shook her head, her gaze piercing. 'I am sorry, Rose. I will not need a companion in the country.'

Her heart shrank. The pain of it made her gasp. 'You are letting me go?'

The old lady looked determined. 'I feel it might be the best thing I can do at this point. I will let Jacob know. In the meantime, will you ask Eleanor to come and see me?'

Blinded by the hot rush of tears and unable to speak another word, Rose made her curtsy and escaped. On her way to her room, she sent the message to Eleanor by way of a footman. She knew she would never keep her composure if she had gone herself.

Did Jake know she'd been dismissed? He must do. He was the Duke. Pain carved an empty space in her chest. Loss. This was what he must have felt when his father and brother had died. How could she not have realised the extent of his pain?

She should not have interfered. She'd only made things worse when all she wanted was his happiness.

Emptiness filled her. She would always miss him.

She drew a deep breath. There was nothing she could do to change what had always been inevitable. As heartbroken as she felt, she had to think of her future, not wallow in misery.

And she could do anything she wished. Jake had shown her a different world and she had proved to herself she could be more than a scullery maid. She just wished there had been something more she could have done for him, to make him happy.

She was packing and mulling over what her next step should be when a knock came at the chamber door.

To her surprise a footman stood outside. He handed her a package. 'From His Grace.' He bowed and marched away.

Slowly she closed the door and then unrolled the fancy scroll tied with a red ribbon. It took her a while to understand what its contents meant. She sat in stunned silence. He'd bought a dressmaker's establishment and put it in her name.

Why on earth would he do such a terrible thing?

Footsore and weary, Rose arrived in the alley behind the V&V. She'd slipped out the moment she'd heard Jake leave the house at eleven. Night was a dangerous time for a well-dressed woman to be wandering the streets near St James's. But she knew her way around here far better than she had ever known her way around the fancy houses in Mayfair.

And at least she'd had the presence of mind to pick up an umbrella on her way out. It would serve to remind any man who thought to accost her of his manners. Fortunately, she knew where she was going and as always her determined stride and confident manner stood her in good stead. What a fool she had been to think Jake might actually care for her.

She'd been a convenience. His mistress. She meant nothing to him but sexual gratification.

The ache in her chest was pure foolishness.

She couldn't even blame him. She'd offered herself. No wonder he'd no respect for her or her opinions and thoughts.

She shuddered.

For years she'd convinced herself that she could earn a living as a servant and not be led astray by some handsome gentleman, as her mother must have been.

More fool her. At least the precautions she had taken meant no children would result from her foolishness. Apart from their last encounter. There had been no time. No thinking.

Surely fate would not be so cruel as to punish her for one night's forgetfulness. She wrapped her arms around her waist, huddling deeper into the shadows, thinking better of this foolish plan of hers. The familiar odours of the gutters filled her nostrils. Offal and stale food and the taste of coal smoke. This was where she belonged, not in a mansion that smelled of beeswax and lemon and roses in vases.

Which was why she was back where she had first met Jake. It was where impossible dreams had started to build themselves like castles amid the clouds. Those dreams now lay in tumbled ruins about her feet.

She almost wished she'd never met him. Never experienced the kind of joy he had brought to her life. Yet, she didn't. Not really. No matter what happened to her in the future, he would remain in her heart. There would never be another man for her. Only Jake.

A sad realisation.

With a deep breath to bolster her courage, she stepped up to the door and knocked. The porter, Ben, opened it with a cheeky grin. 'Back, are yer? Get ye in.'

When the saucy lad gave her an up-and-down look, she ignored him and kept going. Attractive in a rough sort of way, he wasn't above a bit of flirting with the girls who worked at the V&V, but he'd never previously given her a second glance. Was he somehow aware of what she had become? Could Jake have boasted of his conquest? No. She would not believe that of him. The porter was simply being himself.

She made her way down to the Green Room where a couple of dancers she didn't recognise were practising their twirls. No sign of Flo. Music and feet pounded above her head. She must be on stage. She ducked into her old quiet corner. She didn't want Mr Bell seeing her, or Mrs Parker for that matter. They'd quite likely find her something to do. She set her reticule down on the arm of the sofa and took in the cobwebs and dust. It looked as if no one had been here since she left. She picked up the broom leaning in the corner and tidied up.

The rousing crescendo above signalled the end of the act. It wasn't more than a few minutes before a torrent of girls streamed through the door with a chorus of out-of-breath giggles and the usual mutter of complaints. It felt good to be here.

Or it would, if it were not for her mission.

She poked her head out when she heard Flo's voice, grabbed her and dragged her into the secluded corner.

'Rose!' Flo shrieked. She thrust her head back out into the room. 'Hey, everyone, Rose is back.' So much for seclusion.

Several of the girls crowded into the little space. 'Rose, I missed you,' Ginny said. 'No one does hair as good as you.'

'And it's costing a fortune to get the mending done,' someone moaned.

'Where have you been?' asked a third.

'I found a new position,' she said, blushing.

A girl called Lanie, who had never been all that friendly, tipped her chin. 'I should think you did. On your back, if your clothes are any kind of clue.'

The other girls shouted her down.

'I came to speak to Flo,' Rose said. 'If you ladies do not mind.'

'Go on, the lot of you,' Flo said. 'You've had your look-see. If you don't hurry you'll be late for the next act. Rose will help me dress.' She winked at Rose.

There was some good-natured shoving and elbowing as the girls squeezed out. And from one squeak, Rose surmised there had been a pinch delivered to Lanie as well.

Flo turned her back for Rose to untie the tapes. 'How can I help you? That nob of yours treating you right?'

'He's been very kind.' She got the knot undone and started pulling the tapes free of the holes down Flo's back. She stopped at the sight of ugly bruises between her shoulder blades. 'Flo, what happened?'

'Oh, nothing. Tripped down the stairs.' She waved an airy hand.

Rose didn't believe her. 'Flo—'

'Wot about you, missy? Not got a bun in the oven, I hope?' Flo pulled the pins from her headpiece.

'A bun—' Rose gasped at the implication. 'No.'

'That's good, then. Wot did you want?'

'I don't know what to do. We argued and now I'm to leave.'

'He's probably got another girl.'

Her heart wrenched. 'Do you think so?'

'That's usually wot happens.'

Did that explain his sudden withdrawal? The picture had been an excuse. Rose eased the gown down Flo's arms and helped her to step out of it. 'Did you...? Have you seen him with someone?'

'Me?' Flo turned around. 'How would I have seen...? Who is he?'

Rose swallowed and leaned close to her friend's ear. 'Westmoor.'

'The Duke?'

'Hush. Someone will hear you.'

Flo wriggled the next costume up her body and stood waiting for Rose to fasten her up. 'Oh, Rose, you couldn't have picked a worse 'un, I can tell you.'

Her heart sank. 'Why?'

'He's a right one for the ladies, he is. Always a new one on his arm, they say.'

'You *have* seen him, then?'

'Well,' Flo said grudgingly, 'not recently. But a leopard don't change its spots, you know. Off with the old, on with the new.'

Feeling sick to her stomach, she tied the tapes off. 'Do you know if he's here tonight?'

'Oh, he's here every night, according to what I heard Mr Bell say to Mrs Parker. Stays in the office all night. Working.'

Rose knew where the office was. She'd cleaned its grate on many occasions when the gentlemen were absent. They demanded their privacy. But she had to speak to Jake. She just must. She finished Flo's hair and attached the feather plume. 'There you are. All done.'

'I really do miss you,' Flo said, giving her a hug. 'Is there anything I can do for you?'

'You can keep old Mr Bell busy while I sneak past him to have a word with the Duke.'

'Employees aren't supposed to go in there.'

'Well I am not an employee any more, so the rule doesn't apply to me.'

Flo chuckled. 'All right then. And by the way, thanks for that lovely hamper you sent over. It were a proper treat.'

'It was simply a thank you for all your kindness when I first started working here.'

A bell jangled in the corridor.

'Are you ready?' Flo asked. 'I'll have to go up in a minute.'

'As ready as I will ever be.

Flo whisked out of the door and Rose followed a few moments later. As she passed the housekeeper's door, she could hear Flo complaining loudly inside. A moment or two later and she was up the stairs and passing through the green-baize-covered door that led to the owners' inner sanctum.

When she entered the office, a weary-looking Jacob looked up. His eyes flared with something warm and welcoming. But as he shot to his feet, his expression shuttered, revealing only the cold, remote facade she had come to dread.

What little hope she had nurtured around the coming interview dwindled. So be it.

'You should not be here.' Jacob was appalled at the harshness of his tone.

Rose gave him a cold glare. 'Why not? I used to work here. Remember?'

He raked the hair that would insist on falling forward back from his face, using the time to get his brain into some sort of working order. 'You are no longer employed here.'

She flung a bundle of documents down in front of him. 'Apparently, I am no longer employed anywhere.'

She sounded angry. Bitter. He frowned at the papers in their neat red ribbon, the seal dangling off the edge of the table.

'Please, Rose, sit down so we can discuss this like sensible adults.'

For a moment, from the stubborn set of her jaw, he thought she would refuse, but then, to his inordinate relief, she sat.

He followed suit, leaning back, trying to look relaxed. As if nothing was wrong. As if he didn't want to leap across the table and kiss away her anger.

He deserved her anger.

'Tell me why you are here.' He kept his voice cool, distant, barely interested. He could not afford to show any emotion where she was concerned. When it came to Rose, passion begot yet more passion. He could not allow it ever again.

She stiffened. A scowl formed on her face. 'I came about that.' She pointed at the papers.

He curled his lips into a hard smile. 'What, isn't it enough?' An unexpected pang of disappointment struck him behind the sternum. He'd thought she'd be pleased.

She gestured impatiently. 'I want to know why you are giving it me.'

She must be more upset than he'd realised if her grammar was failing her. He wanted to hold her and tell her everything would be all right. He couldn't do it. Not if he were to retain any semblance of common sense. What he had to do was make her take his offer and go away.

Then he might be able to introduce some normality into his life.

'It is a gift, Rose,' he said with a hint of irony he despised the moment he used it. He ploughed on. 'A gentleman always gives a lady a gift when they part company. Most of my other ladies preferred jewels.'

She flinched.

He wanted to hit someone. Or have someone hit him as he deserved for causing her pain. This was for the best, though. He had to keep that in mind. He shrugged with what he hoped was idle nonchalance, though his shoulders felt tight. 'I thought you might like that better. If I am wrong, I would be happy to provide something else. Or more. Name it.' He'd do anything to make sure she was happy. Even let her go.

The fury in her eyes was a good thing, but not the underlying hurt. His fist clenched on his thighs beneath the table. Carefully he relaxed them. It would not do to show his inner turmoil.

He watched her gaze drop to the package, saw her frown. He held his breath, wondering what she would say, hoping she would take his gift. It was what she had said she wanted. That and her family which as yet he'd been unable to find. He had not given up hope on that front, but he would not say anything until he was sure.

Not that he would be saying anything to Rose on any matter. It would be dealt with through his man of business.

'So,' she said, musingly, 'when you decided on this, you thought to give me my heart's desire.'

His heart stuttered in his chest. How easily she saw through him. 'Something of the sort, I suppose. You did mention your dream to open a dressmaker's shop more than once.'

She gave a little nod of acknowledgement.

He started to relax. To feel a sense of satisfaction. She would accept his gift. Relief trickled warm along his veins.

'But you see, Westmoor,' she continued, 'it was a dream I wanted to earn by my own efforts, not have it handed to me on a plate at a mere whim.'

'You did earn it.'

The moment the words came out of his mouth he knew he had fallen into a fatal error. Knew it with every fibre of his being. He didn't have to see the scorn on her face. The repudiation. 'You have been a wonderful companion to my grandmother.' He spoke before she could get out a word.

'I received wages for that,' she spat. 'No, you said only a moment ago that this was a parting gift from you.'

'If you do not find it acceptable on those terms, then look on it as a bonus for your work with my grandmother.'

She shook her head. 'No, thank you.'

No, thank you? Just like that she was turning down a lucrative business in the heart of Mayfair? The terms were so generous, she wouldn't even need to set foot in the shop to make a profit. A manager could handle it all. He wanted to howl. He took a deep calming breath. 'You cannot have read it properly. Perhaps I should explain.'

'Do not patronise me, Jake. I do not want your parting gift.'

'Then what do you want?' Damn. He hadn't meant to ask that. Hadn't intended to give her an opportunity to set her own terms of departure. It was the sort of mistake old Prinny had made with Mrs Robinson. That of a green boy. But the words were out and he waited for what sort of punishment she had devised for him, for she was clearly furious.

It was no more than he deserved.

The wry thought pulled at his lips.

Suspicion filled her eyes. 'Are you laughing at me?'

'No. I am laughing at my own foolishness.' Bitterly.

'Wishing you'd never met me, more like.'

Never that. He had memories of her that he never wanted to forget. He had the feeling they would comfort him into his old age. As long as he knew she was happy. And safe.

'I want you to tell me why you are sending me away with this...this gift. I want to know what I did wrong. It was the picture, wasn't it? I apologised for that and you didn't even cover it up again.'

'You did nothing wrong.'

She shook her head. 'I must have.' She rose to her feet and paced in a small circle. 'But if not, then why?'

She stopped pacing, staring at the back of the door. Spun around to face him. 'That's my bonnet. The one I wore the day I met you in the garden. When I was on the swing. Why is it here?'

He stared at the bonnet. God knew he had been staring at it for days, remembering how she had laughed when he had pushed her on the swing. It was only later that he realised she must never have experienced such a thing before. And she'd let him kiss her. It had been the loveliest kiss of his life. Innocent and fresh and utterly entrancing.

'I meant to return it to you. You can take it if you like.'

Then he would have nothing of hers. Something wrenched at his chest. He pushed the thought back where it belonged. Buried it beneath the cold he used to keep pain at bay.

'You kept my bonnet.' Something glimmered in the back of her eyes. Something suspiciously bright. And come to think of it, her voice seemed a little husky.

God help him, tears would leave him undone and defenceless.

'What of it?'

She returned to her chair and sat down with her hands folded in her lap. 'You haven't yet answered my question.'

'Which was?'

'You know what I am asking. Why would you toss me out on my ear and yet give me everything I said I ever wanted?'

To make you happy.

But it hadn't made her happy, had it? For some unfathomable reason he'd made her angry. And sad.

The only way to make sure she left was to tell her the truth. Make it so she wanted to leave *him*.

'You really want the answer? You want to understand the sort of man I am?'

She said nothing, but her eyes widened. He forged ahead. 'I presume you have heard the rumour about me killing my father and brother in order to take the title?'

Her complexion paled. 'I—it was mentioned. I didn't believe a—'

'It is true.'

Her gasp of shock did not make him feel one iota better. In fact, it felt like an arrow through his heart.

But at least now she would leave him in peace.

Rose stared at him in shock. She couldn't believe, would not believe such a thing about him. 'You are just saying that to make me go away.'

His expression darkened, became grim, hard. He stared down at the desk. 'I wish that were the case.'

Why was she even bothering with him if he was going to lie through his teeth to be rid of her? Then he shot a glance at her from beneath his lowered brows and she saw the pain in his eyes. And the despair.

Why would he want her to believe such an awful thing about him? It didn't make any sense. 'How did you kill them?'

He recoiled. His expression stark with shock. 'What?'

'I heard they were on the way to Brighton when their carriage turned over. You were here at the V&V that night. The girls said so.'

'How would they know? It was a masked ball.'

'Really? You and your friends come and go from this place every day and you think no one knows who you are? They don't blab about you or the goings-on in this place because they are protecting their livelihoods. Not that it's the sort of thing a duke should be doing.'

He grimaced. 'I don't need telling what a duke should or should not do.'

'Nor are you the sort of man who would kill members of his family to gain a title.'

'It's the last thing I ever wanted.' The words came out like a sigh, as if speaking them gave him relief. His shoulders tightened almost immediately. 'But I am responsible for my brother's death.'

The misery in his gaze made her want to hold him. 'I don't understand.'

He squeezed his eyes shut and rubbed a palm down his face as if to wipe away an unpleasant image. 'It was supposed to be me in that carriage,' he said in so low a tone she could scarcely hear him.

She leaned forward in order to hear the softly spoken words and he looked down at the desk, as if too ashamed to meet her gaze.

'I should have been with my father that night,' he said. 'He asked me to go with him to Brighton to visit Prinny.'

'Prinny as in the Prince of Wales?'

'The same. The Prince needed money as usual. Father saw the chance to get him to hand over an estate that had fallen into the Crown's hands when the title died out. My father knew what Prinny did not. The value of that estate. According to Ralph, who was sent to fetch me, I was to go in his place because he had a prior engagement.

'As usual, I was my father's second choice, despite the fact that I read law at university. I'd offered my services on numerous occasions only to be told the Duchy was not my affair. Father only wanted me along to distract Prinny with gossip. One fashionable fribble entertaining another.'

Her eyes widened. Oh, yes, she would be shocked at his callousness.

'To cut a miserable story short, I told Ralph I had invited a lady guest to the annual Vitium et Virtus masked ball and was dashed if I was going to go back on my word.' He clenched his fists. 'That was the last time I saw Ralph alive. Father sent round a pretty stiff note before he and Ralph departed for Brighton. He noted my lack of filial duty, saying as usual Ralph had put the dukedom before his own amusements. Ralph died in the accident, and Father shortly after, but not before he made me promise to do my duty to the title in my brother's place. He could scarcely look me in the eye. He knew as well as I did, it was my fault Ralph died that night. It is my fault they are dead.'

He sat watching her, his expression haughty, indifferent. Defensive. No doubt he expected her to heap coals upon his head.

As if she would blame him. 'I'm so sorry.'

He frowned.

'But you know...' she glanced down at her fingers twisting around themselves in her lap '...you can never replace your brother.'

His jaw dropped. The pain in his eyes intensified. He looked away. 'I know that.'

The despair in his deep voice made her heart contract painfully.

'You should go. Take that with you.' He made a dismissive gesture with his hand at the documents.

How easily he shut her out. But somehow, before she left, she had to make him see what had become so obvious now she knew the whole story. 'Jake, you cannot spend your life thinking about the what if, but only about the what is. I learned long ago not to wonder what my life might have been like if my mother hadn't left me behind. I might have had brothers and sisters. My parents might have been cruel. Or poor. Or rich. I could imagine them for hours on end. But it wouldn't change the fact they never wanted me. All I can do is take my life as it is now.'

His eyes lifted to her face, his gaze intense. Piercing. Almost frightening. She forced herself to continue. 'I never knew your brother. But in the portrait, you seem so different from him.'

He let out an impatient sound. 'You said that before. It is not relevant.' He started to rise.

'Jake, you wear your brother like a mask.' Oh, now that really sounded as if she was a bedlamite.

It stilled him, though. He sank back into his seat. 'Rose—'

'No. The man *you* are is the man who took pity on a lonely girl waltzing in the dead of night. You are the man who gave an innocent miss her first turn on a swing and was not bored by her simple joy in one of the most amazing moments in her life. You are the man who spent an afternoon with his niece explaining a Panorama and eating ices and who made her feel loved. You are the man who took me out of the squalor of the rookeries and asked nothing in return. You are you. No one else. And who you are is a good, kind man.'

At that last, he frowned. 'I am also the man who seduced you.'

She relaxed a little. At last, he was listening. She cast him an arch smile, because he certainly did not want her pity. 'Oh? And did you hear any protests?'

He shook his head.

'And would you have seduced me had I said no?'

He grimaced.

'Of course not. You are who you are, Jake. And life can be hard. Impossibly so. But you have been given an opportunity to use yours for the good of others. To make a difference. But how can you, if you cut yourself off from who you really are?'

His face shuttered.

She unclenched her hands and realised her whole body was tense. Shaking with the passion in her words. She collapsed against the chair back. He must think her such a fool. But she would say what was in her heart or regret it for the rest of her life.

'I understand you cannot love me. Our worlds are too far apart. But please, Jake, do not hate yourself for what happened to your family. Forcing yourself to be someone you are not is hurting you badly. You are no worse or better than your brother. You are different.'

The distant expression remained on his face.

He didn't understand and she wasn't clever enough to make it any plainer. Her throat felt raw from all the talking. Almost as raw as her heart.

A sense of defeat filled her. She pushed to her feet. 'I thank you for your gift. It was thoughtful and kind, but I cannot accept it.' It was worth a king's ransom. 'I will always treasure the time we spent together.' She choked on the words and swallowed. 'I would not spoil those precious memories for anything.'

She turned to leave.

'Rose.' His voice was harsh.

She turned, expecting to see anger. His expression was tortured.

He had risen to his feet, his hands clenched at his sides. His eyes were fixed on her face again. 'Rose,' he said softly. 'If I promised to do better, will you stay?'

Startled, she could only stare. He wanted her to stay? Her heart leaped, driving the breath from her throat.

'Rose?' He came around the desk, holding his hands out for hers.

Reason overcame her joy. She whipped her hands behind her back. 'I cannot.' She shook her head and backed away. She would not stay as his mistress. One day soon he would marry. Must marry. She would not be able to bear parting from him again. She just wanted him to be happy. To be himself.

'I love you, Rose,' he said hoarsely.

'No.' Not this. Not now. 'You are a duke. You cannot be with someone like me.'

'I love you more than my own life, Rose. I should never have told you to go. Marry me.'

She turned to run for the door. On a hook on the back of

it was that sad-looking little straw bonnet with blue ribbons. She turned back to face him.

She frowned. The hat meant something. It had to. 'For a duke, you are a hopeless romantic.'

'It would seem so.' He went down on one knee and took both her hands in his, kissing each one in turn. He looked up at her with a spark of mischief in his eyes, but there was something else there, too. A great deal of love. 'I love you, Rose. You see *me*. I need you to remind me who I am. I cannot do this without you. Will you marry me? Please?'

Longing filled her chest. It was so tight it hurt. Tears filled her eyes, blurring her vision. 'How can I? I'm not even a lady.'

'You are the most beautiful, wonderful, amazing lady in the world to me and that is all that counts. Isn't that what you said only moments ago?'

'But this is different. I can't—'

'You can. You can do anything you want. Rose. Darling, dearest Rose. Can't you see? You are what I needed. Without you, I was lost.'

Blinking away the mist, she looked down into his lovely face, saw the love and slowly sank to her knees before him, throwing her arms around his neck and weeping on his shoulder. 'Oh, Jake,' she said through her sobs.

'Is that a yes?' he asked, half-joking, half-serious.

'Yes.'

He swept her up in his arms and carried to the nearest armchair where she curled up on his lap the way she always did. He proceeded to kiss away her tears, until they were both breathless.

'Darling Rose,' he murmured against her lips, 'I love you so damned much.'

'I love you to bits, Jake,' she said tipping her chin to look into his face. 'I always will.

Chapter Thirteen

The Church of St George was packed to the gunnels. After all, it wasn't every day a duke got married to a lady's companion and former scullery maid at the most debauched club in London. Though no one but Frederick had recognised her, Rose had insisted his family be told the full truth before they got married.

Jake had been worried they might not accept her.

To his surprise, Grandmother had taken it all in stride. Indeed, she had taken quite a bit of pride in her matchmaking efforts and said she always knew Jake would come to his senses and marry the gel.

Bless the old dear.

Jake couldn't have been more proud to walk down the aisle towards the waiting vicar with his bride on his arm. Lucy trailed behind them, ready to hold Rose's posy when it was time to say their vows. The pews rising up on either side of them were festooned with flowers, roses of course at this late season, and crowded with well-wishers, as well as others who simply came to gawk. The galleries above were also team-ing with people. In the very back row he'd spotted a couple of the girls from Vitium et Virtus. Rose's friends. He'd laid on a carriage for them, but he wasn't sure they would come. He was delighted that they had. Rose had so few people to call her own.

'I told you we should have had a quiet wedding at home,' Rose whispered as they approached the altar with its magnificent Venetian window letting the light flow over the awe-inspiring altar piece showing the Last Supper. Her hand trembled beneath his. While any of his friends would have been more than happy to escort her down the aisle, he'd been terrified she might turn tail and run at the last moment and he knew she wouldn't with him at her side.

He smiled at her encouragingly. 'I wanted everyone to see what a lucky man I am.'

She blushed.

The urge to kiss her welled up inside him. He glanced around. There was one person he didn't see. He'd tried everything in his power to get her to come, but she wouldn't promise. Didn't want to intrude. She had also wept copiously.

Then, as they approached the altar, he saw her sitting on the left side of the Church directly opposite from Grandmama and hemmed in between Fred and Georgiana. Today she was smiling mistily. Georgiana apparently had her in hand and shook her head at him.

She was probably right. Better to wait until after the wedding.

Oliver, serving as best man, stood waiting for them. Fred left Georgiana to join them at the steps to the altar, his task to give Rose away in place of a father.

The service went by in a blur. All he could do was watch the woman who had agreed to become his Duchess in wonder and awe. Her courage nigh unmanned him, for he had been daunted by the idea of becoming a duke and he had at least known something about it.

The vicar joined their hands and the feel of her skin through the lacy glove was icy cold. Perhaps she was not feeling quite so brave after all. He slipped the ring over her finger as they had practised and they repeated their vows.

He'd made the vicar promise not to drag it out. He didn't want Rose suffering unduly, for the scrutiny of the crowds was like a hail of arrows. Yet he didn't want anyone thinking there was something havey-cavey about their marriage, either. And finally the vicar stopped droning on and they were married. They were ushered towards the vestry to sign the register.

He caught Georgiana's eye and nodded. She helped the woman beside her to her feet.

Once they were safely away from prying eyes, Jake took that woman by the arm and led her to Rose.

The woman, a neatly dressed lady with a tidy grey bun and the attire of a gentlewoman, hung back, tears forming in her eyes.

'Rose, I want you to meet someone,' Jacob said firmly.

His bride gave him a startled look. Perhaps he had spoken a little too firmly, but he needed her attention. 'Rose, this lady is your long-lost mother.'

For a moment, he thought she might faint, her face went so pale, and her chest rose and fell so rapidly. He reached out to hold her by the elbow. 'Rose, it is all right. Sit down for a moment.'

'Mother?' she said, looking at the modestly gowned woman. 'You are my mother?'

The woman nodded. 'I am.'

Rose sought his gaze. 'You found her?'

'I did. Rose, your mother did come to the orphanage to find you. She has the other half of your token. They told her you had died. Some sort of error in record keeping. Your mother was heartbroken when they gave her the news.'

Still the woman held back. 'I should never have left you in that place.'

Rose lifted her chin. 'Why did you?'

'Your father died at sea. I had another child on the way and I had no way to feed either one. I had to work to support myself. I was a dressmaker before I married, but no one would hire me with a child. The people at the Foundling Hospital promised to care for you until I returned. Five years later, you were gone. Died, they said.'

Rose frowned. 'I was there when I was eight. Did you not ask for me? Rose Nightingale?'

'My married name is Fairclough. Your name was given as Fairclough.'

Understanding dawned on Rose's face. 'A girl around my age named Fairclough died of pleurisy.'

Jacob stemmed the fury rising in his veins all over again. 'Someone made a bad mistake. Muddled the records. It was only my man's digging around that discovered it. Rose, I am sorry.'

Rose stared at the small woman standing so hesitantly beside him, then opened her arms. 'Mother,' she said softly.

The two women clung together, weeping.

He felt awkward. He patted her back. 'I'm sorry I didn't find her before. It took time to get to the bottom of it.' Perhaps she wouldn't have wanted to marry him if she had known she had family who cared.

He stifled the thought, but Rose, as if she sensed his concern, raised her head and drew him into the circle with her mother. 'Oh, Jake, you could not have given me a better gift on my wedding day. Surely, you could not.'

And as quick as that, all was right with his world.

'Now then,' Grandmama said, moving in like a tiger ready to defend her young. 'You and your mother will have many weeks to spend together once you return from your honeymoon. Right now there is a congregation waiting to greet the Duke and his Duchess.'

Her mother stepped back. 'Indeed, Rose. Indeed. You go on. I will be here when you return.'

'You promise?' Rose visibly choked back tears.

'She will,' Jacob said. 'You can be sure of it.' Fred and Oliver would make sure of it, he could see it on their faces.

Mrs Fairclough bobbed a curtsy and smiled. 'No need, Your Grace. Never again will I be parted from my little girl.'

Rose dried her eyes on a handkerchief provided by Georgiana, and together they ran the gauntlet of the waiting congregation.

Sated and lax and lying in her husband's arms later that evening Rose pressed a kiss to her husband's raspy cheek. They had arrived without incident at Dover. Tomorrow they would take the *paquet* to Calais and from there travel to Paris.

'Thank you,' she whispered.

He rolled on his side and drew her closer to his naked body. She sighed at how well they fit together.

'All I want is your happiness,' he said.

A gentle thrill wandered its way along her spine. 'And I yours.'

A vision of the gin-raddled women of St Giles appeared before her eyes. She yawned. 'Jake, what would you have done if she had been absolutely awful?'

'Exactly what I did. No matter what, she is your mother. I despaired of finding her, to be honest. Then my man of business suggested asking the Hospital to open their records and we saw that two girl children were admitted on the same day, Rose Nightingale and Rosalyn Fairclough. After looking at both records, we interviewed one of the older wardens. She admitted the clerk at the time had been a drunkard and had messed up several entries, but that she thought they had caught all of his errors.

'But the more we looked into it, the clearer it became there might have been one mistake they had not seen. The Nightingale child was brown-eyed, for example.'

A heavy weight lifted from her heart and finally, finally she dared to believe. 'All this time I thought they didn't want me.'

'When I found her yesterday, she was so shocked, I honestly wasn't sure she believed me. I have never seen a woman so confused. She didn't know whether to laugh or to cry.'

Rose felt like laughing and crying, too. She kissed her husband's shoulder and hoped he would know how much he had eased her pain. She forced lightness into her voice, for after all, this was her honeymoon. 'It will be interesting getting to know my family when we return.'

'The other half of your family,' he corrected, kissing the tip of her nose. 'You are part of my family now, too.'

She snuggled closer to his warmth and strength. 'I really am the luckiest woman alive.'

'And I the happiest man because of you, my love.'

'I do love you, Jake.'

'I know. I love you more, though.'

She laughed.

They kissed and... Well, anyone could guess what happened next...

* * * * *

A Pregnant Courtesan For The Rake

Diane Gaston

Diane Gaston's dream job had always been to write romance novels. One day she dared to pursue that dream and has never looked back. Her books have won romance's highest honors: the RITA® Award, the National Readers' Choice Award, the Holt Medallion, the Golden Quill and the Golden Heart® Award. She lives in Virginia with her husband and three very ordinary house cats. Diane loves to hear from readers and friends. Visit her website at dianegaston.com.

Books by Diane Gaston

The Society of Wicked Gentlemen

A Pregnant Courtesan for the Rake

The Scandalous Summerfields

Bound by Duty
Bound by One Scandalous Night
Bound by a Scandalous Secret
Bound by Their Secret Passion

The Masquerade Club

A Reputation for Notoriety
A Marriage of Notoriety
A Lady of Notoriety

Three Soldiers

Gallant Officer, Forbidden Lady
Chivalrous Captain, Rebel Mistress
Valiant Soldier, Beautiful Enemy

Linked by Character

The Diamonds of Welbourne Manor
"Justine and the Noble Viscount" *A Not So Respectable Gentleman?*

Visit the Author Profile page
at millsandboon.com.au
for more titles.

Author Note

I've always considered myself very lucky to be among my fellow Harlequin Historical authors. These ladies have been a fount of information, support and, on the rare times we can gather together, sheer fun. So, I was thrilled to be invited to write a book for The Society of Wicked Gentlemen series. It was every bit as enjoyable as I thought it would be. We made a most efficient team, quick to answer each other's questions and to collaborate on our stories. Readers, enjoy The Society of Wicked Gentlemen! We loved telling their stories!

To Christine, Ann and Sophia,
my fellow Society of Wicked Gentlemen authors.
It has been a pleasure!

Prologue

Paris—1816

'He is dead?'

Cecilia Lockhart stood in the doorway of the shabby Paris room where her husband insisted she should be grateful to lodge. Sounds of babies crying, a man and woman quarrelling, and an old woman wailing could be heard from behind closed doors. The scent of cooking meat, urine and sweat filled her nostrils.

A captain of the 52nd Regiment of Foot stood stiffly in the hallway, unable—or unwilling—to look her in the eye.

'Killed,' he said. 'By a Frenchman. In a duel.' His tone was disapproving. Why not? Duelling was forbidden in the regiment. 'He apparently had a great deal to drink.'

Of course he had. What day did Duncan not have a great deal to drink?

'What happened?' she asked. 'Did he cheat at cards? Insult the French army?' Why did she bother to ask? Cecilia did not care about the reason.

The captain stiffened. 'The Frenchman apparently found Lieutenant Lockhart in bed with his wife.'

Oh.

Why that detail should have stung, she did not know. It was merely one more humiliation.

Another slap in the face.

She almost laughed at her little joke, but this stern, disapproving captain would never have understood.

'What happens next?' she asked.

'We'll bury him,' the captain replied. 'You may return home. Do you have enough money to make the trip?' He asked the question without sympathy, perhaps worried he would have to take up a collection among his fellow officers on her behalf.

'I need nothing.' Not from these men anyway. 'Do what you must, and thank you for informing me.'

He nodded and turned away. She closed the door and leaned her forehead against it. The baby cried. The old lady whined. The couple cursed each other. And the captain's receding footsteps sounded on the wooden stairs.

But for Cecilia it was as if the sun had burst through a sky of dark clouds.

She was free. Her husband was gone, never to return.

Never to slam his fist into her flesh ever again, nor throw her against the wall. No more bruises to hide. No more pain.

She had little money, no friends—Duncan had seen to that—and no one in England who would welcome her home. In a moment she might panic at being alone in this foreign country, among people who, a few short months ago, would have considered her the enemy. But for now she felt as light as air.

Free.

Chapter One

Paris—August 1818

Oliver Gregory strolled along the River Seine as the first fingers of dawn painted the water in swirls of violet. The buildings of Paris, tinged a soft pink at this time of day, were even more beautiful than in the brightness of a noonday sun. London at dawn would seem a dark maze of streets and shops.

And Calcutta... Calcutta, the city of Oliver's birth, defied description, except in words whispered in memory—Hindi words.

Oliver struggled to remember those steaming, fragrant, exotic days of his childhood and the smiling woman swathed in brightly coloured silks holding him in her arms and calling him her *pyaare bete*, her sweet boy.

In the quiet of dawn he could bring it all back. He feared forgetting even more than the depths of depression that followed. Lately his decadent lifestyle provided no ease from the blue devils.

He'd crafted his life to distract him from the sadness of loss. What better setting than a gentlemen's club devoted to pleasures of the flesh? Oliver was one of the owners of Vitium et Virtus—Vice and Virtue—the exclusive gentlemen's club he and his three friends started when they were mere students at Oxford. Vitium et Virtus specialised in decadent pleasure, whether it be beautiful women, the finest brandy or a high-stakes game of cards.

To think he'd just left a Parisian club that made Vitium et Virtus look tame. This club featured sexual gratification through pain, whether self-inflicted or inflicted by another. Vitium et Virtus included some fantasy games with one of their tall, beautiful, dark-haired women playing dominatrix, but this French club went way beyond, so far Oliver nearly intervened to stop it. He knew some people found pleasure in pain, but these Parisians flirted with death. He had no intention of bringing those ideas to their club.

His mind flashed with an image of a nearly naked man swallowing a snake. And another man running over hot coals.

Memories from India again.

A cry jerked him back to the present near-dawn morning. In the distance a swarm of street urchins accosted a woman, pulling at her clothes, their demands shrill in the early morning air. He'd seen street urchins in Calcutta rush a man and leave him with nothing, not even the clothes on his back. The dark rookeries of London posed similar dangers.

Oliver sprinted to her aid. *'Arrêtez! Arrêtez!* Stop! Stop!'

The woman lifted her arms. 'No! No!'

The children scattered.

When he reached her, she placed her hands on her hips. 'Look what you've done!'

'You are English?' He was surprised.

She merely gestured in the direction the children had disappeared. 'They've run away.'

'They were attacking you.' At least that was what he'd thought.

She gave him an exasperated look. 'They were not attacking me. I was giving them money so they might eat today!'

'Giving them money?' He turned to where he'd last seen them and back to her. 'Is that wise?'

Her eyes flashed. 'Wiser than having them starve or be forced to steal.'

He could not argue with that. 'Forgive me. I thought— Can you call them back?'

'No, they will be too frightened now. They are gone.'

He shook his head. 'I am sorry.'

She frowned. 'Another time—tomorrow—I will be back.' She turned to walk away.

'Wait.' He strode to her side. 'What is an Englishwoman doing on the banks of the Seine at dawn?'

Now mischief sparkled in those dark eyes. 'Why, I was giving coins to street children until you chased them away.'

She was lovely! Those beautiful eyes were fringed with dark lashes, and her brows, delicately arched. An elegant nose and full, luscious lips adorned her oval face. Her bonnet covered her hair, but as the sky grew lighter, Oliver saw her dress was dark blue and her hair a rich brown.

'What is an Englishman doing on the banks of the Seine at dawn?' she asked, mocking his tone.

Oliver smiled. 'Attempting to rescue damsels in distress.'

She laughed. 'You must keep searching, then. I assure you I am not in distress.'

'But I am at your service.' Oliver bowed.

She kept walking, and he kept pace with her.

She finally spoke again. 'Enjoying the delights of Paris now that the war is over?' Her tone was a mockery of polite conversation, but at least she'd not dismissed him.

'Actually a bit of business.' Although his business was pleasure. 'And you?'

'Moi?' She fluttered her lashes. 'I live here.'

He was pretty astute at perceiving the character of a person, a skill he'd honed so he'd know right away the degree to which a person might accept him as an equal or as a lesser being. She was guarding her own privacy, not giving him any information at all.

He pretended to peruse her. 'I would surmise there is quite a story about why an English lady such as yourself lives in Paris.'

She looked suspicious. 'Why do you say I am a lady?'

His mouth widened into a smile. 'It is not difficult. The way you carry yourself. The way you speak.'

She shrugged at that. 'Well, I am not telling you anything.'

And he would not press her. He understood the need to keep one's privacy, but he also did not wish to say goodbye to her. The sky had lightened, turning the water blue and the stone path to beige. He suspected she would soon leave this path and be gone.

'I have a proposal,' he said impulsively. 'Eat breakfast with me.'

She laughed derisively. 'Why would I do that? I do not know you.'

'Allow me to introduce myself, then. I am Oliver Gregory. My father is the Marquess of Amberford.' He never explained further. People who did not already know his father usually assumed he was a younger son. 'Now you know me.'

She laughed again, this time with more humour. 'I know your name. Or at least the name you deign to give me.'

'I assure you it is my name.'

Her brows rose and she nodded with exaggerated scepticism.

He spread his palms. 'I am telling you the truth.'

She cocked her head. 'It does not matter.'

'So,' he tried again. 'Will you have breakfast with me? I promise to be amusing. We can sit in the open at a café if that will ease your discomfort.'

Her expression sobered and she stared at him for several seconds, as if deciding how to respond. 'At a café?' she repeated.

'Wherever you wish. You choose where you would like to

eat.' He'd dined at Le Procope, a café that had been in existence for two hundred years. Would she choose some place as grand? He was suddenly very eager to find out.

'Very well,' she finally said. 'But you must also give me some coins for the children. They will be even more hungry tomorrow.'

He reached into a pocket and pulled out a leather purse. He loosened its strings and poured out several coins. Then he extended his hand. 'Here.'

She scooped up the coins and slipped them into her reticule. 'I know of a place we can breakfast.'

She walked him past La Fontaine du Palmier, the monument to Napoleon's battles in Egypt, in the Place du Châtelet, to a small café just opening its doors. They sat at a table out of doors. With the sun came warmer temperatures and a blue sky dotted with white puffy clouds. A perfect day.

'The pastries are lovely here,' she said.

'Pastries.' He rolled his eyes. 'Everywhere in Paris I've been served pastries and I do not possess a sweet tooth.'

'Some bread and cheese, then?'

'Ah, oui. C'est bon.' He smiled. 'With coffee.'

The waiter arrived and greeted her warmly. Obviously she was known to him. She gave him their order, selecting a pastry and chocolate for herself, bread, cheese, and coffee for him.

He watched her as she settled herself in her chair. She removed her gloves and rearranged the colourful Kashmir shawl she wore that reminded him of India. She wore a dark blue walking dress and looked as if she'd just spent an afternoon promenading in Hyde Park. Was it only the children who caused her to be on the banks of the Seine at dawn?

'Tell me what your business has been that brought you to Paris,' she asked with some evident interest.

Oddly enough, he did not want to tell her of the business that brought him to Paris lest she disapprove. He'd come to explore the decadence of Parisian gentlemen's clubs to see what they might include at Vitium et Virtus. This trip had not been as productive as the previous one when he'd found a satisfyingly buxom, Titian-haired French songstress eager to come to London to work in their club. He usually did not care if a lady disapproved of his activities. For the ladies who did disapprove of him, the gentlemen's club was the least of their objections.

'Exploring opportunities,' he responded vaguely.

'Opportunities?' Her eyes, lovely as they were, showed little interest.

He challenged her. 'You are making polite conversation with me.'

Her eyes sparkled. 'Yes. I am. But tell me what opportunities anyway.'

Those eyes distracted him. In the sunlight they appeared the colour of fine brandy and just as liquid. A man could lose himself in those eyes.

He glanced away. 'Business, you know, but nothing came to fruition.'

The waiter brought a pot of coffee, a pitcher of cream and a sugar dish, placing it in front of him. He placed a chocolate pot in front of the lady, produced two cups and poured for them.

When he left, Oliver added only some cream. He took a sip of the coffee and nodded to her. 'This is excellent.'

Her captivating eyes appeared to concur. 'It always is here.' She sipped her chocolate and made an appreciative sound.

He faced her, fingering the handle of his cup. 'The topic of business is always a boring one. Perhaps there is something else you would like to ask me?'

Her eyes flickered in surprise, then fixed on him with a challenge of her own. 'Do you mean why you do not look like an Englishman?'

He was not certain if she was asking or not.

Who was he attempting to fool? Women always wanted to know why his skin was so dark, why his hair was so dark. She simply was more direct than most and much quicker.

'See. You are wondering why the son of a marquess looks like something spawned on a foreign shore.'

'Am I?' Her brows rose. 'Or is this what you desire to tell me?'

He paused, unsure of his own motivation. He did want to tell her, though, he decided. 'My father is the Marquess, but my mother was from India.'

He waited. Usually the women with whom he spent the most time found his looks exotic and appealing but, then, such women were typically interested only in sharing the pleasures of the night with him.

Ladies of the *ton* with marriageable daughters steered them away from him, however. Even though they knew he was wealthy. Even though some of those same ladies did not mind sharing his bed.

She took another sip of chocolate. 'That does explain it. Were you born in India?'

'I was. I left when I was ten.' He would not tell her everything about his birth and those first ten years of his life. He never talked about it, although many who knew his father knew some of it. His partners in Vitium et Virtus knew nearly all and they'd accepted him as an equal since their days at school.

'You must remember it then.' She sounded truly interested now.

'I do.' He'd been remembering it that morning when she appeared.

'Tell me,' she said, licking off the chocolate from her lips and nearly driving India from his mind.

'I remember the sounds and the smells and all the bright colours,' he began.

He told her about the man charming the snake and others

sleeping on a bed of nails or walking over hot coals. He told her of the music and the singing and dancing, of statues and paintings of gods. He talked of fragrant gardens and cool houses with pillows.

He did not tell her about his mother. Or about how his father shared his time between his Indian house and his English one on the other side of the garden.

'I cannot imagine it,' she said, her face alight with animation. 'I would love to see such a place some day.'

His insides clenched in a familiar pain. He would never return there, never see those sights again.

He made himself smile. 'Is Paris not enough for you?'

Her expressive face turned sad before she composed it again. 'Paris...has not been unkind.'

How much was hidden in that statement?

The waiter brought a flaky confection filled with whipped cream and jam for her and, for him, a selection of cheeses and a loaf of bread still warm from the oven.

She nibbled on her pastry. 'There is much beauty here in Paris. I gather some of the buildings, statues and art were almost lost during the Revolution. We can credit Napoleon for preserving them.'

'If we must,' he said, smiling wryly.

He was gratified she smiled in return.

'I have seen very little of the city,' he went on. His hosts had taken him to places where pleasure was more valued than architecture. 'And now I have only today left.'

She lowered her pastry from her lips. 'You have only today?'

'I leave tomorrow.' Somehow that information did not seem to disappoint her. 'Tell me what sights I must see before I leave.'

Again her face animated. 'Notre Dame, for certain. It is the most impressive and beautiful church one could ever see. The Louvre, as well. It is a beautiful building filled with beautiful art that once graced the houses of the aristocracy before the Revolution. And I suppose one should see the Palais-Royal. It is now filled with shops and restaurants.'

She went on to describe these sights in more detail as they finished their meal and drank the last of the coffee and chocolate. He paid the waiter and reluctantly stood. He could have remained all day in her presence, even though she'd told him nothing about herself. She wrapped her shawl around her, despite it being warm enough now to go without.

'Thank you for breakfast,' she said. 'I did enjoy it.'

'As did I,' he added.

'I suppose I must say *adieu*.' She did not look happy about it, though.

'I suppose...'

They left their table, but stood together on the pavement. The city had come alive while they'd eaten. The streets were full of carriages, horses and wagons. The pavement was abustle with workmen, servant girls, children and a few finely dressed gentlemen.

He held her elbow and guided her away from the fray.

Then he took her hand. 'Do not say *adieu*. Stay with me. Show me the sights you have so wonderfully described.'

Cecilia glanced into his face. He had a memorable one—as handsome as any woman could wish. That was not what captivated her, however. Duncan had been handsome. After Duncan she'd learned not to be seduced by a handsome face.

His complexion was darker than one would expect from an Englishman. Knowing he was half-caste explained that. His hair was as dark as the night, worn longer than fashionable as if he did not trouble himself to visit the barber overmuch. His eyes were unexpected, though. They were hazel, the kind of eyes that changed colour from green to brown with the hue of his coat. When he fixed his gaze upon her she had the feeling he could see inside her, directly to her thoughts.

Perhaps that was why he asked her no questions about herself. He asked nothing of her, but shared about himself. What other man of her acquaintance would tell of his life before age ten? Duncan certainly had not.

What harm could there be in spending the day with him? She had no other obligations for today and he was leaving tomorrow. She liked his foreign looks and she relished the sound of his English accent, so familiar, so reminiscent of home. He was an easy companion, agreeable, unhurried and undemanding.

With those enthralling eyes.

Her hands started to shake and her knees grew weak, not from his allure, but from her decision. 'I will show you Paris.'

He smiled and her knees grew weaker.

'We should start at Notre Dame,' she said quickly lest he notice he affected her. The famous cathedral was close by, its spire and towers visible from where they stood.

As they neared Notre Dame, she said, 'Before we go inside, we must walk around the cathedral, because it looks very different from each side. You would hardly know it is one structure.'

They first faced the western façade, looking up at its symmetrical towers and carved stone. From where they stood they could see only the tip of the spire.

Slowly, they walked around to the north side. 'See the rose window? How big it is? You will be astounded when we see it from the inside with the sun illuminating it.' They continued walking. 'You can see now how the cathedral is in the shape of a cross. All cathedrals are in the shape of a cross.'

He smiled at her. 'You are quite knowledgeable about this.'

'I suppose I am.' She felt suddenly self-conscious.

She often had days free and the cathedral had become one of her favourite places. Sometimes she wandered for hours inside it, especially when she needed to feel peaceful.

They continued what was a fairly long walk around the building. The Seine was behind them, not too far from where he'd chased away the poor street children, busy now with boats and barges transporting people and goods up and down the river.

'Flying buttresses,' he pointed out, then smiled. 'See? You are not the only one who is knowledgeable.'

Humour. It was as welcome as the clear summer air. She so rarely experienced the levity of humour. She could not help but return his smile.

They concluded their walk around the cathedral, talking of its architecture, and finally went inside. As they entered the church, the bell tolled the hour, its sound echoing against the stone walls.

Cecilia loved the inside of Notre Dame, loved the colours the rose windows cast upon the interior. Oliver Gregory seemed interested in everything she drew his attention to. Was he pretending? If so, he was very good at it.

Others filed into pews and soon a priest and his attendants appeared at the huge altar. They had come at the time of the Catholic Mass.

'Do you mind if we stay?' she asked. There were so many English people who would abhor attending a Catholic Mass.

'Not at all,' he said.

They chose a pew in the back, but with a good view of the altar.

She liked the ritual, a little like her church at home, but different as well. Watching and listening to the Latin service drove other thoughts from her mind and calmed her. It made her forget the strange way she made her living and how lonely she was.

When the service was over he clasped her hand. 'I am glad we stayed.'

They walked around the cathedral some more, marvelling at the windows, peering at the statues until they had seen enough.

As they came towards the long aisle to the door, she stopped him. 'My name is Cecilia.'

Surely it would not hurt to tell him her given name.

She had never told anyone in Paris her real name, not since the day the captain came to tell her Duncan was killed, but she wanted this man to know. For one day she wanted to be herself, as she might have been had she never fallen under Duncan's spell.

This lovely man beside her did not act as if she'd said anything unusual by giving her name so abruptly.

'If I am to call you Cecilia,' he said in a matter-of-fact tone, 'you must call me Oliver.'

'Oliver,' she whispered.

'Cecilia.' He smiled.

It was not the done thing for a gentleman and a lady to call each other by their given names, not unless they grew up together from childhood. She'd known him only a few hours, but still it seemed natural that they should do so.

'We should go to the Louvre next,' she said.

The Louvre was another place Cecilia visited when she needed to remind herself that there was incredible beauty in the world. She loved the Renaissance art, especially the portrait called *La Gioconda*. She tried to imagine any other man of her acquaintance walking through the museum without any sign of boredom.

Was this man—Oliver—really what he seemed? Or was he pretending, hiding his true nature? Every day she pretended to be someone she was not. Every day she hid her real self. Today, though, she would be her real self, even if he were not.

When they again stepped outside, they could hear the bell of Notre Dame strike four o'clock, reminding her of when Oliver had last eaten.

'There are restaurants at the Palais-Royal, if you are hungry.' She was accustomed to going without food.

When she'd followed the drum with Duncan, she'd been allotted half his food rations, but when he could, he ate her portion as well as his own. She'd quickly learned not to complain.

'Do you wish to eat?' he asked.

Throughout the day, he'd checked on her wishes before stating his own, she noticed. Another technique of seduction? Or did he truly wish to fulfil her desires?

'I know it is country hours, but I am quite famished,' she admitted.

'Then we must eat.' He offered her his arm and they leisurely walked to the Palais-Royal, once the home of the Duc d'Orléans and, earlier, Cardinal Richelieu. The *palais* was not far from where she earned her money.

No. Cecilia Lockhart, who strolled by the side of this English gentleman, earned no money.

That was the job of Madame Coquette.

Chapter Two

The restaurant Oliver chose was the Beauvilliers, with its tables covered in white linen, shining silverware and sparkling crystal. He had dined there once already during his visit.

'This restaurant is very expensive,' Cecilia warned him as they were led to a table in a private corner.

'Do not concern yourself,' he told her. 'I can afford it.'

He was used to ladies' eyes kindling with greed when realising he was wealthy, but Cecilia merely nodded sceptically.

He laughed. 'I assure you, Cecilia. Order whatever you desire.'

After they were seated he said, 'There is something to be said about *liberté, égalité, fraternité*. I have yet to have any Paris high servant or shopkeeper regard me with disdain.'

She looked surprised. 'That happens to you—being regarded with disdain?'

'Because of how I look. Like a foreigner.' In England, members of the *ton* and their servants often peered down their noses at him. It happened often enough in London shops as well.

'I do not think you look all that remarkable,' she said.

He laughed. 'Thank you... I think.'

They perused the printed menu with its numerous choices for each course, deciding to begin with an onion soup followed by a platter of oysters and sausages. For the main course they chose beefsteak, then an entrée of duck. They could have ordered additional courses of fish and roast poultry or veal, but Cecilia said she would burst from that much food. Each course was accompanied by a different wine.

'This meal reminds me of dinner parties at home,' she said over the soup.

This was the most information about herself that she'd divulged yet. This was an aristocratic meal, so it was likely she came from an aristocratic family.

'Home meaning England?' he ventured.

Her expression sobered. He surmised she debated how much to disclose.

'Surrey,' she replied.

He smiled inwardly. It was as if she'd bared her soul to him.

'We were practically neighbours, then,' he said. 'My father's estate is in Kent.'

They went on to taste the oysters and sausage and sip the wine before she spoke again. 'I am not welcome back in Surrey. My family disowned me when I ran away to Gretna Green to marry.'

This was a great deal to divulge and it made him sad for her. He knew how it felt to lose someone.

He was also disappointed to hear her mention a marriage.

Oliver usually did not care much about the details of a woman's life, not the least of which was whether or not she was married. The woman's apparent character and disposition of the moment were enough to satisfy him, but his reaction to this woman was different. He was intrigued by Cecilia. Maybe because she kept information about herself so close to her chest, he wanted to know all about her. Mostly he wanted to know what experience had put that sadness in her eyes. Had it been that Gretna Green elopement? Being disowned by her family?

He would continue to tread carefully, though.

'They disowned you,' he repeated as neutrally as he could.

'My parents declared my husband to be unsuitable.'

He certainly knew that feeling. Most noble parents felt Oliver was unsuitable.

'My husband thought they would come around if we were married. He thought my father would relent and turn over my dowry—but my father never did.' She finished her glass of wine. 'My husband had no fortune, no name to speak of, but he was dashing in his regimentals.' Her voice turned sarcastic.

'He was in the army?' he guessed.

She nodded. 'That is how I came to be in Paris. His regiment was ordered to Brussels and I came with him. After the battle at Waterloo, his regiment marched into France and, ultimately, Paris.'

Oliver had honoured his father's wishes and had not purchased a commission. He regretted that decision to this day. He should have been fighting along with his friend Frederick.

She nodded as the waiter filled her wineglass again. 'The battle was a horrific thing!'

'You witnessed the battle?' He was shocked.

Oliver had been there, too. At Waterloo. Unable to enlist, he'd gone to Brussels to be a part of it all, like so many others. Brussels had been filled with the British aristocracy and British tourists at the time. On the day of the battle he and other spectators rode to the site where the troops were amassed. Never had he felt so helpless as he watched the carnage unfold. Cecilia would have witnessed horrors no woman should ever see.

She took a long sip of her wine, and her voice turned to a mere rasp. 'So many men killed.'

Oliver had done what he could to pull wounded men off the field, but it had never felt like enough. After he'd returned to London from Brussels, it had taken him a long time to again lose himself in the pleasures of Vitium et Virtus. In fact, he'd never quite managed to free himself of Waterloo. A part of him always remembered the sights, the sounds. The agony.

'I saw the battle, too,' he told her.

Her eyes turned wary. 'Oh? You were in the army?'

'I was not.' He pushed the food around on his plate. 'My friend Frederick was, though.'

'Did he live?' she asked.

'Yes.' He lifted his glass to his lips. 'Thank God.'

They had barely touched the oysters and sausage, but the waiter removed those dishes and brought the beefsteak, smothered in sauce. Another bottle of wine was opened and new glasses poured.

'And your husband?' he asked. 'What happened to him?'

She shrank back as if his question had been an attack. 'In the battle, do you mean?'

'Yes.' He had meant in the battle, but suddenly realised he wanted to know so much more.

'He came through without a scratch.' She sounded disdaining.

Oliver cut a piece of his beefsteak and brought it to his mouth.

She tapped the stem of her wineglass with her fingernail, making the crystal ring. 'My husband died here in Paris. In a duel.'

'A duel?'

'Two years ago.' She did not say more about the duel. 'Since I was no longer welcome at home, I stayed in Paris.' She drank her wine.

Oliver knew she was not the only British expatriate to find living in Paris more affordable than London.

She turned her attention to her food, apparently consumed by her own thoughts, but it seemed that she was pulling away from him. Perhaps she'd regretted confiding this much to him. He would not press her for more, no matter how he yearned to know.

Finally, she spoke again. 'But what of you, Oliver?' Her tone was defensive. 'I have said all there is to say about me.'

He doubted that. 'There is little to say about me.'

She smiled, but he still felt she'd gone back into hiding. 'Surely you do not expect me to believe that.'

'It is true. I'm a simple man with simple tastes.' He lifted his wineglass, filled with fine, expensive wine, in an ironic salute.

'Come now, Lord Oliver.' She wagged a finger at him.

He frowned. 'I am not Lord Oliver.'

Her brow furrowed. 'But you said your father was a marquess.'

'He is, but I have no honorific.' He was admitting himself to be a bastard.

Understanding dawned on her features. Understanding. Not distaste.

He went on. 'My father was not married to my Indian mother, as you have no doubt surmised.' He was a bastard son—his father's only son. 'But he brought me with him to England when he assumed the title.'

His mother had been an Indian *bibi*, a mistress. A prostitute. The love of his father's life, his father had often said. But his father left her behind when he unexpectedly inherited the title, something his British wife had insisted upon. His wife had also promised to raise Oliver as if he were her own son—a promise she broke as soon as she could.

'Did you ever see your mother again?' she asked.

'No.' He poured himself more wine. 'She died.'

Oliver's mother died shortly after he left India. She died before the ship Oliver sailed on even reached England. His stepmother told him she'd lost her life giving birth to another of his father's bastards. So he'd believed he'd lost a mother and a brother or sister.

It wasn't until he was a young man that his father told him that story was not true. His father had to show him the letter he'd received from India for Oliver to believe him. His mother had died, but from a fever—or perhaps from a broken heart.

Cecilia's face filled with sympathy. 'I am so sorry! How very sad for you.'

He took a gulp of wine. 'It was long ago.'

She had not commented on him being a bastard. She'd hardly blinked at that information. He was not sure why he'd even told her. He never spoke about that. Or about his mother.

He had the illusion that they were old friends who knew each other well and could trust each other. As he knew and trusted Frederick, Jacob...and Nicholas, wherever Nicholas might be. Not dead. He'd never believe Nicholas was dead. The fourth founding member of the gentlemen's club had simply disappeared from Vitium et Virtus one night six years ago, leaving only a pool of blood in the alley and his signet ring.

'I still miss my family.' Her voice turned low. 'Even though—' She stopped abruptly and stabbed at her meat. 'Never mind. It is foolish to wish for what one can never have.'

'I could not agree more.' He lifted his glass as if in a toast.

He turned the conversation to something less emotional for them both—the sights they had seen that day, their favourites and least liked.

Pretty soon the dessert was served, profiteroles and *éclairs* and finally coffee and liqueur.

When they left the restaurant, the shops were still open. To walk off the sumptuous dinner they strolled under the galleries and through the gardens. The Palais-Royal was filled with people and the shops were busy.

Oliver was accustomed to giving gifts to ladies whose company he enjoyed and all the ladies he knew received his gifts eagerly. He wanted something to commemorate this day, this companionship that had been unlike any other he'd experienced.

When they came upon a jewellery shop, he stopped. 'Let us go in.'

She accepted the idea impassively and he was surprised. Most ladies would surmise they were about to receive a gift.

They gazed at necklaces and bracelets with diamonds, emeralds, rubies and garnets, but he could not discern any special interest on her part.

'Beautiful, are they not?' he tried, hoping she would give him a clue as to what she might like.

'Oh, yes,' she agreed dutifully. 'Quite beautiful.'

He pointed out several other pieces, but she showed less interest than she had gazing at the paintings in the Louvre or at the stained-glass windows of Notre Dame.

Finally, he faced her. 'Do you not realise, Cecilia, that I wish to buy you a gift? I am trying to discover what you would like.'

'A gift?' Her voice turned wary. 'Whatever for?'

'To commemorate our day together.' So she might remember him as he would remember her.

She stepped back. 'And what will you desire in return?'

He was startled. 'In return? Why, nothing. It is a gift.'

Her eyes narrowed as if she did not believe him.

'Heed me.' He took a chance at touching her arm. 'This has been a most special day. You've shown me sights I would not have seen nor would have appreciated had I been on my own today.'

He probably would have slept half the day and made his

way to one of the dancing halls or casinos at night. In her company, he'd lost any interest in either.

One of the glass cases displayed gold lockets and other less expensive pieces.

He pointed to a necklace consisting of a single pearl on a long gold chain. 'Let me buy you a token, then? In thanks for this day?'

She still looked leery, but she said, 'Very well.'

He caught the attention of a clerk and purchased the necklace with the coin in his purse. As the clerk opened the glass case to remove the necklace, he turned to her. 'Earrings to match?'

The corner of her lovely mouth quivered as if she was trying not to smile. 'No. Do not say more or I will change my mind.'

No woman of his acquaintance would threaten to refuse a gift, especially such an inconsequential one. It was even less of a gift he might bring to Jacob's sister or her young daughter.

Nothing about this fascinating lady was like other women he knew.

Cecilia glanced into Oliver's hazel eyes, so unexpected paired with his darker skin, but so captivating she had to glance away again. He placed the gold chain around her neck, her skin tingling where his fingers touched as he worked the clasp. Stubble shadowed his cheeks, and his scent filled her nostrils. His face was so close she could feel the warmth of his breath.

She knew this feeling, this attraction that made her want to run her hands over his stubble-roughened chin or plunge her fingers into his hair. She'd once felt a similar attraction to her husband as she felt now. This carnal aching inside her.

She'd forgotten that erotic sensation, but she had not forgotten that just because a man attracted her like a moth to a flame did not mean he was decent or honourable. It did not mean he would not change from loving to...hurtful.

'Thank you for the gift,' she managed.

'My pleasure.' His voice turned low.

He finished fastening the necklace and put an inch more space between them, enough that she could see his smile, which had its own power over her.

'It looks fine,' he said. 'In fact, against your skin, it is even more pleasing than against the black velvet of the glass case.'

As compliments went this was a mild one. Did he know that a more flowery compliment would have driven her away even faster than an expensive gift would have done? Was he that clever to know precisely how to chip away at her defences?

For long moments during this day she had been able to believe he was just as he seemed—gentlemanly, kind, generous—but every once in a while her guard flew up again. Like when he asked about her husband. Like when he wanted to buy her jewels. Somehow, even in those moments, he managed to find a way around the walls she erected to keep from ever being at the mercy of a man again.

They left the shop and strolled out to the gardens, where it seemed there were many gentlemen and ladies engaged in flirtations. That only made her worry again. Was he merely charming her or was he what he seemed to be?

'Do you know what I would like to do now?' he asked.

Some wariness crept in. 'What?'

'I would like to walk along the Seine like early this morning. There is still an hour or so before the sun sets. I watched it rise there; it would be nice to see it set.'

What man desired walking? Duncan had once seemed to enjoy the strolls they took away from prying eyes when he was trying to ingratiate himself with her, but after she married him, he wanted nothing to do with walking. Just bedding.

But, then, that was all she'd wanted at first, too.

'I should go home.' Best she part from him while she could still think and before he did something to burst the illusion that he was a perfect gentleman.

They left the Palais-Royal.

'I will escort you home, then,' Oliver said.

'It is not necessary.' She did not want him to know that she lived in a small room near the theatres, casinos, gentlemen's clubs and *maisons closes* or houses of prostitution.

He frowned. 'I would feel remiss to merely send you on your way alone.'

'I was alone when you met me,' she reminded him.

'Still, I would not forgive myself if any harm came to you.'

She made a face. 'How would you know? You leave tomorrow. We will never see each other again.' Her throat tightened at her words and she feared tears would sting her eyes.

He gave her an imploring look. 'All the more reason not to say goodbye so soon. Stay with me to watch the sunset.'

Those captivating eyes seemed to pull her in.

What harm would it do? Besides, she wanted to stay with him; she wanted to keep this lovely illusion that such a kind, handsome, charming man existed, a man who wanted nothing from her but her company.

'Very well,' she said. 'I will stay with you to watch the sunset.'

They walked through the Paris streets to the stairs leading to the Seine. There were walkways on both sides of the river with other couples strolling, street vendors plying their wares, other men and women hurrying to and fro.

'I am glad to walk off my meal.' He patted his stomach.

'It was delicious.' The best meal she'd had since Brussels three years ago when Duncan had taken her to fine restaurants.

Then Duncan received the letter from her father saying he would never provide her dowry or any money at all. After that everything changed.

But it had not changed in a day. Certainly not in an evening. So, perhaps she could pretend Oliver could be trusted to be a gentleman for one evening.

As the sun dropped lower in the sky, the evening took on a magical quality.

Oliver seemed to catch the magic as well. 'I had been told of the beauty of Paris, but I confess I did not believe in it...' He paused and looked down at her. 'Until this day.'

She fingered the pearl that nestled almost between her breasts. 'You have more than paid me back.'

He touched her arm and made her face him. 'This was not a gift for recompense, but for remembrance.'

As if she would be able to forget him. A man who behaved as a friend and stirred her like a lover.

They resumed their stroll. 'I have been here almost three years and I cannot tire of its beauty.'

The conversation that had come so easily to them when they were sharing the sights lost its ease. There was too much she wished to conceal. Let him think she was an English lady living on a small income here in Paris. Sometimes she felt that was exactly what she was.

She did not fit into this Parisian world any better than he must fit into the British aristocracy. Perhaps that was why she was so drawn to him.

'You told me earlier a little of India, but do you remember what it looked like?' she asked, truly wanting to know about the distant foreign land that was in his blood. 'I have read it also is a beautiful place.'

He took several steps before answering. 'I remember lush gardens filled with fragrant flowers and pools of water. My mother's house was filled with colour, woven carpets, fragrant sandalwood, and soft cushions instead of chairs. My father's house, on the other hand, was typically English. He wore his *jama* when with my mother, but on the other side, he dressed like he'd come from his tailor on Bond Street.'

'What is a *jama*?' she asked.

He laughed. 'A bit like a dress, actually. I wore a *jama* as well. They were cooler than British clothes.'

She threaded her arm through his and rested her head against his shoulder. All the wine they'd consumed made her languorous—and loosened her control. 'Tell me something else about India.'

'I remember the streets of Calcutta being crowded and noisy and alternately perfumed and putrid.' He paused. 'I remember elephants and camels and scantily dressed men charming snakes.'

'Snakes.' She shuddered.

He went on talking about spices and tigers and Hindu gods. His voice lulled her and her eyes grew heavy. It was so comfortable to hold his arm, to lean against him.

To not be alone.

He stopped and put his arm around her. 'You are falling asleep. Time to take you to your home.'

Leave him? She should never have agreed to walk along the river with him. The alchemy of the setting sun turned the sky into yellows and oranges, making the water appear to sparkle with gold. She felt its riches and dreaded going back to the emotional deprivation that was her life.

'Not to my home,' she murmured.

'Where to then?' His voice vibrated inside her.

'To your hotel.'

Cecilia knew precisely what she was saying to him. What she was offering. She wanted to pretend a little longer. She wanted everything that she thought she'd have with her husband, even if for only a night.

'Are you certain?' he asked. 'This is not the wine speaking?'

The wine had given her courage. 'I do not want our night to end, Oliver. I want all it can offer us.'

She did not want the magic to end.

Chapter Three

They crossed the Place Louis XV, which had been called the Place de la Concorde after the Revolution, and walked to Rue Saint-Honoré to where Oliver's hotel, Le Meurice, was located. A doorman opened the huge wrought-iron door for them and the attendant in the hall greeted Oliver by name. Other guests passed them without comment.

In London, a gentleman would have had to sneak a woman up to his room or risk being asked to leave the hotel. In Paris, no one took any notice.

Oliver led Cecilia up the three flights of stairs to his room. It was a comfortable space with a sitting area and a separate bedroom and dressing room. His valet stayed in a room next door and would come only if Oliver summoned him.

Oliver opened the door and stepped aside for Cecilia to enter. She walked to the centre of the room and stood as if uncertain she wanted to be there.

He closed the door and removed his hat and gloves. 'Are you wishing I had walked you home instead?'

She turned to him, looking surprised.

He softened his voice. 'It is not too late, Cecilia. I will take you home if that is what you desire.'

She pulled off her own gloves and removed her bonnet. 'I do not desire you to take me home.'

He stepped forward to take her shawl. His fingers skimmed her determinedly squared shoulders.

'Then tell me why you suddenly seem as taut as a bow-string.'

'Do I?' She attempted a smile, which disappeared as quickly. 'I was remembering something...unpleasant.'

He put his arm around her and guided her to the sofa. 'Come sit and do not think of unpleasant things. I will pour us some champagne.'

He was filled with desire for her, which had surged when she proposed coming to his hotel. He'd been on fire ever since. But she was different from other women he'd pursued. She was not a conquest; he liked her too much.

She was mysterious and sad, but strong, as well. He wanted to know why. He wanted to know everything, so he could make her smile again.

She gazed around while he opened and poured the champagne. 'This is a lovely room.'

He recognised, after this whole day, that she relied on typical society conversation when her guard was up. He knew many women who knew of no other kind of conversation, no matter what.

How was he to put her at ease?

He handed her the glass of champagne. 'It looks remarkably like a room in the Clarendon Hotel on Bond Street, but then, Le Meurice is known to cater to British visitors.'

'It is quite comfortable.'

Oliver felt as if he was losing her.

He sat next to her on the sofa. 'Cecilia, nothing will happen here that you do not want. I have enjoyed this day with you. I will not spoil it now.'

She smiled wanly. 'You must think me very absurd. To offer myself so blatantly, then to act like the silliest ninnyhammer.'

He met her gaze. 'Explain it to me.'

She glanced away and her breathing accelerated. 'I—I do not frequent the hotel rooms of gentlemen by habit.'

He was glad of that, even though he could not say he did not occasionally entertain women in hotel rooms.

She finished her glass of champagne, and he refilled it.

Then he put his hand on top of hers. 'You have promised nothing by coming here, except to spend time with me.'

She gazed at him sceptically.

He smiled. 'Nothing.'

Her eyes softened. 'May I truly believe you?'

He looked her in the eye again. 'I do not lie. I abhor lies.'

She held his gaze for a long time.

He took the champagne glass from her hand and set both glasses on the table next to the sofa. 'So...how do we begin?'

Her lashes lowered and then opened again. She looked directly into his eyes. 'With a kiss?'

He smiled. 'I believe I can comply.'

He gently lifted her chin with his fingers and moved slowly, coming closer and closer until his lips touched hers.

Her lips were soft and warm and they trembled under his. With all his resolve, he held himself back when every fibre of his being wished to pull her body against his and deepen the kiss.

It was she who moved. She wrapped her arms around his neck and came closer. He leaned back and she slid on top of him. Her lips had become hungrier, and he was only too glad to appease her appetite. She opened herself to him, straddling him and pressing against his groin. He was already hard, wanting all of her. He pressed her to him and parted his lips to allow her tongue access. She tasted of champagne, but more intoxicating. His senses reeled.

He could take her here, he realised. Merely unbutton his trousers and free himself to enter her, but he wanted so much more than a speedy release.

He lifted her off him and stood, sweeping her into his arms. 'The bedchamber?' he asked.

She nodded.

He carried her into the bedchamber and lay her on the bed. Making short work of removing his coat and waistcoat, he leaned down for another kiss, which she willingly accepted.

She watched him as he next pulled at his boot, trying to remove it. The boot stubbornly stuck to his foot and he cursed it beneath his breath.

She laughed, a deep, genuine laugh that made his insides quake in joy for it.

She reached for him. 'Let me pull them off for you.'

He climbed on the bed, and she took hold of his boot, twisting and wiggling it before finally pulling. The boot came free.

She grinned at the victory.

She pulled the other boot off with as little difficulty.

He came to his knees. 'Now I shall help you.'

He turned her around and undid the laces of her gown and carefully lifted it over her head, folding it before placing it on the floor. Next he untied her corset and helped her slip out of it. She turned to face him and reached for his shirt, pulling it over his head. He jumped off the bed and removed his trousers and drawers.

She remained seated on the bed, dressed only in her shift, pulling pins from her hair. It tumbled to her shoulders as she watched him, naked before her.

He was accustomed to the appreciative gazes of the women he bedded, but Cecilia set his senses afire.

As she could obviously tell.

He smiled again and twirled his finger at her.

She looked puzzled for a moment, then her brow cleared and she smiled back as she drew her shift over her head. He knew she would be lovely. All creamy skin, narrow waist, full breasts.

'You are a beautiful woman, Cecilia,' he said with complete honesty.

She blushed an appealing pink.

He approached her slowly, climbing back on the bed and lying next to her, drawing her into another kiss, stroking her fine skin, fingering the rich waves of her hair. She touched him, too, placing her palm on his chest, sliding her hand lower to his groin. To his surprise and delight, she wrapped her fingers around his shaft, though it made his resolve to go slow a challenge.

She slithered up to place her lips against his ear. 'How long do you intend to wait?'

Cecilia knew she was behaving wantonly, but she did not care. The wine had loosened her inhibitions and this man had made her yearn for lovemaking. In the early days of Duncan's seduction, he had shown her these erotic delights. She remembered aching for him so acutely she'd have done anything for him. Now she knew it had been his way of making certain she would marry him.

Those early days of lovemaking awakened her to the pleasures of the flesh. She had no doubt she would gladly succumb to such temptations over and over if only she could be certain that the tide would not turn.

Coupling could be transcendental or it could be...brutal.

Since Duncan she'd never taken the risk. Until now.

One night was not too much to ask, was it? One night to re-experience corporeal delights?

'How long?' she whispered again.

He turned his head to face her. 'I should ask first if you have the means to prevent a child?'

She'd not had to worry over that with Duncan. 'I know what to do.'

He smiled teasingly. 'Then have your way with me, Cecilia.' He rolled onto his back.

She immediately climbed on top of him, but, unlike his words suggested, he was not passive. He grasped her by the waist and guided himself inside her. She gasped at the sensation.

Together they moved, forming a rhythm that built her need. He was a skilled lover, she could tell. He knew just how to move her to intensify her sensations. It seemed to her that he also knew just how long he could draw this out to put her into a frenzy.

A pleasurable frenzy.

She felt the change in him, the moment he lost all thought and was in the throes of lust. His thrusts quickened, pushing her to the brink of frustration until her release came in like a lightning storm. She cried out with the acute pleasure just as his release came. His cry joined hers. He held her tight until the wave of pleasure washed away and her body turned the consistency of soft butter.

She collapsed beside him. 'Well, that was rather nice.'

He laughed softly, but the laugh resonated within her. 'I feel damned with faint praise.'

'And assent with civil leer?' She knew that poem. 'Epistle to Dr Arbuthnot' by Alexander Pope.

He countered. 'And without sneering, teach the rest to sneer.'

She smiled. He knew the poem as well.

'Willing to wound, and yet afraid to strike,' she added.

He finished it. 'Just hint at a fault and hesitate dislike.'

She returned his smile. 'What nonsense, to recite that poem after making love.'

He feigned an innocent look. 'You started it.'

She loved this bantering. Would it not be lovely to have a man who always found some lightness and humour wherever he went?

He reached over to her necklace and fingered the single pearl. 'I do not have faint praise, Cecilia. Mine is rather loud, I fear.'

She grew warm all over again. 'I am glad I accompanied you to your hotel.'

His smile grew slowly. 'As am I.'

He turned on his side and pulled her into a kiss that ignited her senses all over again.

This time he rose over her, entering her again and moving slowly as if savouring the experience. As if trying to make the moment as pleasurable as possible for her.

She was glad she'd allowed herself this liberty, this lapse in the tight control she exerted over herself. She'd lived in the winter of her emotions for too long. How lovely it was to let the sun shine in.

As he moved, her need built slowly, a glorious need because it held the promise of fulfilment at the end. All her senses came alive, awakened after a long hibernation. She was delighted she could still experience this pleasure.

And she was delighted with this lovely man who bestowed it like a gift.

His thrusts accelerated and her thoughts flew out of her head, replaced by sensation. Need. Growing. Nearing its promised end.

Her release shattered inside her, sparkling like the sunlight on the rose windows of Notre Dame. Then the release came again and again. And again when he spilled his seed inside her.

He collapsed on top of her, and she relished his weight upon her for the moment he remained there. Before he made it hard for her to breathe, he rolled off her, pulling her into another kiss and another.

He finally faced her, twirling a lock of her hair in his fingers. 'Ah, Cecilia. Words fail me.'

She merely snuggled against him, relishing the scent of him and the warmth of his skin against hers.

'I wonder,' he began.

She could feel his voice through her body as well as hear him with her ears.

'I wonder,' he said again. 'Perhaps I might extend my visit...'

A *frisson* of fear raced up her spine. No. That was not what she wanted. One day, he'd said. One night. More time together and what could happen?

One night did not seem like enough to her either, though.

She did not answer him, instead closed her eyes and let herself drift into sleep. Another pleasure—sleeping naked next to the man who had just joined with her.

She could still pretend for a few more hours, even if he wished to extend that time into days. She was determined not to let go of this wonderful illusion until she absolutely must.

Oliver, too, drifted to sleep with the thought that he had no real reason to start his journey back to England so soon. What would a few more days hurt? Frederick and Jacob could manage things until he returned. One more week would not matter.

He slept deeply, content to hold Cecilia in his arms.

When he woke it was to a loud knocking on the door.

'Sir. Sir.' It was his valet knocking. 'The coach is due in an hour. You must rise now.'

Oliver shook himself awake and sat straight up.

He turned to the space in the bed beside him.

Cecilia was gone. Her clothes were gone.

'Sir!' His valet knocked again.

'One moment,' he answered, climbing out of bed.

He searched to see if she'd left him a note, but there was

nothing in the bedchamber. He entered the sitting room and searched there. To no avail.

There was nothing to indicate she'd ever been with him.

He had no way to find her. No surname. No address.

Perhaps he could find her on the banks of the Seine, giving coins to the children. He must dress quickly. He ran back to the bedchamber and grabbed his drawers, managing to don them as he started towards the door to let his valet into the room.

A glance towards the window depressed his spirits. The sun was high in the sky. He'd slept through most of the morning. She would not be on the banks of the Seine giving coins to street urchins. She would be long gone.

'Sir! Sir!' his valet cried.

'Coming!' He walked to the door and opened it, and knew he would never see Cecilia again.

Chapter Four

Cecilia had left Oliver's bed at dawn and hurried to the river to pass out the coins to the children who, hungry, flocked to her.

Now when she met the children she would be reminded of him for ever. She'd see him running to rescue her. She'd see his smile and remember his laugh.

How would she be able to sit in Notre Dame, listen to the bells, witness the Mass, without remembering him at her side, seeming to understand the special aura of the place? When she gazed at her favourite paintings in the Louvre, would she not think of him standing next to her, listening to her enthuse about what she loved about the work?

As she'd walked back to her room, she fingered the pearl next to her skin. The memory of him would always touch her if she wore the necklace.

How good it was that the memory of her day with him was a happy one. She so much relished having a happy memory to replace the unhappy ones from her past.

On her way she stopped at an apothecary to buy the items

necessary to keep from getting with child. She returned to her room afterwards.

Her room was about half the size of Oliver's sitting room in the hotel, but it was as clean and as cheerful as she could make it, with a pot of flowers she'd impulsively bought from a vendor and the lace curtains on the window it had taken weeks of saving to afford. She reached behind her to untie her laces so that she could pull her dress over her head and folded it carefully.

Next she removed her corset and set about using the items from the apothecary.

When first married to Duncan, she'd pined for a baby, but it did not take long for her to pray a child would never happen. She'd learned what to do to prevent it. Too many times, though, she could not clean herself afterwards. Still, she did not become *enceinte*. She'd concluded his punches had damaged her and she could not conceive. At the time she thought it a blessing.

After completing her task, Cecilia climbed on her bed and burrowed under the quilt she'd crafted from scraps of cloth collected during her years of marriage. Sewing the quilt had helped her endure. It was her prized possession, her badge of honour.

Her mind drifted as she lay on her bed. She'd slept only briefly the night before. In Oliver's arms. Most of the night she'd gazed out of the window, keeping herself awake so that she could be sure she'd rise before him and make her escape.

She'd waited until the first light of dawn appeared, then slipped out of his embrace where she'd felt warm and safe. As quietly as she could she searched for her clothing, scooping it into her arms and tiptoeing to the sitting room to dress. On a table had been a stack of Oliver's calling cards. She took one as a souvenir of the man with whom she'd spent this wonderful day. When she was fully clothed, except for her shoes, which she still held in her hands, she peeked in the bedchamber one last time, for one last look at him.

So handsome. His face was relaxed in sleep, which only accentuated the perfection of his features. His dark hair was in wild disarray. She stared at him a long time, committing his image to her memory.

As if she could ever forget him.

He'd proposed more days together. He'd tempted her especially when her body had still been humming with the pleasure he'd brought her. But she knew she'd reached her limit with one day. One glorious day.

More time was too great a risk. More time making love with him would only bind her to him, a cord that could bring delight, but also great pain. More time and she'd likely fall under the spell of his charm. More time and she might convince herself that she needed him. Before she knew it, he would be able to control her every move. He'd change. Become brutal.

She'd never go through that again.

Even so, as she lay on her small bed, she yearned to be held by Oliver again. He'd opened a door that she'd thought closed for good—one that Duncan had slammed on her—and how was she to lock those feelings away again?

She would, she vowed. She must.

That night Cecilia entered the club through the rear door. The Maison D'Eros was located near the Palais-Royal, which, at this late hour, became quite a different place from the one she'd strolled through with Oliver. She was glad Oliver would never know she was a part of this world. At night courtesans, departing from the theatre, promenaded with their patrons. Prostitutes strolled, hoping to attract clients.

Cecilia might have been one of those unfortunate creatures had she not been rescued by Vincent, her one French ally. When Vincent found her that first desperate night at the Palais-Royal, she'd spent her last *sou*. Her search for employment had been futile. No Frenchman wished to hire an English lady for any reason—except the most wretched and shameful one. So she'd been reduced to that circumstance that night.

Until Vincent took pity on her.

Dear Vincent, the one man she felt comfortable with. Vincent was like a bosom beau and unlike anyone she'd ever met before. A man who adored womanly things, but preferred men to women. He was the very safest sort of ally. He took her under his wing and brought her to the Maison D'Eros, talking the manager into letting her serve drinks for tips.

'You must flirt with the rich gentlemen so that they buy more drinks and pay you more tips,' Vincent had told her, then he showed her how to do it. She managed it by pretending she was someone else, not Cecilia Lockhart. The men started calling her Coquette, so she became Coquette.

Coquette was brave. Coquette could tease men and put them in their place. Coquette could laugh at their silly jokes and admire their braggadocio. Coquette could sing bawdy songs and dance seductively. Coquette spoke only French.

Soon men were begging for her favours and Vincent devised another plan.

'I have a way you might become the rage of Paris! Paris's most selective courtesan!' he'd said to her one night.

She'd been scraping by on her tips. 'I told you, Vincent, I do not wish to be a courtesan. Bedding strange men is abhorrent to me.'

He'd sighed. 'Abhorrent to you, but my greatest pleasure.' He'd placed his hand to his heart for a moment. 'But, never mind. You will not have to bed anyone.'

'How can one be a courtesan without the bedding?' she'd asked.

He'd explained it to her.

And so Coquette became Madame Coquette, Paris's most

selective courtesan, selling her favours a mere two nights a week—without selling her favours at all.

Tonight Vincent greeted her in the back room wearing a purple coat, a deep blue waistcoat and a bright yellow neckcloth—his work costume. His blond hair curled around his boyish face and his lips and cheeks were tinted a pale pink.

'Madame Coquette, *chérie!*' He kissed both cheeks in his flamboyant manner. 'You look ravishing.'

'As do you, *mon cher.*' She kissed him in kind.

'Who do you entertain tonight?' he asked.

'Monsieur Legrand.'

Legrand was a wealthy merchant who had made it a point to ingratiate himself with those in power during the restoration of the monarchy. It was said he courted favour with the Duke of Wellington, but now, with the Occupation near to its end, he'd turned to Frenchmen who were likely to come to power. Procuring a night with Madame Coquette was, no doubt, part of how he intended to impress.

'Legrand,' Vincent repeated. 'He is no challenge at all. You will wrap him around your little finger in no time.'

Her brow furrowed. 'But Hercule will remain nearby, will he not?'

Hercule, large, strong and intimidating, was employed as a flash man to make certain none of the working girls suffered mistreatment. He stayed within shouting distance in case things did not go as planned.

'But of course.' Vincent threaded her arm through his. 'Time to turn yourself into Madame Coquette.'

They walked up the servants' stairs to a room on the first floor where the dresser arranged Cecilia's hair and applied just a light dusting of rouge on her cheeks and lips.

'What dress today, Coquette?' the dresser asked.

'The red, I suppose.'

The red gown was made of fine silk, its neckline, sleeves and hem trimmed in gold embroidery. The neckline dipped lower than what Cecilia would wish, but it was perfect for Madame Coquette. Her gowns were fine enough for a high-priced courtesan, but they were not hers. The manager of the club paid for them.

Once in her gown and slippers, Ceclia said *au revoir* to the dresser. In the hallway with Vincent, there was nothing left to do but meet her customer.

Vincent held her by the shoulders and looked her in the eye. 'Deep breath!' he commanded. 'Breathe in, Madame Coquette!'

She took a deep breath, closed her eyes and let herself become her alter ego.

Lifting her chin, she opened her eyes again and nodded to Vincent who turned her towards the door that led to the drawing room and gave her a little push.

With a slight sway to her hips that had not been there before, she entered the drawing room and made straight for Monsieur Legrand as if she were eager to be in his company.

He gaped at her as she approached him, almost spilling his glass of wine and only remembering to stand when she drew near.

'Legrand,' she said in a voice deeper than she usually spoke, emphasising the *grand*. 'It is my pleasure to entertain you tonight.'

Legrand was a man in his fifties, who obviously enjoyed the fruits of his labour. His round stomach strained at the buttons of his waistcoat, which was well tailored and made of the finest cloth. His nose had the red hue of someone who enjoyed too much wine and his neck disappeared behind his jowls. Yet he displayed himself to her as if she would find him irresistible. No wonder so many courtesans had their beginnings in the theatre. It took a great deal of acting to convince a man such as this that his company was desired.

He'd paid a great deal for this night with her, although the manager of Maison D'Eros took the lion's share. Her goal was to save enough for a modest living somewhere, ideally back in England, for which she was always homesick—even more so since spending the day with Oliver. It would take her a long time to amass such a sum. Years, perhaps. She'd been building Madame Coquette's reputation over the last year and a half and she had little more than what travel expenses to England would cost her.

'Shall we retire to my room?' she asked, taking his arm.

'Yes. Yes,' he stammered.

She led him up to the second floor to a room that was not exclusively hers. Others, including Vincent, used it on other nights of the week.

She gestured for Legrand to open the door and she swept by him to enter the room, decorated in red-silk drapery on the walls and white and gold damask upholstering the *chaise* and sofa. The tables were mahogany embellished with gold and Egyptian motifs made popular by Napoleon's invasion of Egypt. On the tables were crystal decanters of wine and brandy, bottles of champagne, and plates of grapes and cheeses. Prominent in the room was a large bed, its covers and canopy in a white fabric similar to the upholstered *chaise* and chair, trimmed in gold fringe.

Cecilia's silk red gown was perfect for the room. She looked as if she were part of the room's decoration.

Legrand closed the door and lunged for her, throwing himself at her and slamming his lips against hers.

She pushed him away. 'Monsieur Legrand!' She spoke with great indignation. 'How dare you attack me like—like you are a hound in heat. I will not stand for such disrespect!'

'Forgive me, *madame*.' He grovelled. 'I could not help myself. The mere sight of you lights a fire in me that can never be extinguished!'

She straightened her clothes. 'Well, I suggest you compose yourself immediately. Remember the bargain, *monsieur*. You have paid for my time, but that is all. You must win me over if you want any more of me.'

This was the brilliant ruse Vincent had thought up for her. Her customers were required to make her want to bed them. And if she wanted it, she promised them rapturous satisfaction.

Of course, she never wanted any of them.

'What might I do to please you?' Legrand asked.

She lowered herself onto one of the sofas. 'First you may pour me some champagne and amuse me with your repartee.'

'Yes. Yes.' Legrand nearly tripped over his own feet in his haste to reach the champagne bottle and open it.

The champagne always made being Madame Coquette a bit easier.

Legrand babbled of once meeting and advising Talleyrand, the French politician who'd managed to operate at the highest levels of government through Louis XVI, the Revolution, Napoleon and now the Restoration.

As if Talleyrand would accept advice from such a ridiculous man.

'Talleyrand.' She made a sound of derision. 'He is the one no one trusts completely, is that not so? He is a traitor to France. Am I to admire you for associating with a traitor?'

If Legrand had vilified Tallyrand, she would have praised Tallyrand as a great statesman of France.

Because, no matter what Legrand said or did, she was not going to be pleased by him. He would never win her over. That was the point.

Legrand continued to try, attempting to impress her with his wealth and his success as a merchant. Cecilia could almost feel sorry for him, except he was willing to pay for a woman's favours, merely to impress his compatriots.

Conversation inevitably came to an end and Legrand began spouting flattery. '*Madame*, your beautiful skin makes me long to touch you. You are the most ravishing of Paris courtesans. I would have paid double for this night with you. Triple. And considered it worth every franc.'

Cecilia wished her price had been negotiated higher. This was something to discuss with the manager, who might be underselling her services.

'You flatter me, *monsieur*,' she said, dipping her head and fluttering her lashes the way Vincent had shown her.

His expression turned eager. 'Please, I beg you, *madame*. Sit with me.'

'With pleasure.' Cecilia girded herself and moved to the *chaise*.

Legrand put his arm around her. 'This is much better. Much better.'

She pretended to sigh. 'Would you pour me more champagne?'

'More champagne?' He sounded both surprised and disappointed. 'As you wish.'

'For you as well.' She smiled sweetly.

He opened the second bottle of champagne and poured two glasses, handing one to her.

She tapped her glass against his. 'To this lovely night.'

He puffed up with hope. 'This lovely night.'

He drank the contents in one gulp and put his arm around her again. As Cecilia slowly sipped hers, he stroked her arm, then became bolder and put his hand on her thigh.

'May I kiss you?' he asked while he performed the greater indignity of kneading her thigh.

She took her time to drink the last of her champagne, then smiled. 'Of course you can!'

He placed his dry, thin, fleshless lips against hers and held her in both arms.

She made herself remain still for a moment, before starting to cough. And cough. And cough.

He released her. 'What can I do? More champagne?'

She nodded, still coughing.

His hand shook while he poured another glass of champagne. She grabbed it from his hand and drank as if desperate for it.

When she'd composed herself again, she apologised. 'Forgive me, *monsieur*. I—I tried...' She let her voice trail off.

She positioned herself for another kiss and Legrand eagerly complied. This time he opened his mouth.

She made a sound and again pushed him away. 'Did you clean your teeth, *monsieur*?'

'My—my teeth?' He looked befuddled.

'I am sorry, but your mouth—the taste, the smell—it makes me cough.' She reached for her champagne again.

He cupped his hand near his mouth and exhaled, trying to smell his own breath.

'I cannot kiss you, *monsieur*.' She frowned. 'I am so sorry.'

He moved towards her. 'We can proceed without kissing.'

She allowed him to touch her, to fondle her breasts, to run his hands down her body before pushing away again. 'It is no use, *monsieur*. I am certain you are a very fine gentleman and I am so very impressed by your wealth and your importance, but I must feel something for the men I bed. They must stir me and you—you do not.'

He looked as if she'd slapped him.

This was the dangerous moment. When the man was filled with lust, but spurned. This was when Hercule might be needed.

'I am very certain this has never happened to you before,' she said. 'You are such a fine gentleman. I do not know what is wrong with me.'

He puffed up again. 'Never happened before. Never. Women like me. Many women.'

'I am certain they do,' she said soothingly.

He gave her a hopeful look. 'Perhaps we can proceed anyway? I will not hold it against you if you do not—do not get pleasure from it.'

'Monsieur Legrand!' She pretended to be horrified. 'You wish me to bed you without feeling on my part?'

'Well...'

She shook her head. 'No. That is not what I do. Remember the bargain?' The rules set forth for a night with Madame Coquette were very specific. 'I must want to couple with you and now, I simply cannot. I will have another coughing fit and I know you would not wish me to have another coughing fit.'

'No...' He rubbed his face. 'I told all my friends.'

'You told your friends that you had arranged a night with me?' she asked.

He nodded, looking horror-struck.

She reached over and patted his hand. 'It is not your fault. It is entirely mine.' She always tried to take the blame. She had no wish to humiliate the men, although with some of the more unpleasant ones, it was tempting.

'No one will believe that.' His lower lip jutted out like a hurt child. 'Some of them are here tonight. In the card room. If they see me leave early—'

'You must not leave early, then!' she reassured him. 'We will stay the whole night, until just before dawn. Will that do?'

He seemed to be considering it. 'Just before dawn. That might work. My wife will expect me home about then.'

The men always had a poor wife waiting at home.

'And you must tell your friends whatever will impress them,' she added. 'I will never say anything but that my time with you was incredibly passionate. I will say I was impressed by your skill—because I am sure I would be, if it were not for my awful cough. Because of the smell.'

'You would be, that is very true.'

She patted his hand again. 'I am very sure I would be.'

He flushed with pride, as if he really had given her incredible passion.

Cecilia was always surprised how easy it was to talk these

gentlemen out of bedding her by complimenting their supposed prowess. What the man's friends thought of his night with her was always more important to them than the act itself.

'What will we do all night?' he asked.

She opened a drawer and pulled out a deck of cards. 'We can play piquet!'

Chapter Five

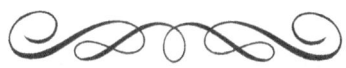

November 1818, three months later

Oliver leaned against the wall in the billiard room of Vitium et Virtus, watching Frederick and Jacob knock the balls in the pockets of the green baize table. The day's weather was cold and drizzling, but the fire in the fireplace kept the room comfortably warm. Frederick was meticulously lining up his next shot, taking long enough that Oliver began tapping his foot.

'Just take the shot, Fred,' he said impatiently. 'This fuss does you no good.'

Frederick ignored him and continued to study the ball some more before placing his cue and executing a perfect shot, sending Jacob's cue ball and the red ball into the pockets.

'That's the game,' groaned Jacob.

Frederick looked up and grinned. 'Does me no good, Oliver?'

'You would have made it without all that fuss.' Oliver picked up his cue and stepped up to the table while Frederick retrieved the balls from the pockets.

Jacob flopped in a chair. 'That is the second game you've won over me.'

'You were distracted.' Frederick turned his grin on the new duke. 'Thinking of your bride, no doubt.'

Jacob laughed.

It was gratifying to see Jacob happy. Oliver had often caught Jacob spending the night hours at Vitium et Virtus, drinking and looking more haggard by the day.

Jacob had been reeling with grief over the accident that killed his father and brother, and lamenting that he was not up to the enormous responsibility of a dukedom.

But then Jacob met his Rose.

Oliver wished them well. He really did.

He wished Frederick and Georgiana well, too.

Both Oliver's friends were obviously besotted with their wives. When Oliver saw them with the women, the loving looks and tender touches between them reminded him of the many gestures of affection he'd long ago witnessed between his mother and father.

But his father had still left his mother behind in India.

Obviously love fled in the wake of expediency. Once gone, love could destroy.

Oliver sincerely hoped the love shared by Frederick, Jacob and their wives would not be so easily shattered. But he would not wager any money on it.

And he was known to wager on almost anything.

Oliver stood next to Frederick and they hit their respective cue balls simultaneously to see who would have the first shot. Oliver's ball stopped closest to the baulk cushion. He went first, hitting both Frederick's cue ball and the red ball.

Oliver concentrated on the billiards. That was what he liked about games or any competition. He could focus on winning and push all other thoughts out of his mind. Unfortunately, Frederick's careful approach to billiards gave Oliver too much time to think.

He frowned and crossed his arms over his chest.

'Back to discussing my wife,' Jacob said in good humour. 'I highly recommend marriage.'

'As do I.' Frederick continued to eye the ball. 'You should try it, Oliver.'

'Not likely.' Oliver's reply came quickly.

'You will change your tune.' Frederick continued to consider the placement of his cue. 'Once you meet the right lady.' He finally hit the red ball and sent it into a pocket.

Did Frederick not see how easily his marriage to Georgiana might have turned to misery? Oliver held his tongue, though.

He took his shot and this time sent Fred's cue ball into a pocket.

'Maybe he already has.' Jacob rose to pour himself some brandy. He turned to Oliver. 'The mysterious Parisian lady.'

Cecilia.

'Nonsense.' He regretted telling them of her, not that he'd said much, and it had taken him some time to divulge even that meagre information. He never discussed the more private elements of his time with women.

'You cannot tell us you do not think of her,' Jacob persisted. 'You've been different since that trip. A veritable malcontent.'

'I dispute that statement.' Oliver tapped his foot, impatient over Frederick's care in executing his shot. Or at least that was the reason he told himself his toe was tapping.

Frederick finally hit the ball. 'I agree with Jake. You've been moodier. And what lady was your last conquest? No one since Paris.'

Frederick was right, of course. 'You assume too much. Perhaps I do not tell you of my every liaison. Perhaps I am discreet.' Oliver took his shot and missed.

His friends exchanged knowing glances.

He played the rest of the game in disgruntled silence. And lost.

Oliver refused to believe that the brief encounter with Cecilia had sent him into this funk. Perhaps the cause was because he'd not accomplished his goal in Paris. He'd not found very much new to offer at their club. Nothing, at least, that was not distasteful to him.

Too much of Vitium et Virtus was becoming distasteful to him.

But that was a worry that had preceded his trip to Paris.

He must admit that the memory of Cecilia did linger in the recesses of his mind. A church bell would call back the image of her in Notre Dame, the sun through the rose windows bathing her face in colour. One of the lady patrons of the club wrapped her Kashmir shawl around her shoulders, just as Cecilia had. Their new French songstress had Cecilia's colour hair.

Reminders were to be expected, were they not? Yet surely that bore no special significance.

'Another game?' Frederick held up a cue ball.

Jacob stood and picked up a cue.

Oliver poured himself some brandy and lowered himself into a chair. The room had been designed for their comfort, his, Jacob, Frederick and Nicholas. The richly carved oak panelling on the walls came from a German monastery. The billiard table, with its fine green-baize surface, filled the room's centre, but around it were the most comfortable chairs in the club and enough tables and cabinets to hold the ever-present brandy. The chandelier's many candles illuminated the billiard table so play could continue all night, if desired.

Very occasionally they offered billiard tournaments, the prize of which was some debauched spree, but most of the time this room was for their own amusement. Oliver preferred it that way. Increasingly he was preferring the days Vitium et Virtus was closed and he had time to himself.

He, Frederick, Jacob and Nicholas began the club back in their Oxford days. It was secret, exclusive and naughtier than the Hell Fire clubs of their grandfathers. Vitium et Virtus also lacked the Hell Fire clubs' anti-religious affectations. No black mass for Vitium et Virtus. No devil worship or paganism or ridiculous rituals. Their club worshipped pleasure and excess, in card-playing, drink and fornication. It had been their highest accomplishment at the University.

When they left Oxford, they brought the club to London.

What did Oliver care that he was not welcome at Almack's? He belonged to Vitium et Virtus.

Life had been good right up until that night six years ago when Nicholas disappeared, leaving only a pool of blood and his signet ring in the alley behind the club.

Oliver, Frederick and Jacob had kept Vitium et Virtus running for Nicholas's sake, but for how much longer? Frederick and Jacob were now married. What honourable gentleman runs a club of Dionysian revels when his wife is waiting at home?

Oliver would keep it going by himself, if necessary. To him, giving up on Vitium et Virtus was like giving up on Nicholas. He refused to believe Nicholas was dead.

He finished his brandy and poured another.

Enough blue devils.

'I do have one new idea for the club,' he began.

Jacob grinned. 'Nothing that involves driving hooks through one's skin and hanging from ropes.'

Oliver had told them of the self-mutilation and flagellation of some Paris clubs.

'Not unless you wish to try it,' he shot back.

Jacob held up both hands. 'Not me!'

'We could have a Vitium et Virtus ball.'

'Oh, that is original,' Frederick said.

'Not the usual sort of ball.' Oliver rose and picked up one of the billiard balls from a pocket. 'We have two baskets of balls like these, only each ball has a number painted on it. There are matching numbers for men and for women. The men pick from the men's basket and the women from the women's. Then they partner up with the person whose number matches theirs. No one knows ahead of time who their partner will be.'

Frederick straightened his spine. 'Georgiana and I will not play.'

Jacob laughed. 'Nor will Rose and I.'

Oliver shook his head. 'Of course not.' In truth, he also had no desire to play that game. 'I think several of our members will relish it, though. We know many married couples who would clamour to be first in line to play.'

Frederick turned back to his game. 'You manage it, if you like, but you had better make certain everyone knows what to expect.'

'What if Bowles shows up?' Jacob asked.

Frederick missed his shot.

Nash Bowles was a nasty fellow they'd known since their Oxford days, who'd joined before they'd become more selective. He'd lately pressed to purchase Jacob's share of the club.

Frederick's lips thinned. 'That reprobate.'

Bowles was the reason Fred had married his Georgiana. Vitium et Virtus had held a virgin auction which was supposed to have been a total farce. The women usually auctioning their wares were certainly no virgins, but instead, those who loved the sexual excess of the club. Instead, respectable, well-bred Georgiana Knight, a viscount's daughter, had climbed up on the table and offered herself. Frederick had bid on her, intending to protect her reputation.

'Bowles.' Fred spat out the name like a piece of rancid meat. 'He had better behave himself or he will answer to me.'

Bowles had threatened to ruin Georgiana for her escapade at Vitium et Virtus unless she married him as her father wished.

Honourable Frederick married Georgiana instead, to rescue her from Bowles. And somehow Fred and Georgiana had fallen in love with each other.

What were the chances that marriage would remain blissful? Especially since Georgiana was so free-spirited.

And how long would Jacob remain besotted with Rose? He was a duke and she had been a maid here at Vitium et Virtus. How long before Jacob left Rose like Oliver's father had left his mother?

'You two should go home to your wives,' Oliver said. His friends had better do right by those good women or they'd have to answer to him.

'I was thinking the same thing,' Fred said.

Jacob looked pensive. 'I was thinking how lucky I am to have this happiness. And how much I wish Nicholas could share in it.'

'Nick.' Oliver's voice rasped with pain.

He placed his hand palm up on the billiard table. Jacob and Frederick placed theirs on his. 'In Vitium et Virtus,' they recited together.

They'd been schoolboys when they first contrived this oath, resurrecting it after the night Nick vanished to remind them that they were still four. Nicholas was somewhere, Oliver insisted. And somehow he'd find his way back to them.

They broke apart, and Frederick poured more brandy. He lifted his glass in a toast. 'To absent friends.'

Oliver and Jacob raised their glasses.

'Be he in heaven or hell—' Oliver continued, a refrain they'd repeated several times in the six years Nicholas had been gone.

'Or somewhere in between—' Fred added.

'Know that we wish you well.' Jake ended it.

If only words could magically bring Nick back.
They downed their brandy in silence.

After Oliver said goodbye to his friends, he made his way to the back door, the private entrance used only by him and his friends. The drizzle persisted, so he dashed across the garden and out the gate, through the alley and the garden of the town house on Bury Street adjacent to the club. Oliver's town house. How lucky he'd been to be wealthy enough to buy a town house so conveniently located to Vitium et Virtus.

When his father became the Marquess of Amberford and inherited the property and riches to go with the title, he'd settled the fortune he'd acquired in India on Oliver, a fortune great enough that Oliver could live more than comfortably. He could afford many pleasures. Fast carriages, matched horses, beautiful women.

Funny that Oliver used to fear he'd be poor. When he was a boy, his father's wife often threatened to put Oliver out on the streets. Eventually he learned about his fortune and that she could not touch it. When his father was not present, she was always nasty to Oliver. He'd absolutely believed he could be tossed out onto the streets like Cecilia's street urchins—

Cecilia.

Again she popped into his mind unbidden. For the last three months the memory of her caught him at odd moments. Why should she inhabit his thoughts so often? He'd only known her one day.

Perhaps the brevity of their time together had enhanced the experience, made it grander, magical. It had seemed as if she'd appeared out of the mist and disappeared as quickly. No liaison of his had ever begun so unexpectedly and ended so abruptly.

He reached the garden door of his town house and went inside, brushing the raindrops off his coat and hair. He greeted his cook and housekeeper as he passed the kitchen and made his way up to the hall where his butler stopped him.

'Sir, you have a caller,' the butler said.

'A caller?' Oliver rarely had callers. He was not on society's circuit of people whose favour one must court.

His butler, only a decade older than he, leaned closer. 'A lady. She declined to give her name.'

Oliver's brows rose. 'You do not know her?'

Irwin typically had an excellent eye for faces and names, especially ladies' names.

He shook his head. 'She has been waiting over an hour.'

'An hour?' What lady would wait an hour for him? 'Why did you not simply say I was out?'

Irwin appeared affronted. 'I did say you were out. She insisted upon waiting.'

Oliver was always very careful that the ladies with whom he associated knew precisely the nature of the relationship. He did not want any of them to consider him so important they'd waste an hour waiting for him.

Irwin inclined his head towards the drawing room. 'She waits in there.'

Oliver shrugged. He might as well discover who it was.

He opened the door, startling the woman who sat upon the sofa facing the fireplace. She stood and turned to him.

For a moment Oliver could not breathe.

'Cecilia.'

Chapter Six

Cecilia had forgotten how his presence affected her. His handsome face. His masculine grace. His riveting eyes. Unwillingly, her body flared in response to him. She'd not wished to seek him out, but what other choice did she have?

He hurried towards her. 'But why are you here? How did you know—?'

'Where to find you?' She finished his question and felt somewhat embarrassed to admit to the answer. 'I took one of your cards before I left. It gave your direction.'

She was wary of him, of how he would respond to her, of his reaction to what she must tell him.

To her surprise, he softened his voice. 'I am delighted to see you, Cecilia. What is wrong? You seem distressed. Do you need my assistance?'

She had to turn away from him. From his kindness.

'I never intended to come to you. I went first to my parents—my mother—' Her voice cracked and she blinked away tears. The last thing she wanted was to weep in front of him. She wrestled her emotions back in control. 'My mother and father refused to see me. I am dead to them, you see.'

She'd yearned for her mother. When everything fell so completely apart in Paris, she'd desperately yearned for her mother. She'd wanted to be enfolded in her mother's arms and soothed and told everything would turn out all right. So many times after Duncan had beaten her she'd wished for her mother's arms, but when Duncan was alive, it had been impossible. This time, though, with Duncan dead, she thought perhaps her parents would forgive her. She'd travelled first to their country house only to be told they were in London.

She then went to London, but they refused to see her.

You are dead to them, their butler, a man she'd known since childhood, had frostily told her.

So she came here. To Oliver.

She'd always known that her ruse as Madame Coquette would end some day. One night the man who'd paid for time did not fall for her excuses. He'd tried to take what he wanted. For a few frightening moments, it was as if her husband had returned from the dead to again force himself on her. Hercule had burst in and stopped him.

The club manager had not been amused. When he learned what really transpired with Madame Coquette, the manager gave her an ultimatum. Provide what the men desired or leave.

Give the manager control over her? No man would control her ever again. Although a part of her despaired, she'd told the manager she would leave. She begged Vincent to look after the street urchins, sold her meagre belongings and her beloved quilt, and journeyed back to England to a mother who refused to see her.

Now her money was rapidly running out. Now she was forced to put herself at the mercy of another man.

Oliver.

'Tell me how I may help,' he said without hesitation.

She faced him again. 'I need money.'

'Money.' His voice turned cautious. 'Am I to know why you need money?'

She took a deep breath and pressed her hand to her abdomen. 'I am going to have a child.' She fixed her gaze on him. 'Your child. And I do not have funds enough to take care of the baby.'

He looked stunned—and not pleased.

'A baby.' His eyes flashed. His entire demeanour changed. 'You said you would take precautions.'

She lifted her chin. 'I did take precautions.'

'This cannot be!' He began to pace. 'Are you certain?'

'Am I certain?' she shot back. 'Am I certain I took precautions? Yes. Very certain. Am I certain I am with child? Yes.'

So much for kindness from Oliver, apparently. Well, she had endured disappointment before. Kind, loving Duncan had turned violent towards her as soon as life became difficult. Why expect Oliver to be different?

She'd thought nothing could hurt as much as being turned away by her parents. Nothing could make her feel so totally alone, so desolate, but now she realised just how acutely she'd hoped Oliver would not fail her. She'd hoped he'd be that man he'd been for one day and night in Paris.

She should have known he would not. How could he be glad she was carrying his child?

'Heed me, Oliver.' She directed her gaze at him. 'I did not want this to happen any more than you did. I tried to prevent it, but my efforts failed.'

He rubbed his face as he prowled back and forth. 'Are you certain I am the father?'

Cecilia felt her face grow hot. What man would not use this excuse to avoid his duty? 'Yes. You are the baby's father.'

Although, it made sense he would expect her to be with other men. She'd fallen into bed with him after only a day, had she not?

'Am I to believe you?' he said in an ill-tempered voice. 'One night. Three months ago?'

'I thought this consequence extremely unlikely. I'd never conceived with my husband.' Even when she had not taken precautions. But this time she'd missed her courses and could no longer deny why her stomach felt so unsettled in the morning. 'It took time for me to realise it was true.'

'Did you see a doctor?' he asked as if trying to prove she was lying.

'I did. He confirmed it.' The doctor's examination had been quite unpleasant.

Oliver turned away from her. He faced the fireplace and put a hand on the mantel as if holding back strong emotions. As if his efforts to contain his rage were fraying.

How many times had she witnessed Duncan in such a state?

She should have stayed in Paris, but how could she raise a child there? What work could she do besides what the club manager required of her? Even if she could endure such an occupation, could she bear raising her child in a *maison close*?

Vincent and the other girls at the club told her to visit a physician who would make the problem go away. That idea was worse than becoming a *fille de rue*.

Instead, she'd gone running to her mother. Surely a mother would help her daughter in such a fix. She'd devised a plan. She'd tell her parents the child was Duncan's, pretend he'd been killed three months ago instead of three years. She could preserve her respectability that way. She'd figured it all out, except she had not anticipated her mother would send her away.

Would consider her dead.

Likely Oliver wished she were dead as well.

She fingered the pearl she still wore around her neck. 'You once told me you are wealthy. If you are wealthy, you can support this child you helped create.'

He continued to face the mantel. 'You say you are with child. You say the child is mine. You say you want money for it.'

'Yes.' Although *want* was the wrong word; *need* was more accurate. 'I will be penniless in a few days.'

She touched the pearl again, her only piece of jewellery. What once was a remembrance of a lovely day would have to be sold.

'You say.' He said it in a voice filled with scorn and disbelief.

She knew that tone of voice. Duncan had used that tone of voice. Scorn quickly led to rage.

She'd made the right choice when she'd left Oliver that night in Paris. Their day together had been delightful, their lovemaking glorious, but never would she risk being the recipient of a man's rage ever again.

She'd risk one more try. 'I do not need anything else from you. Merely enough money to support the child. Make an arrangement to provide me the money and I will never plague you again.'

Oliver was whirling with this news, with seeing Cecilia again. She looked so beautiful in a deep green dress that complemented her pale skin and dark hair. Her hair was primly tucked into a bonnet, but he remembered how glorious it had been that night in Paris, cascading over her shoulders in dark silken curls. He remembered how her naked skin had gleamed in the candlelight. How often she'd appeared in his dreams, looking much like that. How often he'd wished to see her again.

Here she was.

With news he never wanted to hear.

A child.

He'd vowed never to bring a bastard child into the world. No child of his would endure the name-calling and rejection he'd lived through. No child of his would be torn between two worlds.

He'd always been so careful, only bedding women who knew the rules of their sensual game, who did not want a baby any more than he did.

He could not think; his emotions were too high.

In his mind he heard the voices of his friends—Frederick, Jacob, Nicholas—cautioning him. Saying to him, *'How do you know it is your child? How do you know there even is a child? Do nothing,'* they'd say, *'until you know whether or not she is lying. You only knew her for a day, after all.'* A day was no time at all.

His father, too, would say to assume a woman lies. Certainly Oliver's stepmother lied at any opportunity, without any qualms. From her, Oliver knew first-hand how duplicitous a woman could be.

Those voices and memories might be crowding his head, but he could not let them matter.

Cecilia was in trouble of some kind. Even if she was lying, her distress was genuine. And he did have the means to help her.

'Do you know something, Oliver?' Cecilia picked up her gloves and cloak from the side table. 'I was mistaken to come here. I do not need anything from you. Forgive me for wasting your time.'

She swept out of the room.

What? First come and ask for money, tell a tale that, unbeknownst to her, was guaranteed to tug at his heartstrings, then run out?

He would not have her disappear again.

'Cecilia! Wait!' He rushed after her.

His butler still attended the hall.

'Where did she go?' Oliver asked.

Irwin lifted his hands. 'Out the door.'

'And you did not stop her?' he growled.

'I was supposed to stop her?' Irwin asked.

'You do not understand, man.' Oliver strode towards the front door. 'I do not know how to find her.'

He opened the door and ran out, sweeping his gaze up and down the street. He did not see her. His house was near the corner, so he hurried to look on Jermyn Street. He could not see her there either. How could she have disappeared so quickly? How was he to find her again? He must.

Because he needed to tell her it did not matter what trouble she was in, he could and would help her. If she were indeed carrying a child, even if that child was not his, he had no wish to make them both destitute, no wish to force her into the terrible choices with which women in her situation were forced to make.

Without a topcoat or hat, he walked in every hotel on Jermyn Street and asked for her, but no one could recall a guest who matched her name and description.

How was he to find her?

He'd mishandled things, become confused by the voices in his head, voices of his friends and his father. But his friends and his father had never met Cecilia, had never spent time with her. He could not believe he had totally misread her character.

He sensed there was much she was not telling him. No wonder he could not instantly believe her, could not immediately decide how to proceed. Besides, his whole life his father had hammered into him to be wary of women, that they would lie and deceive to get their hands on his wealth.

He'd always wanted to ask his father if his mother had been after his father's wealth. If so, Oliver never saw it. Certainly Oliver's stepmother used his father for his fortune. She relished the heights of society his money and title provided for her—and had always warned Oliver that he would never belong there.

There certainly had been women who were more enamoured of Oliver's money than of Oliver himself, but none had tried to get more out of him than trinkets. None had tried to entrap him with claims they were with child. He'd always supposed the women did not want a bastard half-caste for more than a few passionate nights and some pieces of jewellery, and they certainly did not want the half-caste's child.

Perhaps that was why he'd simply been unprepared for Cecilia and her claim. He'd always believed the women he'd bedded were as eager to prevent a baby as he was.

He'd lost her now, though, so what was he to do?

She thought he'd refused her request. What would she do instead? If she was with child, would she feel forced to give up the baby to the Foundling Hospital? Oliver had visited the Foundling Hospital. He'd donated to it, but, although the hospital did good work raising unwanted children, too many of them died.

The rain had stopped, but the sky was darkening and the air turned even chillier than when he'd dashed out of the town house. Tomorrow he'd go to Bow Street and see about hiring a Runner to track her down. And he'd continue his round of hotels.

Cecilia had hurried into Grenier's Hotel on Jermyn Street, right around the corner from Oliver's town house. Ironic that she should be staying so close to where he lived. The way her luck was transpiring she would encounter him again.

She could not leave it to luck. Tomorrow she would look for somewhere else to live, somewhere cheaper, although how to find such a place, she did not know. She'd only been to London a couple of times when her older sisters were presented at Court.

She pulled off her bonnet and walked to the window overlooking Jermyn Street. Below on the street, Oliver entered the hotel. Her heart pounded. He was pursuing her? Did he see her enter?

Her senses had become finely tuned to other people's moods. Especially men. She'd had to learn to read Duncan or else stumble into something that set him into a rage.

She ran back to her door to make certain it was locked.

Grenier's Hotel catered to French expatriates and she'd registered as a French woman. Coquette Vincent was the name she'd used, although she'd had no good reason to hide her identity. Habit, she supposed. She was glad she had not given her real name. It would make it that much harder for him to find her.

Still, she held her breath when footsteps sounded in the hallway.

They continued past her door.

She hurried back to the window and watched until she saw Oliver leave again, striding down the street away from his house.

Apparently, she was safe.

She walked over to the bed and lay upon it, resting her hand on her abdomen.

'Poor *petit bébé*,' she murmured. 'How am I going to take care of you?'

She refused to say she did not want this baby, now that the baby grew inside her. She knew what it was like to feel unwanted. Her parents had wanted a boy. After two girls, her older sisters, her parents had been certain the third child would be a boy.

But Cecilia had been born instead. Her sisters were never happy they had to share the money for their dowries or their clothes and such. Her father could not be bothered with her at all, but when she was a child, she'd thought her mother cared for her a little.

Until she'd asked to see her mother and father just the day before and they refused.

Her mother had refused to see her.

She sat up and hugged her knees.

'I'll take care of you, *petit bébé*,' she murmured. 'I'll never turn you away.'

She needed money. She could still work at something until her body swelled. She had a few months before that would occur. She'd survived on her own in Paris and she would do so here, as well, she vowed.

She could do what she used to do in Paris. All she needed was a place, a club. She probably did not have enough time to build an interest in her as Madame Coquette. She and Vincent had worked over the course of a year to build Madame Coquette's reputation. First by allowing the occasional man a night with her, then gradually building to more frequent nights as word of her selectivity spread.

It did not matter, though, because she did not wish to be Madame Coquette ever again, but she could work in a club and make the men spend more money there.

Most gentlemen's clubs in London did not allow females anywhere near their establishments, but she had heard of a place that was much like the clubs in Paris. On Jermyn Street, too. She'd met an Englishman at Maison D'Eros who'd bragged about a club on Jermyn Street that he intended to own some day. He'd tried to impress her so she would agree to allow him to have a night with her, but there was something about him she did not trust, so she'd refused.

But she remembered the club and the street it was on. She did not know the number, but how difficult would it be to discover which building was a gaming club?

She rose from the bed, tidied her hair and put on her shoes. She walked down to the clerk of the hotel.

'Pardon, monsieur.' She spoke in French. 'I have heard there is a club near here for playing cards where ladies may also play. Do you know where it is?'

'I have heard of it, *madame*,' the man answered. 'It is on this street, they say, but I do not know what house.'

'Are you certain you do not know?' she persisted. 'I will

not tell anyone else, if that is what worries you.' Really, how could a man who worked on this street not know this?

'Nothing worries me,' he snapped. 'I know nothing of this club.'

Now he knew nothing of it. Before he knew it was on this street.

'Merci, monsieur.' There was no point in pressing him further and making him angry at her.

She would discover the club on her own.

When it turned dark, Cecilia donned her cloak and her half-boots and walked out of the hotel and onto the street.

The pavement was illuminated by the soft glow of gas lamps, an innovation that made this time of night as busy as the day. Pedestrians filled the street, older men with young women on their arms, younger men and their friends, laughing and stumbling from too much drink, women, not unlike herself, unaccompanied, walking with swaying hips and skin exposed. Carriages rumbled by, fine carriages with crests painted on the side and humbler hackney coaches.

It was difficult to discern which of the many houses on the street could be the gaming club for which she searched. She assumed the club would have people coming in and out the door, but people came in and out of several doors.

She walked the street four times and soon received some interested stares from some of the men she passed. Her heart raced. Surely no harm could come to her in such a crowded place?

A man stepped right in front of her. 'How much, doxy?'

She stepped back to get around him and bumped into another man. 'We can pay,' the other man said.

'You are mistaken,' she said in a firm voice. 'I am not game.'

The first man blocked her way. 'I'd say you are as game as they come. What say you, Samuel?'

His companion replied, 'I'd say she ought to give it for free now for causing us trouble.'

She tried to step around, but they would not let her. The first man reached for her.

She jerked back. 'Do not touch me!' she cried in a loud voice. 'Leave me alone and let me pass!'

'Not tonight, doxy.' He seized her arm and she readied her heel to come down hard on his foot.

Suddenly, though, the man was pulled back. Someone had seized his collar and nearly lifted him off the ground.

'Leave her!' a man shouted, shoving her assailant into his friend and knocking them both to the pavement.

Other people stopped to watch.

'Leave,' the man commanded. 'Before you regret it.'

The two scrambled to their feet, pushed their way through the spectators and disappeared down the street.

A woman approached her. 'Are you hurt? They did not hurt you, did they?'

Cecilia wrapped her cloak around her. 'I am not hurt.'

She saw now that her rescuer was a well-dressed gentleman and his lady, a petite young woman with blonde hair and the kindest eyes Cecilia could ever recall.

'Go now,' the gentleman said to the onlookers. 'Nothing to see any more.' He spoke to Cecilia. 'Are you certain you are unharmed?'

Cecilia nodded, though her knees began to shake as the enormity of what could have happened to her struck her.

'You've had a terrible fright,' the lady said. 'Come inside with us and we will get you something to drink.' She turned to the gentleman. 'Won't we, Jake?'

'We certainly will. Come with us.' He walked up to an impressive black-lacquered door and sounded its brass knocker.

A large man opened the door.

'We are back, Snyder,' the gentleman said.

They escorted her inside to a drawing room off a large

marble-tiled hall. Cecilia sat in an upholstered chair in front of a warm fireplace.

Almost immediately the blonde lady poured her a glass from a crystal decanter. 'Have some claret.'

The lady sat on a sofa near Cecilia's chair. 'I am Rose,' she said. 'And this is my husband.' She gave him a worshipful look.

He laughed and placed a fond hand on his wife's shoulder. 'You are not yet used to introductions, are you, love?'

'I am perfectly aware of the correct way to do things, but she doesn't need any fancy introductions, Jake,' his wife retorted. 'Not after what she's been through.'

Cecilia looked from one to the other. 'What fancy introductions?'

The gentleman extended his hand. 'Duke of Westmoor.' He inclined his head towards his wife and his voice grew soft. 'And my duchess.'

Cecilia felt her face drain of blood. She'd never before met a duke. 'Your Grace.' She shook his hand. 'I am Mrs Lockhart.' Her real name slipped out instead of her alias in her shock.

The Duke, a handsome man with dark hair and blue eyes, sat next to his wife.

Cecilia glanced around the room, which appeared nothing like she'd expect a duke's house to appear. On the walls were large paintings of naked Roman gods frolicking in lush green gardens. A statue of a nude in a very suggestive pose stood in the corner.

'I know you must wonder why I was out by myself.' Cecilia felt she owed them some explanation. 'I—I am staying in a hotel nearby and I was looking for—for a place I'd heard of.'

'What place?' the Duke asked, looking eager to help.

She took another sip of her claret. 'I was looking for a gentlemen's club. A gaming place.'

The Duke and Duchess exchanged glances.

'I know it sounds scandalous,' she admitted. 'But I am in rather straitened circumstances and I thought perhaps I might find employment there.'

They exchanged glances again.

'Perhaps you have heard of such a place?' she went on. 'I believe its name begins with a V.'

'Vitium et Virtus,' they said in unison.

Her eyes narrowed. 'Perhaps.'

The Duchess laughed. 'You have found it!'

'This is Vitium et Virtus.' The Duke made a gesture that encompassed the whole room. 'It is closed tonight. It is not open every night.'

The Duchess looked sympathetic. 'Tell us about your straitened circumstances.'

'I—I was widowed—my husband was a soldier. He fought at Waterloo.' British people were impressed by Waterloo veterans, even though Duncan's career as a soldier was nothing heroic. 'I was stuck in France for a while, but when I came home, the only relative I counted upon could no longer help me. I am quite alone.' It was all true, but certainly not the whole of her story. 'I've worked at a club before.'

'What did you do at the club?' the Duke asked, with the slightest edge to his voice.

He wanted to know if she was—was what the two men who accosted her thought she was.

'I worked as a hostess,' she said. 'I flirted with the men, eased their time at the club, brought them drinks and food, made them comfortable, urged them to spend more money. The more important the man, the more attention he received. I never sold my favours, though. Never.'

Explaining Madame Coquette would be too difficult and who would believe it?

'A hostess?' The Duke looked thoughtful. 'We've never had a hostess. What do you think, Rose?'

What did he mean *we've* never had a hostess?

His wife smiled, making her look even lovelier. 'I think it sounds like an excellent idea. And it will help Mrs Lockhart.'

The Duke extended his hand once more. 'You are hired, *madame*. We are closed tonight, as you can see, but you may start tomorrow. We have a gambling and entertainment night tomorrow.'

'She should come before then to meet everyone?' His wife turned to her. 'Come around six in the evening. Six would be good, would it not, Jake? We will introduce you to everyone.'

Cecilia shook her head in confusion. 'I am perplexed. Why does a duke hire a hostess for a gentlemen's club?'

The Duke smiled. 'I am part-owner. It is a long story and we do not have time right now. Our carriage is waiting. Tomorrow? Come at six.'

'We cannot allow her to walk back to her hotel alone,' the Duchess protested.

'Indeed we cannot.' The Duke stood and faced Cecilia. 'You must ride in the carriage with us.'

So Cecilia rode back the short distance to Grenier's Hotel in a duke's carriage.

But she had a job and a chance to work out what to do next.

When she lay in her bed a little while later, sleep eluding her, she pressed her hand to her abdomen. 'We'll survive, *petit bébé*. We will survive.'

Chapter Seven

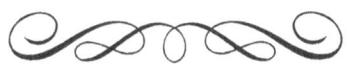

The next evening Oliver walked through the public rooms of Vitium et Virtus, checking on the preparations. The game room was set up with several tables for cards, a hazard table and a faro table. It was important to Oliver that the atmosphere be elegant, tasteful, even if unapologetically bawdy in its painted ceiling, a bacchanalian scene they'd commissioned from an Italian artist.

Oliver continued on to the ballroom, which was set up with a stage at one end. There would be musicians in one of the balconies and the songstresses would appear on the stage.

In his youth, Oliver enjoyed the naughty songs sung at the club. The singing had been one of his favourites of the club's offerings. He'd even joined the women, lending his voice to theirs.

She's Tall and Slender,
She's Soft and Tender,
Some God commend her,
My Wit's too low:
'Twere Joyful plunder,

To bring her under,
She's all a wonder,
From Top to Toe.

But now it seemed rather juvenile. Some of the songs were extremely graphic and those were the ones their members liked the most. Some of the club's employees liked to sing them, too. The women used the songs to entice willing gentlemen to spend more money on them. The women poured compliments in the men's ears, making them think it was their manliness that attracted and not their money.

What would happen if Oliver arranged for *Don Giovanni* to be performed here one night? Something beautiful rather than bawdy.

He suspected it would not do well.

Snyder, the porter, came to the door. 'The new woman is here, Mr Gregory.'

'New woman?' He knew nothing of this.

'His Grace hired her last night,' Snyder said. 'Told her to come at six.'

'Hired her? Where is Jacob? Is he here?' Oliver asked. If so, he'd like to speak to him and ask what the devil was she hired for?

'No, sir,' Snyder said.

'Well, where is Mr Bell? Have Mr Bell deal with her.' Mr Bell was, by title, the club's butler, yet in practice more of a manager. He and Mrs Parker, the housekeeper, saw to most of the mundane details of running the club.

'Mr Bell is delayed,' the porter said. 'And Mrs Bell is on an errand.'

'Zounds, is no one else here?' Oliver did not hire the staff.

'You are here, sir,' Snyder said. 'What should I do with the new woman, then?'

He blew out a breath. 'I'll see her, I suppose. Where is she?'

'I put her in the drawing room.' He bowed. 'Must get back to the door, sir.'

Oliver waited a moment to collect himself. If Jacob had hired the woman, then Oliver supposed he'd go along with it, whatever 'it' was, but they usually discussed these matters first.

He left the ballroom and descended the stairs. He crossed the hall, passing Snyder who again stood at his place by the club's entrance. The drawing room was directly off the hall.

Oliver opened its door.

The woman stood with her back to him, staring at one of the paintings, the one where satyrs cavorted with scantily clad nymphs.

He cleared his throat. 'Mrs Lockhart?'

She turned to him and it was as if he'd been punched in the chest.

'Cecilia!'

'Oliver?' Her voice rose an octave.

She wore the same green dress she'd worn the day before, the one that made her skin glow and her whisky-coloured eyes gleam. He wanted to tell her how glad he was to see her here, how he'd searched for her, both the day before and earlier this day, how he'd hired a Bow Street Runner to help find her.

But what was she doing here?

'I expected the Duke and Duchess.' She sounded affronted.

She knew Jacob and Rose? She'd told him she knew nobody. 'How do you know the Duke and Duchess?'

She lifted her chin. 'I met them by happenstance last night.' She took a nervous breath. 'I will tell you, but I hope you honour me with an explanation of your own. I was looking for this club—to ask for work—and I happened upon the Duke and Duchess who agreed to hire me.'

He stared at her, certain she was leaving something out. 'Hire you for what?'

They had their singers and dancers and their maids. Vitium et Virtus needed no more workers. What could Cecilia do? Especially carrying a child.

'To be a hostess.'

'A hostess? What the devil does a hostess do?'

She sighed as if she found explaining this role tedious. 'It will be my job to make the wealthiest of your members as comfortable as possible, to fuss over them, flatter them, bring them drinks, make certain they spend a great deal of money. I should be able to do this for several months until my condition is too evident.' She paused. 'I did this work in Paris.'

'You worked in a club in Paris?' The clubs in Paris he'd visited were gambling dens and brothels. She'd worked in one? That was a great deal to conceal from him.

'That is why I was by the Seine at dawn. I had just left the club.' She spoke as if he ought to have known that. 'You will next want to ask if I slept with the patrons. I did not.'

He'd thought that would go without saying. Not one of the entertainment staff they employed at Vitium et Virtus had refrained from willingly sharing some gentleman's bed.

'You expect me to believe that?' he shot back.

She held his gaze. 'It is the truth. A hostess is not a courtesan.'

What need did Vitium et Virtus have for a hostess? 'Did the Duke explain the nature of our club?'

She glanced around the room. 'I can imagine.'

'No, you cannot,' he insisted. 'We are not a brothel, but we are a place where men and women can be as free as they desire to seek pleasure in all manner of ways. We take no money from the private arrangements men and women make, even if the women are some of our entertainment staff. We do not allow that licence for the maids, footmen and other kitchen workers. For their protection. They are too vulnerable to being misused.'

'Which would I be, then?' she asked, still sounding defiantly wary.

'You would not be a servant.' He could never see her as a servant.

'So I would be expected to sleep with the members?' Her eyes flashed.

He gritted his teeth. 'You are free to decide for yourself.'

She nodded, as if satisfied.

His anger rose. 'You say you are with child, but you are contemplating—'

She held up a hand. 'I will not sleep with your patrons or with anybody. And after you, I shared no man's bed.'

How could he believe this?

'Now it is your turn for explanations.' She crossed her arms over her chest. 'Why are you running this place?'

'I am part-owner,' he retorted. 'With the Duke and—with two more friends.' Because Nicholas was still part-owner. He stopped himself. 'Wait, Cecilia. We have unfinished business about this baby.'

'I am thinking of the baby,' she countered. 'That is why I need work.'

'You do not need work. I have money to help you. If there is indeed a baby, I will provide for the child.'

Her eyes narrowed. 'What do you mean "if there is indeed a baby"?'

He shrugged. 'I have only your word for it.'

Her eyes flashed. 'And I have only your word that you will provide for my baby. Your baby! Do not prevent me from working, Oliver. I need this job.'

The desperation in her voice was very clear. It tugged at him.

He softened his voice. 'I won't prevent you from working.' He rubbed his face and changed the subject. 'How did you learn of this place?' he asked. Vitium et Virtus was exclusive and secret.

She took a breath before answering. 'I met a gentleman in Paris who told me of it.'

Oliver's heart pounded. Could she have encountered Nicholas? He took an eager step towards her. 'Who was this gentleman?'

She stepped back. 'Sir Nash Bowles.'

'Bowles!' He spat out the name.

Just when he thought this could not get worse. Sir Nash Bowles. The man who'd nearly ruined Frederick's Georgiana. Bowles always had been a nasty character, even at school.

'How do you know Bowles?' Oliver demanded.

She cast him a wary look. 'I do not know him. He came to the club in Paris. I saw him one time. Why?'

Oliver frowned. 'He is not a good man to know.'

'Then I am glad not to know him.' She glanced towards the door. 'May I see where I will work? Unless you have changed your mind about my employment.'

'I have not changed my mind.' Oliver was a man of his word.

She lifted her chin again. 'I will work only for tips if you do not wish to pay me.'

She was starting to irritate him again. 'Of course we will pay you.'

They paid all their people generously. They could afford to do so. Cecilia would be well compensated.

She looked down at her dress. 'I am not dressed for an exclusive gentlemen's club. Do you provide clothes for me to wear?'

'Yes.' He extended his hand. 'Come. I will show you the club.'

Cecilia flinched when he touched her arm to guide her from the room. He released her, which was good. Even though he was obviously not happy to see her or hear of her condition, he still possessed an allure that made her susceptible to him.

As they approached the stairs, he asked, 'Where are you staying?'

She became wary again. 'Why do you need to know this?'

He blew out a breath. 'Only to inform you that our employees are not allowed to entertain in the house when the club is not open. We are not open every night.'

'I will entertain no one.' How many times must she say so?

They climbed the grand staircase.

He spoke in the tones of a displeased tutor. 'Our club is a secret one. Every member is anonymous, so to attend the club each member must wear a mask. Masks do not always perfectly disguise the wearer, of course. Most members know who is behind a mask, but they are honour bound never to disclose who attends. If you learn the identity of a member, you must swear never to disclose who they are.'

She lifted her hand. 'I swear.'

Masks seemed a bit childish to her. But the British were much more concerned about what other people thought of them than the French had been.

'Do I wear a mask?' she asked.

'Yes,' he said curtly. 'But the masks worn by the female workers are more decorative than disguising.'

He brought her to what looked like a ballroom with sofas and divans arranged for an audience. Like the drawing room she'd just left, the ballroom was decorated with paintings of nude gods cavorting in idyllic gardens. The fireplace mantel was a clever sculpture of two couples engaged in copulation.

'Tonight we will have a concert.' Oliver gestured to a raised platform at one end of the room. 'Our singers will perform before mingling with our guests. I warn you the songs will be bawdy.'

Bawdy songs did not distress her. She'd followed the drum, after all. Soldiers rarely sang hymns.

'We always have gambling,' he went on. 'I'll show you that room. Other nights we feature tableaux.'

'Tableaux?' This was something new to her.

'Our ladies pose—let us say that it is our version of Lady Hamilton's attitudes minus the veils and scarves.'

He meant they posed nude.

'Our ladies dance, as well,' he went on. 'As I said before, the singers and dancers are free to accept arrangements with our male patrons. We also do not interfere with the private decisions of our members who wish to be private with each other.'

She bristled. 'Why do you keep saying this to me? Is this expected of me or not?'

He turned to her and grasped her arm. 'It is not. But you must know how matters exist here. We believe everyone should be free to decide for themselves.'

She averted her gaze. 'That is good, because I decide for myself what I will and will not do.'

His lips thinned. 'As you decided with me?'

Her body flushed with the memory. She pretended to ignore his question, but the moment seemed to make the air crackle between them.

They continued through the club's elegantly appointed dining room, featuring small tables for intimate repasts. He brought her up another flight of stairs to show her the private rooms, each decorated to fulfil some erotic fancy. One, all red and gold, reminded her of the room in Maison D'Eros. Another looked like it belonged in an Arabian harem. A third was as dark as a dungeon.

Next he took her below stairs to meet the cook, the kitchen servants and the footmen who served the food and drink.

She watched the other workers carefully as Oliver greeted them and they spoke to him. They seemed pleased and comfortable with him and he with them. That was good.

She'd been shocked to see him in the club, to discover

he, of all people, was one of the owners. Now she must face him every day she would work, when she'd already decided it was not safe to see him ever again. It made it worse to see him through the admiring eyes of others, to have her body flare in response when he touched her.

But she would endure this. She had a job. She'd earn money. And he said he'd give her more.

She and her baby were safe for now.

He stopped in front of a closed door and knocked.

'We call this the Green Room,' he said. 'It is the dressing room for the singers and dancers and other female workers.'

'Come in,' a female voice said.

He opened the door.

The room was lined with mirrors and there were clothes' presses and rails filled with costumes. Seated in a chair facing one of the mirrors sat a pretty young woman dressed in her shift and a wrapper that was off her shoulders.

She smiled and pulled up her wrapper when she saw Oliver. ''Ello, Mr Gregory.' Her accent was like others Cecilia had heard among ordinary London folk.

'How are you, Fleurette?' he responded.

'Well enough, sir,' she answered brightly. Her gaze turned to Cecilia.

'Let me introduce you.' He looked questioningly at Cecilia. 'How do you wish to be known?'

Fleurette laughed. 'We're none of us using our given names.'

Cecilia gave the name that was foremost in her mind. 'Coquette. You can call me Coquette.' She extended her hand to the girl. 'I am happy to meet you, Fleurette.'

The girl laughed again. 'Fleurette. Coquette. It rhymes.' She accepted the handshake. 'But you can call me Flo. Everyone does.'

'You are getting dressed early,' Oliver remarked.

'Aw, I'm not gettin' dressed yet. I—I bruised my arm on—

on a door and I'm trying to cover it up.' She put her hand over her arm, which was already covered by the wrapper.

'Nothing serious?' he asked in a concerned voice.

'Naw. A bruise isn't serious.'

Oliver turned to Cecilia. For a moment his eyes were as warm as when he looked upon Flo, but they quickly turned flinty. She remembered how his eyes had glowed when he'd gazed upon her naked skin. 'I will leave you in Flo's care, then.'

'As you wish,' Cecilia managed.

He spoke to Fleurette—Flo—again. 'She needs a dress to wear tonight. Can you find her one?'

'I can do that,' the girl answered amiably.

'And tell her how things go here?' he went on.

'I can really do that.' She smiled.

He nodded. 'I will leave you to Flo, then... Coquette. But I wish to see you before the club opens. Flo can help you find me.'

'Very well.' She was somehow reluctant to let him go, which was absurd.

At that moment, the door burst open and the Duke and Duchess of Westmoor rushed in.

Flo jumped to her feet. 'Rose!'

'Flo.' The Duchess gave the girl a fond hug. She glanced over at Cecilia. 'I am so sorry we are late.'

'Estate business.' The Duke groaned. 'We got away as soon as we could.'

The Duchess smiled. 'I see Oliver has taken care of you.'

Cecilia curtsied. 'Your Grace.'

Rose released Flo and clasped Cecilia's hand. 'Please do not be so formal with me. Not here, anyway. I am Rose.'

'Rose was one of us, in a manner of speaking.' Flo grinned at the Duchess. 'Before she got so grand.'

Oliver glowered during this display. He turned to the Duke. 'May I have a word with you, Jake?'

'Certainly!' the Duke said jovially. 'Shall I leave you here, Rose?'

'Oh, please do!' She laughed. 'Perhaps some of the costumes need mending!'

This whole exchange meant nothing to Cecilia. A duchess who was not always so grand? Who was one of the hirelings? Who mended costumes?

Oliver left Cecilia without even a nod of goodbye, which only fuelled her wariness of him. Perhaps he would not help her. Perhaps he would turn on her eventually.

'We're to find Coquette a dress for tonight,' Flo told the Duchess.

'Oh, yes.' The Duchess smiled at Cecilia. 'Come, Coquette. Let us look through the costumes and see what might do for you.'

They found her a dress, a lovely indigo confection, which she would don later.

That task complete, the Duchess bade them goodbye. 'I want to say hello to Mrs Parker and cook and the others.' She gave Flo another hug before leaving the room.

'Rose worked as a maid here at the club and then she became companion to the Duke's grandmother,' Flo told her.

She went on to embellish the story with all sorts of drama and romance, ending with a big, envious sigh.

'It is almost time for dinner,' Flo said. 'We eat in the servants' hall.' Her face tensed. 'I—I am going to tend to my bruise, but you can join them now. No need to wait for me.'

Cecilia did not relish walking into a room of other workers alone, even if the Duchess might be there. 'Perhaps I can help you cover the bruises. What are you using for it?'

Flo hesitated before answering. 'Pear's Almond Bloom.' She handed the pot to Cecilia.

Pear's Almond Bloom was a tinted face paint that was supposed to give the face a natural look. Cecilia had used it before.

'Let us try it, then,' Cecilia said.

Flo hesitated again before slipping off her wrapper.

There was not one bruise, but four, all round in shape and reddish-blue in colour. The bruises were on Flo's upper arm. Cecilia's hands trembled. She had seen bruises like this before, in this same pattern. She'd seen them on her own arms.

'Did—did you get the bruises here?' Cecilia asked, trying to sound casual. She opened the pot of Pear's Almond Bloom and put a little on her finger. She gently dabbed it on one of the bruises.

'No,' Flo answered. 'I was out.'

So someone outside the club had inflicted them?

Confronting Flo so soon after first meeting her would be a mistake. If someone had cared enough to ask Cecilia how she got her bruises, she would have lied. If they'd asked her if her husband had inflicted them, she would have denied it. He'd have killed her if she ever told.

Cecilia vowed she'd find out who did this to Flo, though. She'd bide her time. Look for a safe moment to ask the girl who had held her with a grip so tight it caused bruises.

'Do you have any white powder?' Cecilia asked.

Cecilia had become quite experienced at hiding bruises.

Flo took a powder box and powder puff from a drawer in a nearby dressing table. Cecilia dabbed the powder lightly over the Almond Bloom, then dabbed on some more Bloom followed by more powder until the bruises faded from sight.

'Coquette!' Flo exclaimed. 'You made them disappear! How did you learn to do that?'

'I worked in a club before,' she said, which was no explanation at all.

Flo put on her wrapper and tied it with a sash. 'Let us go to dinner, then,' she said.

Chapter Eight

If they had been anywhere else, a dinner table full of diners would be scandalised by a pretty young woman coming to eat in her wrapper and shift like Flo did. Not in a club such as this. Or in the one in Paris.

Just as outrageous, the Duchess sat at the table with these lowly folk. She did not eat, but did introduce Cecilia to the large group of servants and entertainers. Cecilia could not remember all their names. She made a point of learning the names of Mrs Parker, the housekeeper, and Mr Bell, the butler, who would be present throughout the night, and Snyder, the large man who guarded the door.

After dinner, Cecilia, Flo, and the other girls who would perform that evening donned their costumes, each of which had a mask to match. Cecilia's mask was a lacy gold concoction with paste jewels resembling blue sapphires outlining the eyeholes. As Oliver said, it did not totally disguise her face. Most of the girls wore similar masks that showed more of their faces than they concealed. So the gentlemen members could see how pretty they were, Cecilia supposed.

* * *

After she was dressed, Cecilia walked upstairs to report to Oliver as he had requested. She found him in the ballroom standing with another gentleman. They wore black-silk masks, but it took just a glance for her to recognise Oliver. And a second one to see the other man was the Duke. Oliver watched her approach. He, of course, recognised her.

The Duke turned when she came near and smiled. 'Look at you!'

She met Oliver's gaze, made even more intense by the black mask framing his eyes. 'Will this costume do?'

'I think you look lovely,' the Duke said.

Oliver glanced away.

He really did not want her here.

Suddenly he spoke to her. 'Explain how this works. You encourage members to spend more money? There are not many ways this might be done. You might encourage them to play more games of hazard and faro, but that is the extent of it.'

'I will concentrate on the game room, then.' It might be difficult to prove her worth if these were the only ways she could increase revenue. 'I can always challenge them to make larger bets or to linger at the tables a bit longer than they otherwise might have done. I can bring them drinks, so they do not have to take their attention from the games.'

This club was not like Maison D'Eros, where attendance could be gained by paying the price for entrance and where guests were charged for drinks and food and for the privilege of sitting down to a game of cards.

'Have you met everyone?' Oliver asked.

'I believe so,' she responded. 'At dinner.'

The Duke interrupted. 'I beg your pardon. I must bid you goodnight. Rose and I are expected at the theatre tonight.' He took Cecilia's hand. 'I hope this night goes well for you.

Welcome to Vitium et Virtus.' He turned to Oliver. 'We seem to be leaving everything to you.'

Oliver's expression softened. 'Go. Enjoy your evening with your wife.'

Cecilia still had difficulty believing that this Duke had actually married a maid.

'The Duchess is below stairs in the servants' hall,' Cecilia told the Duke.

The Duke grinned. 'So I expected.' He seemed besotted with his duchess and she with him.

Cecilia remembered when she had been besotted with Duncan. Before he used his fist on her. She could even admit she'd spent a day besotted by Oliver, but now...

She and Oliver were left standing alone together and she was acutely aware that he might have the power to dismiss her, no matter what his partner, the Duke, might say. She must make herself seem malleable to his desires—at least as far as her duties on the job required.

He turned to her and the softness in his eyes when speaking to the Duke disappeared, replaced by the hard stare that made her feel him a powder keg that was about to explode.

'Shall I place myself in the game room, then?' she asked.

He nodded.

She was about to turn away when he stopped her. 'Are you certain you wish to do this?' His voice seemed earnest. 'Our members will certainly proposition you.'

She forced herself to look into his eyes and hoped she would not weaken in front of him. 'It will not be much different from Paris. I know what to do.'

She would endure the propositions, the lewd remarks, the groping hands, just as she had in Paris.

'Let one of us know—Mr Bell, Snyder, me—if any member becomes too un-gentleman-like.'

She could not read his expression. Did he think this likely? Would he blame her if it happened?

'If there is something I cannot handle myself, I will alert one of you,' she responded.

She turned and walked away from him, feeling his gaze on her back as she did so.

When she entered the game room, her spirits sank. She'd forgotten how much she detested the flirting and flattering. She'd thought she'd left that all behind in Paris. She thought she could return home again.

She shook herself. She must never allow herself to think of home again.

They—her family—must be as dead to her as she was to them.

She lifted her chin and strode into the room, approaching the croupiers who ran the hazard and faro tables, as well as the footmen in attendance in the room, reminding them of what she would be doing there.

At Maison D'Eros there had always been jealousy and competition among the workers, especially between the women who entertained the men. Someone was always feuding with someone else. Vincent taught her to ignore it and simply serve the patrons. She had only been at Vitium et Virtus a few hours, but, so far, everyone seemed amiable and content. At dinner they'd all insisted to her that they were well paid and well looked after by Oliver, the Duke and the third man whom she had not yet met. They all helped each other, too, they'd said.

Each and every worker in the game room offered that very thing. To help her.

It touched her.

The footman in attendance told her, 'If anyone gets out of hand, you signal me. The owners do not allow any tomfoolery.'

It was more reassurance.

'Would you steer me to the wealthier members? Or the

more important ones? I will ensure they enjoy losing all the coins in their purses.'

The footman laughed. 'I will indeed.' He called out to the croupiers. 'Let us help Coquette find the wealthy and important fellows.'

The two young women at the faro and hazard tables shouted back their agreement. They were an attraction to the tables themselves, with their pretty faces and low-cut necklines that were almost low enough to cover no part of the breast at all, especially when they leaned over. Which they certainly needed to do in the performance of their jobs.

Cecilia had been fortunate to find this place, lucky to have been hired by the kind Duke and Duchess. Her situation could have been so much worse. Perhaps she could relax a bit.

At that moment voices sounded outside the room and men in masks walked in. Cecilia laughed at herself for thinking about relaxation. She took a breath, straightened her spine, planted a smile on her face and became Madame Coquette.

She strode towards the doorway. 'Greetings, gentlemen,' she welcomed. 'I am Coquette, your new hostess, here to see to your pleasure.'

Oliver did not visit the game room right away, although all his impulses propelled him in that direction. With difficulty he resisted, remaining in the ballroom, mixing instead with the members and guests seeking drinks of whisky and brandy poured one after the other by the butler.

After an hour he could wait no longer. He wandered over to the game room and looked in, his gaze riveted on the young woman dressed in deep blue with her sensuous walk and throaty laugh.

Cecilia.

Several men surrounded her at the hazard table while the croupier gathered their markers or doled out their winnings. She cried aloud for the dice to roll the winning numbers and moaned when they did not. It looked to Oliver as if the entire game was played to attempt to please her. Her gaze drifted from the game and she caught him watching her. Her smile faltered a moment before she returned to the dice.

She had transformed herself into a woman he did not recognise. Openly flirtatious, lively and overtly sensuous, as if she had turned herself into her opposite. Which one was genuine? He could not tell.

One of the footmen came to the doorway. 'The concert begins shortly,' he announced.

Oliver followed him out of the room and back to the ballroom. As one of the owners, he would introduce the singers. The orchestra, seated on a balcony overlooking the room, tuned their instruments while the members filed into the room and found seats on the sofas and divans arranged for their viewing pleasure. Many of the members had already linked themselves to a woman, whether they were those employed at Vitium et Virtus who were not performing this night, or other female guests.

Oliver waited until everyone was settled, then he climbed onto the stage. 'Ladies and Gentlemen!' he shouted over the din of conversation. 'Ladies and Gentlemen! The Vitium et Virtus singers!'

Three young ladies stepped forward, Fleurette in the middle. They immediately burst into a pretty but bawdy song sung in Shakespeare's time.

That was a maid this other day
And she must needs go forth to play.
And as she walked, she sighed and said,
'I am afraid to die a maid.'

When the four friends had been at Oxford, they'd made a study of bawdy songs. Elizabethan times were particularly fruitful in this endeavour and, truthfully, Oliver had learned a great deal about that era as he searched.

The ladies continued.

He took this maiden then aside
And led her where she was not spied
And told her many a pretty tale,
And gave her well of Watkins ale.

Oliver glanced over to the doorway of the ballroom and saw Cecilia standing there, listening to the concert, the ghost of a smile on her face. She looked more herself than at any other moment since she'd reappeared to him. Or, at least, she looked more like the woman she had been in Paris. His skin warmed at the sight of her relaxed, enjoying the moment, even if she hovered by the doorway as though she did not belong inside.

He walked over to her and she immediately stiffened.

'The game room is almost empty,' she said defensively. 'I only wished to listen for a minute.'

The Parisian Cecilia had disappeared again. He still did not know which Cecilia was the real one.

'You are free to go wherever you like in the club,' he told her. 'I came over to ask what you think of the entertainment.'

She glanced back to the stage. 'Their voices are lovely. They blend so well. And the song is very pretty.' She looked at him with a hint of amusement in her eyes. 'Not too shocking.'

He smiled. 'Take care. They are only getting started.'

The singers were skilled at connecting with their audience, so that they made each person feel as if they sang for them. The members loved it. Oliver had attended musicales at his father's house, usually with singers hired from the Royal Opera. Though he appreciated the beauty of their music, it lacked this personal touch.

Sometimes, though, when he listened to music, there drifted in a memory of different rhythms, ones that repeated over and over. Different instruments, making different sounds. Different voices singing words he could no longer make out. Music that touched sympathetic chords deep within him.

He had not thought of India, not with this nostalgia, not since he'd been in Paris. Not since right before he'd first seen Cecilia.

He darted a glance to her. She quickly averted her gaze as if she'd been looking at him. He felt his mood mirrored in the expression on her face, the expression of one who'd lost a great deal of what had been most dear.

Cecilia watched the change in him, saw the moment the sadness enveloped him and felt it resonate within her. Why should she feel this so acutely? Why should this moment bring on his sadness? She did not want to be curious about him, to wonder what had come over him, to wonder what had sparked it. The music? The music was gay, pretty and clever in its use of double entendre. It made no sense that it should depress his spirits.

She forced herself to attend to the singers on stage. Of the three, Flo stood out. It was she to whom one's eye was drawn. Flo was so pretty, so lively. If there was a man hurting her, how long would it take before she'd shrink and cower from everything and everyone?

The singers began a new song, this one sung in the Scot's tongue of Robert Burns.

Come rede me, dame, come tell me, dame,
My dame come tell me truly,
What length o' graith, when weel ca'd hame, Will sair a woman duly?
The carlin clew her wanton tail,

*Her wanton tail sae ready
I learn'd a sang in Annandale,
Nine inch will please a lady.*

Cecilia laughed at the last line of the stanza.

Oliver must have heard her, because he emerged from his black cloud to stare at her.

Her guard flew up. Did he object to her finding that funny? Well, she'd told him she'd worked in a club—a brothel, really. Surely he did not expect her to be maidenly. She could never be maidenly again.

At least his sadness evaporated. She could sense it inside herself.

Once Cecilia had learned to be attuned to her husband's moods. That had been a matter of self-preservation. But she could not recall ever *feeling* his moods the way she felt Oliver's.

She mustn't let this draw herself to Oliver, as she had been drawn to him in Paris. She hoped he would make good on his promise to support her and the baby, but she would not even allow herself to count on that. She'd seen his mood change when she told him about her condition; she'd seen his disbelief, his blaming her.

She placed her hand on the doorjamb. Gracious, she was tired. She could not remember being this weary since marching with Duncan from Belgium to France after Waterloo. In some ways this fatigue was even more pervasive than that.

The club stayed open until two in the morning. She still had two hours to go.

'Are you feeling unwell?' Oliver asked.

He startled her. 'I am merely fatigued.' It would not do for him to think she could not perform her job. She pushed herself away from the doorjamb.

She must have moved too quickly, because a wave of dizziness washed over her. She groped for the doorframe again.

And felt his arms encircle her. 'You are unwell. Come.'

He led her through another room to a door that led to what looked like a completely different place. He brought her to a drawing room and sat her in a chair.

She leaned forward. 'I am so dizzy.'

'Did you eat?' he asked, removing her mask and placing it on a nearby table.

'Yes. With the other staff. I ate.' Although some of the food made her stomach queasy.

'Have you had anything to drink?' He pulled off his mask.

She'd brought many a drink to the gentlemen in the game room, but had no more than a few sips for herself. 'Not since dinner.'

'Wait here.' He left the room.

Cecilia held her head in her hands and prayed the room would stop spinning.

Oliver returned with a tray holding a teapot, cup, sugar and milk. He set it down and poured her a cup, adding milk and sugar.

She took the cup from his hand and sipped it slowly, hoping to keep it down.

She'd heard that women who were going to have babies often felt sick in the morning, but this was the first wave of true nausea and dizziness she'd experienced. And, of all inconvenient things, she had to experience it in front of Oliver.

'Feeling better?' he asked.

She did not feel better, but she smiled and replied, 'Oh, yes. I am quite certain I can return to work.' In a few minutes. She hoped.

'No,' he said emphatically. 'No more work for you for tonight. As soon as you are able to walk, I will see you back to your hotel.'

'Truly, I will be well enough to work.' She tried to stand, but sat down again when the room started spinning.

'See? You are not ready yet.' His voice turned low and soft.

Through the walls they could hear the orchestra. Flo's clear, bell-like voice came through as well.

I'll go no more a roving, with you fair maid.
A roving, A roving, since roving's been my ru-i-in,
I'll go no more a roving, with you fair maid.

She remembered her day of roving with Oliver, how perfect he'd been. Would that day, though, be her ruin? She needed this job. She must not appear weak.

'I am able to work.' She stood again and walked to the door, but could not make it without holding on to the furniture.

He came to her side. 'Stop this nonsense,' he said sharply.

Warning bells sounded inside her.

'You will not work the rest of this night,' he said firmly. 'I'll walk you back to your hotel. Now.'

Her anxiety rose. 'Are you discharging me? I can do the work, Oliver. Believe me, I can do it. Let me return.'

'I am not discharging you,' he said. 'But you are not working any more tonight. If you feel well enough tomorrow come back and I will give you the club schedule.'

'You are not discharging me?'

'No,' he said, his voice lower.

She would have another chance. 'I need to change my clothes.'

'No, you do not. Bring the dress back tomorrow.' He placed her in another chair. 'Where is your hotel? Do I need to summon a coach?'

She shook her head. 'Grenier's. Nearby.'

He gave her a puzzled look. 'I asked for you at the Grenier. They did not know you.'

'I gave them another name, Coquette Vincent.' She switched to French. *'Visite de Paris, France.'*

He did not ask her why. Instead, he said, 'Sit here until I

can have Snyder collect your cloak.' He poured her another cup of tea.

She tried sipping it again, but the nausea was worse. All she really wanted was to sleep for a week or more.

He returned, wearing a topcoat and carrying her cloak. He helped her rise from the chair and wrapped her in the cloak. He put an arm around her and supported her while she walked.

They left Vitium et Virtus by a private door that led to the garden. Her dizziness seemed to worsen with each step. Suddenly everything went black. For a moment she could hear the coaches and horses in the street, the music from the club.

Then even the sounds stopped.

Chapter Nine

Cecilia woke in a strange room dimly lit by daylight peeking through curtained windows. She was in a bed, so comfortable she almost did not care that she had no idea where she was. She forced herself to sit up and look around.

She wore her shift and corset, and was still in her stockings. Her hair was loosened from its pins.

The room was not large, but cheerful with brightly coloured birds painted on vivid blue wallpaper. The chairs and bedcovers were a rich red and the mahogany furniture was accented in gold. She'd never seen a room quite like it.

Where was she?

Still feeling shaky and weak, she climbed out of the comfortable bed and found her slippers nearby. A man's banyan was draped over a chair. The dress she had worn at Vitium et Virtus was folded neatly on a chest.

She donned the banyan and tied it with a sash. There was plenty of fabric to cover her. The garment even reached the floor. Her hairpins were in a dish on a dressing table next to a brush and comb. She smoothed her hair back with the brush, twisted it into a chignon, and secured it with the hairpins.

The room had three doors. One revealed a dressing room, another a cosy sitting room. She walked to the last door and opened it to a hallway across from which was another door, presumably another bedchamber. The stairway was in between.

She paused in her doorway, trying to remember what happened. She remembered becoming dizzy at Vitium et Virtus. She remembered Oliver taking her to some private rooms in the club and insisting she go back to the hotel. She remembered him walking with her. After that, what?

Waking to him carrying her. Taking her inside a house and calling for someone to help him. Being undressed and tucked into that glorious bed.

She started down the stairway. Reaching the landing on the first floor, she could see to the hall below.

A manservant stood there, but looked up at her approach. 'Mrs Lockhart.' His greeting was cordial.

She remembered him. 'I am in Mr Gregory's house?' He'd answered the door the day before.

'That you are, ma'am,' the servant said. 'Mr Gregory asks that you join him for breakfast. I will show you the way.'

The man did not seem to take notice of her unusual dress. He led her out of the hall as if nothing was amiss.

He brought her to a small dining room and announced her presence. 'Mrs Lockhart.' Then left her there.

Oliver, the only person seated in the room, rose.

'Cecilia. You are awake.' His greeting was curt, a mere acknowledgement that she was present.

He walked around the table and guided her to the chair adjacent to his. 'Sit. I will fix you a plate.'

At the mention of food her nausea returned. 'Is—is there toasted bread? Please. That is all I want.'

He turned to the sideboard, which seemed to have a variety of foodstuffs, some emitting smells that were making her stomach roil. He placed a plate with two pieces of toasted bread on it in front of her.

'Butter or jam?' he asked.

'Nothing,' she said too sharply. 'Nothing,' she repeated in a more grateful tone.

He lifted a teapot. 'Tea?'

She nodded.

'Why—why am I here?' she asked him.

He poured her tea and placed the sugar and milk within her reach. 'You don't remember?'

'Only a little.'

He returned to his chair. 'I was walking you to your hotel when you fainted. It seemed wiser to bring you here than carry you to the hotel.'

She took a nibble of the toast and hoped it kept her from vomiting. 'I am not by habit so weak.'

He attended to his food. 'My housekeeper assures me that your symptoms are not unusual for a woman who is with child, but, just in case, I have sent for a doctor.'

'A doctor!' She did not wish to endure another examination. 'I—I am certain I am quite recovered. I do not need a doctor.'

'If you faint in front of me and barely regain your wits, I will consult a doctor.' He spoke in that firm, no-nonsense tone that put her guard up.

She was not about to argue the point and risk making him angrier.

Cecilia took another bite of her toast and chewed it carefully. 'So I am not allowed to leave until this doctor arrives?'

'Not allowed?' He looked surprised. 'You are not a prisoner, Cecilia. But the doctor has already been summoned. When he arrives, I want you to be examined by him.'

She nodded, but she did not like this turn of events. He spoke of freedom, then dictated what he wanted her to do.

They finished the breakfast in near silence. Cecilia concentrated on eating slowly and taking small sips of tea. Oliver read a newspaper.

Before they were finished, the butler announced the doctor's arrival.

She met the man in the drawing room. Oliver came with her and introduced himself and Cecilia to the doctor.

'Dr Ebersham,' the man said, shaking first Cecilia's, then Oliver's hand. If he thought it untoward that a single man asked him to examine an unrelated widow, dressed in a man's banyan, the doctor did not let on. 'Now what seems to be the problem?'

'I—I am going to have a baby,' Cecilia admitted. She recounted her symptoms.

Oliver described her fainting spell and her lack of being fully conscious later and then he excused himself.

His departure surprised Cecilia. She had thought he would want to hear everything she and the doctor said, given his doubting of her before.

The doctor listened to her heart with his wooden tube and pressed down on her abdomen. Thank goodness he did not want to examine inside her. He asked a great many questions about what she ate and drank, how much sleep she'd received, how much worry afflicted her.

When he was finished, he asked her if she wished Oliver to hear his conclusions. Her normal instinct was to keep anything about herself private. And she might have insisted upon doing so had he remained in the room. But because Oliver respected her privacy, she was willing for him to hear what the doctor said.

The doctor left the room to ask for him.

When Oliver and the doctor returned, the physician said, 'There is nothing serious. All you have experienced is not unexpected when a woman is *enceinte*.' He smiled at Cecilia. 'I do believe you should not exert yourself, though. Only do what feels comfortable for you to do. Do not fatigue yourself or strain yourself in any way. The nausea should pass after a few weeks. The dizziness may persist if you do not eat correctly and achieve sufficient rest.'

All Cecilia could think was that she must work. She could not just rest!

Oliver saw the doctor out and returned to the drawing room.

'Do not tell me I cannot work!' Cecilia cried as soon as he entered the room. 'I have no money.'

That was precisely what he'd been about to say, but the doctor warned about her getting upset.

'I told you, Cecilia, I will support you, as you asked.'

She averted her face as if he'd slapped her. 'And I have told you, I need money of my own in case you do not.'

Perhaps he should settle a sum of money on her right now. If he did so, he was certain his friends—and his father—would consider him a gullible twit.

Besides, if he gave her the funds now, she would leave and he was not ready for that to happen, not until he knew whatever it was she held back from him. And not until he knew her health was restored and she could give birth to this baby safely.

He sat in one of the chairs.

She still stood, her arms folded across her chest. 'Well?'

He tapped his fingers on the table, trying to determine what he should say to her. Something that would keep her healthy—and here—but would reassure her as well.

Finally, she sat as well, tucking the banyan around her.

'The doctor said you need to rest, to not exert yourself,' he began.

'Being a hostess is no exertion,' she burst out. 'All I do is stand around and talk.'

He'd watched her. It took some energy to feign excitement

over the roll of dice. And he doubted she'd ever sat in a chair. She'd certainly flagged quickly during the singing.

He held up a hand. 'Let me finish.'

Her lovely lips pressed together in a stubborn expression, but she gave him her attention.

'I cannot discharge you, not when Jacob hired you, but I certainly could attempt to exert some influence over his decision.'

Her eyes flashed. 'You would not dare.'

He met her gaze. 'Believe me, if I felt that was what I must do, I would do it and see it through.'

Her defiance flickered.

'Here is what I propose.' He was making this up as he went along. 'You may work, but you must rest in between. And if you cannot finish out an evening you must stop and leave before you make yourself ill.'

She lifted her chin. 'I'll make it through next time. I'll show you.'

Did she not understand? 'I don't want you to show me, Cecilia. I want you to take care of yourself and the baby inside you.' After the doctor's visit, he at least knew there was a baby. 'If you are worried about money, then it would behove you to leave that expensive hotel.'

'I intend to find a less expensive place to live,' she assured him.

Any place less expensive was likely to be further away which meant she would be travelling the roads of London at two in the morning.

'I can offer you a place to live that will cost you nothing.' What was he thinking? 'You will be close to Vitium et Virtus so if you do get fatigued you can quickly go home.'

'Where can there possibly be a place that will cost me nothing?' she scoffed.

He fixed his gaze on her. 'Here. Come and live here.'

Her eyes widened. 'Here? In this house?'

He nodded. 'In this house. It is not a large town house, but there is room enough for you. You saw the second bedchamber. It has a sitting room. When you are here, you can be as private as you like.'

She peered at him. 'What sort of payment is expected of me?'

'Cut line, Cecilia,' he said sharply. 'I may not look like a gentleman, but I am one.'

He'd heard his stepmother call him names because of his appearance. Even some of the women with whom he'd had affairs called him savage.

'I am not talking about how you look,' she shot back. 'Gentlemen of all shapes and sizes give gifts so they might get something in return.'

He glared at her. 'You have been around me enough to take that much measure of my character.'

She crossed her arms over her chest. 'Then are you not worried it is too scandalous to share a house with a widow?'

He shrugged. 'By whose estimation? I am a bastard son and you work in a gentlemen's club that I part-own. I do not think anyone expects propriety from either of us.'

Her eyes flashed at him. 'At least you did not say it was my interesting condition that makes me scandalous.'

'Your *interesting condition* makes it sensible for you to live here.'

'I do not see how,' she protested.

'Because it is free and you are close.' He was puzzled by her, but exasperated as well. 'What is your objection?'

Her brow furrowed and she pursed her lips.

'You say it is my child inside you,' he went on, because his doubts about her story were growing again. 'But perhaps it is not and that is why you do not wish to accept my offer.'

'The baby is yours,' she insisted.

'Then live here.' If he was ever to discover the truth about her, he needed her close by. 'You do not need to return to the hotel. I will send Irwin to collect your things and pay your bill.'

'Irwin?'

'My butler,' he explained. 'You stay here and rest.'

'Where will you be?' she asked.

'I need to go to the club for a while.' He did not *need* to go to the club, but her reluctance to share his house kindled memories of his stepmother refusing to live with him as soon as they reached England. He was immediately sent away to school.

She stared at him. 'What will the rules be if I live here?'

'Rules?' He'd always been against rules. He gave her a blank look. 'Do not destroy the furnishings?'

She blew out an exasperated breath. 'I mean, I must be free to come and go as I please.'

'Of course.' He thought more about this, though. 'I may want to restrict who may visit you, however.'

She caught on right away. 'No scores of men in my bed, do you mean?'

He met her eye. 'That is precisely what I mean.'

'That is hardly a worry.' She laughed drily. 'Even if I wished to entertain gentlemen—which I most assuredly do not—who would call upon me?'

Men she met at Vitium et Virtus, perhaps?

She took a breath. 'So... I will abide by your terms.'

He should not be this glad. 'We have a bargain, then?'

He reached over to her, extending his hand.

She hesitated. 'Will I have to pay for food?'

'No,' he responded. 'You will not have to pay for your rooms or your food. I offer them at my pleasure.'

She finally clasped her hand with his.

Her touch set off a flare of desire within him and a memory of bare skin against bare skin, of lovemaking and shared pleasure.

He released her and wondered what he had done to himself by inviting the intimacy of sharing this house.

* * *

Cecilia could still feel the warmth of his hand on hers even though their handshake was quick. In Paris she'd thought he would merely be a pleasant memory. Never did she conceive of actually living with him day after day. She'd never wanted to live with a man again. Never wanted to be under a man's control again.

But this was simply too tempting an offer. Free food. Free room. She could save every bit of what she made at Vitium et Virtus. And if he did give her enough money for her and the baby to live on, all the better.

But not expecting anything of her in return? That made her suspicious.

'Is there pen and paper?' she asked. 'I will write a note for the hotel.'

He rose and walked over to a table with a drawer. He took out a sheet of paper, an inkpot and a pen. He handed them to her and sat back in his chair.

She leaned over to write the note on the side table. When she was finished she handed it to him. 'I have some coins stitched in my valise. If Irwin could pay the hotel bill, I will pay back the money when he returns.'

Oliver took the note. 'I am well able to afford your hotel bill.'

He would pay her hotel bill? That meant even more obligation to him. She knew how it would be. The more he did for her, the more control he would have over her.

But she must go along with it for the baby's sake.

'Irwin should have no difficulty,' she said. 'My valise is packed with everything I own.' In case she had to leave in a hurry—a habit she'd acquired from living with Duncan.

'I am certain Irwin will have no difficulty,' he assured her.

She stood. 'May I retire to the bedchamber now?'

He stood as well. 'You do not need my permission, Cecilia.'

She nodded. 'It is just that I am suddenly fatigued again.'

'You do not need to explain.' He gave her a concerned look. 'Are you feeling unwell? Do you require anything?'

'Nothing.' She wished he would not be so solicitous. It confused her. And warmed her towards him. 'Sleep, perhaps.' She walked unsteadily to the door.

He came to her side. 'I'll escort you.'

He gave her his arm. Holding on to him did steady her. It also reminded her of their day in Paris when she'd held his arm and they'd seen so many wonderful sights together.

His strength made it so much easier to climb the two flights of stairs to the bedchamber where he'd taken her the night before.

'Who undressed me?' she asked.

His mouth turned up in a half-smile. 'I am tempted to set you into a pique and tell you Irwin and I did it, but Mrs Irwin, my housekeeper, and Mrs Smith, the cook, were the ones.'

This little tease reminded her of his light banter in Paris. She did not want to feel amused by him again.

They reached her room, and he opened the door.

'I'll leave you now, Cecilia, unless there is something I may do for you.' He stepped away.

She crossed the threshold, but turned to see him already at the stairs.

'Oliver?' she called.

He turned.

Her throat felt suddenly tight. 'Thank you,' she managed, though it came out sharper than she intended.

He nodded, turned and descended the stairs.

Cecilia slept until the light dimmed in the room and the clock chimed five o'clock. Five o'clock! She'd slept the day away.

She stretched and sat up, feeling more rested than any time she could remember. Even the nausea had disappeared. Was it the bed? she wondered. Or was it because Oliver had taken away most of her worries?

For the moment.

There was a soft rap at the door. Cecilia jumped out of bed and quickly donned the banyan. 'Who is it?' she asked.

A young woman, little more than a girl, opened the door and peeked in. 'You are awake, ma'am! May I come in?'

'Yes?' Cecilia said uncertainly.

The girl entered, carrying Cecilia's valise. She promptly curtsied. 'I am Mary. Mary Driscoll, ma'am. I'm to be your maid, if you'll have me. Mr Gregory told Mr Irwin you should have a maid and as he is my uncle—Mr Irwin, that is—he asked Mr Gregory if it could be me and Mr Gregory said yes. So I can learn and all.'

Cecilia had not had a maid in years, but this one looked young and fresh and untouched by the world.

'How old are you, Mary?' Cecilia asked.

'Sixteen, ma'am, but I've worked a little here, cleaning and that sort. And I learn fast.' The girl was earnest. 'I want to be a lady's maid, y'see.'

'Oh, Mary.' Cecilia sat down on the chair by the dressing table. 'I do not think that I am the sort of person who can help you be a lady's maid.'

The girl's face turned crestfallen. 'But I love to do hair and mend clothes and such. I am good at it, Aunt Irwin says.'

'It isn't that.' How was she to explain? 'I am simply not the sort from whom anyone would want a reference. In fact, serving me might be an impediment.'

Mary seemed to cogitate on this. 'Do you mean because you are an unmarried lady living with Mr Gregory? Or because you work in the club? Or because you are going to have a baby?'

'You know a great deal about me,' Cecilia said with some dismay.

'Oh, we all do. My uncle and aunt and Cook, at least. Mr

Gregory explained it all. None of that worries us, though. My mum was never married to my dad, y'see. And my sister once worked at the club.'

Had Cecilia ever been that unguarded? She supposed she had. Unguarded and naïve and easily manipulated.

Mary went on. 'And Uncle Irwin says when the time comes, Mr Gregory will get me work in the Duke of Westmoor's house and nobody will question a reference from a duke.'

Cecilia was not so certain of this. Rose had been a maid herself. Surely society was less than accepting of her, even if she had married a duke. A commoner duchess was certainly better than a scandalous widow, though.

She smiled. 'Then I would be delighted for you to be my lady's maid.'

Mary gave an excited whoop and jumped up and down. When she settled, she asked, 'May I start right now? I can arrange your hair and put you in a gown.'

The few dresses Cecilia had brought with her would be terribly wrinkled from being in the valise, but she supposed they'd have to do.

'May I suggest the green dress?' She spoke as if she were a lady's maid of vast experience.

'It is here?'

Mary went into the dressing room and brought it out. 'Mr Gregory brought it from the club. I tiptoed in here while you were asleep. I also brought in fresh water for you to wash.'

It had been a long time since a maid had cared for her clothes, helped her bathe and dress and fix her hair. Not since she'd lived at home with her parents and sisters. She'd never had a lady's maid of her own, but she'd always had help with dressing and with her hair. Until she married Duncan.

'Mr Gregory said I was to ask you if you wanted your dinner sent up here or if you would join him in the dining room,' Mary told her while pinning up her hair.

Cecilia did not know what to say. 'I don't know. What do you think he wanted me to do?'

'Why, for you to join him for dinner, of course!' Mary cried, then seemed to question whether she'd been too boisterous. 'Ma'am.'

'Then dress me for dinner with Mr Gregory, Mary.'

'Yes, ma'am!'

Chapter Ten

A week later Oliver and Jacob rose early to give their best horses a good run on Rotten Row. After a friendly race at full gallop on the bridle paths of Hyde Park, the two men cooled their horses at a sedate pace. Rotten Row this early in the morning was a busy place with other riders and groomsmen exercising their masters' horses.

It had been an eventful week and a sad one. Queen Charlotte's death had been announced and the country again plunged into mourning, as they had done the year before for her granddaughter and namesake, Princess Charlotte, the Prince Regent's only daughter, the heir to the throne.

The royal mourning meant that usual social events were suspended or greatly subdued. As a result, more members came to Vitium et Virtus for entertainment. Oliver and his friends did not require the women in their employ to wear black, but they did dress them in various shades of purple and gave them black armbands. Snyder, their porter, always wore black, but he and the other male servants also donned black armbands.

As the Duke of Westmoor, Jacob was expected to participate in the royal funeral. The Queen had died in Kew Palace and there would be a funeral procession from there to Windsor where she would be interred in St George's Chapel.

'I am not made for all this ceremony,' Jake complained. 'I mean no disrespect for the late Queen—she was quite beloved by my grandmother who'd served her in their younger days—but the whole pageant sounds gruelling and tedious. You've no idea how many will participate!'

'It will be elaborate, I am certain,' Oliver agreed. He did not like to dwell too much on the Queen's death. On any death of a mother.

Had his mother had a funeral? Had someone placed her body on a pyre and set it aflame?

Jacob shook his head. 'Enough of the funeral.'

It wasn't as if Oliver brought up the subject. He hadn't started any part of their conversation this morning. The last time he'd seen Jacob, he'd told him about inviting Cecilia to live in his town house. They'd exchanged sharp words over it. Jake warned Oliver that this was bound to cause trouble among the other women at Vitium et Virtus. Worse, he worried that Oliver might not treat Cecilia well, given his history of dalliances with women. Jake did not believe for a moment that there would be no dalliance.

For reasons Oliver could not explain, even to himself, he had not told Jacob or Frederick or anyone that Cecilia was the woman he'd met in Paris, nor had he mentioned she was carrying a child—his child.

Or so she claimed.

'So...' Jake began in a cautious tone. 'How are you faring with Cecilia?'

Oliver did not wish to reopen this discussion.

'Splendidly,' Oliver replied. 'Truly, we see little of each other.'

This was the truth. Cecilia kept to herself in her room and

sitting room a great deal of the time. Oliver did not intrude upon her privacy. They did share breakfast occasionally and dinner almost every night.

But he certainly was not going to tell Jacob that sharing meals with her was actually pleasant.

'And at Vitium et Virtus?' Jake persisted. 'Any problems?'

'None of which I have been made aware.' Oliver shook his head. 'I am still not certain a hostess makes any sense at all, though.'

Not any more sense than how much Oliver disliked seeing her in that role.

'Does she help make money?' Jake asked. 'How's the take for the hazard and faro tables? Is it up?'

'Up, but not by much.' His horse lagged behind Jake's and Oliver urged the mare to catch up. 'I will say that the members appear to have taken to her.'

Some of the gentlemen even sought her out. She was attentive to several of them, bringing them drinks and cheering the play at the tables. Sometimes Oliver would spy her seated at a table with one of them, listening intently as the man seemed to prattle on. She had been true to her word, though. She never sought to be private with any of them.

'Does the increased amount cover her wages?' Jacob asked.

'More than covers it,' Oliver replied. At least the part of her wages Oliver took from Vitium et Virtus. That amount was on a par with the singers and dancers. The rest came from his pocket.

'Well, then, as long as we are not losing money, no harm is done to have her there,' Jake said. 'She needed the employment. I would hate to think where she would work otherwise.'

So would Oliver.

This moment was a perfect opportunity for him to tell Jake of meeting Cecilia in Paris.

But he kept his mouth shut.

Jake also did not know Oliver had been discussing with

his banker how to set up some sort of annuity for her. Or that he'd indulged her by sending for the modiste the club used for their singers' and dancers' costumes and was having Cecilia fitted for several new dresses, not only for the club, but mourning clothes for day as well. He'd paid extra for them to be completed in a rush. The first of the dresses would be ready tomorrow.

'Will you come to Vitium et Virtus tonight?' Oliver asked.

Jacob looked dismayed. 'Forgive me, Oliver. I cannot. Grandmama has taken to her bed.'

'She is ill?' Oliver was fond of the elderly lady. She'd always been kind to him.

'Mourning more than ill, I am certain, but I think I should stay at home.'

'Of course,' Oliver said.

Jacob turned to him. 'Tonight features the dancers, is that not right?'

The dancers frolicked through the ballroom showing lots of leg and bosom and sensuality in their performance. It was one of the most sought-after entertainments at the club. Oliver would have them subdue their enthusiasm tonight out of respect for the deceased Queen.

They rode a few paces in silence before Jacob said, 'I am ashamed to say I cannot muster much interest in our club entertainments. Not since marrying Rose.'

Oliver could not muster interest in the entertainments and he had no wife.

So much had changed since Nicholas disappeared. The club used to be the friends' shared passion and they relished partaking in whatever boisterous debauchery they'd conceived. But now they were older and Nicholas was gone, and Frederick and Jacob were married. The club had become more of a business venture in Oliver's eyes than his preferred playhouse. There was nothing particularly carefree and daring about a business venture.

They exited the park at Hyde Park Corner, now more crowded with other riders, carriages, and wagons than when they'd set out.

When they reached Park Lane, Jacob said, 'This is where I must leave you.' He leant over and shook Oliver's hand. 'I am sorry we have abandoned you to run Vitium et Virtus alone, Oliver.'

Oliver smiled at him. 'Do not apologise. What else would I do, if not for Vitium et Virtus? Come when you can. Otherwise stay with your family.'

Jake grinned. 'With pleasure!'

That night after a pleasant dinner, Oliver escorted Cecilia to Vitium et Virtus. They walked the back way, through his garden and out of the gate to the alley, then through another gate into the garden of the club. The night was damp and cold and they walked briskly, entering through the door that led to the private part of the building. In the entryway, Oliver helped Cecilia off with her cloak. She felt the touch of his hands on her shoulders even as he turned to hang her cloak on a peg by the door.

She pulled off her gloves and left them on a table where Oliver had placed his hat.

'I will leave you here,' Cecilia told him.

She would paint her face a little and put her mask in place before again becoming Coquette.

To her surprise, he touched her hand. 'Are you feeling well enough tonight?' he asked.

She nodded. 'I am feeling quite well, actually.'

Perhaps he meant the touch as a goodbye. Whatever his reason, it set her heart dancing.

He had been so kind these last days, ever since she agreed to live in a room in his house. The room, sitting room and dressing room gave her more space than she'd ever lived in since leaving her parents' houses. She told herself that it made sense for her to eat with him, if only to save the servants from climbing the stairs to bring her a meal. She breakfasted in the small dining room for the same reason, although he was often out by the time she rose.

At meals they talked of the events written in the newspapers or chatted about at the club. Cecilia had followed closely the news of the Queen's death and the plan for her funeral, as well as news of financial hardship around the country and of society people and events.

Meals were so comfortable they became her favourite part of the day.

And being Coquette again was her least favourite.

She made her way to the Green Room where the dancers were busy dressing in lavender gowns. Her new lady's maid, Mary, had already arranged her hair and dressed her in her costume, a gown of deep purple.

'There she is,' one of the dancers said scathingly. 'Oliver's choice.'

'Hello, Lanie,' she responded in a friendly tone. 'How are you faring today?'

Cecilia was sorry she upset Lanie, who so obviously wished Oliver favoured her. Lanie's jealousy put a pall on the otherwise genial atmosphere among the workers. Jealousy was so unnecessary. Cecilia kept her distance from Oliver and he seemed content for her to do so.

They might converse comfortably at dinner, but that was more like a truce than an affair. She could not convince Lanie of that fact, though.

Lanie glowered. 'I'd fare a lot better if I were sharing the boss's bed like you do.'

'Leave her alone, Lanie,' came a voice from the back of the room.

It was Flo.

'Never mind, Flo,' Cecilia assured her. She turned to Lanie. 'I share his house, not his bed, Lanie.' Not now, at least.

'I am not a fool, Coquette.' Lanie flounced past her and left the room.

'Ooh,' the other girls said, laughing.

Cecilia walked over to Flo, who was seated in a chair, but had wrapped her head and shoulders in a shawl. 'I am surprised to see you here, Flo. Are you working tonight?'

Flo shook her head. 'I came to see you.'

'Me?' Cecilia pulled up a chair and sat near her.

Flo glanced at the dancers as if to check if they were watching. She lifted the shawl away from her face. There was a bruise from her temple to her cheek.

'Flo!' Cecilia said in alarm.

Flo covered her face again. 'I—I bumped into a door.'

'You did not bump into a door!' Cecilia touched her own cheek, again feeling the pain of Duncan's fist.

Flo gave her an obstinate look. 'All I want is for you to help me cover it up. I am to visit my mother tomorrow and I do not want her to see it.'

She'd helped Flo cover up bruises on her neck one night, as well as the ones on her arms that first time they met.

'Why? What would your mother think if she saw such a bruise on your face?'

'It—it would make her worry over me and she has enough to worry over feeding my brothers and sisters.'

Cecilia shook her head. 'She'd think someone hit you.'

Flo's hand went to her face. 'Oh, no. I bumped into a door.'

How many *doors* had Cecilia bumped into during her marriage? Her teeth ached as she remembered the pain of Duncan's fist.

Cecilia took Flo's hands in hers and made the girl look into her eyes. 'Heed me, Flo. I know someone hit you. I know, because my husband used to hit me. He used to squeeze my arms until they bruised just like the bruises on your arms when we first met. And the ones on your neck? My husband made marks like that when he choked me.' She released one of Flo's hands and gently touched her face. 'I'll cover your bruise, but we should do it tomorrow morning. What I do tonight will not last.'

Flo's eyes filled with tears. 'Do you think Mr Gregory and Mr Bell would let me stay here tonight? I do not wish to go back to my rooms.'

Cecilia raised her brows. 'Because he knows where you live? Or is he waiting for you there?'

Flo clamped her mouth shut.

There were bedrooms in the club, the rooms where willing men and women could retire and indulge their passions. Or in the case of some of the women, make some money.

'I will ask.' If Oliver refused her, Cecilia would take her to her own rooms to spend the night. 'Will you wait here?'

'Here or in the servants' hall,' Flo said.

Cecilia nodded. 'Tomorrow morning I will come back here and we will cover your bruise.'

They would be alone, then. Maybe when they were alone, Flo would tell her who was beating her.

She hugged Flo and left to put a dusting of powder on her face and tint on her cheeks and lips like Vincent had taught her, with a light touch. She found her mask, made from feathers dyed purple. She filed past the dancers and wished them a good performance.

Lanie waited for her in the hallway. 'How did you manage it, Coquette? Coquette. Such a silly name.'

'I agree,' Cecilia responded, determined not to make an enemy of the girl. 'Coquette is a silly name.'

'That is not my question.' Lanie looked peeved. 'How did you manage to snare Oliver? He has refused any attachment to the rest of us.'

'Lanie.' Cecilia spoke as kindly as she could. 'Do not fret over this. I've explained the nature of my relationship with Mr Gregory. There is no reason to be in such a high dudgeon.'

'The nature of your relationship?' Her voice mimicked someone haughty.

What truly was the nature of her relationship with Oliver, though? Cecilia did not know. His actions were kind and generous, but she often caught him looking at her with anger in his eyes. He did not trust her or believe her.

But if he touched her, even to help remove her cloak, her senses flared in response as if there was still something romantic between them. Like in Paris.

She shook the thought from her head.

'Leave it, Lanie,' she said.

She continued down the corridor to the stairs leading to the hall where Snyder stood guard. At least that was how Cecilia always thought of it. She was pleased the large man was always nearby. Just in case.

She had been propositioned many times by the men in the game room. Some were very displeased she did not accept their offers. Some offered her as much as Madame Coquette earned in Paris.

She passed the ballroom and glimpsed Oliver standing near the stage. He turned and watched her walk by. She felt his gaze upon her as if it were a touch.

Members and guests were already arriving. The Queen's death increased attendance, as if mourning the Queen was less important than card-playing, gambling and watching bawdy entertainment.

At the door of the game room she hesitated. Taking a breath, she closed her eyes and transformed herself into Coquette.

Oliver walked to the door of the ballroom after Cecilia passed. At the door to the game room her demeanour changed. She became more fluid, her posture more relaxed, her neck looser. When she entered the room, her hips swayed.

She'd become Coquette.

He watched this transformation almost every night the club was open. Could she feign such sensuality?

How could she be two such different women?

Coquette was sensual, approachable, light-hearted. She drew men out so that suddenly they were talking with her, confiding in her. Cecilia was guarded, wary and cool.

No, she was three women, not two. The Cecilia he'd met in Paris was vulnerable, sad and passionately loving.

These changes intrigued him as much as they fed his suspicions of her. Who was she really? And why did she hide her true self?

He entered the game room, but remained at its doorway, pretending to check the room, but really watching her.

She greeted several of the members she undoubtedly recognised and soon was laughing with them and encouraging them to play hazard. Was she pretending to be excited by each roll of the dice? She must be, although she did it so well she had him believing it.

After a few minutes she left the men at the hazard table and walked towards the door. When she saw Oliver there, she seemed to lose Coquette for a moment and become Cecilia.

'Fetching drinks,' she said to him as she passed him.

She brought two of the members at the hazard table glasses of brandy, watched them for a little while and made her way to the faro table. There were only three members there. Two of them greeted her. The third man sidled up to her, effectively separating her from the other men.

Oliver tensed. He recognised a man attempting a conquest. Why should it bother him? He had no claim on Cecilia.

Still, it roused his emotions to think she might accept.

Instead, she stepped away from the man and abruptly left the table. She walked swiftly to the doorway, her expression one of distress.

She passed Oliver without seeming to see him.

He went after her, catching up to her in the hallway. 'What is it, Cecilia? What did that member say to you?'

'Nothing.' She could not look at him, though, and she backed away as if wanting to flee.

He seized her arm. 'Come with me.'

He brought her into the private rooms of the club and removed his mask. 'Now, tell me what happened.'

She pulled her mask off as well. 'Nothing happened. It is just that…' She paused and seemed to have difficulty composing herself enough to speak. 'I—I recognised him.'

'Someone you knew from before?' he asked cautiously.

She laughed with disdain. 'I should say so.'

She'd met Bowles in Paris. But the man who'd spoken to her was not Bowles; Oliver could tell. There must have been other men. 'Who is he?'

Her eyes narrowed. 'You told me never to reveal a member's identity.'

'Cecilia, tell me who it is.'

She met his eye again, but this time hers were full of pain. 'My father.'

'Your father?' Her father was a member? 'Who is your father?'

She glanced away as if considering whether or not to tell him. She glanced back. 'Baron Dorman.'

Dorman? She was Dorman's daughter? A member of the aristocracy?

'He did not recognise me.' Her voice cracked.

Oliver took her in his arms and held her tightly against him. She clung to him and repeated in a more agonised tone, 'He did not recognise me.'

He wanted only to soothe her. 'Of course he did not recognise you. You wore a mask.'

'I recognised him!' she cried.

He probably did not look above her neck, Oliver thought.

She pulled out of Oliver's embrace. 'How dare he gamble! When I was at home, all he did was complain about how much my sisters and I cost him. How he could not afford decent dowries for us. How dare he be so foolish as to play faro!'

Faro was simply a game of chance. The cards were either with you or against you, no skill involved whatsoever.

She paced in front of him. 'I hardly know what to say or do!'

'Would you like me to confront him, Cecilia?' he asked.

She stopped and faced him, obviously considering this. Finally, she met his eye. 'No. Not you. I want to confront him.'

'Then I will bring him to you.'

'Here?' she asked.

'Here.'

She had a look of steely resolve. 'Yes. Bring him here.'

'I will remain nearby.' In case that feeling of panic returned, the one with which she entered the room. Her panic had swiftly transformed into anger, her apparent feelings of weakness, into strength.

She nodded.

He tied his mask on once more and left the room to make his way back to the public rooms and to Lord Dorman who was still at the faro table, losing his money.

'Sir?' Oliver did not call him by name. 'Coquette would like a private word with you.'

The man puffed up like a rooster. 'Coquette? Private? Yes, indeed. Thought she would.' He followed Oliver eagerly. 'Back in the private rooms, no doubt.'

'My private rooms.' Oliver escorted him through the owners' entrance, taking off his mask as he crossed the threshold.

'Should I remove my mask?' Dorman asked.

'If you so desire,' Oliver replied. 'It is entirely up to you.'

Dorman removed his mask and combed his thinning hair with his fingers.

When they reached the door to the drawing room, Cecilia stood with her back to them. She turned as they entered. She'd donned her mask again.

Her father approached her and bowed. 'Lord Dorman at your service, my dear.'

She lifted her chin. 'I know who you are.'

The man simpered. 'Then I am excessively honoured.'

'Are you, sir?' she responded haughtily.

This was yet another Cecilia, Oliver thought. Strong and sure. He could not help but be fascinated.

She smiled at Dorman, slipping back into Coquette's seductive style. 'How has your luck been at the faro table?'

'About to turn at any moment.' Dorman laughed. 'But you must not worry your pretty little head over it.'

'Must I not?' she simpered.

She was playing him with finesse, Oliver thought. He had no idea where she was leading the man, but he admired her for it.

She smiled again. 'Are you pleased that I asked to see you in private?'

Dorman lowered his voice. 'I am very pleased, my dear. I trust you will not be disappointed that you requested me.'

Dorman took another step towards her. Cecilia took a step back and Oliver braced himself to intervene on her behalf, should it become necessary.

'I am disappointed.' Her tone turned sharp.

'Disappointed? But, why? How can I change your mind?' Dorman sputtered.

She fixed her gaze on him. 'You do not recognise me, do you?'

'Should I?' he asked.

'You should.' She pulled off her mask.

Chapter Eleven

It took several painful seconds for Cecilia to finally see recognition dawn on her father's face. Had she truly been so unimportant to him that he had not committed her face to memory?

'You!' he said breathlessly, his face blanched.

Not even using her name.

'I know I am not so altered that a father would not remember me after a little more than three years,' she said. 'A loving father, that is. Not one who declares me dead to him.'

He turned red. 'You disgraced the family!'

'You could have prevented that if you had accepted the marriage.' That had been what Duncan expected. If her father had accepted the marriage, society would have forgiven the elopement and that would have been an end to any scandal.

'Accept the marriage?' Her father huffed. 'He was a nobody!'

She glanced over at Oliver, who stood by the door in the shadows so she could not see his reaction. She'd told him about her marriage, at least about eloping and being disowned.

'Look at you now,' he said scathingly. 'He has you working as a strumpet. I dare say if anyone does recognise you, it will be more scandal for your sisters and your mother.'

'Take care, sir.' Oliver spoke in a sinister tone. 'Your daughter works here as a hostess, nothing else. And, since you were so eager to accept her favours, do not think your hypocrisy is lost on either of us.'

Cecilia added, 'What is more, I would not be forced into this position if you and Mama had taken me in. Mr Gregory was kind enough to hire me so I would not starve.'

Her father laughed derisively. 'What? That no-good husband of yours is not even supporting you?'

'He is dead.'

Cecilia touched her abdomen and thought of the baby growing inside her. She once thought that her parents would welcome her back because of the baby. Now she did not consider her father worthy of learning of the baby's existence.

She went on. 'I wonder how much money you have lost gambling at this club? As much as my dowry would have cost you? How very convenient to refuse to provide that money to Duncan so you could lose it gambling. Tell me, are my sisters still fighting over the dwindling resources?'

'Your sisters married. Respectably,' he shot back. 'But, if it had not been for you, they could have married much higher.'

She ignored that statement. 'Does Mama know you gamble at Vitium et Virtus? Is she still forced to make economies? To deny herself?'

His eyes flashed in panic. 'You would not tell your mother I am a member!'

'Or that you were ready for a dalliance with your own daughter?' she added with sarcasm.

Oliver stepped forward. 'Except you are no longer a member of Vitium et Virtus.'

'What?' Her father sounded outraged. 'You have no cause to expel me.'

'I do not need a cause, except that I do not like the way you treat your daughter,' Oliver said.

Her father took a step towards him. 'Why, you half-caste bastard! Wait until I take this to the Duke. Or to Challenger. We will see who is expelled.'

Oliver stood his ground. 'I implore you to take this to the Duke. Or to Frederick. Do not forget to explain how eager you were to be private with Coquette.'

'I am certain Mama would like to know about that,' Cecilia added. 'As well as about the gambling.'

Oliver extended his arm towards the door. 'Unless Cecilia has more to say to you, let me show you out.'

'I am quite finished,' she said.

Oliver escorted Lord Dorman to the door to the club's rooms.

'Put on your mask,' he ordered, pulling his own from his pocket.

Dorman fumbled for his mask and managed to affix it well enough. When he again wore the disguise required by Vitium et Virtus, Oliver opened the door and led him to the hall where Snyder was in attendance.

'This guest is leaving,' Oliver said. 'And he is not welcome to return.'

'As you wish, Mr Gregory.' Snyder was particularly astute in recognising members under their masks. If he was not certain, he could take them to a more private area and have them remove the mask and verify their identity.

'I'll not forget this, Gregory,' Dorman snapped.

Oliver gave him a contemptuous smile. 'I'll not forget either, Dorman. Neither will my friends. Cause me or the lady trouble and neither will the other members of Vitium et Virtus.'

Dorman's eyes flashed in alarm.

Snyder handed the man his topcoat, hat and gloves. When

Dorman had donned them, Snyder walked to the door to the outside and opened it.

'An abomination! That is what this is. An abomination!' Dorman strode out, and Snyder closed the door behind him.

'So what did he do?' Snyder asked.

Since Snyder was the gatekeeper, he needed to know. It helped him bar members if they tried to return.

'Coquette knew something about him, about his mistreatment of his family,' Oliver responded. 'If he tries to return, simply inform him that we will tell his wife all about him.'

Snyder smiled. 'I dare say I could threaten any of them with that statement.'

Oliver answered in the same tone, 'Unless the wives attend, as well.'

'Indeed.' Snyder grinned.

Oliver returned to Cecilia, finding her seated on the sofa, her hands pressed against her abdomen.

Without thinking, he sat down next to her and put his arm around her. 'That cannot have been easy for you.'

She leaned against him. 'I cannot stop shaking.'

He held her tighter.

'I always knew I meant little to him,' she said. 'This was not a surprise.'

But it hurt anyway. Just as his stepmother's cruelty once hurt him. 'He is a detestable man.'

She turned to him so she was able to look him in the face. 'You expelled him. I never expected that.'

He shrugged. 'I could not have him come back.' Not to hurt her all over again. 'The chances he would cause trouble are too great.'

She shivered. 'He gambles away large sums without blinking an eye. I know that would cause my mother hardship. And I am sure my sisters will have suffered. Their dowries must have been limited by his losses.'

Oliver once relished the excitement of a game of chance, of

risking large sums and hoping for the big win. He was lucky that he could always stop himself from risking more than he could afford. He saw it over and over in the game room of other establishments, the men and women whose losses were devastating, but still they could not stop.

She sighed. 'I suppose he will find some other place to gamble.' She leaned against him again. 'I should not care about it.'

But she did no matter what she said.

'You do not need to return to the game room tonight, if you do not wish to,' he told her. 'I will walk you home now, if you like.'

She straightened. 'No. No. I can go back.' She laughed scornfully. 'If I do not, those gentlemen in the game room, who certainly knew my father's identity, will think I went to spend the night with him.'

'You do make a point.'

She put on her mask. 'I wish I knew how my mother and sisters are faring. It sounds like life has been difficult for them.'

'Would you like me to make enquiries about them?' he asked.

She shook her head. 'No. At least I do not think so.'

They walked out of the room and into the hallway.

Cecilia touched Oliver's arm and he faced her.

'I—I did not deserve the kindness and support you showed me with my father,' she said to him. 'I do not know how to thank you.'

'It was not so difficult a thing for me.'

He found his senses surging at her closeness. He glanced at her neck and noticed the pearl necklace, remembering her thanks in Paris for that trifling gift, remembering what had come after.

He leaned down, closer. Her scent filled his nostrils. He wanted her and her lips were tantalisingly close.

Her eyes dilated.

But he pulled back and continued walking.

'He called you vile names,' she said a moment later. 'I am so sorry. You did not deserve that.'

He smiled. 'I have heard such names my whole life, Cecilia.' Bastard. Half-caste.

'That is dreadful!' she exclaimed.

He lifted a shoulder. 'It is what I am, is it not?'

She resumed walking this time, but he heard her murmur, 'You are much more.'

His heart swelled at that.

They reached the door to the club's rooms, but she stopped again.

'I forgot to ask you something,' she said, her tone changing. 'A favour, really.'

His mistrust was roused. Was she manipulating him? A compliment, then a request? 'What is it?'

A wariness flickered in her eyes. 'Um...when I was in the Green Room... Flo was there.'

'This is not her night to perform,' he said.

'I know.' Cecilia continued. 'She asked me to ask you if she could spend the night here. Alone. Just this once. She cannot go back to her rooms tonight.'

'Why not?' he asked. He'd not expected the request to be on another's behalf.

'She did not tell me, but she seemed...upset...and a little frantic about what she would do.'

It was not something that he could allow on a regular basis, lest the workers move in completely, but it seemed churlish to refuse. Or perhaps it was merely difficult for him to say no to Cecilia.

'Just this once, if she doesn't make a thing of it with the others.' His tone turned sharp. 'I'll tell Snyder and Mr Bell.'

She shrank from him. 'Thank you, Oliver.'

They proceeded to the club's rooms and he walked her

to the doorway of the game room. He watched her take a breath and loosen her limbs and again turn herself back into Coquette.

The next morning Cecilia rose early and, with Mary's assistance, dressed in one of her old dresses, her hair in a simple plait down her back. She hurried down to breakfast and learned that Oliver had already gone out.

She ate quickly and told Irwin that she was going over to Vitium et Virtus to help Flo with something.

'As you wish, ma'am,' Irwin said.

She tried the door she and Oliver always used, but it was locked. She crossed the garden again and walked back to the alley and to the front of the house. She sounded the knocker, and Snyder answered the door.

'Coquette,' he said by way of greeting.

'I've come to see Flo,' Cecilia told him.

That seemed to be enough of an explanation for him. He let her enter, even took her cloak.

'Flo is below stairs,' Snyder said.

'Thank you, Snyder.' She walked down the stairs to the dressing room, but Flo was not there. She walked back out to the hallway and saw one of the kitchen workers.

'Morning, Coquette,' the girl said.

'Good morning, Sally,' she responded. 'I'm here to see Flo. Do you know where she is?'

'I do,' the girl responded. 'She's finishing breakfast in the kitchen. Poor thing. She bruised her face. She bumped into a door.'

'Yes,' Cecilia said. 'She told me.'

She came to the kitchen and the cook offered her a cup of tea, which Cecilia gratefully accepted. They all chatted amiably until Flo, hiding her bruised face with her hand, finished eating.

She and Cecilia returned to the dressing room, and Cecilia sat Flo down in front of a mirror and started to work on covering her bruise. Yesterday it had been red and blue; today it was purple.

Flo flinched when Cecilia touched the injured area. Cecilia remembered the pain of a new bruise and she winced in sympathy.

Cecilia started by dabbing Almond Bloom on the bruise. 'A fist made this bruise.' How well she remembered.

Flo tensed.

Cecilia continued. 'I told you. I know how it feels. The fist hitting you. It feels like the pain will explode in your head. Your eyes blur. And then he hits you again.'

She mixed a tiny bit of lip tint to the face powder and put the powder over the Almond Bloom. She repeated this.

And kept talking. 'You wonder what you did wrong. Maybe you should have known not to say what you said, or do what you did. After a while you start to think maybe you deserved to be punched in the face.'

Flo's eyes glistened with tears.

Cecilia put on another layer of powder.

'Won't you please tell me about it?' she asked Flo, keeping her voice low and soft.

''E— 'E is a gentleman,' she began, her accent making her sound like a little girl. 'He gave me presents and said I was pretty and that I was special.'

Cecilia felt a pang of pain.

Duncan's flattery had fallen on grateful ears. Cecilia had been so lonely. Her mother had been preoccupied by money. Her sisters resented and excluded her. She'd been so ripe for someone to pay attention to her and Duncan, so handsome, had told her everything she'd yearned to hear.

Flo went on. 'He asks me about Vitium et Virtus all the time. About Mr Gregory and the Duke and Mr Challenger— they are the owners, you know. He asks if they talk about him and he gets very angry when I say I never hear them say anything.'

This was odd. The man's connection was obviously with Oliver and the other owners, not with Flo.

'Lately I've been thinkin' he doesn't care a fig about me; he just wants to hear about them. But he said he'd never let me go, so I might as well do as he asks, but I can't because I don't ever know anything!' Her words were rushing out now.

And her tears were flowing, washing away Cecilia's handiwork. She started sobbing, and Cecilia took her in her arms and held her, smoothing her hair and trying to soothe her, but instead of being comforted Flo seemed to unfurl her pain and confusion and fear all at once.

There was a loud knocking on the dressing-room door. Cecilia handed Flo a handkerchief and went to answer it.

She opened the door a crack.

It was Oliver.

'What is this?' he asked. 'Snyder said you were here. I heard weeping.'

'Fleurette is a little upset,' Cecilia said.

'Let me talk to her.' He pushed on the door.

She opened it. He walked in, but she hurried to Flo first.

'Mr Gregory wants to see you,' she said.

Flo cowered. 'No! I mustn't talk to him.'

Oliver reached the girl's side. He crouched down so his face was even with hers. 'Why not, Fleurette? Whatever it is that makes you cry so, you must tell me.'

'It is about a gentleman who has been paying her particular attention,' Cecilia said. She did not want to say too much for fear Flo would clamp her lips shut for good.

Oliver handed Flo his handkerchief.

Flo wiped her eyes with the handkerchief and rubbed off the careful cover Cecilia had made over her bruise.

Oliver's gaze darted to Cecilia and back to Flo. He touched Flo's cheek very gently. 'Did the gentleman cause this bruise?'

Flo's eyes grew very wide, but she nodded.

He took Flo's hand. 'We cannot have this, can we? I do not allow anyone to hurt my entertainers, do I?'

''E— 'E would not want me to tell,' Flo said.

'What he wants does not matter a fig, does it?' Oliver responded. 'We cannot have you being hurt. You are too important to the club.'

Cecilia felt tears burning her eyes. She'd remained dry-eyed when her father blatantly rejected her, but Oliver's kindness to Flo was turning her into a watering pot. She knew how much such kindness meant. She'd needed it so desperately when Duncan went into a rage.

''E said he'd hurt me if I told anyone. He'd hurt me and never come back to me,' Flo said, her voice small.

'You cannot want him back!' exclaimed Cecilia. She used to pray Duncan would leave her.

'He wasn't always mean,' Flo shot back. 'Sometimes he was very sweet to me.'

That was how it was at first. The beatings came without warning, but afterwards Duncan had been so sweet and loving. She'd wanted so much to believe he was sweet and loving. Eventually, though, he beat that out of her as well.

Oliver squeezed Flo's hand. 'You must have a man who treats you well all the time, is that not so? There are many men who admire you. Bide your time and another, better man will love you.'

But, in this club, love would be fleeting. Or soiled by the knowledge that the man had a wife he would never leave.

Oliver made Flo look directly at him. 'Tell me who this man is. I promise you he will not hurt you. He will go away.'

She nodded solemnly. 'He is a member. He wants to own the club.' She swallowed. 'He is Sir Nash Bowles.'

'Bowles?' Cecilia exclaimed.

She felt the emotion in Oliver change. 'Bowles.' His voice

turned into a growl. He released Flo's hand and it felt like rancour poured out of him. 'Where is he likely to be?'

Flo shrank back. 'He could be at my room.' She gave him the direction. 'He stays there, waiting for me, lots of times.'

He stood and put a hand on Flo's shoulder. 'Do not fear, Flo. He will leave you alone from now on. He will never hit you again.'

He turned and strode towards the door.

Cecilia caught up to him in the hallway. 'What are you going to do, Oliver?'

'I'm going to take care of Bowles,' he responded in a rough voice.

The rage inside him was palpable. He frightened her, suddenly so violent and untamed.

She could not even say goodbye to him. She fled back to the Green Room.

Flo, though, looked as if a heavy weight had been lifted off her shoulders. 'I never thought Mr Gregory would be so nice.'

She seemed oblivious of the violent change in him.

'He's going to protect me.' Flo sighed. 'Nobody ever protected me before, not even Mum when that man she lived with made me bed him.'

'Flo!' Cecilia exclaimed. 'How old were you?' She seemed about nineteen now.

'I was eleven.' Her expression changed. 'Do you know Sir Nash?'

'I met him once,' Cecilia responded, her mind horrified by what Flo had just told her. 'That is how I learned about Vitium et Virtus.'

Flo shook her head. 'He sure talks about Vitium et Virtus a lot. Question after question about it, too.'

Cecilia remembered taking an instant dislike to Bowles in Paris. She'd avoided him and was grateful he'd not tried to hire her for the night. Now she wondered if she'd sensed his similarity to Duncan. Both abusive, violent men.

But there was violence in Oliver, too. She'd felt it.

Oliver brought Snyder with him to see Bowles, but they did not find him in Fleurette's room. It took some searching to discover him at the Union Club, reading a newspaper and sipping tea.

Bowles greeted Oliver with a pleased expression. 'Gregory. A pleasure to see you.' He gestured to the second chair at the table. 'Do sit down. Shall I have the servant bring you some tea? Something stronger?' He spoke with that slight lisp that always struck Oliver as a slippery affectation.

Snyder remained standing a few feet away. When Bowles noticed the large man, his friendly countenance momentarily faltered.

Oliver did not sit. 'I'd rather you come with me.'

Bowles looked alarmed. 'Where?'

Oliver signalled to Snyder, who strode over. They flanked Bowles, each taking an arm.

'Not far,' Oliver said.

They lifted Bowles to his feet.

'See here!' the man protested.

They half-walked, half-carried him out.

Once outside Oliver said, 'I learned something about you.'

Bowles blanched. 'What did you learn? It is not true. Not true. Who is talking about me?' His words rushed out.

They carried him to an alley at the back of the club and released him.

He started to back away. 'Two against one, Gregory? That is not a fair fight.'

Oliver didn't heed him. He advanced on Bowles, drew his fist back and punched him in the face.

Bowles fell backwards to the ground, clasping his cheek.

Oliver stood over him. 'How does that feel, Bowles?'

Bowles glared up at him.

Oliver held his ground. 'If I ever hear that you have struck any of the women who work for Vitium et Virtus, Snyder and I will return to finish this job once and for all.'

Bowles looked puzzled, then relieved, which made no sense at all. 'Who has said this?' he demanded.

'Never mind who. I have known you since school, Bowles. I've seen your cruelty.'

Bowles had been behind many a cruel stunt in school, but always slithered his way out of being caught. When they were boys, he'd picked on the younger ones, anyone weaker than he. Now he was older, he'd not changed, obviously.

Bowles's lip curled. 'Boyhood pranks. A long time ago.' He rose to his feet. 'Think, man. I want to own a share of Vitium et Virtus. Why would I damage the goods? Let me buy in to the club. I am certain I could find many creative roles for your beautiful women. If you, Westmoor and Challenger would allow me the opportunity, we could make a fine profit.'

Bowles was one of the men who perceived the club as a brothel, which it was not. It represented freedom, but not profit and certainly not exploitation.

Oliver advanced on him again, seizing him by his coat and lifting him to within inches of his face. 'Heed me, Bowles. You will not approach any of our workers. Unless you want more than this sample of what Snyder and I can do, you will stay away.'

Bowles lifted his hands. 'Easy. Easy. I am a peaceable man. If it pleases you, I will avoid any liaisons with your women. Will that do?'

Oliver released him with a shove. 'Stay away completely. Your membership is revoked.'

'That goes too far, Gregory,' Bowles snapped. 'I have been a member since the beginning.'

They'd made him a member all those years ago so he would keep the club secret, not because they'd wanted him there.

'No matter,' Oliver said. 'You are a member no longer. Do not set foot in the club or Snyder will toss you out. Do not engage with any of our women, or we will both be back.'

Oliver turned away and he and Snyder walked away, leaving Bowles in the alley to stew in his own juices.

They would return to Vitium et Virtus. Oliver would tell Flo that Bowles promised to leave her alone. He hoped she would inform him if Bowles ever broke that promise.

He also hoped that Cecilia would approve of his action here today.

Chapter Twelve

Cecilia spent that afternoon in her sitting room, mending the purple costume she'd worn the night before. After she'd covered Flo's bruise and the girl went off to see her mother, Cecilia was left with a Gordian knot of emotions inside her. She envied Flo's easy trust of Oliver; she'd believed his word that he could make Bowles leave her alone. She also envied Flo's eagerness to see her mother, who would undoubtedly welcome her. Cecilia was glad of both those things. She was glad Flo's abuse had not escalated to a more dangerous level. She was glad Flo had a loving mother from whom Flo wished to hide her problems. Just because Cecilia could not say the same did not mean she was not happy for Flo.

She was confused about Oliver, which perhaps disturbed her the most. Which was he? A man capable of such kindness and tenderness towards a wounded girl? Or a man with violence inside him?

She'd not sensed that level of anger when he'd spoken to her father, but the fear she used to experience with Duncan returned when Oliver left in pursuit of Bowles.

He'd been angry enough to kill.

She pushed the needle through the fabric and tried to banish that thought from her mind.

A knock sounded at the sitting room door.

'Come in,' she said.

To her surprise, it was Oliver who stepped into the room. She held the needle poised in the air.

'I thought you might wish to know what happened,' he said.

Her hand shook. She immediately stuck the needle into the fabric and set the dress aside.

'Please sit, Oliver,' she managed, but her insides trembled at what she might hear.

He sat in the sofa across from her. 'Bowles was not at Flo's room, but we finally did find him.'

'We?' Who had gone with him?

'I took Snyder with me.'

Snyder, the flash man of Vitium et Virtus. Snyder was intimidating on first sight. Tall. Muscular. Unsmiling. But she was always grateful he was there at the club.

She nodded. 'So what did you do when you found Bowles?'

She sensed the violence again and gripped a fold in her skirt.

'I hit him.'

'You hit him?' She touched her cheek, feeling the memory of Duncan's fist against her face.

'Of course I hit him. I know Bowles. He would not have listened otherwise. I told him if he touched any one of my workers, Snyder and I would finish the job.'

She felt his ferocity. 'Finish the job?'

Oliver nodded. 'Bowles knows I never back down in a fight.'

'You—you've fought him before?'

He laughed drily. 'Not Bowles, but he's seen me fight many times.'

She'd heard of gentlemen who engaged in boxing matches, ridiculous contests of who could hit his opponent until his opponent was knocked out.

'Exactly where did he see you fight?' she asked.

He shrugged. 'On the fields of Eton and in its hallways. There were plenty of other boys who wished to show me my place. At Oxford, as well.'

'In school?' Was that where men learned to punch so hard the victim could see stars? 'You have known Bowles since school?' Was his anger at Bowles that long lasting?

He nodded. 'I knew it would take more than a threat to deter him. He needed to know we meant what we said. But we'll have to be vigilant. Bowles is a snake. He'll slink back as soon as he thinks we are no longer looking. I think I'll warn the entertainers and servants about him. We don't have to mention what happened to Flo.'

Her heart was pounding in anxiety. This image of Oliver striking Bowles roused memories of her husband. Duncan fought everyone, even the man who killed him in a duel.

'Bowles is a member of the club?' she asked.

'No longer,' he replied. He glanced at the door. 'Is Fleurette still at the club?'

Cecilia pulled herself away from memories. 'She is visiting her mother, but she is supposed to return to spend the night at the club tonight.' Cecilia insisted Flo return here and not to her room, just in case Oliver had not succeeded.

'I'll have Snyder tell her she is safe now.' He stood. 'Will I see you at dinner?'

She looked up at him, so tall, so handsome. So strong and powerful. 'Of course.'

'I will see you then.'

When he left the room, she dropped her head onto her hands.

He was a wonderful protector. Why did he also have to frighten her so?

***

Over the next week, Cecilia settled into a routine, dining with Oliver, walking to the club with him. The nights at Vitium et Virtus had been uneventful, and Cecilia fell into the familiar role of Coquette. Her father, apparently accepting his exile, did not return. There was also no sign of Sir Nash Bowles. Flo moved from her room to one closer to her mother. She'd not seen Bowles since Oliver had intervened. With each day, Flo grew happier and Cecilia allowed herself to be lulled into a comfortable sense of well-being.

Cecilia herself felt physically marvellous. This was her fourth month of pregnancy and she rarely experienced nausea any more. She suddenly had energy again, so much so that she made herself useful in Oliver's house. Helping with the mending. Putting his bookshelves in order. There was not much on his shelves that she wished to read, though. The poetry of Wordsworth and Coleridge was the lot.

Today Oliver invited her to come with him to the shops on Bond Street. She was always suspicious of invitations, but the weather was clear and crisp, making it a fine day for stretching one's legs and exploring the myriad shops that led Napoleon to call England a *nation of shopkeepers*.

She could not resist.

She wore a black dress that had been hastily made after the Queen died, a colour that did not reflect her current feeling of well-being, but was not unflattering. Her bonnet was also black. Both were gifts from Oliver and she was grateful. It meant she would not stand out from the other Mayfair shoppers, the aristocrats who would undoubtedly respectfully mourn the Queen.

What a great deal that lady had endured, she thought. The madness of her husband. The death of a daughter, a granddaughter and a great-grandchild. The excesses of her sons. No wonder she kept her remaining daughters so confined.

Such motherly devotion. Cecilia dared not dwell on that subject lest she miss her mother all over again.

Never mind. She would have her baby and she'd love her baby with all her heart. She'd devote her life to her child's happiness.

If Oliver fulfilled his promise to support them.

She really was at his mercy as far as the support of her child was concerned and if she thought about that subject too much her feeling of well-being vanished.

She stood in front of the mirror in her bedchamber to check her appearance one more time, pressing the skirt of her dress against her belly to see if it looked as if her belly had swelled. It did.

But not enough to worry about showing under the generous material of her skirt. Enough, though, to remind herself that soon it would become obvious she was carrying a child. She did not know enough about childbearing to say when that would be. Another month? Two? Another worry she tried not to think of.

Instead, she smoothed out her skirt again, picked up her gloves and hurried out to the stairway.

Oliver waited at the bottom of the stairs, dressed in a black coat, waistcoat and black trousers. The dark coat and white linen shirt and neckcloth set off his dark skin and green eyes in a manner that took Cecilia's breath away.

She wished she would not have this reaction to him.

His magnetic eyes followed her down the stairs. Was the expression on his face approval? She could not tell.

'Am I presentable?' she asked warily.

His eyes scanned her. 'Very presentable.'

Irwin helped Cecilia on with her cloak and Oliver with his topcoat and black armband. He held the door as they left the house. Once on the pavement, Oliver offered his arm.

She accepted it. It would seem churlish not to.

'Where would you like to shop?' he asked as they approached Jermyn Street.

'Me?' she responded. 'I will go wherever you wish.'

They turned on to Jermyn Street and walked past the windows of Floris perfumers.

'Do you need some scent?' he asked.

She made do with lavender water. 'I do not like to spend my money on scent.'

He stopped at the doorway. 'I told you in Paris. I am rich. I can buy you scent.'

'Why would you, Oliver?' she asked. Perhaps her lavender water was not to his liking.

'Let us go in. I will purchase a throwaway for you. You can wear it at the masquerade.' He pulled her towards the door.

A throwaway was a small sample of a scent. Perhaps he wished a new scent to be part of her costume. The masquerade was planned to be the last big Vitium et Virtus event before Christmas, when most of the members travelled to their country houses or to house parties.

She acquiesced.

A clerk stood behind a long mahogany case that displayed scent bottles of all shapes, sizes and designs. 'May I be of assistance?' he asked.

'A throwaway for the lady,' Oliver said.

The clerk showed them a variety of scents and offered to make a special blend if she chose. She selected a scent, which was a blend of jasmine and other fragrances that seemed exotic and that met with Oliver's approval. The tiny cylindrical glass bottle was adorned with hand-painted gilt and enamel. It was wrapped in brown paper and tied with string. Oliver carried it in his pocket.

Next they stopped at Hatchard's bookshop, where Cecilia browsed through the first volume of a novel that caught her eye. She'd forgotten the pleasures of reading novels.

'What is that book?' he asked, coming to her side.

'It is two books in one,' she replied. '*Northanger Abbey* and *Persuasion* by the author of *Pride and Prejudice*.'

'Something you would enjoy?'

'I did enjoy *Pride and Prejudice*.' She'd read it an age ago when she'd still had stars in her eyes and dreams of romance and marriage.

'Will you allow me to buy it for you?' Oliver asked.

She closed it. 'No, indeed. Stop offering to buy me things.'

'Why?' he demanded.

Because it made her uncomfortable. Because it reminded her of Paris.

She touched the pearl that hung at her neck. 'It is not economical to buy a novel. One generally reads them just once.'

He shrugged. 'I have no need to be economical.'

What else could she say? 'Gifts come with obligation.'

He sobered. 'I have asked nothing of you. It is you who ask of me. You want me to support you.'

She leaned even closer. 'Not me. The baby.'

Their eyes caught and gazes held and the flush of arousal rushed through her. Like Paris all over again.

She glanced away and put the book back on the shelf.

'Did you find anything for yourself?' she asked.

He gently extended his hand and touched her arm, but just as quickly withdrew it and shook his head.

After they left Hatchard's they passed many ladies and gentlemen of Oliver's acquaintance on the street. He tipped his hat in greeting. The gentlemen tipped their hats in return; the ladies smiled appreciatively.

'I thought you were ostracised from society,' Cecilia said. 'There seem to be many people willing to acknowledge you.'

'I am not entirely a pariah,' he admitted. 'Because of Frederick and Jacob—' and Nicholas '—I actually have mixed in society quite a bit. Even my father has included me in invitations from time to time.'

She laughed. 'And here I thought you as scandalous as I am.'

He did not like to hear her speak of herself that way.

'Oh, I am perfectly acceptable if some young buck wants a phaeton race or a sparring match or sword fight. Or if his father enjoys a high-stakes game of cards or wishes membership in Vitium et Virtus. Or his mother or married sister wishes a flirtation.' He frowned. 'But no one wishes me anywhere near their marriageable daughters. No one wants the family line tainted by a half-caste's blood.' He glanced down at her and made himself smile. 'No vouchers for Almack's for me.'

She gave him a look of sympathy. 'None for me either. I cannot imagine I'd ever receive any society invitation.' She grimaced. 'Except the sort of invitation the patrons of Vitium et Virtus offer me.'

They walked on.

'Does it bother you?' she asked.

'Not always,' he admitted. Not when he could distract his mind from the memories of the time in India when he'd known love and security.

He did not ask if it bothered her, but she answered anyway.

'Sometimes I wonder what my life would have been like if I had not eloped with Duncan.' She blinked. 'But I will never know, will I?'

He made himself smile again. 'Better to enjoy the fine weather, the exercise—' he felt his skin warm as he gazed at her '—and the company.'

Her gaze met his and held. 'Yes. It is a fine day.'

This moment felt like Paris. He would cherish it.

They crossed Piccadilly and walked down Old Bond Street, stopping in a grocer's to purchase tea and pausing to look at all the prints displayed in Ackermann's windows.

He spied another place. Hookham's. 'Let us go in here,' he said.

She did not realise what sort of establishment it was until they crossed the threshold.

'A Circulating Library!' she cried.

This was one way to give her the pleasure of the book she'd examined in Hatchard's. 'You cannot object to me signing you up for the Circulating Library.'

This ploy worked in Paris. Why not here? She'd refused his offer of jewels, but accepted the necklace with a single pearl. It had worked at Floris, too. No bottles of expensive scent, but she had agreed to a small throwaway.

She would not allow him to purchase a book for her, but how could she refuse a subscription to a circulating library? It only cost one pound and fourteen shillings for a subscription for two persons for six months.

After six months, he did not know what would happen.

He walked her to the counter and arranged for a subscription for eight volumes at a time.

'And what books would the lady like to borrow?' the clerk asked.

He turned to her. 'Do you want the one you looked at in Hatchard's?'

'Very well, Oliver.' She sighed. To the clerk, she said, '*Northanger Abbey* and *Persuasion*.'

'Volume one?' the man asked.

'All volumes,' Oliver said.

Books were often in four volumes. It stood to reason to borrow them all at once.

'Any other?' the clerk asked.

He might as well borrow the book he'd looked at in Hatchard's. '*The Principles of Political Economy and Taxation*.'

'Excellent choices, sir,' the clerk said.

Oliver supposed he said that to every subscriber.

The clerk extended his hand. 'Please have some refreshment while I fulfil your request.'

They left the counter. 'Do you want some refreshment?' Oliver asked.

'No,' she responded. 'But I would not mind sitting for a moment.'

'We can wait in the reading room,' he said.

The reading room was a place where subscribers could pass the time until their books were found. Some read the newspapers, which were made available. Others read the books they'd selected to borrow to see if they really wanted them.

In the reading room were a gentleman engrossed in a newspaper and two ladies standing in conversation. One lady had her back to them and she blocked a view of the other. When the lady moved slightly, the other woman's face was visible for a moment.

Cecilia emitted a small sound of alarm and abruptly pulled away from Oliver. She fled back to the main room and retreated to the front of the shop where there was a window display.

He hurried after her.

'What is it, Cecilia?' he asked.

She appeared to be gazing out the window. 'The lady—the lady in the reading room.' She seemed to have trouble breathing.

'What of her?'

She faced him and her eyes filled with pain. 'She is my mother.'

Her mother?

Cecilia seemed to shrink before his eyes, becoming a frightened child. 'May—may we leave?'

Leave? She'd once gone in search of her parents for their help. Her father had his chance to embrace her and return her to the family. He'd lost that chance.

But she must not give up on the possibility that she might

reunite with her mother! What he would give for even one brief moment with his mother.

He gripped her arm. 'You confronted your father. Now confront your mother. Say to her all the things you wish to say. You may not get another opportunity.'

She straightened and he watched her transform herself yet again, this time from weakness to strength. 'You are right.'

He released her.

She strode to the reading room. The two women were still conversing. One was older—Cecilia's mother, he presumed. The other, the one whose back was to them, was younger.

Cecilia walked directly up to them. 'Hello, Mama,' she said.

Her mother gazed at her and it took a moment for her eyes to widen in surprise.

It was the younger woman who spoke first. 'Cecilia!'

'Hello, Agnes.' Cecilia's voice sounded flat.

Her mother took a step forward. 'Cecilia!'

The younger woman stopped her. 'Mama! Remember what Papa said when she eloped?' Cecilia's sister, obviously.

Her mother pushed her aside and came up to Cecilia. Tears were in her mother's eyes. 'My darling daughter! How are you?' She touched Cecilia's arms, as if to test whether they were in one piece. Her gaze swept over her daughter. 'I cannot believe you are here.'

'Mama!' Agnes broke in again.

Cecilia was speechless.

Her mother ignored Cecilia's sister. 'But why did we not hear a word from you? Where have you been all these years?' She seemed to notice Oliver. 'This is not your husband?'

'My husband is dead, Mama.' She turned to Oliver. 'This is Mr Gregory. A—a friend.'

'Lady Dorman.' Oliver bowed. He nodded to Agnes. 'Ma'am.'

He seemed to be too much for the baroness to take in. She

turned to Cecilia again. 'My condolences,' she said, not very sincerely. 'Why did you never write to me?'

Cecilia looked puzzled. 'I wrote many times, Mama. I had only the one letter from Papa.'

Her mother stumbled and looked as if she could not keep her balance.

Oliver caught Lady Dorman before she fell. 'Come, you should sit.'

He supported her until she lowered herself onto a sofa. She reached for Cecilia's hand so she would sit beside her. Agnes primly took a seat nearby. Oliver stepped back.

'I—I never received a letter from you,' her mother said.

Cecilia glanced at Agnes, who blinked and turned her head.

'Do you know anything of this?' Cecilia asked her sister.

The sister lifted her nose. 'Papa told Joan and me to consider you dead, so he destroyed any letters from you.'

'He destroyed letters?' her mother cried.

The clerk stood in the doorway, looking hesitant. Oliver was not sure how long he'd been there. The man reading the newspaper was still reading.

'Your books, sir,' the clerk said uncertainly.

Oliver walked over to him and took the books, which were wrapped in brown paper.

'Mama,' Cecilia said gently. 'Do not be distressed.'

Her mother looked at her again, a reverent expression on her face. She stroked her daughter's cheek. 'I thought you were lost for ever.'

'I—I've been living in France,' Cecilia said.

As with her father, she had not mentioned that she was expecting a child. There was much she left out. How much had she left out for him?

Her mother grasped her hands. 'Now you are a widow, you can come home!'

Cecilia winced in pain. 'You must ask Papa about that.'

She knew, of course, she was not welcome home. 'But tell me, Mama. Are you in good health?'

Her mother continued to hold Cecilia's hands as she related a list of minor complaints to which Cecilia listened sympathetically. When her mother finished, Cecilia turned to Agnes. 'What of you, Agnes? How do you fare?'

Agnes seemed surprised Cecilia asked about her. 'I am married to Mr Higgins, Sir William Higgins's son.'

'How nice,' Cecilia said. 'Do you have any children?'

Agnes faltered. 'Not yet.' She changed the subject. 'Joan is married, too. To Mr Pottinger, an earl's younger son. She has no children either.'

Cecilia gave her a warm smile. 'I wish you both happy.'

Agnes turned her face away.

'Where are you staying?' Lady Dorman asked. 'Are you living here in London?'

Cecilia glanced to Oliver before answering, 'I rent a room in Mr Gregory's property.'

'How do you live?' her mother asked, then gave an answer. 'I suppose you have a widow's pension.'

Agnes interrupted. 'Mama, can you not see she is in Mr Gregory's keeping? She is his mistress.'

Cecilia paled.

Oliver calmly spoke up. 'She is not in my keeping, Mrs Higgins. She does let a room, however.'

'What a silly thing to say,' her mother chastised Agnes, who gave an obstinate look.

'Mama, we should go,' Agnes said, rising from the chair. 'Lady Ashton is expecting us to call.'

Lady Dorman clasped Cecilia's hands again. 'You will call upon me soon, will you not?'

'Mama,' Cecilia replied. 'I cannot. Papa has forbidden me.'

Her mother looked puzzled. 'You have seen him?'

'I called once,' she prevaricated. 'I was told not to call again.'

Oliver stepped forward and handed Cecilia's mother his

card. 'If you should need to speak to your daughter, you can send a message to me. I will see she receives it.'

Agnes gestured with her hand. 'Mama, we must go.'

Cecilia helped her mother to stand.

'I am quite all right now,' her mother said. 'It was the shock, you know.' She embraced Cecilia. 'My darling daughter. You are alive.'

'Goodbye, Mama.' Cecilia's voice cracked.

'Mama!' Agnes demanded.

Her mother bustled out of the room behind her other daughter, turning at the doorway for one more glance at Cecilia.

Cecilia collapsed on to the sofa as soon as her mother left. She was a hair's breadth from bursting into tears. Her mother had not disowned her! Her mother had cared about her.

Oliver sat at her side, but said nothing.

She could not look at him. 'You made me confront her. I would never have known otherwise.' It meant everything to her.

His voice turned soft and low. 'She is your mother.' He cleared his throat and his tone turned more conversational. 'I liked her better than your father. I cannot say the same about your sister, though.'

'She was brought up to despise me.'

Their father had reminded her sisters frequently that Cecilia, the youngest, was the reason they did not have more dresses, more visits to London, a larger dowry. If only she had not been born.

Cecilia suspected her father had not mentioned to them that Cecilia had been given no dowry. That money was certainly lost to gambling.

'I would like to write to my mother again, when—when I go away,' she said.

'Go away?' he asked.

'After the baby is born,' she said quietly. 'I plan to move away where no one knows me.'

He frowned and turned away from her. When he turned back his eyes were filled with resolve. 'If you ever want your mother to receive a letter from you, send it to me. I will make certain she receives it.'

She believed him.

Chapter Thirteen

The next day turned cold and rainy and Oliver could think of no reason to go out, not even to Vitium et Virtus, which would be closed this night. He holed himself in the small room that was his library and opened the book he'd borrowed from Hookham's.

It was hard reading, but intriguing. Oliver had never paid much attention to things like the value of land and how much workers should be compensated. It stimulated his thinking. It also expanded his thinking beyond the offerings of Vitium et Virtus, to ideas about producing food and manufacturing essential items, of paying wages based on the value of the tasks performed, and a concept of minimum wage that provided workers enough for food, clothing and shelter.

Perhaps there was more to life than a scandalous gentlemen's club.

His butler came to the door. 'Sir, do you recall the gentleman you asked me to take heed of?'

Bowles? It would be like Bowles to make more trouble.

Irwin went on. 'The gentleman who might ask for Mrs Lockhart?'

Not Bowles. Lord Dorman.

'Is he here asking for her?'

'That he is,' Irwin said. 'What do you wish me to do?'

Irwin would probably throw the man out if Oliver wanted him to.

'I'll see him,' he said instead. 'Did you put him in the drawing room?'

'That I did, sir. He was complaining all the way.'

Oliver closed his book. 'Tell him I'll be down directly.' He rose from his chair and entered the drawing room a minute behind Irwin.

Dorman swung around to him. 'I asked to see my daughter, not you.'

Oliver raised his brows. 'Now she is your daughter? I thought she was dead to you.'

Dorman huffed. 'You know my meaning.'

'Why call here to see her?' Oliver asked.

Dorman gave him a smug look. 'I asked around. I know she lives here.' He sneered. 'With you.'

There was no use in denying it. 'What is this business you have with Mrs Lockhart?' Oliver asked.

'Why should I tell you?'

Oliver came close to him. 'Because I will not have you distressing her. You have done damage enough.'

'What concern is it of yours?' Dorman persisted.

'She is my employee and my friend,' Oliver said. 'Both mean I care that she is not distressed.'

'Humph!' Dorman's expression was of disdain. 'My daughter Agnes tells me she's more than that.'

'Ah.'

Cecilia's sister informed her father about the meeting at the circulating library. And, of course, his wife now knew he had destroyed Cecilia's letters.

'Perhaps you can tell me what you wish to say to Mrs Lockhart. I will pass on the message...' Oliver paused. 'Unless it is hurtful.'

'She is never to contact any member of this family again!' Dorman cried. 'Tell her that. Or show me where the chit is hiding and I will tell her.'

'I doubt she finds it necessary to hide from you.' In fact, Oliver had no more right to keep her from seeing her father than her father had to order her presence.

It should be up to Cecilia to decide.

'If you care to have a seat, I will ask if she wishes to see you.' He gave Dorman a steely glare. 'But I warn you, if you are not civil, you will be tossed out on your ear.'

'You wouldn't dare!' Dorman lifted his chin. 'A man of my station.'

Oliver gave him a sarcastic smile. 'Ah, but I have no station, as you indicated in our last...encounter. What trouble can you cause me?'

Dorman pursed his lips, no doubt frustrated that he had no clout at all with Oliver.

'If you pardon me, I will speak to Mrs Lockhart.' Oliver did not give Dorman a chance to say another word. He walked out of the room and went in search of Cecilia.

Cecilia sat reading by her window when there was a knock at the door.

Oliver.

The last time he'd knocked on her door had been after dealing with Sir Nash. 'Come in,' she said.

He entered the room and sat in a chair near her. 'Your father is downstairs.'

Her stomach turned to lead. 'My father.'

'He wishes to see you. I almost tossed him out, but the choice should be yours. Do you wish to see him?'

He made it her choice? Considered her feelings? She felt a crack in her resolve not to let down her guard about him.

'Did he say why he came?' she asked.

'I suspect he wishes to speak to you about seeing your mother and sister.'

Of course.

'If you do not wish to see him, I will deal with him for you,' Oliver said.

'I will see him.'

He stood and extended his hand to help her rise. His hand was warm. And strong.

They walked out of her room together and descended the stairs. Irwin, looking serious, was attending the hall.

'Stay nearby,' Oliver told him.

Irwin nodded.

Cecilia hesitated before entering the room. She straightened her spine and lifted her head. Her father would not see how much his rejection wounded her.

She strode into the room. 'You wished to see me, Papa.'

As before, at the club, and at the Circulating Library, Oliver remained by the doorway, but she knew he was there.

Her father turned to her. 'You've caused me more trouble,' he spat out. 'Talking nonsense to your mother.'

'Nonsense?' Her eyes widened.

Her father went on, 'We washed our hands of you, remember.'

She crossed her arms over her chest. 'Oh, I remember. Did you come merely to remind me?'

His nostrils flared. 'I came to forbid you to see your mother or your sisters. You stay away from them. I said you are dead to us. Stay dead.'

She placed her hand on her abdomen for a brief moment, before saying coolly, 'You can no longer order me, Papa.'

He went on. 'I'll not have you filling your mother's head with your stories and making life difficult for her.'

'Do you mean telling her of your membership at Vitium et Virtus? Of your gambling and debauchery? Of destroying my letters?' She kept her gaze steady. 'Or of sending me away when I came to call upon you?' When she'd felt in such need of her mother.

'You have already told her about the letters,' he snapped.

It was Agnes who had told their mother, but Cecilia did not have the heart to put her sister in her father's black books.

'And I am free to disclose anything I know to my mother or to anyone else. I have been disowned by you. I have been married and widowed. You have no say in what I do.'

He took several steps and leaned into her face, but she did not back away. From behind her she heard Oliver move closer.

Her father shook his finger in her face. 'You will do what I say or else.'

She did not flinch. 'Or else what?'

His expression turned smug. 'I will tell your mother you work in a brothel.'

Oliver stepped up, his eyes shooting fire. 'Enough, Dorman!'

Her father backed off.

Oliver's voice rose and shook with anger. 'You dare to threaten us? Recall that I have powerful friends. You cannot harm me. I will not allow you to harm your daughter. I assure you, I will destroy you if you try!'

Cecilia trembled at Oliver's fierce tone and dangerous expression. She felt his repressed rage. It frightened her.

Her father stormed out without another word.

Oliver still seemed like a powder keg that might explode at any minute. 'He had better not threaten you again.'

She was too shaken to say anything. She nodded and fled the room.

That evening, for the first time, Cecilia asked to dine alone in her rooms. Oliver's anger had frightened her and she simply could not sit in the dining room with him.

After Mary took away her dinner dishes, however, she'd calmed down and guilt seeped in. Oliver's anger had been in her defence, after all. Running off and avoiding him were shabby ways of expressing her gratitude.

She ought to apologise. She rose with resolve and left her rooms to go in search of him, hoping he had not gone out.

She found him seated at a table in the drawing room, gazing down at it and apparently not hearing her approach.

'Oliver?'

He raised his head. A desolate expression on his face changed to a neutral one. He nodded a greeting.

She walked over to where he was sitting and glanced down at the table. It was made of light and dark wood inlay forming long triangles on two sides, their points meeting in the middle. There were chips of white and black marble on the triangles and two sets of dice, one set white, one black, with cups in which to shake them.

'It is a game!' she exclaimed, glad for something else to talk about than explaining why she'd avoided him at dinner.

He moved one of the pieces. 'Backgammon.'

'I have seen this game before,' she said. 'Some of the soldiers played it.'

He looked up at her. 'Do you know how to play?'

She shook her head.

'Would you like to learn?' he asked.

The anger she'd sensed in him seemed to have been supplanted by a sadness that evoked sympathy, not fear. She ached to dispel it. Perhaps to ease her guilt.

'I'd be delighted to learn,' she said.

He gestured for her to sit and rearranged the game pieces. 'Backgammon is an ancient game, known to the Romans and before, but I'd never heard of it until I found this table. I bought it and found a book about the game—*A Short Treatise on the Game of Backgammon*. I taught myself to play.'

'Can only one person play?'

He gave a soft laugh. 'If one plays both sides. You'll be my first true opponent.'

He showed her the rules by playing a couple of practice games. The game was simple enough, easier than chess where each piece moved differently. It took her a few games—a few losses—to grasp that there was strategy involved. She focused even more on her play, wanting to win.

They began to compete in earnest. Both ignored anything but the roll of the dice and moving the pieces. Cecilia let go of her fear of his anger and forgot her guilt at avoiding him. She merely wanted to protect her game pieces as she moved them around and off the board.

'Gammon!' she cried, taking her final two pieces off. Oliver was left with all his pieces still on the board. Gammon gave her an extra point. 'I won!'

'That you did,' he said with some dismay. He immediately set up the pieces again. 'You caught on quickly.'

'I've played some chess and draughts,' she responded. 'When I was following the drum.'

'Not as a child?' He handed her one of the white die.

'Not really.' She put the die in the cup. 'My sisters hated it when I won, so I rarely had an opportunity to play.'

'You have a talent for this game,' he said.

Oliver put his black die in the cup, shook it and rolled it onto the table.

Earlier he'd been plunging into depression when she had come into the room, willing to play.

He'd missed her at dinner. He relished her company then and it had been lonely without her.

It would be even lonelier when she left for good. He did not want to think about it. He wanted only to enjoy this moment with her.

She rolled her white die. 'Did you play games as a child?'

From the time he could remember he'd played games. With his friends at school. Occasionally with his father. But his earliest memories were playing games with his mother.

He smiled. 'In India, I used to play a game called Snakes and Ladders.'

'Snakes and Ladders?'

'Snakes and Ladders.'

He closed his eyes and could see the board with its black snakes crisscrossing the squares and ladders. The writing on the board was foreign, but he could remember reading it.

He opened his eyes again. 'The board consisted of squares. Each square was a house and each house represented an emotion. You threw the dice to see how far you could go. The ladders represented good feelings and you could rise to the top of the ladders on good feelings, but if you landed on a snake, a bad feeling, you slid back down the board and slipped further and further from *nirvana*.'

'What is *nirvana*?' she asked.

Another memory, this time of his mother, flashed into his mind. Wrapped in her brightly coloured sari, her face beatific, she told him of *nirvana*. 'It is the highest happiness, but also perfect quietude, oblivious to the world of pain and worry.'

Cecilia looked at him with a sober expression. 'Imagine a game all about emotions where one tries to win happiness and peace.'

He held on to the memory as if it were a precious jewel. Emotions had been free-floating in his mother's house. She displayed them generously. Joy. Love. Anger. Sadness.

Grief.

When he arrived in England, though, expression of emotion was forbidden.

Cecilia reached across the table and grasped his hand. 'You've turned sad, Oliver.'

He blinked. 'I was remembering India.'

She kept her hand in his, and he held on to her until the wave of unbidden and forbidden emotion washed through him.

She did not speak until he relaxed his grip. 'Shall we put the game table away?'

He smiled. 'Not until you give me a chance to win another game.'

She returned a smile, reminding him of Paris. 'If you think you have a chance. I believe I have caught on.'

She won the first move.

Halfway through the game, in which he was ahead, she leaned back and put her hand on her abdomen. 'Oh!'

He dropped his dice. 'What is it?'

Was something wrong?

She looked at him with wonder in her eyes. 'The baby moved! I felt the baby move.'

She took his hand and pulled him from his chair to come closer to her. She placed his hand on her abdomen.

She smiled. 'Can you feel it?'

He knelt on the floor next to her. Her hand covered his, holding it in place. There was the faintest flutter beneath his fingertips. He kept still and the flutter happened again.

He met her gaze, feeling a connection as strong as they'd experienced in lovemaking.

'It is real,' she whispered. 'A real life inside me.'

A real life. Had this life come from that extraordinary night they shared in Paris? Was this new life a part of him?

He did not dare believe it.

He stood abruptly. She pulled her hand from his, her expression wounded and confused.

Chapter Fourteen

The next two weeks settled into a routine. Oliver dined with Cecilia, walked to Vitium et Virtus with her and even played backgammon with her, but he kept himself at a distance. He wanted what he could never possess. He wanted a family with her. He wanted the baby to be his. He wanted them to be together.

Everything she did not want and could not guarantee.

At least there had been enough to keep him busy. Vitium et Virtus was preparing for their annual masquerade ball, the last event before the club closed for Christmas. All members were invited and were encouraged to bring guests, making for larger crowds than the club was accustomed to.

The Queen's death made it the only ball anyone could attend, because no one hosted such a lavish party while the country was in mourning—except for Vitium et Virtus, that is.

In previous years Oliver would have been delighted to flout any of society's rules. That was expected at Vitium et Virtus. But the old Queen had been the mother of the country and it seemed unnecessary, disrespectful and simply juvenile to defy the decree to mourn her.

It was not only up to him, though. Both Jacob and Frederick expected Vitium et Virtus to hold the masquerade. All the members counted on it. Oliver supposed the club did have a reputation of irreverence to uphold.

He decided to honour the Queen by dedicating the ball to her. The Queen loved the bucolic life, so Oliver gave the masquerade that theme. The male workers of Vitium et Virtus dressed as peasants or farmers. The singers dressed as milkmaids; the dancers, shepherdesses and the girls in the game room, peasants. Their costumes were, of course, idealised versions of these characters about whom many bawdy songs were sung. Their skirts were short, showing plenty of ankle, and were made from colourful printed fabric. His workers wore their hair unbound, tied back only with brightly coloured scarves. The singers carried milk pails, the dancers, shepherd's crooks.

Cecilia's costume, a dress of red and white stripes with a huge white apron flounced across her middle, was not as revealing. Her skirts reached the floor, although the neckline dipped low enough to show a tantalising glimpse of bosom. She wore her hair unbound, too, reminding Oliver too much of that night in Paris when her mahogany tresses were splayed across the white bed linens.

Masks, of course, were required and, because of the numbers of non-members attending, many attendees covered their faces more carefully. Oliver knew that the more the attendees' identities were disguised, the looser their behaviour would become.

This was a night to stay vigilant.

Once he would simply have joined in and relished the bacchanalia, but ever since Nicholas's disappearance, he'd regarded the club more seriously. No harm to anyone should come from attending the club. Or from working there. Fleurette had been hurt and Oliver had put a stop to that, but he'd not been able to stop the harm that had come to Nicholas.

Yes, tonight he would be vigilant.

The guests started arriving. Snyder and Mr Bell were busy collecting the vouchers that had been issued for admittance. That task was not too onerous at the moment, but when the guests all arrived at once it would be more difficult.

Oliver walked from the ballroom to the game room, checking on things, watching things. Making certain food was plentiful and the drinks flowed.

The singers and dancers made a show of entering. They would perform during breaks in the dancing. Discordant sounds came from the orchestra as they tuned their instruments. More guests arrived.

Oliver stepped into the hallway and glanced over the stair railing down to the entrance.

What an incongruous sight. Vitium et Virtus masquerade balls typically were a potpourri of finery, of outrageous excess, a contest of who might have the cleverest, most outlandish costume of all. This view from above reminded him more of a county fair. Although costumes were exaggerated—hats were larger, trousers baggier, aprons and caps puffier—it looked more like everyone had come from farms and villages for a market-day festivity. Instead of costumes of brilliant reds, yellows, and blues, or dominoes of the deepest black, the guests' costumes were mostly shades of brown and grey.

Not very festive.

Amidst the stream of faux farm workers entering the hall, he spied Cecilia, who appeared like a flower blossoming out of the bare earth. As she made her way through the crowd, she greeted the arrivals and spoke to them, probably encouraging them to come to the game room and try their luck at the faro and hazard tables.

Although, she was not Cecilia at the moment. She was

Coquette, seductively slinking through the crowd, lightly touching men on their arms, leaning close, smiling at them.

He watched her climb the stairs, hips loose, dark hair flowing down her back.

His senses flared. This version of Cecilia was a man's dream.

His dream.

He remembered how she'd looked when she'd asked to come to his hotel that night. He remembered how she'd relished their lovemaking, how he'd relished it.

God help him, he wanted her all over again. He wanted her now. He did not want to let her go, alone to raise a child who could not claim a father's name.

She reached the top of the stairs and started for the game room, but turned back and walked up to him instead. 'Is anything amiss, Oliver?'

He was taken aback by the question. 'No...why do you ask?'

'You looked—I don't know—distressed.'

Not distressed. Aroused.

He attempted a smile. 'Much to think about tonight.'

Her brows knitted. 'Let me know if I can help.'

Impulsively, he put his arms around her and pressed her to him. 'Save a dance for me.'

She nodded, her eyes wide. He released her and she backed away, turned and melted into the crowd.

Cecilia wound her way through the growing crowd, her body still throbbing from Oliver's sudden embrace.

Gentlemen greeted her as Coquette, forcing her to act as Coquette.

She smiled. 'Come see me in the game room,' she said, making the invitation sound seductive.

There would be large quantities of wine and spirits flowing tonight and likely a great deal of money wagered. No doubt there would be sexual excesses of all types. She'd heard from the other workers that Oliver used to indulge in every excess, that he'd been linked with the many women eager to bed him.

She could understand why.

She flushed with the memory of making love with him, of feeling his body against hers in that sudden embrace. A mere touch of his hand brought it all back. How his hand felt on her naked flesh, how his lips tasted, how it felt when he entered her—

She must stop thinking of this.

She'd glimpsed him as she climbed the stairs to the first floor. She felt his unease. The masquerade was supposed to be the foremost event offered at Vitium et Virtus, but she could sense no excitement or enjoyment in Oliver to attest to that impression.

She certainly did not expect to enjoy it.

She'd attended masquerades in Paris as required by the manager at Maison D'Eros. The men in Paris took a costume and a mask as licence to behave in as debauched and depraved a manner as possible. She'd endured many an unwanted kiss and incessant groping at a masquerade. The neckline of her dress tonight was too low for her comfort, especially since her breasts seemed to have grown larger. Wearing her hair down made her feel as if she were getting ready for bed.

In any event, the gentlemen who frequented the game room at Vitium et Virtus were typically well behaved once they understood she was not available for licentious purposes. Tonight, though, she suspected they'd behave just as badly as their Parisian counterparts.

She stood at the hazard table, encouraging the players to roll the dice, pretending to be excited or disappointed, depending upon the roll. One of the gentlemen who wore tight buckskins and tall boots, with just a loose shirt and vest, threw his arm around her. She waited a moment before manoeuvring her way out of it. Another clodhopper patted her derrière when he stepped up to the table. She pretended to be amused. She sidled away, but the man moved closer, this time stroking her behind.

She glanced up and saw Oliver in the doorway. Had he seen that bit of intimate contact? Her face burned at the thought. But why? Was that not why she was hired? So the men would remain at the table and wager their money?

Oliver called loudly so everyone in the room could hear, 'The dancing will begin in the ballroom.'

The card players did not even look up.

The announcement gave Cecilia an opportunity to escape the man with the busy hands.

'Oh, dancing!' she cried. 'I adore dancing.'

She hurried out the door and away from groping fingers, hands and arms.

When she stepped into the hallway, Oliver was there.

'May I watch the dancing for a while?' she asked. 'I need to get away for a bit.'

'I saw,' he said.

He brushed against her as they walked to the ballroom, and her body flared in response. Odd that the men groping her in the game room left her cold, but even the barest of contact with Oliver could arouse her.

When the first set began, he touched her arm.

'Save a waltz for me,' he murmured into her ear before she left his side and mingled with others who watched the dancers perform the figures of the quadrille.

Cecilia had never been to a London ball, but she'd always imagined it to be an exciting, glittering affair, with beautiful gowns on graceful ladies and gentlemen in exquisitely fitting formal attire. This ball seemed colourless and affected. It made her sad.

She glanced over at Oliver, who frowned as he watched the dancers. Was he feeling the same? Too often it seemed as if she could feel what he felt.

* * *

When the set ended, he walked through the crowd towards her. Her insides fluttered.

'The next set is a waltz,' he said, extending his hand. 'Shall we?'

She put her hand in his, her fingers tingling. 'As you wish.'

He escorted her onto the ballroom floor.

To her surprise, the Duke and Duchess of Westmoor stood near them.

'How do you fare?' the Duchess asked her. 'Is Oliver taking good care of you?'

The Duchess's tone was light-hearted, but did she know more than she let on? Did she know about the baby? Would Oliver have told her?

'I am well, thank you,' Cecilia answered politely. 'And you?'

She and the Duke were already facing each other. Her hands were on his shoulders and the Duke's were on her waist.

'I am very well,' the Duchess answered, smiling at her husband.

Oliver regarded them both with a fond expression. 'Will it not cause a scandal that the Duke and Duchess are seen dancing the waltz at Vitium et Virtus?'

The waltz was still considered scandalous by some, because the man and woman faced each other, touched each other and danced alone rather than doing figures in groups of four or more.

The Duke laughed. 'Nothing matters but we are together and happy.' He smiled. 'Besides, we are in costume and masked. Who will know us?'

Another joke. Certainly both she and Oliver had instantly recognised them.

The music began.

With hands held, Cecilia and Oliver began the dance with

a short march, then faced each other. Cecilia curtsied; Oliver bowed. Then Cecilia put her hands on his shoulders; his hands touched her waist. As the music played its sweeping tune, Oliver led her twirling around the room.

Cecilia forgot the Duke and Duchess. She forgot the colourless dancers. She faced Oliver, his hands in near embrace, music transporting them. His black mask intensified his green eyes. She felt his gaze upon her more acutely than his hands at her waist. Her body hummed with wanting him.

How glad she was that he was her baby's father. How she wished she could repeat the lovemaking that had created that child.

'Your thoughts?' he asked, his voice deepening.

She shook her head. 'The dance.'

He gazed down at her, his eyes warming her. Thrilling her. She wished the music would never end.

When it did end, it took her a moment to realise it. She leaned towards him and his head dipped down. But the noise of the other couples leaving the dance floor woke her to where she was. She took her hands from his shoulders and stepped back.

'I—I should return to the game room,' she said.

Before he could respond she turned and fled.

It was a bit difficult, but she turned herself back into Coquette, entered the game room and forced herself to approach each of the tables of card players to ask after their comfort. She brought several men drinks and replenished others with a carafe of brandy. At least busying herself helped pass the time. Helped calm herself.

She walked to the faro table, passing out more drinks and encouraging the players to increase their wagers. A short, thick-set man with dark hair and dark, beady eyes stood watching the play. She'd not seen him before, she did not think, but there was something familiar about him.

'May I get you a drink, sir?' she asked the man.

His eyes shifted as if in alarm, but he finally smiled. 'Some brandy, perhaps, would be very nice, my dear.' He spoke with a lisp.

'My pleasure,' she said, turning away and walking to where the drinks were. She brought another carafe of brandy and a glass and returned to the faro table.

'Here you are, sir,' she said in Coquette's cheerful voice.

She poured him some brandy and refilled the glass of the man beside him.

'Thank you, Coquette,' the man said.

'Coquette?' the stranger piped up. 'Have we met before, Coquette?'

She suddenly knew him. He was Sir Nash Bowles. The man who had beaten Flo. He remembered her from Paris, she was certain.

Her hand trembled, but she poured him more brandy and made herself smile seductively. 'Perhaps we have met, sir. I have been many places. Met many gentlemen.'

He nodded, but looked thoughtful.

Did he remember her as Madame Coquette? The courtesan? What would Oliver think if he knew of Madame Coquette?

She could not worry about that. Bowles posed a danger to Flo.

Cecilia strolled to the hazard table and emptied the carafe in other glasses before returning it to the bar and sauntering out of the room. Once in the hallway, she dashed to the ballroom, searching for Oliver.

She found Flo. 'Have you seen Oliver?'

Flo was arm in arm with some gentleman. 'He was here a while ago.'

Cecilia leaned down to whisper in Flo's ear. 'Stay here. Stay with this man. Do not go in the game room.'

Flo's brow creased in confusion, but she nodded and clutched the man's arm tighter.

Cecilia wound her way through the crowd, which was becoming louder and more raucous. She finally spied Oliver at the door of the ballroom. She had to fight the crowd to reach the doorway again, but he'd already left. She caught up with him on the landing as he was descending the stairs.

'Oliver!' she called.

He turned, and she ran down the stairs to him.

She tried not to raise her voice. 'Bowles is here! I saw him in the game room.'

His gaze caught hers. He bounded back up the stairs, and Cecilia ran behind him. They hurried to the game room, but Bowles was no longer there. They searched in the ballroom, but how could they find him among so many like-costumed men?

From the ballroom, she glimpsed him in the hallway.

'There!' she cried to Oliver, pointing to the door.

They went after him, but as they reached the stairs, he had crossed the entrance hall to the front door.

'Stop him!' Oliver cried, but no one was near. Snyder was not at his post.

Oliver raced down the stairs. Cecilia hurried after him, but he was out the door before she reached the hall. Where was Snyder? She searched for him, but he was not near. What else was there to do but follow Oliver outside? The street was busy enough even at this late hour. She searched up and down the pavement to no avail. When she passed the entrance to the alley leading to the rear of the buildings on Jermyn and Bury Streets, she heard a man's cry. The alley was dark, but she entered it, walking carefully until she could make out two men in the darkness.

One man was beating on the other with his fists.

'Stay away, Bowles!' she heard Oliver shout. 'Did you not think me serious?' He held one of Bowles's arms in one hand and punched him with the other.

'No!' she gasped, but her voice was too soft to carry.

She couldn't breathe. Oliver was beating Bowles! She cowered, remembering how it felt to be hit over and over.

Stop, Oliver! she wanted to cry, but fear locked her throat. Oliver could kill Bowles with his bare hands, just as Duncan could have killed her. She could not bear to watch and was too frightened to try to stop it. She turned on her heel and ran, her heart pounding wildly.

She could not return to Vitium et Virtus and pretend to be Coquette, not while Oliver might be killing Bowles. She went instead to Oliver's house and pounded on the door until Irwin let her in.

Chapter Fifteen

Oliver pulled off his mask and looked down on Bowles, seated in a puddle in the alley. Blood dripped from his nose and one eye had already swollen shut.

It served Bowles right.

Bowles had pulled a knife on him, but Oliver had been quick enough to deflect the blade from stabbing him in the chest.

He picked up the knife and pointed it into Bowles's face. 'Shall I show you what the blade of this knife feels like?' Oliver growled.

Bowles glared at him, but gave no answer.

Oliver gripped the handle of the knife for a moment, angry enough to consider using it. Blood dripped from his hand, pooling on the ground.

Like the pool of blood they'd found in this same alley six years before when Nicholas disappeared.

'Nicholas,' Oliver murmured.

Bowles rose to his feet. 'Nicholas Bartlett? What of him?'

'Never you mind about Nicholas,' Oliver shot back.

He hurled the knife as far as it would go, over the fence and into someone's garden.

Bowles made an unintelligible sound.

'You won't be pulling that knife again,' Oliver told him.

Bowles never heeded the rules of a fair fight.

Oliver's hand throbbed and more blood dripped onto the ground. He pulled a handkerchief from his pocket and wrapped it around his hand.

Oliver spoke low and menacing. 'Stay away from Vitium et Virtus. You cannot best me, so do not try again. Next time I may not let you off so easy.'

'First tell me why you mentioned Nicholas Bartlett,' Bowles demanded. 'He's...he's dead, correct? Everyone says so.'

'Forget Nicholas,' Oliver said sharply. What business was it of Bowles's? 'Leave here now and do not come back. Ever.'

Oliver held the handkerchief tightly against the bleeding cut on his palm as he watched Bowles limp out of the alley. He followed him to the street and watched until Bowles turned the corner at St James's Street.

Oliver walked through the alley again and entered Vitium et Virtus through the private entrance. One of the footmen attending the kitchen was passing by and noticed his bloody hand.

'Sir!' the man cried. 'What happened to you?'

'A cut,' Oliver said.

'Come, sir.' The footman gestured towards the kitchen. 'We'll fetch Mrs Parker. She'll bandage it for you.'

Oliver followed the footman to the doorway of the kitchen, which was a chaos of activity preparing food for the masquerade. The footman strode up to the club's housekeeper and spoke to her, glancing over at Oliver.

Mrs Parker dropped what she was doing and ran over to him. 'Mr Gregory, let us bandage that up.'

She led him to her sitting room where she cleansed the

wound and wrapped his hand in strips of linen. It hurt like the devil.

Oliver thanked her and put on his mask again. He needed to find Cecilia, to tell her he'd caught up with Bowles, who would not likely be bothering them again.

He looked for Cecilia first in the game room, but no one had seen her since she'd left with him. He next searched the ballroom, where Flo approached him.

'Mr Gregory, have you seen Coquette?' Flo asked.

'No. I was about to ask you if you had seen her,' he responded.

'Oh.' She bit her lip. 'She made me worry. Told me not to leave the room.'

He leaned over to Flo's ear. 'Bowles was here, but he is gone now.'

Flo's eyes widened. 'Sir Nash was here?'

He nodded. 'Do not fear. He'd be a fool to return.'

One of the other workers approached Oliver to deal with a drunken guest, and for the rest of the night he was kept too busy to look for Cecilia. When the masquerade was finally over, Snyder told him Irwin walked over to say Cecilia had come home early. Irwin told Snyder she'd appeared upset and Irwin thought Oliver should know.

Oliver left Vitium et Virtus through the private door and walked to his house. He used his key to let himself in. Irwin and the other servants would be abed at this hour. He climbed the stairs to his bedchamber, but paused at his door, turning instead to Cecilia's.

He knocked softly on her door and entered. Coals glowed in the fireplace casting enough light for him to see her in the bed.

How innocent and vulnerable she appeared. Her face was relaxed in repose and, in the dim light from the fireplace, she was almost too lovely to behold.

He made himself call softly. 'Cecilia?'

Her eyes flew open and grew wide with fright. She half rose.

'It is only me.' Oliver wanted to touch her, but held back.

'What?' she said, blinking.

'Sorry to wake you, but are you unwell? You came home early.' Had the commotion about Bowles made her ill? Hurt the baby?

She sat up, holding the bed linens around her. 'I'm fine. I—I just wanted to come home.'

He sensed she was not fine. She was unsettled and disturbed.

He tried to reassure her. 'I came to tell you Bowles will not be a problem any more.'

She clutched the bed linens even tighter. 'Why not?' She seemed even more disturbed. 'What happened to him?'

'I taught him a lesson.' She did not need to hear the details.

'A lesson?' she asked uncertainly.

'He won't be returning.'

Her eyes grew huge and looked frightened. 'What do you mean?'

Her reaction made no sense. 'I mean, I sent him away and he'd be a fool to return.'

The tension in her body eased a little. 'Oh,' she said. 'Very well.'

On the dance floor when he'd almost kissed her, her lips had seemed ready for him. Not now. Something had changed.

'I'll say goodnight, then.' He backed away.

She lay down again, burrowed under the blankets and turned her back to him.

It was near noon by the time Oliver sat alone at breakfast, lingering over the newspapers and cups of coffee, not in any hurry to go over to Vitium et Virtus to survey the damage and disarray that always came in the wake of a special event.

Mr Bell and Mrs Parker would see to the clean-up, but Oliver felt an obligation to be there.

Even if his hand still throbbed from the blade of Bowles's knife.

A knife fight. When had a masquerade included a knife fight?

Could there have been a knife fight the night Nicholas disappeared from that same alley?

Oliver wished he could return to those youthful days when he, Nicholas, Frederick and Jacob conjured up one wild idea after another for their secular version of a Hell Fire club. Even then it had been the camaraderie shared among the four good friends that Oliver valued the most. The belonging. As if they were his family.

When Nicholas disappeared, they lost that. And, with Nick gone, Oliver gradually lost pleasure in Vitium et Virtus.

At least last night he'd had the pleasure of waltzing with Cecilia. Holding her in his arms again.

He wished he'd kissed her.

From her reaction to him last night when he woke her, the chance of kissing her again was somehow lost.

The door opened and Cecilia walked in.

He'd not expected her.

He stood. 'Good morning.'

'Morning.' Her gaze was averted as if she did not wish to look at him.

Why? What had happened between that almost-kiss and now?

He gestured to a chair. 'Sit. I'll fix you a plate.'

She went to the sideboard instead. 'I'll do it.'

She selected her food and poured her tea. He stood the whole time, waiting for her to sit. She finally lowered herself into a chair, not across from him, but adjacent to him. So she would not have to look at him?

He felt as if she were four leagues away.

He returned to his newspaper. What other choice did he have? Until she told him what disturbed her, what else could he do?

She finished her cup of tea and glanced at the teapot, which was not in her reach. She started to rise to walk over to it.

'Allow me.' Oliver picked up the teapot with his bandaged hand.

Her voice rose. 'What happened to your hand?'

He poured her a cup.

'Nothing serious,' he assured her, passing her the cream and sugar. 'A cut.'

She made no effort to fix her cup of tea. 'Last night? How?'

He rubbed the bandage. 'Bowles drew a knife.'

Her eyes grew huge. 'You fought with knives?'

'Bowles pulled a knife. I disarmed him.' *And then pummelled him with my fists*, but she did not need to hear the unpleasant details.

She reached out as if to touch his hand. 'How bad is the cut?'

It still hurt like the devil. 'It will not kill me.'

'May I see?'

Cecilia watched him unwrap his hand, the strips of linen closest to the wound showing new red blood.

Bowles had attacked him with a knife? All Oliver had were his fists. No wonder he used them so fiercely against Bowles.

She moved her chair closer and took his hand in hers. The cut was a long gash across his palm.

'How did Bowles cut your hand?' She had a difficult time picturing it.

Oliver shrugged. 'He was aiming for my heart. I stopped him.'

She shivered. Oliver hadn't been a killer; he'd almost been killed.

The wound's edges were smooth, but there was a gap from which blood still oozed. The skin around the cut was very red and a little swollen.

'I think you need this stitched,' she told him, still holding his hand. 'Would you allow me to sew the sides together? They will heal better.'

His eyes narrowed. 'Do you know how to stitch wounds?'

She nodded and looked directly into his face for the first time this morning. 'After Quatre Bras and Waterloo, the surgeon had me sewing up the easier wounds. I had the needle and thread, you see.'

'You stitched up wounds after Waterloo?' His brows arched.

The sight of wounded men came back to her. 'There were so many.' What she'd done had been such a small thing. 'At first it was a little difficult, but I became accustomed to it.' She examined his wound again, gently touching the edges with her finger. 'Come up to my room. I have needle and thread there.'

She gathered the bloody bandage in her hand. He stood and extended his uninjured hand to help her rise.

As they walked to her room, her emotions were in a jumble. He might have been killed! On the other hand, she'd witnessed him angry enough to kill.

When they reached the top of the stairs, he opened the door to her bedchamber. She led him to her sitting room.

'Please sit, Oliver. I'll gather what I need.' She brought a clean towel, a basin and her bottle of lavender water. When she'd tended to the soldiers at Waterloo, she'd not had the luxury of lavender water.

Her sewing box was on the table in the sitting room.

She sat on the sofa with him and drew one of the tables to the sofa's side. Sitting so close, she felt her body hum again, teasing her with desire. She blinked, trying not to lose focus on his wound.

'Let me wash the blood away.' She held his hand over the basin and poured lavender water on it, carefully wiping off dried blood and new blood with the towel.

If she kept her attention on the task and not on the lime and bergamot scent of his soap, she'd endure this.

She took a needle from her etui and a length of black thread from a spool. She threaded the needle and wet the thread with the lavender water. 'It will go through easier this way.'

'I am delighted to know that.' His voice was strained.

She glanced into his eyes. 'This will hurt, but it will go faster if you do not move.' She folded the towel and placed his hand on top of it on the table. 'Are you ready?'

He smiled at her. 'As ready as I have ever been to have my hand sewn together.'

His good humour reminded her of Paris. That was not going to help her complete this task.

She took a breath and pushed the needle into his skin.

He flinched and gritted his teeth, but kept his hand steady.

She continued, riveting her attention to the wound, as she had managed after Waterloo. She worked quickly, but carefully.

As she was concentrating, the baby inside her moved, startling her into pausing.

'Why are you stopping?' he asked, his voice tight.

'The baby,' she said. 'The baby moved.'

How much tougher could this be? The baby reminding her that Oliver was the father.

'There!' she said when finished.

She glanced up at him. His face was taut. She'd seen that look before on countless men trying to endure pain.

Oliver expelled a pent-up breath and more colour returned to his cheeks.

She rose from the sofa. 'Wait here. I need some bandages. I'll be right back.'

She found Mary down in the kitchen with Mrs Irwin. 'Do we have some strips of cloth to use as bandages?'

'Bandages?' Mary cried. 'Who needs bandages?'

'Mr Gregory cut his hand.' It was enough of an explanation.

'I don't think we have bandages,' Mrs Irwin said.

'But I know some cloth we can use.' Mary popped out of her chair.

They ripped an old, laundered bedsheet into strips, and Cecilia brought the bandages to Oliver, who was lying on the sofa, one arm over his face.

He sat up when he heard her enter and extended his arm.

Cecilia started wrapping his hand, a hand that had once caressed her. A hand that had been capable of a brutal beating.

Oliver felt her withdraw again as she finished bandaging. For a very few moments, they had been as they were in Paris. At ease with each other. That was worth the several minutes of pain he'd endured.

'Do you have plans for today?' he asked, trying to delay having to leave her.

'I planned on returning books to Hookham's,' she responded. 'Do you need any returned? Any you wish me to pick up?'

'No.' He had heard of a book he wanted to read, *The European In India*, but to mention it seemed too revealing a disclosure.

The clock struck one. 'I should go now,' she said, standing. 'Oh,' she exclaimed.

'What is it?' Princess Charlotte died in childbirth. So could Cecilia.

Her smile was beatific. 'The baby moved again. Very active baby today.'

'Is that good?' He hoped so.

'I have no idea.' She put her sewing items back and picked up the basin and lavender water.

A hint he should leave, he believed.

But she did not rush him out. 'What about you, Oliver? What are your plans today?'

'Back to the club. It is likely a shambles today.' He would rather walk to Hookham's with her.

'Well, do not use your hand overmuch.' She nodded towards it.

He pushed himself up from the sofa and started for the door of the sitting room, but turned around before crossing the threshold. 'Thank you, Cecilia.' He lifted his hand. 'That was quite remarkable of you.'

He left her bedchamber and continued down the stairs. There was no reason for him to delay going over to the club. Keeping busy would prevent him from thinking of her.

He crossed through the garden and into the alley where he had tussled with Bowles the night before. In the sunlight he could see a small pool of blood from the bleeding of his hand. He touched his bandages, remembering the flash of silver that warned him of Bowles's intent.

He crossed through the club's garden and entered the building through the owners' entrance. As he passed through the rooms to the door through to the public side, a figure stepped into the hallway.

It took a moment for Oliver to recognise who it was. 'Frederick!' He quickened his step. 'When did you get back?'

When they reached each other, a handshake was ready. Frederick and his wife had been away in the country for a couple of months.

'We arrived this morning.' Frederick's lips twisted in dismay. 'I'd planned to be here for the masquerade, but one of the carriage wheels broke and we tipped over.'

'Good God! Was anyone hurt?'

'With God's luck, no,' Frederick said. 'It was just Georgiana and me inside. One of the coachmen was thrown off, but suffered only bruises.'

Oliver frowned. When Frederick purchased his commission in the army after Oxford, Oliver actually prayed his friend would survive. His prayers had been answered, apparently not only during the war, but also on the road to London.

'Suffice to say,' Frederick went on, 'we were delayed. But I was sorry to leave that chaotic event in your hands alone. I know how hectic it can be.'

'Jake and Rose came, so I was not alone.' Although they had been so wrapped up in each other, he'd not had the heart to disturb them.

'From the disarray I just surveyed, it was a wild night,' Frederick said.

Oliver took a deep, resigned breath. 'I might as well see for myself.'

The two men walked together to the door to the public part of the club. They entered the hall, which was in reasonable shape.

'The ballroom is what you should see,' Frederick said.

The ballroom floor was filled with scattered oddments. Masks. Gloves. Scarves. Shoes. Broken glasses and spilled drinks. Remarkably, some undergarments, as well. Some maids were already busy with brooms and dustpans. One maid went ahead of the others and picked up the items of clothing. Nothing seemed valuable enough to save for an owner to collect it. The maids would sell the clothing on Petticoat Lane and make a few extra pennies.

'Take care,' Oliver said to the maid gathering up clothing. He pointed to the broken glass.

The maid glanced up and smiled. 'I will, Mr Gregory.'

'Mary?' The girl he'd hired as Cecilia's lady's maid was assisting in the cleaning up.

'My uncle asked Mr Bell if I could help. The extra money will help me a lot.'

Frederick pointed to Oliver's bandaged hand. 'What happened to you?'

'Ah…' Oliver laughed sarcastically. 'It is quite a story. Let us look at the other rooms first and I'll tell you over a drink.'

It appeared that Mr Bell had matters well in hand. He'd hired extra help for the day. So far nothing too alarming had been found, except one hungover gentleman who'd passed out on the floor in one of the bedrooms and had gone unnoticed. The singers and dancers had all taken off and would not return until after Christmas.

Back in the private owners' rooms, over brandy, Oliver told Frederick about Sir Nash Bowles.

'That reprobate!' Frederick banged his fist against the table. 'I thought we'd rid ourselves of him after his treachery with Georgiana.'

'I am reasonably certain he will not return,' Oliver said.

'I think we should be watchful,' Frederick said. 'The singer, Fleurette—will he leave her alone, I wonder?'

'He had better,' Oliver said fiercely. He poured them each another brandy.

Oliver had not mentioned Cecilia. How to talk about her with Frederick? He must, because Fred would eventually see Jake and Jake or Rose would speak of her.

'We have a new worker,' Oliver began. He gave a very short version of the events that led to Cecilia being hired, leaving out any mention of his meeting her in Paris.

'We need a hostess?' Frederick looked sceptical.

Oliver could not disagree, but of course, he knew Cecilia's reasons for wanting to work. And he knew her employment would be temporary.

'One thing more.' Oliver could not leave this out. 'She is living at my house.'

'Your house?' Frederick's brows rose. 'Is there more to this?'

Much more. 'She is an employee and a lodger.'

Frederick laughed. 'Since when do you take in lady lodgers?'

'It is complicated.'

'And you do not want to talk about it,' Frederick added.

'That is so.'

His friend leaned forward. 'Well, here's the thing. Georgiana and I want you to come to dinner. The rest of the family are still in the country, so that should keep things calm. Come to dinner the day after tomorrow. Bring this hostess lodger with you.'

'She will not come.' Oliver was certain of that.

'Then invite us to dinner at your house in two days. I want to meet this hostess.' Frederick grinned. 'We will be showing up on your doorstep, so refusal is out of the question.'

There was no sense in countering Frederick when he acted like that. He took it upon himself to oversee the welfare of Vitium et Virtu and his friends.

'Very well. Dinner in two days' time.'

Chapter Sixteen

Cecilia did not see why she must attend this dinner with Oliver's friends. Oliver said this Frederick Challenger was one of the owners of Vitium et Virtus and he wanted to meet the new hostess. If so, she could merely appear and be introduced.

They had a little row over it.

'You are making it seem as if we are attached and we are not,' she protested.

'Are we not? If you claim the baby is mine, does that not mean we are attached?' he shot back.

'I don't *claim* it,' she countered. 'It is the truth.'

They went on like that for a good quarter of an hour.

Finally, Oliver said. 'I've given you a place to live, allowed you to work at the club and have promised to support you and the child. I think you could do this one thing for me—attend this dinner with my friend and his wife.'

Cecilia could not counter that argument.

The night of the dinner she wore a purple dress, one of the ones she wore at Vitium et Virtus, because the black one he'd bought her was not fancy enough for a dinner dress. She cared that his friend's wife approve, but, at the same time, it irritated her that it mattered to her.

Mary finished arranging her hair, stared into the mirror and spoke to Cecilia's reflection. 'Will that do, do you think?'

It looked effortless and not as fancy as she might wear as a hostess, but not as plain as she wore every day. Mary had pulled her hair into a coil at the top of her head and picked out a few tendrils to caress the back of her neck. The only jewellery she wore was the only jewellery she still owned—her pearl necklace.

'It is perfect, Mary.' The girl had done precisely what Cecilia wanted.

She stared at her reflection and frowned. 'The neckline is too low.' It was suitable for Madame Coquette, but not Cecilia.

Mary stepped back. 'I have just the thing!'

She ran out of the room and returned with a piece of black net with black embroidered flowers on it. 'A fichu!' she called triumphantly.

'Where did you come by this?' Cecilia asked.

'At Vitium et Virtus,' Mary responded. 'Uncle Irwin got Mr Bell to hire me to clean up after the masquerade. Mr Gregory let us keep some of the things we found that was not likely to be sought by the owners.'

'This does not fit in at all with the masquerade's costume theme.' But it was perfect for Cecilia.

Mary helped her tuck in the netting around the neckline of the dress. When Cecilia again looked in the mirror this time it made the gown even more elegant.

'It is perfect, Mary. Thank you.' Cecilia stood. 'I suppose I should go downstairs.'

The maid gave her a sympathetic look. 'I do not know why you are so unhappy about this. Mr Challenger seemed like a nice man when he was at the club with Mr Gregory. Maybe his wife will be nice, too.'

Cecilia sighed. 'I am sure she will be nice. That is the problem. What am I doing sharing dinner with nice people?'

To her surprise, Mary gave her a hug. 'You have been more than nice to me, Mrs Lockhart. There is no reason why they should not like you very much.'

Except that she worked in a decadent club and was bearing a child out of wedlock.

'I suppose I should go and find out.'

Oliver said he'd not told his friend and his wife that she was carrying a child. He'd not told anyone outside of this house. Though, they would still assume she and Oliver were a couple, would they not? Especially since she'd be dining with them.

She left the bedchamber and went downstairs with butterflies in her stomach, chastising herself for feeling nervous. She knew they'd already arrived because she saw their carriage pull up while she was dressing. As she approached the drawing-room door she decided to borrow a little confidence from Coquette. She straightened her spine and entered the room.

They all turned to her and rose from their seats.

Mr Challenger, who stood next to Oliver, was tall like Oliver, but he was light to Oliver's dark with light brown hair and brown eyes that did not exactly welcome her as much as they assessed her. His wife had the sort of looks Cecilia always envied as a girl. Blonde with blue eyes, taller than was fashionable, though, but with an elegant figure.

'Allow me to present Mrs Lockhart,' Oliver said. 'Cecilia, Mr and Mrs Challenger.'

They would notice, of course, that Oliver addressed her by her given name.

Cecilia curtsied.

Mrs Challenger stepped forward, extending her hand.

When Cecilia accepted it, Mrs Challenger held on in a friendlier manner than a handshake. 'Oh, but you must call us Frederick and Georgiana. Oliver does and it will be so much more comfortable.'

Comfortable for her, perhaps, but it reflected an equality that Cecilia could not feel.

'Yes,' Mr Challenger said less enthusiastically. 'Call me Fred.'

'How do you do,' Cecilia managed. She would endeavour not to address them by name at all.

'Some claret, Cecilia?' Oliver asked, having already poured a glass.

She reached for it. 'Thank you.' She'd take a few sips and leave the rest. Since her pregnancy, wine unsettled her stomach, but she did not wish to call any attention to herself by refusing what everyone else was drinking.

Though why she cared what these people thought of her was a puzzle. And yet she wanted them to accept her as if she'd stepped out of her parents' house, never having met or married Duncan.

'Come sit with me,' Georgiana said.

Could she refuse?

'Where are you from?' Georgiana asked.

'Surrey,' she replied.

'Oh, Surrey?' Georgiana smiled. 'Where in Surrey?'

'Near Haslemere.'

'I have never been to Haslemere,' the lady said.

All the better. Think how hard it would be if Georgiana had lived in Haslemere and knew people she knew. Or maybe she should tell her whole story. What difference would it make? If Oliver supported her as he promised to do, she'd go where no one knew her and never see these people again.

Never see Oliver again.

Cecilia suspected Georgiana wished to ask more about her, but could not do so without showing she was pushing for information like a concerned mother interviewing a woman her son wished to marry.

Except marriage was certainly not what Cecilia and Oliver were about.

'Have you spent much time in London?' This was more conversational.

'Not before this.'

Irwin appeared at the door. 'Dinner is served.'

Cecilia did not expect the evening to improve over the dinner table.

But it did.

Instead of continuing to interview her, they talked of Vitium et Virtus, how it began when Oliver, Frederick, the Duke and another friend were all attending Oxford. The other friend, Nicholas, had originated the idea and put up the most money. This was the first Cecilia had heard of Nicholas. She'd heard talk of Frederick and of his marriage to Georgiana, but no one had ever mentioned Nicholas.

'What happened to him?' she asked.

'To whom?' Oliver responded.

'To Nicholas. I never heard of him before.'

Oliver lowered his head and tension filled the room.

Finally, Frederick spoke. 'Nicholas disappeared six years ago. We do not know where he is or if he is even alive.'

'He is alive.' Oliver's voice turned low and firm.

His was obviously the final word, because a pall spread over the room after he spoke.

Georgiana broke it. 'Cecilia, did you know that Vitium et Virtus is the reason Fred and I married?'

'No, I didn't.' She was glad of the change of subject and disturbed by Oliver's change in mood.

Georgiana told of how she contrived to expose the perverted character of the man her father was insisting she marry.

'I knew he would be at Vitium et Virtus, so I came and set up an auction,' Georgiana said.

Cecilia was not following this logic. 'Auctioning what?'

'Her virginity.' Frederick groaned. 'We do not do such things at Vitium et Virtus. There was nothing for me to do but stop it.'

'So he outbid everyone and ruined everything!' Georgiana cried. 'Then that odious man threatened to expose what I'd done and ruin my reputation—'

'So I had to marry her.' Frederick grinned.

'Do you know who the odious man was?' Oliver asked her.

She was glad he spoke. 'Who?'

'Sir Nash Bowles.'

'No!' She swung a look to Georgiana. 'You are lucky you did not marry Bowles. He would be a brutal husband.'

'Yes, he would be,' Georgiana agreed, going on to let Cecilia know she and Frederick had heard of Bowles's latest escapades.

Cecilia lifted her glass. 'May he stay away for good.'

They all joined her in that toast, finishing the wine in their glasses. Cecilia merely sipped hers.

When the pudding was served and even more wine was poured, Frederick leaned towards Cecilia.

'You look familiar,' he said. 'I wonder if we have met before?'

Her heart started to pound. He did not look familiar to her. She remembered every one of the men who'd sought Madame Coquette's favours, but there were others who might have seen her at Maison D'Eros. Sir Nash Bowles, for example.

'I think I would remember *you*, sir,' she said cheekily, making herself smile.

Georgiana laughed and the dangerous moment passed.

After the pudding, the ladies returned to the drawing room. Oliver and Frederick stayed in the dining room, sipping brandy.

'She is not what I expected,' Frederick said.

'I was not asking,' Oliver countered.

Frederick grinned. 'I do not care a fig. You'll hear what I have to say about it anyway.'

Oliver took another sip of his drink, letting the amber liquid warm his throat. 'Of course I will.'

Frederick stared into space as if tallying up a list of figures. 'She is a mystery, is she not? Not much for talking about herself.'

'She probably resented the inquisition.' Oliver could share a lot more about Cecilia. About her husband. Her parents. That she was carrying a child. It seemed disloyal to her, though, even with his good friend. 'But, I agree. There is much she holds back.'

Frederick went on. 'I liked her, even so. Georgiana liked her, too, I could tell. She would have persisted in her inquisition, if she'd not liked her.'

Georgiana was fearless when she wanted something. He thought of the virginity auction. Or the reckless curricle race to which she challenged Frederick. A challenge he, of course, readily accepted.

'Something about your Cecilia...' Frederick gazed into the air again.

Oliver lifted his glass to his lips. He wanted to tell Frederick that she was not his Cecilia. Better to just change the subject. 'How long will you and Georgiana be in London?'

'We'll stay through Christmas,' Frederick answered. 'Our primary reason for travel here was for the masquerade, you know. But we thought it would be nice to have Christmas just the two of us here in London.' He finished his brandy. 'Out of the chaos, you know.'

Frederick came from a family who thought drama and discord were everyday events.

Christmas was only days away.

Christmas was not a holiday Oliver looked upon with any

eagerness. Growing up, he made the obligatory trip to his father's country house, where his stepmother did not want him. She always planned a house party so, as a boy, he could not attend, and as he got older, he felt no more welcome. His father always managed a nice present, usually presented in haste before going off to the next planned activity for the guests.

Oliver finished his brandy and stood. 'We should return to the ladies.'

Frederick grinned. 'Just in case Georgiana is firing more questions at Cecilia.'

The next day Oliver met Frederick at Vitium et Virtus so they could discuss club business. They'd sent a message to Jacob to meet them there, as well, but one never knew if Jacob would be free of ducal affairs and able to attend.

They met in the drawing room. The ledgers were on the table in front of them, but neither Oliver nor Frederick were particularly interested in figures, costs and profit. That was Jacob's forte.

'So...' Fred began. 'What did Cecilia say about us after we left last night? Will she speak to us again?'

'I cannot say,' Oliver replied. 'She retired to her room as soon as you left.' And not before giving Oliver a withering look.

She did not come down for breakfast, either.

'I have not seen her today.'

She'd looked so beautiful the night before. So elegant and ladylike. No reason she should not look ladylike; she was a baron's daughter. He'd even admired her skill at evading Georgiana's questions. He respected a sense of privacy.

Even so, it rankled that she held back from him.

Frederick drummed his fingers on the table. 'Will Jake come, do you think?'

'Jacob stops by when he has the time.' Truth was Jacob

rarely stayed for more than a few minutes when he was able to come.

Frederick looked around. 'What are we doing with this place? Can we keep it up?'

Oliver gave him a direct look. 'We must.'

It went without saying. They could not sell or end the club, not with Nicholas the owner with the most shares.

Fred took another sip of his drink. 'At least for another year.'

In another year, if Nicholas did not return, he could be declared dead.

They both lapsed into a depressed silence that was not going to help anything.

The silence was broken by loud footsteps in the hall and a voice shouting, 'Where are you?'

They both jumped to their feet. Jacob was here.

Frederick reached the door and threw it open. 'Jacob!'

It had only been a matter of weeks since they had been together, playing billiards, the day that Cecilia showed up on his doorstep, in fact. Like they'd done since they were boys, they hugged each other and laughed at themselves for such an emotional excess.

'I am surprised you made it,' Oliver said.

'Some things are more important than others.' Jacob looked from Oliver to Frederick to a missing space in between. 'Friends, for example.'

They caught up on family matters. The delights of their marriages, the health of their families. Any news.

'How is Eleanor?' Oliver asked.

Eleanor was Jacob's sister, who'd been married to some sort of northern laird and widowed a short time after. A boating accident, Oliver thought. She bore the man's darling daughter whom Oliver and his friends now doted on.

'She's doing well,' Jacob said. 'Busy with Lucy, you know.'

He shared the latest antics of the child, now five years old and bright as a copper coin.

'By the way, how is your father, Oliver?' Frederick asked.

Oliver shrugged. 'I assume he is in the country, having their usual house party.' He had not heard from his father since informing him he'd returned from Paris.

Frederick and Jacob knew better than to ask him about the stepmother. Nicholas had long ago told Oliver to simply pretend she did not exist, an idea that worked remarkably well.

They finally settled down to the business of Vitium et Virtus, looking through the books, talking of the events they'd held.

'Did you ever do that idea you had?' Frederick asked. 'You know, the one where men and women pick balls with matching numbers?'

Oliver had forgotten all about it. 'No. Not yet.' He was not even sure he liked the idea any more.

Frederick hit Oliver on the arm. 'Does Jake know about Bowles?'

'Bowles?' Jacob sat up straighter.

Oliver held up his bandaged hand and told the whole saga of Sir Nash Bowles.

'He cut you?' Jake frowned.

'Say it,' Oliver teased. 'Tell me I'm slipping. I let the likes of Bowles cut me.'

The afternoon wore on as they talked over plans for the club after Christmas.

'I'll try to help more,' Frederick said. 'We'll stay in London through the Season. I should be able to come often.'

Jacob shook his head. 'I will try to stop by as much as I can. We leave most of the work to you, Oliver.'

Oliver shrugged. 'Do not worry over it.'

As the sky darkened with the setting sun, they lit one lamp after another, but finally they could not deny that the hour was late and it was time for Frederick and Jacob to return to their wives.

'We should go,' Jacob said.

Without saying a word, Oliver leaned forward and placed his hand, palm up, at the centre of the table they sat around. Jake placed his hand on top of Oliver's, and Frederick lay his on top of Jake's.

'In Vitium et Virtus,' they chorused. In vice and virtue, the words that bound them together.

They broke apart, and Frederick poured them each a glass of brandy. They lifted their glasses.

'To absent friends,' Jacob said.

'Be he in heaven or hell—' Oliver continued.

'Or somewhere in between—' Frederick added.

'Know that we wish you well,' Jacob said, his voice turning low.

Their ritual, their incantation. For Nicholas.

They all stood and made their way to the door. Instead of using the side door, as they were accustomed to doing when the club was open, they entered the public parts of the building to the marble-tiled hall. Snyder, typically a fixture in the hall, was absent and they retrieved their own topcoats, hats and gloves.

Frederick punched Oliver's arm again. 'You've gone the whole afternoon without mentioning Cecilia to Jacob.'

Jacob smiled. 'How is our Coquette doing?'

'Coquette?' Frederick's brow furrowed.

'That is the name she goes by.' Jacob peered at him. 'Did not Oliver tell you she works here?'

'He told me,' Frederick said. 'Not the name Coquette, though.'

Here was another opportunity for Oliver to tell his friends about meeting Cecilia in Paris, that she was the woman he'd told them about when he returned, that she said she bore his child.

But the hour was late and they needed to go home.

'Coquette,' Frederick repeated. 'Coquette.'

'What the devil is wrong with you?' Oliver asked him. 'Most of the singers and dancers use false names.'

'Yes, but something about that one.' Fred looked as if he was struggling to remember. His face relaxed. 'I cannot think. But I do need to return home. Georgiana will believe I fell into the Thames—' He stopped abruptly, realising he was joking about what might have been a real possibility for Nicholas.

He nodded uncomfortably. The three men dressed for the cold, damp evening air and walked outside together.

'Wish I would have arranged for my carriage,' Jacob said.

Frederick gave him a playful push. 'Getting soft in all your ducal splendour, are you?'

They said goodbye and started to walk in the opposite direction from Oliver, who merely needed to turn the corner.

Oliver was about to put his hand on the door handle, when he heard running footsteps behind him. He turned.

It was Frederick. 'Wait, Oliver!'

It had started to drizzle, but Oliver waited for Frederick to reach him. 'What is it?'

'I remembered.' Fred took a moment to try to catch his breath. 'I remembered where I saw her.'

'Saw who?' Oliver asked.

'Your Cecilia.' Fred took a deep breath and expelled it slowly. 'It was when I was in Paris. I went to a club called Maison D'Eros. All the men there were talking about a courtesan, the most desirable courtesan in Paris, they said. Very selective and exclusive. I saw her. She went by the name of Coquette. Madame Coquette!'

Oliver went cold.

'She accepted maybe one or two men per week, they said. And the men paid well for a night with her. They paid for the chance to please her. If they did not please her, she sent them off, but kept the money.' Frederick shook his head. 'I do not know why I did not realise it when I first saw her. Her demeanour was so different at dinner.'

Oliver had witnessed Cecilia's transformation many times.

'It was Cecilia,' Frederick said. 'Did you know? Did you know she was a courtesan in Paris?'

'No.' Oliver's voice deepened. 'I did not know.'

Chapter Seventeen

Oliver stood by the door while Frederick dashed away. The rain thickened, falling like needles in the cold air and still he did not move.

She'd told him there had been no other men since him, yet she'd been a courtesan, selective and exclusive, but a courtesan none the less. Was he to believe she'd stopped her liaisons with men after meeting him?

That was how she earned her money.

Rainwater streamed from the brim of his hat and the wet was soaking through his topcoat. He finally turned and put his key in the lock. The hall was empty, but that was no surprise. The servants had a day off.

He peeled off his wet topcoat and dropped it on to a chair; his hat and gloves he left on the table. He climbed the stairs to the second floor where his bedchamber—and Cecilia's— were located. He paused at the top step, his hand resting on the banister.

With sudden resolve he surged towards her door and, restraining himself, knocked mildly.

'Come in.' Her voice sounded unconcerned.

He opened the door and stepped inside.

'I am in the sitting room,' she called.

He walked to the door of the sitting room.

She sat on the sofa, a book in her hand, her face illuminated by the light of a nearby lamp. Her legs were tucked underneath her, her hair merely tied back with a ribbon. She wore a morning dress, a loose-fitting garment of what might once have been white muslin, but had turned grey with time. Even from the doorway he could see where she'd mended it.

'Oliver,' she said with some surprise, although she must have known the servants were out.

'I am back from meeting Frederick and Jacob at the club.' He could not quite keep all the emotion from his voice.

Her relaxed expression tensed. 'Is something wrong there?'

'Not there,' he said.

Her brows rose.

He meant to ease into this discussion, but his anger pushed words out of his mouth. 'Why did you lie to me, Cecilia?'

Her eyes widened. 'I've never lied to you.'

'You are lying now.' He was burning inside, remembering all the lies his stepmother had told, lies that were meant to make him suffer or to make him look the fool.

Cecilia lifted her chin. 'What is this lie you say I told you?'

He laughed derisively. 'Madame Coquette.'

The colour drained from her face. She uncurled her body and placed her feet on the floor. Her feet were bare. She did not avert her gaze from his.

'Madame Coquette,' he repeated, sarcasm dripping from every syllable. 'The most desirable courtesan in Paris. Very selective and exclusive. Frederick told me all about her.'

She did not flinch. 'There was no need to speak of her. She was not real.'

He laughed again. 'Apparently she took real men to her bed.'

'Did she?' Cecilia stood.

He took a step into the room. 'You said you'd been a hostess, not a courtesan.'

'That was the truth.' She moved away from him. 'I had been a hostess and—and later a courtesan.'

'Later. At the time you met me.' He moved closer, but she edged away.

'Yes,' she admitted.

'So did you seek out those other men, when you found your belly swelling?' This was the lie that hit him hardest. 'Did they laugh at you? So you came to find me?'

'I came to find my mother. You were a last resort.' Her voice trembled. 'But you are the father. Whether you believe me or not!'

'Do not play me for a fool, Cecilia!'

'I am not!' She continued to edge away, trying to circle behind him. She was trying to escape from him, he realised.

Well, they would have this out now, he vowed. He'd not go another day believing her nonsense.

'You will stay here, Cecilia!' he shouted. 'We will deal with this now.'

'No!' she cried.

She made a lunge towards the door, but he was quick. He grabbed her by the arms. 'Now! Cecilia!'

She fought like a dervish to be free of his grip. Twisting. Turning. Pulling away. Her eyes filled with terror. 'No! No! Don't hurt me! Don't hurt me.'

It was as if she was in a different place, a different time. Too hysterical to see what was around her. Who was with her.

'I won't hurt you!' he cried, loosening his fingers to prove it.

She wrenched from his grip and bolted for the door, slamming it behind her.

He took chase, reaching the stairs as she was nearly to the hall. He slid down the banister, but she'd run to the servants' door, closing that behind her, as well. He opened the door and ran after her down the stairs and through the hallway.

He'd done well in many a foot race, but he was no match for her panicked flight. Her bare feet helped her, while his boots could not gain purchase on the polished floor.

She reached the door to the garden and ran outside into the cold, now pouring rain, nothing covering her but her thin dress.

He finally caught her in the alley, the same alley where he'd fought with Bowles, the alley from which Nicholas had disappeared.

He seized her arms again, but she slipped on the wet surface and they both wound up on the ground.

'No! No! No!' she cried.

He feared someone in the surrounding houses would hear her and think he was attacking her.

She thought he was attacking her.

He held her fast and tried to make her look at him.

'I will never hurt you, Cecilia. Look at me! Look at me!'

She finally focused on him.

'I will not hurt you,' he said, slowly and calmly. 'You are safe. But we must get out of the rain.'

Her dress was soaked through and, even in the dim light in the alley, he could see that it clung to her body. The rain drenched through his coat, waistcoat and shirt. It felt like ice, it was so cold out. Her flight, her terror and the cold rain could not be good for the baby.

He repeated, 'You are safe. Now stop fighting. Calm down.'

She nodded, but her eyes still looked fearful.

'We'll go back to the house now and get you warm.'

She started to shiver, a sign, he supposed, that she was calming down.

'Are you ready?' he asked. 'We'll go back now.'

She nodded.

Afraid to let go of her, Oliver continued to firmly grip one of her arms. He rose to his feet and helped her up. He put an arm around her, but as they walked, her wet skirts caught on her legs and tripped her.

He stopped and made her face him. 'I'm going to carry you. Will you allow it?'

Again she nodded. Her teeth chattered.

He lifted her into his arms and carried her back to the garden behind his town house and through the kitchen door, which he'd left open in his rush to catch up to her. He carried her all the way to her bedchamber and placed her in a wooden chair in front of the fireplace. She was shivering and dazed and he feared she would lose consciousness. He needed to get her out of her wet clothes in a hurry. He tried to untie the laces on the back of her dress, but the knots just became tighter. He took a penknife from his pocket and cut them. He pulled off the dress and cut the laces of her corset, as well. Tossing those soaking garments aside, he peeled off her chemise, which was clinging to her like an extra layer of skin.

Her clothing gone, he carried her to her bed and wrapped her in the bed linens and blankets. He pulled the whole bed closer to the fireplace. Near the washbasin, he found a dry towel and wrapped it around her hair.

Her teeth no longer chattered, but she still had not said a word.

'Stay here,' he told her in a gentle but firm voice. 'I will be back quickly.'

Cecilia remained in her bed as Oliver ordered and gradually the mists in her brain cleared and she was able to keep two thoughts together. The cold made her body ache. She loosened the cocoon of covers enough to place her hand on her abdomen.

The baby was so still.

Please, baby, move. Show me you are unharmed.

What had happened? She vaguely remembered being outside in the alley. Oliver carrying her in his arms. She remembered running.

From Duncan.

But that was impossible.

Baby, please move!

The door opened and Oliver entered carrying a tray. He wore the banyan he'd given her to wear that first night she'd worked at Vitium et Virtus.

'Good. You are awake.' He placed the tray on the table beside her bed. It held a teapot, cup and saucer, cream and sugar. He poured her a cup of tea.

She sat up. 'I can't feel the baby move.'

He paused, holding the teapot in mid-air. Her worry seemed reflected on his face. 'Is—is the baby quiet sometimes?'

She'd never paid attention before. 'I suppose so.'

'Try not to worry.' Although he looked worried. He finished fixing the tea and handed her the teacup. 'Drink. It will warm you.'

The blankets slipped from her shoulder and she covered herself again. She took a sip of tea.

She looked up at him. 'What happened, Oliver? I cannot remember.'

'Do you remember that I learned about Madame Coquette?' he asked in a stiff voice.

That part came flooding back. 'You became angry.' It was like a curtain slowly opening in her mind, revealing a little at a time. Her heart pounded and it became difficult to breathe. 'You hit me!'

'Cecilia, no!' His eyes flashed in alarm. 'I never hit you. I would never do that. I seized your arms, but all I wanted was for you to stay and answer my questions.'

She did not remember it that way. She remembered him being angry and lunging at her. She'd had a flash of a memory of him hitting Bowles in the face the night of the masquerade, and then she'd felt the jarring pain of a fist connecting to her own cheek.

She touched her cheek. There was no pain now. She scrambled off the bed with only a blanket to cover her. The towel covering her hair fell to the floor and her still-damp hair tumbled to her shoulders. She walked to her dressing table. Leaning down, she gazed in the mirror. The light in the room was dim, but there was no bruise. She leaned closer, but still—nothing.

'No bruise,' she murmured to herself.

She'd pulled away and ran, but in her mind she had been fleeing Duncan.

'I did not hit you, Cecilia,' he repeated, his voice soft and low. 'I only tried to stop you.'

She turned to him. 'It was you?' She closed her eyes and tried to remember. She remembered terror. She remembered Duncan. 'I thought you were—someone else.'

'Who, Cecilia?' he asked.

'My husband.' She saw Duncan's face again and her legs started to tremble.

'Your husband?' He walked over to her, crouching down so that she could look directly at him. 'Your husband is dead, is he not?'

She nodded.

He searched her face with his green eyes, so piercing framed by his dark skin. 'Why did you think I was your husband?'

Her brows knitted. All she truly remembered was being terrified that this time he would beat her to death. 'I thought you were going to hit me.'

Understanding suddenly filled his eyes. 'Your husband hit you.'

'Yes.'

One of his arms wrapped around her shoulder. 'Come. Let us sit in a more comfortable place.'

She let him help her rise and he led her to the sofa in her sitting room—where her distorted memory had begun. Where he had been so angry with her.

She wrapped the blanket more tightly around her and tucked her feet beneath her. She was shaking, but not from the cold.

He left the room, but returned immediately, carrying the tea tray from the bedroom into the sitting room. He fixed another cup of tea for her and handed her the cup before settling in a chair.

'Tell me about your husband hitting you,' he said.

She stared into her teacup. He'd not asked her *why* Duncan had hit her. To ask her why would have assumed she'd done something to deserve it. Which she once thought she had. It had taken her many months of freedom from him for her to realise he would have beaten her no matter what she'd done.

'He was charming at first. All charisma and solicitude. The first person I truly believed loved me.' She paused. 'But I was wrong. First he merely complained. Scolded me for something I'd done. Or neglected to do. One day I answered impudently and he hit me. Across the face. After that, he hit me often.'

He stared at the floor, but his whole body tensed and she sensed anger in him. Finally he looked up at her. 'Why did you not leave him?'

'How could I?' That trapped feeling came back to her. 'We'd left Brussels, marching to France. I had no money. I knew no one.'

'Why not tell his commanders?'

'Duncan would have killed me!' She hugged herself. 'He told me so. Eventually he would have killed me anyway. I was merely fortunate that he was killed first.'

He stared at the floor again. 'How many times?'

'How many times did he hit me?' And throw her across the room? And choke her? Goodness. She'd lost count. 'Most of the year we were married.'

The disillusionment hit her again. She'd been so convinced that Duncan loved her like no one else ever had. After all, he'd been the kindest, most devoted suitor a girl could want. She'd searched her mind over and over. Had she missed something? How could she have been so thoroughly duped? There had been no love. It had all been a hoax. How could she ever believe in love again? How could she know a man would not change, would not hit her?

She'd been right to fear Oliver. He'd been angry at her. He'd seized her arm. She had only his word for it that he would not have hit her. He might hit her now if she piqued his anger, but she was not in a panic now, like before, and he deserved an explanation.

Not that he would believe it.

She took a deep breath. 'Shall I tell you about Madame Coquette?'

He glanced up at her, but his sympathetic expression disappeared.

And her nerves fired again.

She pressed her belly again.

Please move, petit bébé.

She must not be distracted. 'I was widowed in Paris. I was alone. No one would hire an Englishwoman for any respectable position. I had no money, no food and was in imminent danger of losing my room. I went to the Palais-Royal…and… and there I met Vincent—'

'Your protector?' His voice was grim.

'Yes. But not in the way you mean. Vincent preferred men.' It had been a shock to learn of Vincent's preferences, but she quickly became used to it. He was not so very different for it. 'He helped me, though. He taught me to be a hostess and he invented Madame Coquette.'

'The most desirable courtesan in Paris,' he said scathingly.

She looked him straight in the eye. 'Madame Coquette never bedded anyone.'

He gave a derisive laugh.

She went on, even though she had little hope he would believe her. 'Madame Coquette was paid for her time, not for bedding. She never promised to bed the men, only to consider it. But Madame Coquette always found some fault in the men and would not bed them. She did, however, promise to tell everyone they were wonderful lovers so they could save face. That was how her reputation was built. No man ever wanted to admit he was the one she'd refused, so they boasted about her and she went along with it.'

He gaped at her. 'You expect me to believe this?'

She closed her eyes and rubbed her forehead. 'No. I expect nothing.' She had learned from Duncan to expect nothing.

A part of her yearned for more from Oliver, but that was folly, too, was it not?

She drank her tea.

'Why would a man not demand his money back?' he asked.

She set down the cup. 'The agreement was very clear. Madame Coquette promised her time, not her favours, but that is not why. No man wanted his friends to know that Madame Coquette did not want to bed him.'

His brow creased. At least he seemed to be considering what she said. 'That was enough?'

She rearranged the blanket around her. 'Such is a man's vanity.'

His mouth twitched.

She wrapped her arms around herself. 'I am not proud of this, Oliver, but I did not starve.' And she'd tried to make certain her street urchins did not starve. 'Really, though, the men were mere victims of their own vanity. They thought it fine to pay money to bed a woman. And most of them left a wife at home to do so.' She pulled up her knees and rested her head on them. 'At least I was not at their mercy.' She sighed.

'Did no man protest?' he asked.

'Take me by force, do you mean?' she responded. 'Only one. The flash man had to intervene. That became the end of the game, though. I was discharged. By then I knew I was with child, so it would have been only a matter of time before I would have had to leave.'

'How long did you get away with this?'

Was he believing her?

'Almost a year. I always knew it would end, though. It always surprised me that the men did not complain to the club owner. When he learned I was not bedding the men, he tossed me out.'

He looked at her with scepticism. 'You say you did not bed the men—'

She interrupted. 'I did not want to bed them. The idea was repugnant to me.'

In a swift movement, he leaned towards her. 'But you bedded me.'

She gave a cry and flinched, curling up into a ball and turning away from him.

He reached out a hand, but she tried to back farther away.

'I will not hit you,' he said in a soft voice.

She realised as much this time, but her body had reacted on its own.

He leaned back again, but she still trembled.

'Why did you bed me, Cecilia?' he asked in that soft, calm voice that helped quell her fears.

She could barely look at him. 'I wanted to bed you.'

His expression turned sceptical again.

How could she explain? 'In Paris, we were having such a lovely day. I wanted to pretend a little longer.'

'Pretend?' He crossed his arms over his chest.

'It wasn't real, was it? That lovely day we shared? It was

like a dream. I wanted the dream to last longer. I wanted to pretend for merely one day that love existed and I was worthy of it.'

'But you left,' he accused. 'I would have delayed my departure. We could have had many days.'

'No!' She hadn't meant to speak so sharply. 'No,' she said more mildly.

At the time it had taken all of her courage to trust in that one whole day.

'I—I left before everything changed.' Before he changed. 'Every good thing changes.'

Chapter Eighteen

Oliver gazed at her wrapped in a blanket, hair tumbled down to her shoulders, the very picture of vulnerability. How difficult it was to believe she could have worked in a brothel. Or that any man would hit her with his fist.

His head was still swimming. It was hard to fit the pieces of the day's events together, learning she was a courtesan who did not bed her patrons. A manipulator of men.

A victim of an abusive husband.

He did not doubt her husband hit her. Her terror had been too real. No wonder she'd seen through Flo's excuses; Cecilia had already lived through it.

He had a strong impulse to touch her. Not only touch her, but enfold her in his arms and tell her he'd make everything all right again.

He resisted, still reeling from all she'd withheld from him.

'Has the baby moved yet?' he asked.

She placed her palm against her abdomen and shook her head.

Had her frenzy injured the baby? If so, Oliver was to blame. That idea sickened him.

He rose to put more coal on the fire, to keep the room warm for her. The light from the fireplace made her face glow with golden beauty. He remembered in Paris in his room that same glow on her face.

These weeks she'd lived with him, she'd been different people. One guarded and remote and untrusting. Another the seductive Coquette who could easily have passed as the most desirable courtesan in Paris. Now, though, sad and vulnerable, she seemed the Cecilia of Paris.

'I do not have anything left to say,' she told him. 'You know everything now.'

He doubted that.

She lay back on the sofa. 'I want to rest for a little while. You do not have to stay. I—I'm not cold any longer. I'm not ill. I'll ready myself for bed in a little while. Mary is not waiting on me tonight.'

Oliver had given his valet a long leave to visit family. The Irwins and Mary would stay out late.

'Will you eat dinner?' Cook had left food for them.

She rearranged her blanket. 'No, I want to sleep.'

She clearly did not want him to stay.

He'd endured many rejections in his life, but none wounded him to the quick like this one. She did not want him.

'I'll say goodnight, then,' he rasped, placing her teacup on the tray and carrying it out with him.

Once in the kitchen, he spooned out some mutton stew Cook had left on the hearth. He sat at the kitchen table, dipping pieces of bread in his stew until it had cooled enough to eat with a spoon and fork.

The house seemed deadly quiet. Another night he might have gone out seeking some kind of entertainment. He could not remember when he'd last been alone in the house.

Of course, he was not alone, but Cecilia was as distant as Paris.

Memories came back to him as they inevitably did when

he was alone. Another kitchen smelling much different from this one, a kitchen filled with the scents of exotic spices. He remembered sitting on rich carpets to taste spiced stews made with meat, cream, vegetables, fruit and nuts poured over rice. He could hear his mother saying, 'Eat more, *pyaare bête*. Grow strong.'

He rose and strode to the wine cellar, selecting a bottle of brandy. Finding a glass, he carried both with him to his bedchamber, sat in his comfortable upholstered chair and drank.

The brandy warmed his throat and spread heat throughout his body. He'd still been cold, he realised. No wonder. His feet were bare and the banyan did little more than cover him up.

His thoughts drifted back to Cecilia. He went over her story and her telling of it. He supposed he could verify it. He could send someone to the club where she'd worked, perhaps find this Vincent she spoke of. Would that help him believe the baby was his?

But what did any of it matter? She did not want him.

He started to pour another glass of brandy, but put the bottle aside. Drinking was not the answer. Nothing would stop the whirling thoughts in his mind, especially the one thought he most guarded against.

He loved her.

He loved her more than any other woman he'd been with. He cared about her future and the future of her child. He never wished her to again experience the terror she'd experienced today.

He heard a door slam and the sound of pounding feet. The door to his bedchamber opened and Cecilia burst in. He jumped to his feet and she ran directly to him.

'The baby moved!' She ran into his arms and he held her. 'Oh, Oliver. The baby moved. I didn't hurt the baby.'

Neither had he. He thanked God for that.

'I'm delighted,' he murmured. 'Delighted.'

She pulled away enough to look up at him, smiling. How

rare it was for him to see her smile so genuinely, he realised. He wanted to keep her smiling. He wanted to make her happy.

The nightdress she wore was a mere thin layer of cloth, like his banyan, so thin it was as if they were skin to skin. Still, the cloth seemed too great a barrier. His desire for her, held back so long because of the even greater barriers of mistrust and suspicion, slammed into him. He loved her and he wanted—*needed*—to join with her.

But he held back.

The decision must be hers alone. Like it had been in Paris.

Her smile faded, but she continued to stare at him. His arousal was painfully acute, but he held himself in check. Through the thin material of her nightdress she must have felt it.

She pressed against him more tightly, rubbing against him. He held his breath to maintain control over himself. She rose on tiptoe so that her lips were mere inches from his, but she looked into his eyes.

'Would—would you despise it if we made love?' she asked.

Joy burst inside him. He smiled. 'I believe I might be able to tolerate it.'

He took possession of her lips like a man greedy for gold. He poured his need for her into the kiss, as well as his realisation that he wanted her in his life for ever.

Oliver picked her up and carried her to his bed. When he set her down, she pulled his head towards hers and placed her lips on his again.

The kiss set his body aflame, but he banked his desire and waited to see what she wanted. If a kiss was all she desired, a kiss would be what she'd have. But she broke away long enough to remove her nightdress. Only then did Oliver throw off his banyan. He climbed onto the bed and lay next to her, waiting again to have this lovemaking proceed exactly as she wished. She sat up only to lean down for another kiss. He could not help himself. He lifted her on top of him, but she did not resist. She straddled him and positioned herself to ease him inside her.

He guided her, lifting her on his erection and feeling himself slip inside her. This joining was more than pleasure—this joining was a connection, a belonging to another. This joining banished loneliness.

His need grew even more acute. Still, he strained to hold back, but she took pity on him. She began the primitive rhythm for which he yearned. They moved together with Cecilia setting the pace, moving gradually faster and faster as his need grew stronger. Emotions swirled inside him, his genuine love for her swelled like the urging of his body.

Thought fled and sensation took over with each stroke. Only the quickness of their breath filled the air. His need grew stronger and stronger still until he thought he'd perish if this exquisite agony did not reach its apex soon.

Suddenly she cried out and writhed above him. A guttural sound escaped his lips and he erupted inside her, spilling his seed and slaking this intense hunger for her. Their climax held them suspended in this ecstasy, lasting longer than any he could remember.

Because he shared it with her, he thought.

She slid to his side and lay next to him, one leg still wrapped around him.

'Cecilia,' he murmured. It was as much as he could manage.

He cared so much for her, could he really burden her with the realisation of his love for her? As in their lovemaking, should he wait for her to show him what she wanted, what she could safely handle?

He felt her withdraw suddenly, slipping her leg away, crossing her arms over her chest, no longer touching him.

'You must think me wanton,' she said.

He rose on one elbow so he could look her in the eye.

'There is something between us, Cecilia. That is what I think. It was there in Paris and is here now.'

Her forehead creased in concentration. 'I do not understand it. But yes, there is something.'

He dared to draw a finger gently down her cheek. 'I love you, Cecilia. I want us always to be together.'

Her head whipped away from his touch. 'No!' Her eyes turned panicked. 'No, Oliver. Do not say it!'

He felt the distance between them grow once more. He wanted desperately to stop it, to stop the loneliness that would return in its wake.

'Wait,' he said, trying not to sound desolate. 'That is what I feel. What I want. I mean no pressure. You must decide what you want.'

She sat up and hugged her knees. 'I don't want to try to understand it. Or to decide. I merely wish to enjoy it. Enjoy being with you. For the time we have.'

He'd said words similar to this many times to other women. *Enjoy it while it lasts*, knowing he did not wish the liaison to last. She was reminding him that she would leave him.

If he could, would he take another month, another week, or even a day with his mother? He'd take even an instant.

He carefully reached out and touched Cecilia's hair, stroking it with his fingers. 'Very well. Let us enjoy this while it lasts.'

He had no other choice.

Cecilia lifted her head and gazed into his eyes, his lovely green eyes. They could do this, could they not? Enjoy each other for a little while?

She wanted to feel his arms around her again. To make love with him again. And again.

She moved closer so her lips were near to his. He closed the gap and kissed her, his warm tongue tasting of brandy as it slipped into her mouth. His hand cupped her breast, his palm rubbing against her nipple and creating an ache that could only be eased by his touch.

Or his joining with her.

He held her against him, pressing her against his male member, making her ache even more intense.

'I do not know what is wrong with me,' she murmured. 'It feels so—different. As if I will perish if you do not couple with me right now.'

He rose on top of her. 'I do not wish you to perish.'

He entered her, slowly, almost reverently, and the passionate ache doubled.

'Oliver.' Her voice was a plea.

He complied, moving inside her in a stroking that was at once easing the ache and intensifying it at the same time. It was a glorious, confusing mixture.

He'd said they might merely enjoy this for the time it lasted. She could not do otherwise. He seemed wholly present with her in this moment, ready to relieve her fears and deepen her pleasure. Could she not muster that much courage to stay with him until her condition prevented it?

She tossed away her caution and stopped resisting, stopped trying to comprehend. She gave in to every sensation he created and let the pleasure build even further to impossible heights until the pleasure exploded inside her, like the rockets she'd seen in battle. Oliver spilled his seed inside her once more and collapsed heavy on top of her for only a moment before moving to her side where they both languished in the afterglow of their frenzied act.

She lay still, so relaxed that she doubted her limbs could hold her upright. Her thoughts were quiet, as if the thrill of lovemaking had driven them from her mind. She merely relished the heat of his body next to hers, the sound of his breathing.

She might have drifted off to sleep, except a fluttering inside her roused her.

'Oh!' she exclaimed, touching her thickened belly.

He rose on to an elbow. 'What is it?' His voice was worried.

'The baby moved again,' she whispered. 'I can feel it.'

This time she felt the movement beneath her fingers as well as inside her.

As she had done once before, she took his hand and placed it on her abdomen, holding it still until the fluttering repeated.

'Did you feel it?' she asked.

'Yes,' he rasped.

The baby moved again and she and Oliver exchanged knowing smiles.

She carried life insider her, a life that began with lovemaking much like this. With Oliver.

She turned to him and cuddled against him. Yes. She would enjoy a little more time together with him.

Feeling a new life beneath his fingertips, Oliver experienced a fierce sense of protectiveness towards her and this child. In his mind she and the baby were his. For ever. No matter that she would leave him.

'I feel happy,' she said in a surprised voice.

He held her closer. He felt happy, too.

'I cannot remember when I last felt happy,' she went on.

He could remember. He'd last felt happy in Paris, on that day they shared together. Could they recreate it?

He had an idea. 'Tomorrow would you like to explore London?' As they had explored Paris. 'We could visit St Paul's Cathedral and walk through the city. It would not compare with the Louvre, but we could visit Bullock's Museum. What do you say?'

She moved so they were face to face. 'It sounds like a lovely idea.'

The next day Oliver took Cecilia to St Paul's Cathedral. Like Notre Dame, it dominated the skyline of the city. From almost anywhere in the city, one could turn and see its great dome, which was gleaming white on this rare brisk and sunny winter day. St Paul's had been built over three hundred years later than Notre Dame, replacing a Gothic cathedral on the same site that had been destroyed in the Great Fire of 1666. St Paul's was classical architecture, with its dome, columns, arches and symmetry.

They explored the three naves inside the church and all its chapels, examined the beautiful masonry and ran their fingers over the woodcarving of the choirs. St Paul's lacked the magnificent stained-glass windows of Notre Dame casting rainbows of colour, but its interior was bright, in part due to the windows on the great dome.

Oliver savoured the time with Cecilia—enjoying her while he could. In Paris, he'd known their time together would end—so, too, would it end in London.

Ironically, he'd vowed never to marry, believing no woman would want to marry a bastard half-caste for anything other than his money. Under such circumstances a marriage like that was doomed to unhappiness. It never particularly bothered him not to marry, because he preferred to be free to pursue pleasure and women did not mind his half-caste self in bed, only not as a husband.

But he wanted to marry Cecilia. He wanted to raise the baby as his own. He wanted to spend his life making them both happy.

She did not want it, though. And not because of his birth.

As they walked the long distance of the nave's white-and-black-chequered stone floor, he shook himself out of these musings and decided to enjoy the moment, as she'd asked. As they'd done in Paris.

'What did you think?' Oliver asked her as they reached the great doors of the cathedral to go outside again.

'It is grander than I expected,' she replied. 'But I miss the stained-glass windows of Notre Dame.'

He opened the door. 'It is Christopher Wren's crowning achievement,' Oliver said.

They walked back onto the street in the midday sun. The weather, though much colder, rivalled that beautiful day they'd spent in Paris. It was crisp and cool and windy enough to blow the air clean of the usual veil of smoke that covered the city.

'Could we walk back?' Cecilia asked him. 'It is such a fine day!'

Was she reading his thoughts? 'We could indeed.' He smiled at her. 'I need to let my groom know.'

He'd driven them to the cathedral in his phaeton and his groom waited for them nearby, tending to the horses.

'We have decided to walk,' Oliver said to the man. 'Drive them home, would you?'

'Right you are, sir.'

Oliver and Cecilia started walking along Fleet Street.

'It is not all that far, is it?' she asked.

'Two miles or so.' It felt good to be outside, stretching his legs, walking with her.

She took his arm and they strolled together as they had done in Paris. She did not know London, so he pointed out buildings of interest along the way. St Bride's Church. The various inns of Fleet Street. St Clement's, standing where Fleet Street became the Strand.

'Are you hungry?' he asked.

She did not answer; merely lifted one shoulder.

She must be. '*I* am hungry,' he declared. 'Let us detour to Covent Garden. There will be food there.'

In the early mornings, wagons filled with produce grown outside the city and other wares descended on Covent Garden for a market that had existed for years. It was as rowdy a place as St Paul's had been peaceful. A cacophony of vendors hawked everything from vegetables, fruits and herbs, to hedgehogs.

Oliver spied an old woman tending a still. He pulled Cecilia over to her stand. The old woman was filling bowls with some steaming hot liquid.

'We must have some *salop*,' he said.

Salop was a hot drink made from sassafras wood and infused with milk and sugar. It was like nectar for the gods.

On many a pre-dawn hour Oliver and his friends had soothed aching heads with hot *salop* after imbibing too much liquor at one of the disreputable gambling houses or houses of ill repute in Covent Garden.

Oliver gave the old woman a coin and she poured the steaming liquid into two bowls. Oliver handed one to Cecilia.

She tasted it cautiously, then looked up at Oliver in surprise. 'It is good!'

'Who could dislike it?' Oliver lifted his bowl to his mouth.

The *salop* not only tasted wonderful, it warmed him inside.

They walked on, looking at the displays of vegetables and fruits, stopping at another vendor to purchase ginger cakes.

When they neared the flower sellers, Cecilia exclaimed, 'Oh! Smell the evergreens!'

She hurried to the wagons selling lush cuttings of holly, pine, hawthorn and juniper.

She turned to Oliver. 'Might we purchase some? I have some money with me. It has been so long since I have decorated a house for Christmas. Might we do so?'

She looked as excited as a little girl.

Christmas had never been a happy time for him. He'd either been left at school while his father and stepmother attended a country house party or he'd been stuck staying out of the way when the house party had been at his father's estate. He did remember some enjoyment gathering evergreens to adorn the house on Christmas Eve. He'd been able to climb high in the trees to cut branches or gather mistletoe.

The scent of this greenery reminded him of those days.

'Of course, if you desire it,' he answered her. 'But I will pay.'

She danced in front of him, her cloak coming open. He caught a glimpse of the pearl she wore around her neck, the one he had bought her in Paris. It pleased him that she wore it. It pleased him, as well, that small things like a pearl necklace or fragrant evergreens made her smile.

He'd buy her a forest of greenery if it kept that smile on her face.

He followed her as she flitted from wagon to wagon, trying to decide on what she wanted.

'Buy it all,' he said, laughing. 'I'll pay a lad to bring it to the house.'

While she picked branches of holly, hawthorn and pine, he spied a ball of mistletoe and purchased it when she was not looking. He hired a couple of boys to help them carry the greenery to the house. By the time they neared the town house, Cecilia's cheeks were tinged pink and her eyes sparkled.

Oliver could not have been more gratified.

'I have an errand,' she said suddenly. 'Just a quick run to the shops. I—I want to buy something for Mary. She has been such a help to me.'

'I will come with you if you wait a moment.' All he needed to do was hand off the boys and their bundles to Irwin.

'No. No.' A nervous edge came into her voice. 'It will only take a moment. I'll buy her pretty muslin or something at Harding, Howell and Company, perhaps. And ribbons and things for our decorations.'

She sounded secretive. It raised his suspicions.

'As you wish.' He pulled out his purse and handed her some coin. 'For the decorations.'

She looked at the money in her palm, gave him a smile and dashed off.

Chapter Nineteen

It had been such a lovely day, Cecilia's heart was floating on air. Even more than the cathedral she'd enjoyed the market at Covent Garden, so filled with pretty vegetables and fruits and tantalising treats. She'd loved the *salop* and the ginger cakes, but mostly she adored Oliver for buying all the evergreen cuttings.

She intended to go to Harding, Howell and Company, a linen draper just a couple of streets away on Pall Mall, but her real errand took her first down Jermyn Street to Floris.

She entered the shop and the same clerk, who had served Oliver and her a few days before, greeted her again. 'Good day, madam. May I assist you?'

'Yes.' She stepped forward. 'I would like to purchase a nice gift for a gentleman. Would you help me decide?'

'Some scent?' he asked.

'No. Something more enduring. Something he would use.' She wanted something he would remember her by, like the pearl necklace.

'Let me show you our combs.' The clerk displayed a variety of combs. She selected one made of tortoiseshell and silver. The clerk wrapped it for her.

She hurried to the draper's and purchased ribbons to adorn the evergreens and a length of a pretty sprigged muslin for Mary.

When she headed back to the town house, she felt like skipping along the pavement as she'd done when a little girl. She was excited about her gift to Oliver, excited to decorate and to share Christmas with him.

But she kept a normal pace. When she turned to walk to the town-house door, a man approached her, taking her by surprise.

Sir Nash Bowles.

'There you are.' He moved towards her with an unsteady gait.

She tried to edge towards the door.

'I remembered you.' His words were slurred, adding even more emphasis to his rasping lisp. 'You are Madame Coquette. From Paris. I know all about you.'

He came close enough for her to smell liquor on his breath.

'Leave me alone, Sir Nash.'

She reached the door, but he seized her arm and pulled her away. She dropped her packages and cried out, 'No! Let me go!'

Bowles cried, 'I want to learn what Gregory knows. You find out or I'll make trouble for you.'

She tried to pull away, but his grip was surprisingly strong.

The door flew open and Oliver charged out. He grabbed Bowles by the collar and wrenched him away from Cecilia.

Bowles came back at Oliver, leaping on him, fists flying. Oliver took some blows before he was able to hit him back. He knocked Bowles to the pavement and the two men rolled on the ground and into the street.

Cecilia screamed.

A carriage narrowly missed running over them. Oliver

made it to his feet first and went to hit Bowles again, but Cecilia could stand it no longer.

'Stop! Stop!' She ran over to Oliver and tried to pull him away.

Oliver backed off, breathing heavily. Bowles got to his feet and limped away.

Oliver turned to Cecilia. 'Are you harmed?' He rubbed the hand that Bowles's knife had cut.

She glanced at his hand in alarm. 'Are you hurt?'

He shook his head. 'I aggravated the cut.'

'I'm not hurt,' she finally responded. 'Frightened, though.' Frightened at his violence.

He put an arm around her shoulders. 'Come inside.'

Irwin was in the doorway, looking alarmed.

'Have Mrs Irwin bring tea up to Mrs Lockhart's room,' Oliver told him.

Oliver walked Cecilia up the stairs and entered the room with her. He untied the ribbons of her cloak. He took it off her shoulders and laid it down on a chair.

'Sit down, Cecilia. There will be tea here soon.' He walked her to the sitting room. 'Or would you prefer some claret? Or brandy?'

'Tea.'

There was a knock on the door. Mrs Irwin brought tea.

She placed the tray on the table near the sofa.

'How are you, dear?' she asked. 'That was such a fright!'

Cecilia made herself smile. 'I am a little shaken. Your tea will fix me up.'

Mrs Irwin nodded. 'Nothing tea cannot help.' She patted Cecilia's hand. 'Now you tell us if you need anything else.'

The woman was kind. 'Thank you, Mrs Irwin.'

After Mrs Irwin left, Oliver sat in a chair opposite Cecilia. 'What did Bowles want?'

'He was drunk. Not making sense. He wanted to know what you know.'

He looked puzzled. 'Know what I know? About what?'

'He did not say.' She did not add that Bowles threatened to make trouble for her.

'He's been trouble from the first. I banned him after learning about Flo, but we should have banned him years ago.' He opened and closed his injured hand. 'How many times must I fight him?'

'Do men always fight?' she murmured.

It was not meant as a question for him, but he answered anyway. 'More than not.'

His answer did not reassure her.

Oliver watched her. He'd seen the panic in her face when she pulled him away from Bowles. Now she looked pale and drawn.

What a damnable end to their perfect day.

She pressed her hand to her abdomen and turned even paler.

'What is it?' Something was wrong.

'I—I need to be private for a moment.' She stood.

He left the room, but remained by her doorway waiting, his alarm growing.

She finally opened the door, but clung to the door jamb.

'Oliver...' Her voice shook. 'Find Mary. I am bleeding. I do not know what to do.'

Bleeding?

'Mary!' His voice boomed. 'Mary! Come here this instant!' He put an arm around Cecilia. 'Let me take you to your bed.'

When they reached the side of the bed, he picked her up and placed her on it. 'I'll find Mary.'

He ran out of the door, only to discover Mary hurrying up the stairs.

'What is wrong, sir?' she asked.

'Cecilia is bleeding. Tend to her. I am sending for the doctor.' He bounded down the stairs and found Irwin and his wife at the bottom staring up to see what the commotion was about.

'Get the doctor,' he said to Irwin. 'Quick. She's—she's bleeding.'

'Oh, my goodness!' Mrs Irwin bustled upstairs.

Oliver paced the hall outside Cecilia's bedchamber door while the women tended her.

He'd lost too much already. His mother. His childhood home. His trust. His friend Nicholas. He did not want to lose this baby.

Or Cecilia.

He could give them what he'd lost in India. A name. Security. Love.

He heard voices in the hall below. Irwin had found the doctor quickly.

He leaned over the banister. 'Up here, Doctor!'

The doctor left his coat, hat and gloves with Irwin and hurried up the stairs.

'What seems to be the trouble?' he asked, out of breath from the climb.

'She is bleeding. I do not know how badly or why.' Oliver stepped quickly to Cecilia's door and knocked. He did not wait for permission to enter, but opened the door. 'The doctor is here.'

The doctor strode into the room and someone shut the door behind him.

Oliver was left to wait alone.

Cecilia sat up in bed as the doctor came to her side. Mary and Mrs Irwin had helped her change into a nightdress and they placed rags between her legs.

'You have been bleeding, young lady?' he asked. 'How badly?'

'I—I do not know.'

'It looks a lot like if she started her monthly courses,' Mary offered.

'Still bleeding?' the doctor asked.

'Some, I think,' Mary answered.

Mrs Irwin wiped Cecilia's forehead with a damp cloth. 'The poor dear is very frightened.'

'Well, let me look.'

The doctor examined her, felt her abdomen, and listened for the baby's heart with his wooden tube.

Cecilia's own heart was pounding so loud she did not see how he could hear the baby's. Had she done too much? Walked around London too much? Rushed too fast to the shops? Or was it the tussle with Bowles, her struggle to get away from him?

'Is my baby harmed?' She was afraid to hear the answer.

The doctor touched her hand. 'Your baby seems to be doing very well.'

'But the bleeding?' she asked.

'It could be many things. Not all are to worry over. In fact, I do not believe you have to worry, for now. If you bleed more, send for me. If you have pains, send for me, but, at the moment, I expect you will have no further trouble.'

She released a pent-up sob. Her baby was unharmed.

The doctor stepped away and put his tube back in his bag. 'Stay in bed tonight and do not exert yourself tomorrow, just in case.'

'We'll make certain of that,' Mrs Irwin said in a determined tone.

'I'll bring anything she wants, anything she needs,' Mary added.

Cecilia slid under the covers. Mrs Irwin and Mary tucked her in. She felt suddenly exhausted. 'I promise I will rest.'

The doctor smiled. 'Good day, then.'

Oliver alternately paced the hallway outside Cecilia's bedchamber and leaned against the wall, his eyes riveted on the door.

Finally, it opened and the doctor walked out.

Oliver straightened. 'How is she?'

The doctor gestured for him to move away from her door. Oliver walked with him to the stairs.

'She and the baby are stable now,' the doctor said as he descended the stairs. 'But one never knows about these things. I've seen women who bleed regularly throughout their carrying of the baby and have a normal birth and I've seen others who bleed once and lose the baby.'

'There is a chance she could lose the baby?' A chance they would both lose the baby.

The doctor lifted both shoulders. 'There is always a chance.'

They reached the first floor.

'May I offer you some refreshment before you leave, Doctor?' Oliver asked. 'Some tea? Or brandy.'

The doctor's face lit up. 'Brandy would be most appreciated.'

He brought the doctor to the drawing room and invited him to sit while he removed the decanter of brandy and two glasses from a cabinet. He poured the doctor a glass and handed it to him.

The doctor sipped, then glanced heavenward. 'Mmm. That is a fine brandy.'

Oliver was still too agitated to sit. He stood by the cabinet, fingering his glass. 'What can be done to save the baby?' he asked.

The doctor sipped again. 'Likely she need do nothing, but I do recommend she not exert herself.'

'Should she stay in bed?' He'd keep her in bed if he had to sit on her.

The doctor lifted one hand. 'Not necessary. But it would be best if she remains calm. Nothing to distress or upset her.'

Like fearing another attack.

'She will remain calm.' Oliver would make certain nothing distressed her.

The doctor finished his brandy and lifted his glass towards Oliver, who promptly refilled it.

'I cannot pretend to know the relationship between the two of you,' the doctor said. 'And I am not in a position to judge, but I will tell you that society treats unmarried women with bastard children very badly.' He tasted the brandy and looked over his glass at Oliver. 'I trust you will at least support the woman and her child? A father's duty, you know.'

The doctor had no right to presume anything—except he was correct on all counts.

'I do my duty, sir,' Oliver answered curtly.

'Excellent!' The doctor finished his brandy, this time placing the glass on the table and standing. 'I should take my leave. I am certain someone else will have need of me today.'

Oliver accompanied him to the hall where Irwin brought the doctor's hat and coat.

Oliver shook his hand. 'I thank you for coming.'

'Send for me again if you need me,' the doctor said.

After he left, Oliver took the stairs two at a time, slowing down as he reached Cecilia's door. He knocked softly.

The maid opened the door a crack.

'Good day, sir.' She curtsied.

'Ask if she will see me, Mary,' he said.

She closed the door and returned a minute later.

'Come in, sir.' She stepped aside for him to pass her, then she and Mrs Irwin left the room, closing the door behind them.

Oliver walked up to Cecilia's bed. 'How are you feeling?'

She sat up against the pillows, now wearing a nightdress. 'I feel like nothing happened.'

Her face, however, was taut with worry.

He tried to smile reassuringly. 'The doctor said you should be fine. Just do not exert yourself.'

She raised her knees and hugged them. 'Think how much better it would be if I'd lost the baby.'

'Better?' He recoiled in surprise. 'Do not say you wish you'd lose the baby.'

'No.' She gave him a direct look. 'Not me. You. You must have wished for it, though.'

'Unfair, Cecilia,' Oliver shot back. 'I have never said anything like that.'

'But you thought it,' she persisted.

He tried to remain calm. To keep her calm. 'Cecilia, I will not debate with you on this. What do you need? Would you fancy something special to eat? Shall I ask Cook to fix you something?'

She shook her head. 'I am sorry I snapped at you, Oliver.'

He stepped closer and lightly touched her arm. 'It is forgotten.'

'Will—will it be acceptable for Mary to sleep here in the dressing room tonight?' she asked.

Why be so reluctant? Until this moment he'd given her whatever she'd wanted. What made her think he would stop now? 'Of course it will. Shall I have Irwin find a cot to set up in there?'

'That would be good,' she murmured, lowering her legs and again leaning against the pillows. 'And tomorrow we can decorate the house?'

Tomorrow was Christmas Eve, a traditional time for arranging evergreens throughout the house. 'If you promise not to overdo it. The doctor said—'

'I know,' she said solemnly.

'I'll bid you goodnight, then, unless you need to summon me for any reason.'

She looked up at him, her eyes wide and still filled with uncertainty.

He leaned down and kissed her on the top of her head. 'It will be all right, Cecilia.'

She did not look so sure.

He left her, although he wanted to stay. He wanted to be the one who stayed with her this night instead of her maid.

Instead, he took his latest book—*Description of the Character, Manners, and Customs of the People of India*—to the drawing room and, lighting a lamp, opened the book to where he'd last read.

He read of how a Hindu girl and her family were expelled from their caste, simply because the young man who she was to marry died before the marriage took place and she married another. According to the rules, she was supposed to live as a widow for the rest of her life.

Oliver closed the book. Had his mother been expelled from her caste for being his father's mistress? When his father took him to England and left her in India, had she been completely banished from anyone who might care for her?

He pinched the bridge of his nose. He must not think of this. Not now.

He glanced around the room and a profound loneliness descended upon him, a familiar loneliness suffered when he was taken from India and many times afterwards when he seemed not to belong.

His typical means of dispelling these feelings was to engage in a torrid affair, or challenge himself to some dangerous escapade, a race, a bout of fisticuffs, a high-stakes card game.

He had no taste for any of those distractions.

What he wanted most at the moment was to be seated at Cecilia's bedside, sharing her fears and her hopes.

Chapter Twenty

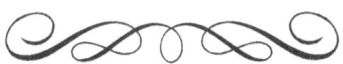

Upon waking the next morning, Cecilia immediately checked to see if she'd bled during the night. She hadn't! It was enough to fill her full of energy and vigour. The baby must be safe or why would she feel so well?

Mary was already awake and dressed and carrying in a jug of clean water. 'Good morning,' she said cheerfully. 'I hope you slept well, because I did not hear a peep from you the whole night.'

Cecilia had slept well. Better than many nights here in London.

And before.

'I slept,' she responded. 'And I feel remarkably well this morning.'

'That is good.' Mary poured the water into a basin on a nearby chest of drawers. 'But remember what the doctor said. You mustn't do too much.'

Too much? She felt as if she could dash across fields as she'd done when she was a child. She felt as if she could climb to the highest bell tower of Notre Dame. It would be difficult to force herself to rest.

'Mr Gregory and I are going to decorate the house for Christmas today,' Cecilia said.

She climbed out of bed and pulled off her nightdress.

'Well, you must take care.' Mary sounded much like a concerned mother.

Cecilia had wished for her mother when she discovered the bleeding. She was certain Oliver would have sent for her mother, if she'd asked. But she'd thought of all the trouble it would cause her mother to come to her. It was not worth putting her mother through that.

Besides, her mother did not know of the baby and Cecilia intended to keep it that way.

And Cecilia had Mary, Mrs Irwin...and Oliver to help her. She was no longer alone.

She rose from the bed and washed herself with the fresh water Mary had brought.

Mary stood nearby, holding a towel.

'I think one of my old dresses will do,' Cecilia said. No need to dress up this day, not while working with plant cuttings.

'Oh.' Mary raised her voice more than necessary. 'They— they need mending.' She blinked. 'I'll tend to them today, but you'll have to wear one of the pretty ones now.'

Cecilia could not remember her dresses needing mending, but she supposed it did not matter much. Mary chose a pale rose morning dress Cecilia had not worn yet, since it was unsuitable to be worn during the Queen's mourning, but she would not be going outside the house, so what difference did it make?

Mary helped her into her shift and corset. She put the dress on Cecilia over her head and adjusted the laces in the back.

Cecilia sat at the dressing table and Mary twisted her hair into a knot at the top of her head. She tied a pink ribbon around Cecilia's head. 'There!'

Cecilia rose and glanced at herself in the full-length mirror. 'Thank you, Mary. I'm sure this will do.'

Mary grinned and curtsied.

Cecilia left her room and walked down to the dining room. Oliver was seated there, reading a newspaper.

He stood at her entrance and his eyes scanned her up and down. 'You look beautiful, Cecilia.'

Her cheeks grew warm. She usually detested a man's admiration.

'Thank you,' she murmured.

He cleared his throat. 'I hope that means you are feeling better.'

'I am feeling quite well.' She quickly turned to the sideboard and selected an egg and a slice of bread with butter and jam. She poured a cup of tea.

'Might we still decorate today?' she asked.

She was asking permission, just as she'd done in her marriage. For every little thing.

She spoke with more strength. 'I would like to decorate today.'

He glanced up. 'As you wish, Cecilia.'

'And before you scold me about it, I will not overdo.'

He nodded. 'Good.'

Why did he seem so distant?

'Do you not wish to decorate?' she asked.

He looked up from his paper again. 'Me? No. I am willing.'

'You are not obligated, though, Oliver,' she went on. 'I am certain Mary or Irwin could help me.'

He laid down his paper. 'Would you prefer that?'

'No,' she admitted.

Why was she going on about this? She longed to spend the day with him, as they had done the day before. Decorating his house for him for Christmas day seemed a delight.

Unlike the one Christmas she'd shared with Duncan. That had been a horror. He'd beaten her for mentioning the day.

After that she'd been alone on Christmas and her celebration had been confined to attending the services at Notre Dame. This year she would not be alone.

She would share the holiday with Oliver.

When they'd walked through St Paul's or browsed the stalls at Covent Garden, catching a glimpse of him had taken her breath away. He was so handsome, so different and so kind. She longed for his lovemaking again, that singular joy, a connection that made her forget every unhappy event she'd ever experienced. With the bleeding she didn't dare to share his bed again.

She glanced at him and her breath fled. Even in something as ordinary as breakfast, he was extraordinary.

But she must not be seduced by him. Duncan had been charming and kind once upon a time. And Oliver was capable of violence, just like Duncan.

What harm could come from sharing the best of the Christmas festivities with him, though? Just this once.

She gulped. 'I—I want very much for us to decorate your house together. You seem disturbed, though. Perhaps angry at me for causing so much commotion yesterday.'

'Commotion?' He straightened. 'Not commotion. You thought something had happened to the baby.'

That worry came sneaking back. 'Let us not talk about that. I am well today. The baby is well.'

The baby *must* be well.

Something was amiss with Oliver, though. She felt it.

'I am not imagining this,' she blurted out. 'You are not happy. I must be the cause.'

His gaze softened. 'You are not the cause, Cecilia. Sometimes unbidden sadness permeates every part of me. I start thinking of what I've lost.'

She reached over and touched his hand. 'We must not

think of what we have lost. If we do, how can we ever lift our chins from the floor?'

He clasped her hand.

'There is nothing to do but see if we can enjoy today.' How many times had she told herself just think about today? Not tomorrow. Not yesterday. Today.

She ought to heed her own advice.

He smiled, though his smile seemed a sad one. 'Then let us enjoy today.'

She squeezed his hand. 'We shall adorn every room!'

He lifted his cup. 'After we finish breakfast?'

She laughed. 'As *you* wish, Oliver!'

He returned to his newspaper and she finished her egg.

'Is there anything noteworthy in the newspaper?' How nice it was to merely have a conversation.

He looked up. 'Two men were apprehended for the murder in Hornsey.'

'There was a murder in Hornsey?'

'About a week or so ago. A young man was robbed and killed when he walked through Hornsey wood at night.'

'How dreadful.' She shivered. She used to walk through Paris at night. Not in London, though. Oliver always walked her home from Vitium et Virtus.

He put down the newspaper. 'How do you wish to proceed with the decorating?'

'I want to arrange the greenery in each of the rooms. Decorate with lace and ribbon—' She put a hand to her mouth. 'The ribbon! What happened to the packages of ribbon and— and other things that I purchased yesterday?'

After the altercation with Bowles, she'd forgotten all about them. Her gift to Oliver was one of them.

'Irwin collected them,' he said.

She again saw the ferocious fight between Oliver and Bowles, but did not wish to remember it.

She stood. 'I want to find Irwin and get my packages. Then perhaps we can start in the drawing room?'

He smiled and her spirits lightened. 'I will carry up the greenery.'

Oliver walked below stairs to the room where they'd stored the cuttings they'd purchased.

Both Mrs Irwin and Cook stopped him.

'How is our young lady today?' asked Mrs Irwin.

'She says she is feeling very well.' He was touched by their concern.

'I fixed her a posset last night,' Cook said. 'I am certain it was my posset that helped.'

'It very well may have been,' he agreed.

Cook beamed. 'I'll make her another for tonight.'

'She will be grateful.' He looked around. 'I've come for the greenery. We thought to start decorating.' He turned to Mrs Irwin. 'Will you send your husband on an errand for me?'

'I will, sir,' she replied. 'What will it be?'

'I want to procure firewood for the fireplace in the drawing room for tonight and tomorrow. It won't be a Yule log, but at least it will smell like one.' He wanted to fill the house with as many delights as he could think of, all to please Cecilia.

'Well, won't that be the thing.' Mrs Irwin smiled in approval.

She helped him carry up the greenery Oliver and Cecilia had purchased the previous day. He had two projects that needed to be done without her seeing. Hanging the mistletoe and shopping.

He walked into the drawing room. 'Here we are.'

They were laden with holly, ivy, hawthorn and flowering Christmas rose.

'Oh, I'd forgotten how beautiful they are. They smell heavenly.' Cecilia stood by the mantel, which she had cleared of its decorative pieces. 'Put them on the floor. We can select them easily from there.'

Mrs Irwin placed her bundle, wrapped in a sheet, in the middle of the floor. 'Would you be needing any help?'

Cecilia smiled at her. 'Thank you, Mrs Irwin. It is kind of you to offer. I think Mr Gregory and I can manage.'

She glanced at Oliver, who added his bundle to the pile on the floor.

Mrs Irwin gave her a knowing, but cheerful look. 'That is it, then. Ring for us if you change your mind.'

'Thank you. We will.' Cecilia turned to the pile of cuttings. 'Where to begin?'

'We should begin with you sitting and directing me.' He pointed to a chair.

To his surprise she did as he asked without an argument.

She pointed to which piece of greenery he should use and told him how to arrange it. When he finished she rose and added bows and ribbons. They placed greenery on the mantel and window sills and in vases on the tables.

The scent of the hawthorn and pine brought back memories of gathering cuttings from his father's country estate. He always accompanied the footmen charged with the greatest portion of the task. His father, stepmother and their houseguests made a show of collecting cuttings, but he was not encouraged to join them.

His father had sent him an invitation to their Christmas house party this year, as he had every year since Oliver turned twenty-one. Oliver knew his stepmother did not want him to attend. She'd always gone out of her way to make him miserable. Once he reached his majority, he saw no reason to put himself through that ordeal. His father used to profess to missing him, but he quickly became accustomed to Oliver's absence.

Oliver never had any reason to acknowledge Christmas after that. He and Nicholas, who also had been at loose ends on the holiday, used to spend it together, drinking, gambling or carousing.

Until Nick disappeared.

This Christmas was different. He was not alone and Cecilia's delight in filling the house with evergreens was infectious. Had the ancient Celts felt that same enthusiasm for Winter Solstice, the rebirth of the sun?

Oliver knew of rebirth. His life had changed dramatically several times. Leaving India. Being befriended by Nicholas, Jacob and Frederick. The creation of Vitium et Virtus.

Now, with Cecilia, his life had changed again. When the baby was born, Oliver would be reborn into the role of father, reborn into a new family of his own.

Even if she would not allow it.

When the drawing room was finished, he and Cecilia moved on to the dining room and the hall. Cecilia arranged some holly cuttings in a vase and climbed the stairs to weave ivy through the banister.

'Are you certain you are up to finishing that task?' he asked her.

She sat on the stairs, weaving ivy in and out of the wrought-iron banister. 'I'm sitting. That is not too much, is it?' She smiled. 'Does it not look pretty?'

It did dress up the hall.

'What else do you wish me to do?' he asked.

'After this we are finished.' She gestured to the extra cuttings left over. They had plenty. 'Perhaps you could remove what we did not use?'

'I'll take them to the servants. They will want to decorate below stairs.' He picked up the bundle.

She gave him a very approving look that felt surprisingly gratifying.

It was his pleasure to please her.

* * *

While Oliver gathered the remainder of the branches and cuttings and carried them to the servants' door, Cecilia finished with the ivy.

The scent of the greenery filled the house, just as it had in her childhood. They always spent Christmas in the country. Had her parents returned to the country house for Christmas? she wondered. Would her sisters and their husbands be joining them?

She would never be a part of their Christmas again.

Oliver re-entered the hall and looked up to where she was seated on the stairs. 'Would you like me to finish that?' he asked.

'I'm done.' She pulled herself up by the banister. 'But I am fatigued. Would you object if I took a rest?'

There she went again, asking permission.

She spoke with more force. 'I mean, I am going to take a rest now.'

'I have no objection.' He frowned. 'Perhaps you have done too much.'

'I've been careful, Oliver,' she assured him. 'But that is why I think I should rest.'

He nodded. 'I have some errands, but I will be back later in the day. Do you need anything? Is there anything I can do for you?'

His concern warmed her heart. She believed he meant it. For now.

She smiled down at him. 'You have done enough by helping me decorate.'

She walked up the stairs, suddenly wishing she could go on his errands with him and remain in his company the whole day.

She entered her room and gasped.

Holly, hawthorn and pine cuttings adorned her mantel

and filled a vase near her bed. Ivy vines wound around her bedposts.

Mary came from the sitting room, carrying a basket of cuttings. 'Oh, you are here!'

'Mary, did you do this?' The room was filled with the heady scent of pine.

Mary grinned. 'I did. Mr Gregory set me to the task. I must say, it was a great deal of fun.'

'Thank you,' Cecilia said. 'It is lovely. Very lovely.'

She'd never had many cuttings in her childhood bedchamber. Her sisters took the extra cuttings for themselves and she'd had to pull small pieces from the decorations in the other rooms and sneak them upstairs.

This room was lavish with greenery.

'I am weary. I plan to rest a little,' Cecilia said.

Mary's brow furrowed. 'Are you feeling ill?'

'No.' It was a lovely sort of weariness. 'But I will retire to the sitting room and read for a while, I think.'

'Anything you require from me?' Mary asked.

Cecilia noticed that the basket had more greenery in it. 'I need nothing. Please use the extra cuttings for yourself.'

Mary grinned and left the room.

Cecilia opened a cabinet and removed the fabric that she'd purchased for Mary. It was wrapped in brown paper, but she added a red ribbon and tied it in a bow. She added a green ribbon to Oliver's gift and wished now that she'd found something of even more value to give to him.

She stared at the package and thought about their day. If all days could be like this one, how pleasant life could be. How pleasant life could be if only one could depend upon another person to be constant, to never change.

She put the gifts back into a drawer and kicked her shoes off, putting her feet on the sofa and hugging her knees.

The baby moved inside her. She lowered her legs and

placed her hands on her rounding belly, vowing to be as constant as the sun and moon for her baby.

'I promise, baby,' she whispered.

At least she could give her baby what she could not have. She let that thought cheer her.

There was a knock on the door and Mary entered. 'Uncle Irwin said this letter came for you.'

'A letter? For me?' She rose from the sofa and met Mary halfway.

Mary handed her the envelope.

Cecilia examined it. It appeared to be from her mother. 'Thank you, Mary.'

Her maid smiled, curtsied and left the room. Cecilia carried the letter back to the sitting room. She sat on the sofa and stared at it. She'd not had one piece of mail since the one from her father three years ago, the one disowning her.

She took a deep breath and carefully broke the seal.

It was from her mother.

She read:

Dear Cecilia,
We are back in the country, but I managed to devise a way to get a letter to you from here without your father knowing.

It will be a quiet Christmas for us. Both your sisters will be spending the day with their husbands, but that is as it should be. We will have our usual guests over for Christmas dinner. The parson. Squire Watson. And their wives, of course. They are dull company, but your father insisted we invite them.

If you could be with us it would make me so very happy, but I fear your father would never allow it.

We will be back in town for the Season, of course, and I hope I am able to contrive to see you. Your father was impossible after we met, checking my every move, but I suspect he will be too busy in the Season to think of where I am.

My love to you, my dear daughter.
Regards to your friend, Mr G—
Happy Christmas,
Your loving mother

Cecilia refolded the letter and blinked away tears. That her mother thought of her, cared for her, meant a great deal, but her mother was so much under her father's thumb, would Cecilia ever see her again? Perhaps a snatched visit in a Circulating Library? By then it surely would be obvious she was with child.

It was probably best that she disappear and never see her mother again.

She put the letter in the drawer with the presents and returned to the sofa, feeling more fatigued than before.

She'd told Oliver not to think of the past. She should heed her own advice. Right now, this day, she'd been happy. That was what mattered. She and Oliver would share Christmas together and they would be happy in each other's company.

For as long as it lasted.

Chapter Twenty-One

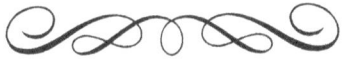

Cecilia dozed on the sofa, waking when Mary came in to dress her for dinner.

'I suppose I was tired.' Cecilia sat up and waited for her head to clear. She determinedly pushed the thought of her mother's letter out of her mind.

'Do you wish to dress for dinner?' Mary asked.

'Oh, yes.' She would make dinner with Oliver as enjoyable as possible for them both. 'I want to wear something nice.'

Mary grinned. 'Let us make you fancy tonight!'

Cecilia frowned. 'Like a lady, though, Mary. Not like a worker at Vitium et Virtus.' Not like Madame Coquette.

Mary chose an emerald-green dress. Its design was simple with few embellishments, but the silk fabric shimmered in the candlelight. Cecilia's pearl pendant became her only ornamentation. Mary fixed her hair high upon her head and fashioned bands of ribbon for a very Grecian look, elegant and simple.

'I have an idea!' Mary went to the vase and snipped off a sprig of holly and pinned it in her hair.

Cecilia gazed at her image in the full-length mirror. 'I look festive, do I not?'

Mary nodded. 'Very festive.'

She felt an unexpected fit of nerves. 'I suppose I am ready.'

Cecilia left the room and the distinct scent of burning firewood reached her nostrils. A Yule log? It could not be. Not in Oliver's small fireplaces. She hurried down the stairs to the hall to see.

Oliver stood leaning on the doorjamb to the drawing room.

'I smell burning wood!' she exclaimed.

'Reminiscent of a Yule log,' he said. 'Best I could do.'

'It smells wonderful.'

He moved to the doorway of the drawing room. 'Shall we have some wassail before dinner?'

'Wassail?' She laughed. 'You have wassail?'

'I do,' he responded. 'To celebrate our decorations.'

She hurried to the doorway. 'Perhaps just a sip.'

He blocked the doorway. 'Not so fast.'

'What?'

He pointed above them.

She glanced up and then met his eye. 'You've hung mistletoe.'

He nodded. 'You know what that means.'

She rose on tiptoe, and he bent down and touched his lips to hers in a kiss so tender it caused an aching in her heart.

She wound her arms around his neck and deepened the kiss while her body flared with need. He lifted her and carried her into the room, still kissing her. They were prone on the sofa, him beside her, but he broke off.

'We had better stop,' he said, his voice rasping.

She nodded. 'The baby.'

Not after the scare of her bleeding could they do anything that might hurt the baby.

He rose and she sat up, her body still humming with need

for him. He walked to the wassail bowl and brought her a cup of the hot mulled cider.

He poured himself a cup and sat in a chair across from her. He looked like she felt. Unsettled. She took one sip before putting her cup down on the table. It seemed wassail made her stomach turn as well as wine.

'The wassail is good.' She did not tell him she could not drink it. She picked up the cup again and let it warm her hands. 'Did you complete your errands?' she asked, trying for conversation instead.

'I did.' He sipped his drink. 'I know wassail is more typical of Twelfth Night, but I felt as if we deserved a reward for working all day.'

He'd also dressed for dinner, wearing an impeccably tailored coat of deep blue, a striped waistcoat and blue pantaloons.

'I enjoyed it, Oliver. Very much. And everything looks so beautiful.' She looked into the fireplace where flames licked the wooden logs and embers glowed bright orange. 'The fire is such a special touch.'

'I am glad you like it.' He smiled. 'Cook has saved the special meal for tomorrow, but tonight we'll still eat well.'

'Like every night.'

She would miss sharing dinner with him. The thought of leaving this little town house and the people in it—Oliver—made her eyes sting with tears.

She blinked them away. 'I am looking forward to Christmas pudding.'

'I know Cook has made some.'

Irwin came to the door and announced dinner.

Cecilia turned to him. 'You had better not tarry in the doorway, Irwin. I might have to kiss you.'

He almost cracked a smile. 'Mrs Irwin would ring a peal over my head if I let that happen.'

'Or more likely over mine.' She smiled.

Oliver rose and extended his hand. She placed hers in his and let him help her up. It brought her close to him, close enough to smell the soap he used and the spice of the wassail on his breath. He threaded her arm through his and they walked towards the door.

He paused under the mistletoe and gave her the lightest, sweetest kiss she had ever received. She touched her lips and thought of all the men she'd been forced to kiss when pretending to be Madame Coquette. Never again. She'd be happy if Oliver were the last man she ever kissed.

Their dinner had been special enough, Oliver thought. Roast lamb and turbot. Parsnips and broccoli. Chestnuts, grapes and walnuts. And cake for dessert. Their conversation had been light-hearted, confined to their experiences of the day before—not counting Bowles—and the decorating they'd done today.

After dinner they returned to the drawing room and played backgammon. Cecilia won most of the games. They laughed and teased each other and Oliver could not think of an evening he'd enjoyed more.

He wanted the feeling to continue.

When it came time for them to retire, they climbed the stairs to their bedchambers arm in arm. At the top of the stairs, Oliver stopped Cecilia and made her face him.

He touched her cheek. 'Come sleep with me, Cecilia. I do not want this day to end.'

Anxiety filled her eyes. 'I cannot. We cannot.'

He held her face in his hands. 'I am not talking of lovemaking. Come be with me. We will sleep and nothing more.'

She looked into his eyes as if searching for her answer. Finally, she nodded. 'I'll come to you after Mary readies me for bed.'

He leaned down and kissed her lips. 'I'll be waiting for you.'

He watched her enter her room before he opened his door.

In his room he undressed, washed and donned his banyan, all without the services of his valet, still in Yorkshire with his family. Oliver put on a fresh pair of drawers underneath his banyan, a barrier to help him keep his promise to Cecilia. He poured himself a glass of brandy and waited for her.

He heard a soft knock on his door and sprang to his feet. When he opened the door to her, all he wanted was to pull her into an embrace and taste her, but his body was already humming with desire and he dared not push himself to a point where they would find it difficult to stop.

'Come in,' he said instead. 'Would you like some brandy?'

She shook her head. She wore a long white nightdress that showed the silhouette of her body when she stood in front of the fireplace. 'I have had enough. We—we perhaps should sleep, like you said.'

She was nervous, he could tell. She had taken quite a chance in coming to him and trusting he would not make love to her.

'Come to bed, then,' he said, taking her hand.

They climbed into his bed and he spooned her against him, his arms around her.

'This is nice,' he said. Nice? It was perfect.

'Mmm-hmm,' she said.

Gradually he felt her body relax.

Why should this have to end? he wondered. Why could they not continue this way? Why not really be a family? He could give the child his name. He could make the child legitimate, something he would never be. He and Cecilia could spend every day together. And every night.

'Cecilia?'

'Hmm?'

'Remember when I said I wanted us to go on this way?'

She stiffened and pulled away, rolling over to face him. 'Do not, Oliver. Do not speak—'

He cut her off. 'I mean marriage, Cecilia. Marry me. We will be a family.' He was never so sure of anything as he was of this.

Cecilia panicked. 'Marriage?'

'Marriage.'

She jumped out of the bed, her heart racing. 'No, Oliver. No marriage. I won't marry you!'

She loved him. She had no doubt of that. She'd even been considering staying with him. But marriage? Marriage changed everything.

He rose from the bed. 'Why not, Cecilia? I love you. I—I believe you have some regard for me. We could be happy together.'

She hugged herself. 'No marriage, Oliver. I don't want to.'

He'd control her. She'd be his property.

His whole body tensed. 'Is it because I am a half-caste? Half-Indian? Too dark for you?'

Too dark? His complexion, his dark hair, only made him more handsome.

'Of course it is not that,' she retorted. 'Do you not know that?'

'Then it is because I am a bastard.'

'Do not be ridiculous,' she shot back. Why would she care about that?

'Then tell me why you do not care for me,' he challenged.

How could she explain?

'I care for you.' She more than cared for him. She loved him. 'But I won't marry. I won't!'

His eyes flashed in pain. 'Consider the baby, then. You profess I am the baby's father—'

She lifted her chin. 'You *are* the baby's father.'

'You make that hard to believe, Cecilia.' His voice turned hard.

'It is true.' Had they not moved past this?

He leaned towards her. 'I do not care if the child is mine or not. I am offering to *be* his father. Or her father. To give the child my name. Would you deprive this child of a father?' His anger was growing; she could tell. 'You would rather the child go through life being called a bastard?'

'He won't be a bastard,' she shot back. 'I plan to tell everyone I am a widow, which I am.'

'You'll pretend that the baby's father was your husband? The man who beat you?' He scoffed. 'Wonderful legacy. Father was a wife-beater. What happens when the child discovers his supposed father died before he was ever conceived?'

There would be records, certainly, but would her son or daughter ever see them?

'That won't happen.' She felt uncertain, though.

'Let me tell you what that child's life will be like, Cecilia.' He stood, arms akimbo, naked from the waist up. 'He will be ridiculed, ostracised, bullied. Servants will consider him beneath them. Tutors will treat him with disdain. No matter where he is, he will never quite belong. Is that what you want?'

Her anger flared. 'I'll tell you what I do not want. I do not want a husband telling me what to do and when to do it. A husband forbidding me, restricting me, confining me. Hitting me if I displease him. I will protect my child.'

'Protect your child?' His gaze pinned her. 'Do you truly believe you will be able to protect your child? I know I can protect you both. I do not want you out there alone.'

'You promised to support us, Oliver. That is all I need.' She'd take her chances on being a woman alone. She'd managed in Paris. She could manage in a small village somewhere in England. 'I have been married. I know what it did to me. I know what it does to my mother. Maybe even my sisters.'

His face flushed with anger. 'I am nothing like your husband. I am nothing like your father.'

She edged towards the door, fearing his escalating anger. 'But you could become like them.'

Oliver was losing *her*.

The familiar ache of loss started deep within him and spread until it hit every part of him.

She put her hand on the door handle. 'I am leaving.'

He would not stop her.

She opened the door, but hesitated, turning back to him. 'In fact, I think it best that I leave completely. Return to the hotel. I should not stay here any more.'

A knife in his gut could not have hurt more.

'You do not have to go to a hotel, Cecilia,' he said. 'We can live separately. I'll stay at Vitium et Virtus, if you like.'

'No.' She looked frantic. 'I need to leave completely.'

She would never allow him to love her, to belong to him. She would always have left him.

He nodded. 'As you wish. I'll have Irwin arrange a room and payment with the hotel.'

She frowned. 'I would pay if I could.'

He held up a hand. 'I gave you my word I would support you and I will. I'll arrange the funds for you and the child.'

The child who now would never be his.

'Thank you, Oliver,' she murmured.

She walked out and closed the door behind her.

Oliver strode over to the table where his decanter of brandy stood. He threw it into the unlit fireplace.

She did not want him. He loved her and she did not want him. All he could do now was provide for her and make certain she and the child would want for nothing. Rather than accept him, she'd choose a harder life for herself and especially for the child.

He'd lived that life, a life of loss and exclusion. Even Vitium et Virtus was falling apart. Nicholas was gone and Frederick and Jacob were making their own families.

At least the women they loved had been happy to marry them.

Chapter Twenty-Two

The next morning Oliver rose early. As he walked down the stairs to the hall, Cecilia's bag was already packed and ready to go. Her maid had just carried it down.

'She says she is leaving today and won't take any of the dresses you bought for her.' The maid frowned. 'Just what she came with.'

Foolish gesture. He was going to pay for her clothes for the rest of her life, why not now?

'Can you contrive to pack the new dresses as well?' he asked.

'I believe so,' she said.

'I'll provide a bag to pack them in. We'll send them with her whether she wants them or not.'

The maid nodded. 'Very good, sir!'

He returned to his room and found a bag for Mary to pack the dresses in. As he brought it into the hallway where Mary was waiting, he spied the items he'd purchased the day before, wrapped in paper.

His Christmas gifts.

He wanted Cecilia to have them, no matter what. If he handed them to her, she'd likely refuse them as she'd refused the dresses.

'Here, Mary, this should do, should it not?' He handed the bag to the maid.

'I'll make them fit,' she replied in a determined tone.

He returned to his room, pulled out pen, ink and paper from a drawer and quickly wrote a note, drying the ink with sand. He gathered the gifts and note and brought them downstairs with him.

Irwin stood in the hall, looking grim.

Oliver nodded to him. 'You have heard that Mrs Lockhart is leaving this morning?'

'Indeed, sir.' Irwin frowned. 'Very bad news, sir.'

Oliver agreed. 'Well, it is what she desires. I need you to go to Grenier's Hotel and arrange a room for her and bring her two bags with you—Mary is packing the second bag right now.'

'As you wish, sir,' Irwin said.

'And if you would be so good as to bring me my topcoat and hat before you leave.' Oliver intended to escort Cecilia to the hotel, something she probably would not want.

Mary brought down the second bag.

'That was quick,' he remarked.

She smiled. 'I am quick!' She curtsied and left the hall to go below stairs.

Oliver opened the second bag and placed the packages and note on top.

Irwin returned with coats, hats, gloves and scarves. 'It is cold outside today.'

Oliver took his things and placed them on a nearby chair. He gestured to the second bag. 'I placed two packages and a note in the bag. When you are in her hotel room, take them out and place them where she will see them.'

'As you wish, sir,' Irwin responded while donning his topcoat. He wrapped a woollen scarf around his neck. 'Are you certain of this, sir? I thought—'

Oliver waved a dismissive hand. 'It is what she wants.'

The butler sighed. 'Very well, sir.' He put on his hat, opened the door, picked up the two bags and stepped out.

Oliver walked over to close the door for him. Outside the sky was grey and fat flakes of snow fluttered to the ground, not yet sticking to the pavement, but tingeing the tops of the wrought-iron gates white.

Oliver and Cecilia might have strolled through the snow to St James's Church on Piccadilly to attend Christmas services. He would have liked that. Afterwards, they could have returned to the town house and stayed cosy and warm inside and shared Christmas dinner together.

He did not close the door until Irwin disappeared through the thickening snow, heading to the hotel on Jermyn Street.

Oliver lowered himself into a wooden chair in the hall and waited for Cecilia.

Cecilia stood in the servants' hall, Cook, Mrs Irwin and Mary surrounding her. She'd given Mary the pretty fabric for a dress and gifts of money to them all.

'Yours is to share with Irwin,' she told the housekeeper.

'Did I hear my name?' Irwin's voice came from the corridor. He popped his head in the servants' hall and saw Cecilia. 'Are you in need of me, ma'am?' His eyelashes glistened and he smelled of being outside.

'I am just saying goodbye,' she said, her throat tight.

The butler nodded. 'I know it. Your room at Grenier's is all arranged and your things are already in it. Mr Gregory's orders.'

How unexpected. 'I should go, then.'

Both older women were wiping their eyes with their aprons.

'You cannot stay for Christmas dinner?' Cook asked.

Cecilia shook her head. 'I will miss your cooking very much, though.'

'Then I'll pack you a basket! You should have some pudding—'

Cecilia lifted a hand. 'No. No. Do not disturb the pudding. I will be very cross if you do.'

Cook scowled. 'I'll find something else to give you.' She hurried back to the kitchen.

'How will we know about the baby if you leave?' Mrs Irwin asked. 'You should stay and let us take care of you.'

'I must go,' Cecilia insisted. 'But I will send word about the baby. I'll—I'll write you a letter.'

Mrs Irwin tried over again to convince her to stay. Cecilia wished she could. She'd loved being in this house, cared for by these servants.

And Oliver.

Cook returned with a basket. 'I've packed some bread and cheese and some of my jam.'

'That will be lovely.' Cecilia's voice cracked. She'd known them such a short period of time, but leaving them was turning out to be painfully difficult. She turned to Mary, who'd been silent during this exchange. 'I must go.'

Mary blinked rapidly. 'I think you are acting like a witless ninny!'

'Mary!' Mrs Irwin scolded.

'Well, she is!' Mary protested. 'Mr Gregory is a nice man! He loves you. Any fool can see that.'

Cecilia shook her head. 'I—I cannot explain. I simply must leave.'

She gave Mary a quick hug, grabbed her cloak and rushed away, climbing the stairs to the hall. When she entered the hall, things only became worse.

Oliver was there.

'Irwin arranged the room,' he told her, his voice stiff. 'I have the key. Your things are already there.'

She could not look at him. 'Thank you, Oliver.' She put on her cloak and pulled on her gloves. 'I'll be leaving then.' She put her hand out for the key.

He did not give it to her. 'I will escort you. See you safely there,' he said. 'One last time.'

She wanted to grab the key and run out, but that seemed childish. What harm in having him walk with her?

He donned his coat, hat and gloves and opened the door for her.

'Oh!' she exclaimed. 'It is snowing!'

The pavement and street were white with about an inch of snow, making everything look new and clean.

'Hold my arm,' Oliver insisted. 'It will be slippery.'

This would be her last time to touch him.

He did not talk to her, except to caution her about a slippery spot or to warn of a curb. The street was empty of people and carriages and the scent of Christmas cooking wafted from kitchens along the way.

She'd be alone this day and so would he.

She could not marry him, though, and she could not stay, because all she wanted was to be with him. It was a splendid trap, loving him, but being shackled with velvet ribbons would still mean being shackled.

They reached the hotel, and she released his arm.

'I am seeing you to your room,' he said to her.

She took his arm again and they entered the hotel. He announced her to the clerk in the hall of the hotel, the same man who had been so unhelpful to her when she'd needed to search for Vitium et Virtus. The clerk directed them to her room on the first floor, one flight up.

Oliver put the key in the door and opened it. 'I will say goodbye to you here.'

She looked up at him, words failing her.

He turned quickly and walked away. She waited until he descended the stairs.

Her last glimpse of him.

She swung back to the doorway. It was better this way. She was better for being free.

She entered the room and removed her cloak and gloves. This room was much more lavish than the one she'd rented before and much more than she needed. Oliver was generous. She fingered the pearl she still wore at her throat. He'd been generous that first day she met him.

Two bags were in the room. She opened the one that was not hers and saw all the dresses Oliver had purchased for her, more reminders of his generosity.

On a table nearby were two small packages and a folded piece of paper. She picked up the paper and unfolded it.

A note from Oliver.

Dear Cecilia,
Do not refuse these gifts. I want you to have them to remember me. They are trifles. The dresses, too. Those are yours. My man of business will be in touch with you within days. You and the baby will be comfortable. I promise.

I beg a promise from you. If you are in any need, send word to me. I will come. I want no harm to come to you or the baby ever. Do not hesitate to ask for my help.

Remember that I love you and that fact will not change.
Yours, O.

A tear slid down her face.

She tore open the larger package, opened the box and gasped. Inside was a teething rattle. Not just any teething rattle. The finest sort, made of exquisitely engraved sterling silver with silver bells all around and a red handle of coral for the baby to teethe on. The other side was a whistle. She placed it on her mouth and blew softly, producing a shrill sound. It was the finest object she'd ever possessed and it was for her baby.

Oliver's baby.

She put the rattle down on the table and picked up the smaller package, untying the string and removing the paper. Its box was covered in blue velvet. She opened it. Inside were two pearl earrings, a match to her necklace. Not precious. Not even as valuable as the rattle, she guessed, but so personal a sob escaped her mouth.

What sort of man would do this? Send gifts after she rejected him, such dear, perfect gifts? What sort of man would make certain she had a comfortable room after she'd walked out of his? Or agree to support her and a baby he did not even believe was his? A baby to whom he offered to give his name?

Ever since she met Oliver, he'd been kind and generous to her, unfailingly so. He'd been there for her when she confronted her father. When she saw her mother. He'd protected her from Bowles—

She inhaled sharply.

He'd protected her. He'd fought Bowles for Flo's protection. Twice. And was stabbed for it.

He wanted to protect her and the baby. He did not want to confine or control her. When had he ever tried to control her? He'd always given her the choice.

She stared at the rattle and the earrings. She read the note again.

If you are in any need, send word to me. I will come...

Even after she'd rejected him, he'd come to her aid.

She lifted the paper in which the gifts were wrapped. What of her gift to him? It was still in the drawer in the sitting room. She'd hurriedly grabbed Mary's gift from the drawer, but not Oliver's.

Cecilia picked up her cloak and gloves and quickly put

them on. She hurried out of the room, locking it behind her and putting the key in her pocket. She ran down the stairs and out the hotel door.

Even in this short period of time, the snow had deepened. She wanted to rush, but the snow impeded her. It fell so thick now she could hardly see two feet in front of her. Her half-boots quickly became caked with snow and her feet felt like icicles. Only a short walk, a couple of streets. The wind picked up and blew the hood of her cloak from her head. She reached Bury Street and tried to walk faster, but it was too hard.

It was Christmas day and she needed to give Oliver his gift.

After leaving Cecilia at the hotel and returning home, Oliver had gone straight to his bedchamber and closed the door.

He imagined he'd figure out a way to put one foot in front of the other again, but for the moment all he could think to do was stand in front of his window and watch the snow fall. He watched it accelerate and thicken, watched the wind toss the flakes into erratic swirls. The pavement was covered with snow and growing deeper. A carriage drove by and was nearly silent. Everything was quiet.

He tried to empty his mind and was fairly successful, except for one thought.

Cecilia was gone. The world was empty. Bleached white.

Something moved at the end of the street. He watched a figure emerge from the white curtain. A woman. In a cloak. Barely visible in the falling snow.

He ran out of the room, down the stairs. He flung open the door as the snowy figure faced the house.

He ran to her and she flew into his arms.

'You came back!' he rasped.

She was weeping into his shoulder and she clung to him.

Finally, she looked up and brushed snowflakes from his hair. 'You do not have a hat or coat.'

'I do not care. You came back.' He held her tighter.

He lifted her into his arms and carried her inside, putting her down and removing her snow-caked cloak.

'I need to go upstairs,' she said. 'I forgot something.'

He released her. He'd got it wrong. She'd merely forgotten something.

He would have to endure her leaving all over again.

He followed her upstairs but stood in the hall while she went into what he would always think of as her room. She emerged as quickly.

'This is for you.' She handed him a package tied with a ribbon.

He opened it and discovered a silver-backed tortoiseshell comb.

'It is a silly gift, I know,' she said. 'But I wanted something you would use every day so you would not forget me.'

He met her gaze. 'I will never forget you, Cecilia.'

Her breathing accelerated. 'I—I learned something. Or rather, I finally put pieces of a puzzle together the correct way.'

He had no idea what she was talking about. 'What is that?'

'You protect; you don't hurt. You give; you don't take. You release who you love; you don't confine them.'

Why was she speaking so? 'I love you, Cecilia. I want you to be safe and happy.'

'I know,' she said. 'I am so sorry. I was wrong.'

'Wrong?' His insides twisted. This felt riskier than a carriage race on a twisting country road.

'I was wrong to believe I cannot trust anyone. I can trust you.'

He narrowed his eyes. 'Be clear, Cecilia. I will be. I love you. I still want to marry you. I will never hurt you and I will not control you. I'll protect you and the baby with my life.'

Her eyes widened. 'Do you mean it? You are not angry with me after—after all I've said and done?'

'I am not angry with you.' Wounded, not angry. 'Marry me.'

She flew into his arms once again. 'Yes! Oliver, yes! I've been afraid to love you, but I do. I do.'

He swung her around in a circle, laughing, the knot inside him loosening and releasing joy. He took her face in his hands and kissed her, a kiss full of the promises he'd made to her.

She kissed him back.

He held her tightly against him, but suddenly released her. 'I felt it!' he cried. 'I felt the baby move.'

'Yes. The baby moved.'

He hugged her again. 'A family,' he murmured.

Epilogue

May 1819

Oliver stood in the hallway of his town house while behind the closed door of Cecilia's room, the doctor, Mrs Irwin and Mary attended Cecilia.

His wife.

Her labour had started three hours before, but in the last few minutes her cries of pain grew louder and longer. Each one reached into him with a mirroring pain.

He paced back and forth.

Princess Charlotte died in childbirth. Both her and the baby. Lots of women died in childbirth.

Cecilia cried again and he could not bear it. He entered the room.

'Sir!' Mrs Irwin scolded. 'You should not be in here!'

'I'm not leaving,' he growled.

The doctor did not take notice of him. Neither did Cecilia.

'Push!' the doctor cried.

Cecilia cried again, her face red with strain.

'The baby's coming!' Mary cried. 'I see the head!'

'When the next pain comes, push again,' the doctor said.

The pain came immediately. Cecilia cried and pushed.

Oliver was riveted to the scene. He could see the top of the baby's head.

All of a sudden the baby's whole head emerged and the baby slipped out into the doctor's hands.

'A boy!' the doctor cried.

A boy?

The baby looked so tiny, but it let out a cry of its own and Oliver exhaled a relieved breath.

Half an hour later the baby and Cecilia were cleaned up and resting on clean bed linens. Cecilia gazed adoringly at her baby boy and Oliver gazed in wonder at both of them.

'Little Nicholas,' she murmured.

There'd been no other name to consider for a boy. Oliver wanted to honour his friend.

Cecilia examined every finger and toe on little Nicholas and rewrapped him in his blanket. She traced her finger over the baby's cheek and forehead.

She laughed. 'Look, Oliver!'

He came closer.

She traced her finger over the baby's ear. 'His ear is just like yours.' The ear came to a tiny point, hardly noticeable. 'Look in the mirror. Your ear is the same.'

Oliver walked over to the mirror. She was right! His ear was the exact same shape.

She sobered for a moment. 'Now do you believe me? You are Nicholas's father.'

He walked over to her and kissed the top of her head. 'It has not mattered for a long time,' he told her. 'I belong to both of you. We are a family. I am content.'

She pulled him down into a kiss.

* * * * *